Divine Rivals

Divine Rivals

A Novel

Rebecca Ross

WEDNESDAY BOOKS
NEW YORK

First published in the United States by Wednesday Books,
an imprint of St. Martin's Publishing Group

DIVINE RIVALS. Copyright © 2023 by Rebecca Ross LLC. All rights reserved.
Printed in the United States of America. For information,
address St. Martin's Publishing Group, 120 Broadway, New York, NY 10271.

www.wednesdaybooks.com

The Library of Congress Cataloging-in-Publication Data is available upon request.

ISBN 978-1-250-85743-9 (hardcover)
ISBN 978-1-250-85744-6 (ebook)

Our books may be purchased in bulk for promotional, educational, or business use.
Please contact your local bookseller or the Macmillan Corporate and
Premium Sales Department at 1-800-221-7945, extension 5442, or by email at
MacmillanSpecialMarkets@macmillan.com.

First Edition: 2023

20 19 18 17 16 15 14

For Isabel Ibañez,
who read this book as I wrote it,
who convinced me to add Roman's POV,
& who occasionally lets me get away with things.

P.S. I'm talking about Chapter 34.

Contents

Write me of hope and love, and hearts that endured.
——EMILY DICKINSON

Prologue

Cold fog had settled over the depot like a burial shroud, and Iris Winnow thought the weather couldn't have been better. She could hardly see the train through the gloom, but she could taste it in the evening air: metal and smoke and burning coal, all woven together with a trace of petrichor. The wooden platform was slick beneath her shoes, gleaming with rain puddles and piles of decaying leaves.

When Forest came to a stop at her side, she stopped as well, as if she were his mirror. The two of them were often mistaken for twins with their wide-set hazel eyes, wavy chestnut hair, and the freckles that spilled across their noses. But Forest was tall, Iris petite. He was five years her senior, and for the first time in her life, Iris wished that she were older than him.

"I won't be gone long," he said. "Only a few months, I think."

Her brother glanced at her in the fading light, waiting for her to respond. It was eventide, the moment between darkness and light, when the constellations began to dust the sky and the city lamps flickered to life in reply. Iris could feel the draw of it—Forest's concerned stare and the golden light that illuminated the low-hanging clouds—and yet her eyes wandered, desperate for a distraction. A moment to blink away her tears before Forest could see them.

There was a soldier to her right. A young woman dressed in a perfectly starched uniform. Iris was struck by a wild thought. One that must have traveled across her face, because Forest cleared his throat.

"I should come with you," Iris said, meeting his gaze. "It's not too late. I can enlist—"

"No, Iris," Forest replied sharply. "You made me two promises, remember?"

Two promises, hardly a day old. Iris frowned. "How could I forget."

"Then speak them back to me."

She crossed her arms to ward off the autumn chill and the strange cadence in Forest's voice. There was a hint of desperation she hadn't heard in him until now, and gooseflesh rippled across her arms beneath her thin sweater.

"*Take care of Mum,*" she said, mimicking his baritone. It brought a smile to his face. "*Stay in school.*"

"I believe it was a bit more than a gruff '*Stay in school,*'" Forest said, nudging her foot with his boot. "You brilliant academic who has yet to miss a day of class in all her years. They give awards for that, you know."

"Fine." Iris relented, a blush nipping her cheeks. "You said, 'Promise me you'll enjoy your final year of school, and I'll be back in time to see you graduate.'"

"Yes," Forest said, but his smile began to wane.

He didn't know when he'd return. It was a promise he couldn't keep to her, although he continued to make it sound as if the war would end in a matter of months. A war that had only just begun.

What if I *had been the one to hear the song?* Iris thought, her heart so heavy it felt bruised against her ribs. *If I had encountered the goddess and not him . . . would he let me go like this?*

Her gaze dropped to Forest's chest. The place where his own heart was beating beneath his olive-green uniform. A bullet could pierce him in a split second. A bullet could keep him from ever returning home.

"Forest, I—"

She was interrupted by a shrill whistle that made her jump. It was the last call to board, and there was a sudden shuffle toward the train cars. Iris shivered again.

"Here," Forest said, setting down his leather satchel. "I want you to have this."

Iris watched as her brother opened the clasp and withdrew his tan-colored trench coat. He held it out to her, arching his brow when she merely stared at it.

"But you'll need it," she argued.

"They'll give me one," he replied. "Something war approved, I imagine. Go on, take it, Little Flower."

Iris swallowed, accepting his trench coat. She slipped her arms into it, belting the worn fabric tight across her waist. It was too big for her, but it was comforting. It felt like armor. She sighed.

"You know, this smells like the horologist's shop," she drawled.

Forest laughed. "And what, exactly, does a horologist's shop smell like?"

"Like dusty, half-wound clocks and expensive oil and those tiny metal instruments you use to fix all the broken pieces." But that was only partly true. The coat also held a remnant of the Revel Diner, where she and Forest would eat dinner at least twice a week while their mother waited tables. It smelled of the riverside park, of moss and damp stones and long walks, and Forest's sandalwood aftershave because, no matter how much he wanted one, he couldn't grow a beard.

"Then it should keep you good company," he said, slinging his satchel over his shoulder. "And you can have the wardrobe all to yourself now."

Iris knew he was trying to lighten the mood, but it only made her stomach ache to think about the small closet they shared in their flat. As if she would truly store his clothes somewhere else while he was gone.

"I'm sure I'll need the spare hangers, since—as you well know—I keep up with all the current fashion trends," Iris countered wryly, hoping Forest couldn't hear the sadness in her voice.

He only smiled.

This was it, then. The platform was nearly empty of soldiers, and the train was hissing through the gloom. A knot welled in Iris's throat; she bit the inside of her cheek as Forest embraced her. She closed her eyes, feeling the scratch of his linen uniform against her cheek, and she held the words she wanted to say in her mouth like water: *How can you love this goddess more than me? How can you leave me like this?*

Their mother had already spoken such sentiments, angry and upset with Forest for enlisting. Aster Winnow had refused to come to the depot to see him off, and Iris imagined she was at home, weeping as the denial wore away.

The train began to move, creeping along the tracks.

Forest slipped from Iris's arms.

"Write to me," she whispered.

"I promise."

He took a few steps backward, holding her gaze. There was no fear in his eyes. Only a dark, feverish determination. And then Forest turned, rushing to board the train.

Iris followed until he disappeared into the closest car. She lifted her hand and waved, even as tears blurred her vision, and she stood on the platform long after the train had vanished into the fog. Rainwater was seeping into her shoes. The lamps flickered overhead, buzzing like wasps. The crowd had dispersed, and Iris felt hollow—*alone*—as she began to walk home.

Her hands were cold, and she slipped them into the coat pockets. That was when she felt it—a crinkle of paper. Frowning, she assumed it was a candy wrapper that Forest had forgotten about until she pulled it out to study in the dim light.

It was a small piece of paper, folded crookedly, with a vein of typed words. Iris couldn't resist smiling, even as her heart ached. She read:

Just in case you didn't know...you are by far the best sister I've ever had. I'm so proud of you.

And I'll be home before you know it, Little Flower.

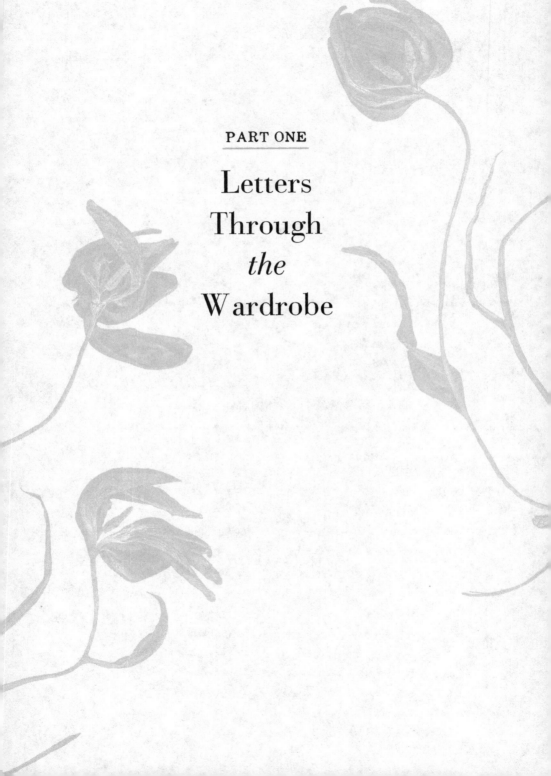

PART ONE

Letters Through *the* Wardrobe

1

Sworn Enemies

FIVE MONTHS LATER

Iris dashed through the rain with a broken high heel and a tattered trench coat. Hope was beating wildly in her chest, granting her speed and luck as she crossed the tram tracks downtown. She had been anticipating this day for weeks, and she knew she was ready. Even soaked, limping, and hungry.

Her first pang of unease came when she stepped into the lobby. This was an old building, constructed before the gods were vanquished. A few of those dead divines were painted on the ceiling, and despite the cracks and the faint light of the low-hanging chandeliers, Iris always glanced up at them. Gods and goddesses dancing among the clouds, dressed in long gilded robes with stars gleaming in their hair, their gazes sweeping the ground. It sometimes felt like those painted eyes were watching her, and Iris stifled a shiver. She removed her mangled right shoe and hurried to the lift with a stilted gait, thoughts of the gods swiftly fading when she thought about *him*. Perhaps the rain had slowed down Roman too, and she still had a chance.

She waited a full minute. The confounded lift must be stuck, of all days, and she decided to take the stairs, hustling up to the fifth floor. She was shaking and sweating when she finally pushed through the heavy doors to the *Oath Gazette,* greeted by a wash of yellow lamplight, the scent of strong tea, and the morning hustle of preparing the newspaper.

She was four minutes late.

Iris stood amidst the hum, her gaze flickering to Roman's desk.

It was empty, and she was pleased until she glanced at the assignment board and saw him standing there, waiting for her to appear. As soon as their eyes met, he gave her a lazy smile and reached up to the board, yanking a piece of paper from a pin. The last assignment.

Iris didn't move, not even when Roman Kitt wound around the cubicles to greet her. He was tall and lithe with cheekbones that could cut stone, and he waved the piece of paper in the air, just out of her reach. The piece of paper she so badly wanted.

"Late again, Winnow," he greeted her. "The second time this week."

"I didn't know you were keeping tally, Kitt."

His smirk eased as his gaze dropped to her hands, cradling her broken shoe. "Looks like you ran into a bit of trouble this time."

"Not at all," she replied, her chin tilted upward. "I planned for this, of course."

"For your heel to break?"

"For you to get this final assignment."

"Going easy on me, then?" He arched a brow. "That's surprising. We're supposed to duel to the death."

She snorted. "A hyperbolic turn of phrase, Kitt. Which you do often in your articles, by the way. You should be careful of that tendency if you get columnist."

A lie. Iris rarely read what he wrote. But he didn't know that.

Roman's eyes narrowed. "What's so *hyperbolic* about soldiers going missing at the front?"

Iris's stomach clenched, but she hid her reaction with a thin smile. "Is that the topic of the last assignment? Thanks for letting me know." She turned away from him and began to weave around cubicles to her desk.

"It doesn't matter if you know it," he insisted as he followed her. "*I* have the assignment."

She reached her desk and flicked on her lamp. "Of course, Kitt."

He wasn't leaving. He continued to stand by her cubicle, watching her set down her tapestry bag and her mangled high heel like it was a badge of honor. She shed her trench coat. He rarely watched her this attentively, and Iris knocked over her tin of pencils.

"Did you need something?" she asked, hurrying to gather the pencils before they rolled off the desk. Of course, one did, landing right before Roman's leather brogues. He didn't bother to pick the pencil up for her, and she swallowed a curse as she bent down to retrieve it, noticing the spit polish of his shoes.

"You're going to write your own article about missing soldiers," he stated. "Even though you don't have the full information on the assignment."

"And that worries you, Kitt?"

"No. Course not."

She glanced at him, studying his face. She put her tin of pencils on the back side of her desk, far from any chance of spilling again. "Has anyone ever told you that you squint when you lie?"

His scowl only deepened. "No, but only because no one has spent as much time looking at me as you do, Winnow."

Someone snickered from a nearby desk. Iris flushed, sitting down in her chair. She grappled for a witty reply but came up short, because he was unfortunately handsome and he often drew her eyes.

She did the only thing she could; she leaned back in her chair and granted Roman a brilliant smile. One that reached her eyes, crinkling the corners. His expression darkened instantly, just as she expected. He hated it when she smiled like this at him. It always made him retreat.

"Good luck on your assignment," she said brightly.

"And you can have fun with the obituaries," he countered in a clipped tone, at last departing to his cubicle, which was—regrettably—only two desks away.

Iris's smile melted as soon as his back was turned. She was still absently staring in that direction when Sarah Prindle stepped into her field of vision.

"Tea?" Sarah asked, raising a cup. "You look like you need some, Winnow."

Iris sighed. "Yes, thanks, Prindle." She accepted the offering but set it down with a hard clunk on her desk, right next to the stack of handwritten obituaries, waiting for her to sort, edit, and type them. If she had been early enough to snag the assignment, Roman would be the one sifting through this heartache on paper.

Iris stared at the pile, remembering her first day of work three months ago. How Roman Kitt had been the last to shake her hand and introduce himself, approaching her with a hard-set mouth and cold, keen eyes. As if he were measuring how much of a threat she was to him and his position at the *Gazette*.

It hadn't taken long for Iris to learn what he truly thought of her. In fact, it had taken only half an hour after she had first met Roman. She had overheard him saying to one of the editors, "She'll give me no competition. None at all. She dropped out of Windy Grove School in her final year."

The words still stung.

She hadn't expected to ever be friends with him. How could she, when they were both competing for the same columnist position? But his pompous demeanor had only sharpened her desire to defeat him. And it had also been alarming that Roman Kitt knew more about her than she knew of him.

Which meant Iris needed to dig up his secrets.

On her second day of work, she went to the friendliest person on staff. Sarah.

"How long has Kitt been here?" Iris had asked.

"Almost a month," Sarah had replied. "So don't worry about him having seniority. I think you both have a fair shot at the promotion."

"And what does his family do?"

"His grandfather pioneered the railroad."

"So his family has money."

"Heaps," Sarah said.

"Where did he go to school?"

"I think Devan Hall, but don't quote me on that."

A prestigious school where most of the rich parents of Oath sent their spoiled brats. A direct contrast to Iris's humble Windy Grove. She had almost winced at this revelation, but pressed on with "Is he courting anyone?"

"Not that I know of," Sarah had answered with a shrug. "But he doesn't share much about his life with us. In fact, I don't really know that much about him, other than he doesn't like anyone touching the things on his desk."

Partly satiated with her newfound knowledge, Iris had decided the best course of action was to ignore her competition. She could pretend he didn't exist most of the time. But she soon discovered that would be increasingly difficult as they had to race each other to the bulletin board for weekly assignments.

She had triumphantly snagged the first one.

Roman had then obtained the second, but only because she had let him.

It had given her the chance to read a published article of his. Iris had sat hunched at her desk, reading what Roman had written about a retired baseball player—a sport Iris had never cared about but suddenly found herself ensorcelled by, all due to the poignant and witty tone of Roman's writing. She was transfixed by his every word, feeling the stitches of the baseball in her hand, the warm summer night, the thrill of the crowd in the stadium—

"See something you like?"

Roman's haughty voice broke the spell. Iris had startled, crumpling the paper in her hands. But he knew *exactly* what she had been reading, and he was smug about it.

"Not at all," she had said. And because she was desperate for something to distract her from her mortification, she noticed his name, printed in small black type beneath the column headline.

ROMAN C. KITT

"What does the C stand for?" she asked, glancing up at him.

He had only lifted his cup of tea and taken a sip, refusing to reply. But he held her gaze over the chipped edge of the porcelain.

"Roman *Cheeky* Kitt?" Iris had guessed. "Or maybe Roman *Churlish* Kitt?"

His amusement dimmed. He didn't like to be made fun of, and Iris's grin broadened as she leaned back in her chair.

"Or perhaps it's Roman *Cantankerous* Kitt?"

He had turned and left without another word, but his jaw had been clenched.

Once he was gone, she had finished reading his article in peace. It made her heart ache—his writing was extraordinary—and she had dreamt about him that night. The next morning, she had promptly torn the paper to shreds and vowed to never read another one of his pieces again. If she did, she was bound to lose the position to him.

But she was reconsidering now as her tea went cold. If he wrote an article about missing soldiers, she *might* be inclined to read it.

Iris yanked a fresh sheet of paper from the stack on her desk, feeding it into her typewriter. But her fingers hovered over the keys as she listened to Roman pack his messenger bag. She listened to him leave the office, no doubt to gather information for his article, his footsteps muffled amongst the clack of typebars and the murmur of voices and the swirl of cigarette smoke.

She clenched her teeth together as she began to type out the first obituary.

By the time Iris was almost done for the day, she felt heavy from the obituaries. She always wondered what had caused the deaths, and although that information was never included, she imagined people would be more inclined to read the eulogies if it was.

She gnawed on a hangnail, tasting a faint trace of metal from the typewriter keys. If she wasn't working on an assignment, she was elbow deep in either classifieds or obituaries. The past three months at the *Gazette* had seen her cycle through all three, each drawing different words and emotions from her in turn.

"In my office, Winnow," said a familiar voice. Zeb Autry, her boss, was walking by, and he tapped the edge of her cubicle with his golden ringed fingers. "*Now.*"

Iris abandoned the obituary and followed him into a glass-walled chamber. It always smelled oppressive here, like oiled leather and tobacco and the strong sting of aftershave. When he sat at his desk, she settled in the wingback chair across from him, resisting the urge to crack her knuckles.

Zeb stared at her for a long, hard minute. He was a middle-aged man with thinning blond hair, pale blue eyes, and a cleft in his chin. Sometimes she thought he could read minds, and it made her uneasy.

"You were late this morning," he stated.

"Yes, sir. I apologize. I overslept and missed the tram."

By the way his frown deepened . . . she wondered if he could sense lies too.

"Kitt got the final assignment, but only because you were late, Winnow. I posted it on the board at eight o'clock sharp, like all the others," Zeb drawled. "You've been late to work *two* times this week alone. And Kitt has yet to be tardy."

"I understand, Mr. Autry. It won't happen again, though."

Her boss was quiet for a beat. "Over the past few months, I've published eleven articles of Kitt's. I've published ten of yours, Winnow."

Iris braced herself. Was it truly going to come down to the numbers? That Roman had written slightly more than her?

"Do you know that I was going to simply *give* the position to Kitt after he got his feet wet here?" Zeb continued. "That is, until your essay won the Gazette-in-Winter Competition. Out of the hundreds of essays I sifted through, yours caught my eye. And I thought, Here is a girl who has raw talent, and it would be a shame if I let that slip away."

Iris knew what came next. She had been working at the diner, washing dishes with muted, broken dreams. She hadn't once thought the essay she submitted to the *Gazette*'s annual competition would amount to anything, until she returned home to find a letter from Zeb with her name on it. It was an offer to work at the paper, with the tantalizing promise of columnist if she continued to prove herself exceptional.

It had completely changed Iris's life.

Zeb lit a cigarette. "I've noticed that your writing hasn't been as sharp lately. It's been quite messy, in fact. Is there something happening at home, Winnow?"

"No, sir," she answered, too swiftly.

He regarded her, one eye smaller than the other. "How old are you again?"

"Eighteen."

"You dropped out of school this past winter, didn't you?"

She hated thinking about her broken promise to Forest. But she nodded, sensing that Zeb was digging. He wanted to know more about her personal life, which made her tense.

"You have any siblings?"

"An older brother, sir."

"And where is he, now? What does he do for a living?" Zeb pressed on.

Iris glanced away, studying the black and white checkered floor. "He was a horologist's apprentice. But he's at war now. Fighting."

"For Enva, I presume?"

She nodded again.

"Is that why you dropped out of Windy Grove?" Zeb asked. "Because your brother left?"

Iris didn't reply.

"That's a pity." He sighed, releasing a puff of smoke, although Iris knew Zeb's opinion on the war, and it never failed to irk her. "What about your parents?"

"I live with my mother," she replied in a curt tone.

Zeb withdrew a small flask from his jacket and poured a few drops of liquor into his tea. "I'll think about giving you another assignment, although that's not how I usually do things around here. Now, I want those obituaries on my desk by three this afternoon."

She left without another word.

Iris set the finished obituaries on his desk an hour early, but she didn't leave the office. She remained at her cubicle and began to think of an essay to write, just in case Zeb did give her a chance to counter Roman's assignment.

But the words felt frozen inside of her. She decided to walk to the sideboard to pour herself a fresh cup of tea when she saw Roman Conceited Kitt walk into the office.

He had been gone all day, to her relief, but he now had that annoying bounce in his stride, as if he were teeming with words he needed to spill across the page. His face was flushed from the chill of early spring, his coat speckled with rain as he sat at his desk, rummaging through his messenger bag for his notepad.

Iris watched as he fed a page to his typewriter and began to furiously type. He was lost to the world, lost to his words, and so she didn't take the long way back to her desk, as she often did, to avoid passing him directly. He didn't notice her walking by, and she sipped her overly sweetened tea and stared at her blank page.

Soon everyone began to leave for the day, save for her and Roman. Desk lamps were being turned off, one by one, and yet Iris remained, typing slowly and arduously, as if every word had to be pulled from her marrow, while Roman two cubicles away was pounding into the keys.

Her thoughts drifted to the gods' war.

It was inevitable; the war *always* seemed to simmer at the back of her mind, even if it was raging six hundred kilometers west of Oath.

How will it end? she wondered. *With one god destroyed, or both of them?*

Endings were often found in beginnings, and she began to type what she knew. Snippets of news that had drifted across the land, reaching Oath weeks after they had happened.

It began in a small, sleepy town surrounded by gold. Seven months ago, the wheat fields were ready for harvest, nearly swallowing a place called Sparrow, where sheep outnumber people four to one, and it rains only twice a year due to an old charm cast by an angry—and now slain—god, centuries ago.

This idyllic town in Western Borough is where Dacre, a defeated Underling god, was laid to sleep in a grave. And there he slept for two hundred and thirty-four years until one day, at harvest time, he unexpectedly woke and rose, sifting through the soil and burning with fury.

He came upon a farmer in the field, and his first words were a cold, ragged whisper.

"Where is Enva?"

Enva, a Skyward goddess and Dacre's sworn enemy. Enva, who had also been defeated two centuries ago, when the five remaining gods fell captive beneath mortal power.

The farmer was afraid, cowering in Dacre's shadow. "She is buried in the Eastern Borough," he eventually replied. "In a grave not unlike your own."

"No," Dacre said. "She is awake. And if she refuses to greet me…if she chooses to be a coward, I will draw her to me."

"How, my lord?" the farmer asked.

Dacre stared down at the man. How does one god draw another? He began to

"What's this?"

Iris jumped at Zeb's voice, turning to see him standing nearby with a scowl, trying to read what she had typed.

"Just an idea," she replied, a bit defensive.

"It's not about how the gods' war began, is it? That's old news, Winnow, and people here in Oath are sick of reading about it. Unless you have a fresh take on Enva."

Iris thought about all the headlines Zeb had published about the war. They screamed things like THE DANGERS OF ENVA'S MUSIC: THE SKYWARD GODDESS HAS RETURNED AND SINGS OUR SONS AND DAUGHTERS TO WAR or RESIST THE SIREN'S CALL TO WAR: ENVA IS OUR MOST DANGEROUS THREAT. ALL STRINGED INSTRUMENTS ARE OUTLAWED IN OATH.

All his articles blamed Enva for the war, while few mentioned Dacre's involvement at all. Sometimes Iris wondered if it was because Zeb was afraid of the goddess and how easily she recruited soldiers, or if he had been instructed to publish only certain things—if the chancellor of Oath was controlling what the newspaper could share, quietly spreading propaganda.

"I . . . yes, I know, sir, but I thought—"

"You thought what, Winnow?"

She hesitated. "Has the chancellor given you restrictions?"

"Restrictions?" Zeb laughed as if she were being ridiculous. "On what?"

"On what you can and cannot feature in the paper."

A frown creased Zeb's ruddy face. His eyes flashed—Iris couldn't tell if it was fear or irritation—but he chose to say, "Don't waste my paper and ink ribbons on a war that is never going to reach us here in Oath. It's a western problem and we should carry on as normal. Find something good to write about, and I *might* consider publishing it in the column next week." With that, he rapped his knuckles on the wood and left, grabbing his coat and hat on the way out.

Iris sighed. She could hear Roman's steady typing, like a heartbeat in the vast room. Fingertips striking keys, keys striking paper. A prodding for her to do better than him. To claim the position before he did.

Her mind was mush, and she yanked her essay from the typewriter. She folded it and tucked it away in her small tapestry bag, knotting the drawstrings before she scooped up her broken shoe. She turned her lamp off and stood, rubbing a crick in her neck. It was dark beyond the windows; night had settled over the city, and the lights beyond bled like fallen stars.

This time when she walked by Roman's desk, he noticed her.

He was still wearing his trench coat, and a tendril of black hair cut across his furrowed brow. His fingers slowed on the keys, but he didn't speak.

Iris wondered if he wanted to, and if so, what he would say to her in a moment when they had the office to themselves, and no one else watching them. She thought of an old proverb that Forest used to invoke: *Turn a foe into a friend, and you'll have one less enemy.*

A tedious task, indeed. But Iris paused, backtracking to stand at Roman's cubicle.

"Do you want to grab a sandwich?" she asked, hardly aware of the words spilling from her mouth. All she knew was she hadn't eaten that day, and she was hungry for food and a stirring conversation with someone. Even if it was *him*. "There's a delicatessen two doors down that stays open this late. They have the best pickles."

Roman didn't even slow his typing. "I can't. Sorry."

Iris nodded and hurried on her way. She was ridiculous for even *thinking* he'd want to share dinner with her.

She left with bright eyes, hurling her broken heel into the dustbin on her way out.

2

Words for Forest

It was a good thing Roman had turned her down for a sandwich.

Iris stopped by a corner grocer, feeling how light her handbag was. She didn't realize she had stepped into one of Oath's enchanted buildings until the food on the shelves began to shift. Only items she could afford worked their way to the edge, vying for her attention.

Iris stood in the aisle, face burning. She gritted her teeth as she noticed how much she *couldn't* afford and then hastily grabbed a loaf of bread and a half carton of boiled eggs, hoping the shop would now leave her alone and cease weighing the coins in her purse.

This was why she was wary of enchanted buildings in the city. They could have pleasant perks, but they could also be nosy and unpredictable. She made a habit of avoiding unfamiliar ones, even if they were few and far between.

Iris hurried to the counter to pay, suddenly noticing the rows of empty shelves. Only a few cans remained behind—corn and beans and pickled onions.

"I take it your shop has been overly keen to sell tinned vegetables lately?" she asked dryly as she paid the grocer.

"Not quite. Things are being shipped west, to the front," he said. "My daughter is fighting for Enva and I want to make sure her company has enough food. It's hard work, feeding an army."

Iris blinked, surprised by his reply. "Did the chancellor order you to send aid?"

He snorted. "No. Chancellor Verlice won't declare war on Dacre until the god is knocking on our door, although he tries to make it *appear* like we're supportive of our brothers and sisters fighting in the west." The grocer set the loaf and eggs into a brown bag, sliding it across the counter.

Iris thought he was brave to make those statements. First, that their chancellor in the east was either a coward or a Dacre sympathizer. Second, to tell her which god his daughter was fighting for. She had learned this herself when it came to Forest. There were plenty of people in Oath who supported Enva and her recruitment and thought the soldiers courageous, but there were others who didn't. Those individuals, however, tended to be the ones who regarded the war as something that would never affect them. Or they were people who worshipped and supported Dacre.

"I hope your daughter remains safe and well at the front," Iris said to the grocer. She was glad to leave the nosy shop behind, only to slip on a wet newspaper in the street.

"Haven't you had enough of me for one day?" she growled as she bent to retrieve it, assuming the paper was the *Gazette*.

It wasn't.

Iris's eyes widened when she recognized the inkwell and quill emblem of the *Inkridden Tribune*—the *Gazette*'s rival. There were five different newspapers scattered throughout Oath, but the *Gazette* and the *Tribune* were the oldest and most widely read. And if Zeb happened to catch sight of her with the competition in her hands, he would surely give the promotion to Roman.

She studied the front page, curious.

MONSTERS SIGHTED THIRTY KILOMETERS FROM THE WAR FRONT, the headline announced in smudged type. Beneath it was an illustration of a creature with large, membranous wings, two spindly legs hooked with talons, and a horde of sharp, needlelike teeth. Iris shivered, straining to read the words, but they were indecipherable, melting into streaks of ink.

She stared at the paper for a moment longer, frozen on the street corner. Rain dripped from her chin, falling like tears onto the monstrous illustration.

Creatures like this didn't exist anymore. Not since the gods had been defeated centuries ago. But, of course, if Dacre and Enva had returned, so could the creatures of old. Creatures that had long only lived in myths.

Iris moved to drop the disintegrating paper in the rubbish bin but then was pierced by a cold thought.

Is this why so many soldiers are going missing at the front? Because Dacre is fighting with monsters?

She needed to know. And she carefully folded the *Inkridden Tribune* and slipped it into her inner coat pocket.

It took longer than she would've liked in the rain, especially without proper shoes, but Oath was not a simple place to travel by foot. The city was ancient, built centuries ago on the grave of a conquered god. Its streets meandered like a serpent's path—some were hard-packed dirt and narrow, others wide and paved, and a few were haunted by trickles of magic. New construction had bloomed during the past few decades, though, and it was sometimes jarring to Iris to see the brick buildings and shining windows adjacent to the thatched roofs, crumbling parapets, and castle towers of a forgotten era. To watch trams navigate the ancient, twisting streets. As if the present was trying to cobble over the past.

An hour later, Iris finally reached her flat, sore for breath and drenched from the rain.

She lived with her mother on the second floor, and Iris paused at the door, uncertain what would greet her.

It was just as she expected.

Aster was reclining on the sofa wrapped in her favorite purple coat, a cigarette smoldering between her fingers. Empty bottles were strewn across the living room. The electricity was out, as it had been for weeks now. A few candles were lit on the sideboard and had been burning so long the wax had carved a way free, puddling on the wood.

Iris merely stood on the threshold and stared at her mother until the world around them both seemed to blur.

"Little Flower," Aster said in a drunken lilt, finally noticing her. "You've come home at last to see me."

Iris inhaled sharply. She wanted to unleash a torrent of words. Words that tasted bitter, but then she noticed the silence. The roaring, terrible silence, and how the smoke curled within it, and she couldn't help herself. She glanced at the sideboard, where the candles flickered, and noticed what was missing.

"Where's the radio, Mum?"

Her mother arched her brow. "The radio? Oh, I sold it, honey."

Iris felt her heart plummet, down to her sore feet. "Why? That was *Nan's* radio."

"It could hardly pick up a channel, sweetheart. It was time for it to go."

No, Iris thought, blinking back tears. *You only needed money to buy more alcohol.*

She slammed the front door and walked through the living room, around the bottles, into the small, dingy kitchen. There was no candle lit here, but Iris had the place memorized. She set the dented loaf of bread and the half carton of eggs down on the counter before reaching for a paper sack and returning to the living room. She gathered up the bottles—*so many bottles*—and it made her think of that morning, and why she had run late. Because her mother had been lying on the floor next to a pool of vomit, in a kaleidoscope of glass, and it had terrified her.

"Leave it," Aster said with a wave of her hand. Ash fell from her cigarette. "I'll clean it up later."

"No, Mum. I have to make it to work on time tomorrow."

"I said to *leave* it."

Iris dropped the bag. The glass chimed within it, but she was too weary to fight. She did as her mother wanted.

She retreated to her dark room and fumbled for her matches, lighting the candles on her bedside table. But she was hungry, and eventually had to return to the kitchen to make a marmalade sandwich, and all the while her mother had lain on the sofa and drunk from a bottle and smoked and hummed her favorite songs that she could no longer listen to, because the radio was *gone*.

Back in the quiet of her chamber, Iris opened the window and listened to the rain. The air was cold, brisk. A trace of winter lingered within it, but Iris welcomed its bite and how it made her skin pebble. It reminded her that she was alive.

She ate her sandwich and eggs, eventually changing out of her wet clothes for a nightgown. Carefully, she laid the sopping *Inkridden Tribune* on the floor to dry, the monster illustration more smudged now after being carried in her pocket. She stared at it until she felt a sharp tug within her chest, and she reached beneath her bed, where she hid her grandmother's typewriter.

Iris pulled it out into the firelight, relieved to find it after the radio's unexpected departure.

She sat on the floor and opened her tapestry bag, where the beginnings of her essay now sat crinkled and damp from the rain. *Find something good to write about, and I might consider publishing it in the column next week,* Zeb had said. Sighing, Iris fed a new page to Nan's typewriter, fingers poised over the keys. But then she glanced at the ink-streaked monster again, and she found herself writing something entirely different from her essay.

She hadn't written to Forest in days. And yet she wrote to her brother now. The words spilled out of her. She didn't bother with the date or a *Dear Forest,* as she had with all the other letters she had typed to him. She didn't want to write his name, to see it on the page. Her heart felt bruised as she cut to the chase that night:

Every morning, when I wade through Mum's sea of green bottles, I think of you. Every morning, when I slip into the trench coat you left behind for me, I wonder if you thought of me for even a moment. If you imagined what your departure would do to me. To Mum.

I wonder if fighting for Enva is everything you thought it

would be. I wonder if a bullet or a bayonet has torn through you. If a monster has wounded you. I wonder if you're lying in an unmarked grave, covered in blood-soaked earth that I will never be able to kneel at, no matter how desperate my soul is to find you.

I hate you for leaving me like this.

I hate you, and yet I love you even more, because you are brave and full of a light that I don't think I will ever find or understand. The call to fight for something so fervently that death holds no sting over you.

Sometimes I can't draw a full breath. Between my worry and my fear...my lungs are small because I don't know where you are. It's been five months since I hugged you goodbye at the depot. Five months, and I can only assume you are missing at the front or are too busy to write me. Because I don't think I could rise in the morning—I don't think I could get out of bed—if news came to me that you were dead.

I wish you would be a coward for me, for Mum. I wish you would set down your gun and rend your allegiance to the goddess who has claimed you. I wish you would stop time and return to us.

Iris yanked the paper from the typewriter, folded it twice, and rose to approach her wardrobe.

Long ago, Nan had hidden notes for Iris to find in her room, sometimes slipping them under the bedroom door or beneath her pillow, or tucking them into a skirt pocket for her to find later at school. Small words of encouragement or a line from a poem that Iris always delighted to discover. It was a tradition of theirs, and Iris had grown up learning how to read and write by sending her grandmother notes.

It felt natural to her, then, to slide her letters to Forest under the wardrobe door. Her brother didn't have a room in their flat; he slept on the couch so Aster and Iris could have the two private bedrooms. But he and Iris had been sharing this closet for years.

The wardrobe was a small recess in the stone wall, with an arched door that had left a permanent scratch on the floor. Forest's garments hung to the right, Iris's to the left. He didn't have many clothes—a few button-down shirts, trousers, leather braces, and a pair of scuffed shoes. But Iris didn't have many outfits either. They made the most of what they had, patching holes and mending frayed edges and wearing their raiment until it was threadbare.

Iris had left his clothes in the closet, despite his teasing her that she could have the whole wardrobe space while he was gone. She had been patient the first two months he had been away at war, waiting for him to write to her as he had promised. But then her mother had started drinking, so profusely that she had been fired from the Revel Diner. The bills could no longer be paid; there was no food in the cupboard. Iris had no choice but to drop out of school and find work, all the while waiting for Forest to write to her.

He never had.

And Iris could no longer bear the silence. She had no address; she had no information as to where her brother was stationed. She had nothing but a beloved tradition and she did as her nan would have done—Iris gave the folded paper to the closet.

To her amazement, the letter had been gone the next day, as if the shadows had eaten it.

Unsettled, Iris had typed another message to Forest and slid it under her closet door. It too had vanished, and she had studied the small wardrobe closely, disbelieving. She had noticed the old stones in the wall, as if someone centuries ago had decided to close off an ancient passageway. She wondered if perhaps magic in the conquered god's bones, laid to rest deep beneath this city, had risen to answer her distress. If magic had somehow taken her letter and carried it on the western wind, delivering it to wherever her brother was fighting in the war.

How she had hated enchanted buildings until that moment.

She knelt now and slid her letter beneath the wardrobe door.

It was a relief to let the words go. The pressure in her chest eased.

Iris returned to her typewriter. As she lifted it, her fingers touched a ridge of cold metal, bolted on the inside of the frame. The plate was the length of her smallest finger and easy to overlook, but she vividly remembered the day she had discovered it. The first time she had read the engraving in the silver. THE THIRD ALOUETTE / MADE ESPECIALLY FOR D.E.W.

Daisy Elizabeth Winnow.

Her nan's name.

Iris had often studied those words, wondering what they meant. Who had made this typewriter for her nan? She wished she had noticed the engraving before her grandmother had passed away. Now Iris had no other choice but to be content in the mystery.

She shifted the typewriter back to its hiding place and crawled into bed. She drew the blankets to her chin but left the candle burning, even though she knew better. *I should blow it out, save it for tomorrow night,* she thought, because there was no telling when she would be able to pay the electricity bill. But for now, she wanted to rest in the light, not in the darkness.

Her eyes closed, heavy from a long day. She could still smell the rain and cigarette smoke in her hair. She still had ink on her fingertips, marmalade in the grooves of her teeth.

She was almost asleep when she heard it. The sound of paper rustling.

Iris frowned, sitting forward.

She looked at her wardrobe. There, on the floor, was a piece of paper.

She gaped, thinking it had to be the letter she had just sent. A draft must have pushed it back into her room. But when she rose from the bed, she could tell it wasn't her letter. This piece of paper was folded differently.

She hesitated, then rose and reached down to take it into her hand.

The paper trembled, and as the firelight seeped into it, Iris could discern typed words on the inside. Very few words, but distinctly dark.

She unfolded and read the letter. She felt her breath catch.

This isn't **Forest**.

3

Missing Myths

This isn't Forest.

The words echoed through Iris as she walked down Broad Street the next morning. She was in the heart of the city, the buildings rising high around her, trapping cold air and the last of dawn's shadows and the distant ring of the trams. She was almost to work, following her normal routine as if nothing strange had happened the night before.

This isn't Forest.

"Then who are you?" she whispered, hands fisted deep in her pockets. She slowly came to a halt in the street.

The truth was she had been too intimidated to write them back. Instead, she had spent the dark hours in an eddy of worry, remembering all the things she had said in her previous letters. She had told Forest she'd dropped out of school. It would be a blow to him—a broken promise—so she had quickly followed it up with her coveted job at the *Gazette,* where she was most likely going to earn columnist. Despite that personal information, she had never given away her true name; all her letters to Forest ended with her moniker. Little Flower. And she was most certainly relieved that—

"Winnow? *Winnow!*"

A hand grabbed her upper arm like a vise. She was suddenly yanked backward with such force that her teeth pierced her lower lip. Iris stumbled but found her bearings just as the oiled whoosh of a tram passed by, so close she could taste metal in her mouth.

She had almost been hit.

The realization made her knees quake.

And someone was still holding her arm.

She glanced up to behold Roman Kitt with his fashionable fawn-colored jacket and shined leather brogues and slicked-back hair. He was staring at her as if she had sprouted a second head.

"You should pay attention to where you're going!" he snapped, releasing her as if the contact had scorched him. "I was one second away from watching you be smashed on the cobblestones."

"I saw the tram," she replied, straightening her trench coat. He had nearly ripped it, and she would have been devastated if he had.

"I beg to differ," Roman said.

Iris pretended she hadn't heard him. She *carefully* stepped over the tram rails and hurried up the stairs into the lobby, blisters blooming on her heels. She was wearing her mother's dainty ankle boots, which were a size too small, but they would have to do until Iris could purchase a new set of heels. And because her feet were throbbing . . . she decided she needed to take the lift.

Roman was unfortunately on her trail, and she realized with an inward groan that they would have to ride the elevator together.

They stood waiting for it, shoulder to shoulder.

"You're here early," Roman finally said.

Iris touched her sore lower lip. "So are you."

"Autry give you an assignment I don't know about?"

The lift doors opened. Iris only smiled as she stepped inside, positioning herself as far away from Roman as possible when he joined her. But his cologne filled the small space; she tried not to breathe too deeply.

"Would it matter to you if he did?" she countered as the lift began to rumble upward.

"You were here late yesterday, working on something." Roman's voice was measured, but she swore she heard a hint of worry in him. He leaned on the wood paneling, staring at her. She kept her gaze averted, but she was suddenly aware of the scuffs on her mother's shoes, the wrinkles in her plaid skirt. The stray hairs escaping her tightly wound bun. The stains on Forest's old coat that she wore every day like armor.

"You didn't work all night in the office, did you, Winnow?"

His question jarred her. She brought her gaze back to his with a glare. "*What?* Of course not! You saw me leave, right after I offered to buy you a sandwich."

"I was busy," he said.

She sighed, glancing away.

They were just now approaching the third floor. The lift was slow, and it paused as if it sensed Iris's distress, let out a clang, and then opened the doors. A man dressed in a derby suit with a briefcase in hand glanced from Iris to Roman and the vast space between them before he gingerly stepped inside.

Iris relaxed a fraction. Having a stranger join them would make Roman hold his tongue. Or so she thought. The lift continued its laborious ascent. And Roman broke elevator etiquette, asking, "What assignment did he give you, Winnow?"

"It's none of your concern, Kitt."

"It actually *does* concern me. You and I want the same thing, in case you forgot."

"I haven't forgotten," she said tersely.

The derby-suited man fidgeted, caught in the middle of their argument. He cleared his throat and reached for his pocket watch. The sight of it made Iris think of Forest, which made her dwell once more on her current dilemma of the mysterious correspondent.

"I don't see how it's fair if Autry gives you assignments without my knowledge," Roman carried on. "This is supposed to be an even draw between you and me. We play by the rules. There shouldn't be any special favors."

Special favors?

They were almost to the fifth floor. Iris tapped her fingers against her thigh.

"If you have a problem with it, then go speak to Autry yourself," she said, just as the doors yawned. "Although I don't know why you're so worried. In case you need to be reminded . . . '*She'll give me no competition. None at all. She dropped out of Windy Grove School in her final year.*'"

"Excuse me?" Roman demanded, but Iris was already three steps away from the lift.

She hurried down the hall to the office, relieved to see that Sarah was already there, brewing the tea and emptying all the crumpled paper from dustbins. Iris let the heavy glass door swing closed behind her, right in Roman's face, and she heard the squeak of his shoes and his grunt of annoyance.

She didn't spare him another glance as she settled in at her desk.

This day had brought her far bigger problems than Roman Kitt.

"Are you happy here?"

Sarah Prindle seemed startled by Iris's soft question. It was noon, and the two girls had found themselves on lunch break together in the small kitchen. Sarah was sitting at the table, eating a cheese and pickle sandwich, and Iris was leaning against the counter, nursing her fifth cup of tea.

"Of course I'm happy," Sarah said. "Isn't everyone who gets a job here? The *Oath Gazette* is the most prestigious paper in the city. It pays well, and we get every holiday. Here, Winnow, do you want half of my sandwich?"

Iris shook her head. Sarah cleaned and ran errands and took messages for Zeb. She organized the obituaries and the classifieds and the announcements that came in, setting them on either Iris's or Roman's desk to edit and type.

"I guess what I meant to say was . . . is *this* what you envisioned for yourself, Prindle? When you were a girl and anything seemed possible?"

Sarah swallowed, pensive. "I don't know. I guess not."

"What was your dream, then?"

"Well, I always wanted to work in the museum. My dad used to take me

there on weekends. I remember loving all the old artifacts and stone tab-
lets, teeming with lore. The gods were quite vicious in their time. There were
the Skywards—Enva's family—and then the Underlings—Dacre's family.
They've always hated each other. Did you know that?"

"I unfortunately don't know much about the gods," Iris said, reaching
for the teapot. "They only taught us a few legends in school. Mainly about
the gods we killed, centuries ago. But you could still do that, you know."

"Kill gods?" Sarah's voice cracked.

"No," Iris said with a smile. "Although that would bring an exhilarating
end to this bloody war. I meant you could go and work in a museum. Do
what you love."

Sarah sighed as a piece of chutney fell from her sandwich. "You have
to be born into that profession, or be very, very old. But what about you,
Winnow? What is your dream?"

Iris hesitated. It had been a long time since someone had asked her such
a thing.

"I think I'm living it," she replied, tracing the chipped edge of her teacup. "I've always wanted to write about things that matter. To write things
that inspire or inform people." She suddenly felt shy, and chuckled. "But I
don't really know."

"That's swell," Sarah replied. "And you're in the right place."

A comfortable silence came between the girls. Sarah continued to eat her
sandwich and Iris cradled her tea, glancing at the clock on the wall. It was
nearly time to return to her desk when she dared to lean closer to Sarah and
whisper, "Do you ever pay attention to what the *Inkridden Tribune* publishes?"

Sarah's eyebrows shot upward. "The *Inkridden Tribune*? Why on earth
would you—"

Iris held a finger to her lips, heart quickening. It would be her luck if Zeb
happened to walk by and hear them.

Sarah lowered her voice, sheepish. "Well, no. Because I don't want to
get fired."

"I saw the paper yesterday," Iris continued. "On the street. They were
reporting on monsters at the front."

"Monsters?"

Iris began to describe the image from the paper—wings, talons, teeth. She couldn't stifle her shudder as she did, nor could she untangle the image of Forest from it.

"Have you ever heard of one?" Iris asked.

"They're called *eithrals,*" Sarah said. "We touched on them briefly in my mythology class, years ago. There are a few stories about them in some of the older tomes in the library . . ." She paused, a startled expression stealing across her face. "You're not thinking to write your own report on them, are you, Winnow?"

"I'm debating. But why are you looking at me that way, Prindle?"

"Because I don't think Autry would like it."

And I don't care what he thinks! Iris wanted to say, but it wasn't completely true. She *did* care, but only because she couldn't afford to lose to Roman. She needed to pay the electricity bill. She needed to purchase a nice set of shoes that fit. She needed to eat regularly. She needed to find her mother *help.*

And yet she wanted to write about what was happening in the west. She wanted to write the truth.

She wanted to know what Forest was facing at the front.

"Don't you think Oath needs to know what's truly happening out there?" she whispered.

"Of course," Sarah replied, pushing her glasses up her nose. "But who knows if eithrals are truly at the front or not. I mean, what if—" She abruptly cut herself off, her eyes flickering beyond Iris.

Iris straightened and turned, wincing when she saw Roman standing on the kitchen threshold. He was leaning on the doorframe, watching her with hooded eyes. She didn't know how much he had overheard, and she attempted a smile, even as her stomach dropped.

"Conspiring, are we?" he drawled.

"Course we are," Iris countered brightly, holding her teacup like a toast. "Thank you for the tip, Prindle. I need to get back to work."

"But you haven't eaten anything, Winnow!" Sarah protested.

"I'm not hungry," Iris said as she approached the doorway. "Pardon me, Kitt."

Roman didn't move. His gaze was fixed on her as if he wanted to read her mind, and Iris fought the temptation to smooth the stray tendrils of her hair, to anxiously roll her lips together.

He opened his mouth to say something but thought better of it, his teeth clinking shut as he shifted sideways.

Iris stepped over the threshold. Her arm brushed his chest; she heard him exhale, a hiss as if she had burned him, and she wanted to laugh. She wanted to taunt him, but she felt scraped clean of words.

Iris strode back to her desk and set down her lukewarm tea. She shrugged on her coat and grabbed her notepad and pencil, feeling the draw of Roman's suspicious gaze from across the room.

Let him wonder where she was going, she thought with a snort.

And she slipped away from the office.

Iris wandered deep into the library, where the oldest books sat on heavily guarded shelves. None of these volumes could be checked out, but they could be read at one of the library desks, and Iris choose a promising tome and carried it to a small table.

She flicked on the desk lamp and carefully turned the pages, which were so old they were speckled with mold and felt like silk beneath her fingertips. Pages that smelled like dust and tombs and places that could be reached only in the dark. Pages full of stories of gods and goddesses from a time long ago. Before the humans had slain them or bound them deep into the earth. Before magic had begun to bloom from the soil, rising from divine bones, charming certain doorways and buildings and settling into the rare object.

But now Enva and Dacre had woken from their prisons. Eithrals had been spotted near the front.

Iris wanted to know more about them.

She began to write down the lore she had never been taught in school. The Skywards, who had ruled Cambria from above, and the Underlings, who had reigned below. Once, there had been a hundred gods between the two families, their individual powers fanning across the firmament, land, and water. But over time they had killed each other, one by one, until only five remained. And those five had been overcome by humankind and given as spoils to the boroughs of Cambria. Dacre had been buried in the west, Enva in the east, Mir in the north, Alva in the south, and Luz in Central Borough. They were never to wake from their enchanted sleep; their graves were markers of mortal strength and resilience, but perhaps most of all were rumored to be places of great enchantment, drawing the ill, the faithful, the curious.

Iris herself had never visited Enva's grave in the east. It was kilometers from Oath, in a remote valley. *We'll go one day, Little Flower,* Forest had said to her only last year, even though they had never been a devout family. *Perhaps we'll be able to taste Enva's magic in the air.*

Iris bent over the book, continuing to search for the answers she craved. *How does one god draw another?*

Dacre had started the war by burning the village of Sparrow to the ground, killing the farmers and their families. And yet such devastation had failed to attract Enva to him, as he thought it would. Even after seven months of conflict, she remained hidden in Oath save for the moments when she strummed her harp, inspiring young people to enlist and fight against her nemesis.

Why do you hate each other? Iris wondered. What was the history behind Dacre and Enva?

She sifted through the book's leaves, but page after page had been removed, torn away from the volume. There were a few myths about Enva and Alva, but no detailed records of Dacre. His name was mentioned only in passing from legend to legend, and never connected to Enva. There was also nothing about eithrals—where they came from, what controlled them. How dangerous they were to humans.

Iris sat back in her chair, rubbing her shoulder.

It was as if someone wanted to steal the knowledge of the past. All the myths about Dacre, his magic and power. Why he was furious with Enva. Why he was instigating a war with her, dragging mortal kind into the bloodshed.

And it filled Iris with cold dismay.

4

Dustbin Revelations

Her mother was asleep on the sofa when Iris got home that evening. A cigarette had burned through the threadbare cushion, and the candles on the sideboard had almost melted into stubs.

Iris sighed but began to clean up the empty bottles and ashtrays. She removed her boots, wincing to see that the blisters had bled through her stockings. Barefoot, she stripped her mother's wine-stained sheets off the bed and then gathered a few garments to launder, carrying everything down to the common area. She paid a few coppers for water and a cup of soap granules and then selected a washboard and bucket and began to scrub.

The water was cold, pumped up from the city's cistern, and the soap turned her hands raw. But she scrubbed away the stains, and she wrung out garment after garment, her anger fueling her long after her stomach ceased groaning its emptiness.

By the time Iris had washed everything, she was ready to write the *This isn't Forest* person back. She returned to the flat and hung everything up to dry in the kitchen. She should eat something before she wrote them, or who knew what might come out of her. She found a tin of green beans in one of the cupboards and ate it with a fork, sitting on her bedroom floor. Her hands ached, but she reached for Nan's typewriter beneath the mattress.

She'd kept the note she'd received last night, and it sat open by her knee as she furiously began to type a reply:

> You claim who you are not, but without further introducing your-
> self. How many of my letters have you received? Do you make it
> a habit to read other people's post?

Iris folded the paper and slid it beneath the wardrobe door.

Roman was reading in bed when the paper arrived.

He had come to know the sound of Iris's letters well, how they slipped like a whisper into his room. He decided he would ignore this one for at least an hour, his long fingers hidden in the pages of the book he was reading. But from the corner of his eye, he could see the white patch on the floor, and it eventually bothered him so greatly that he rose from bed, shutting the tome with a sigh.

It was late, he realized as he checked his wristwatch. Shouldn't she be in bed? Although if he were honest . . . he had been waiting for her reply. He had expected it last night, and when it failed to appear, he halfway believed she would cease sending letters.

He didn't know if it would be more of a relief or a regret, to no longer have her letters mysteriously arrive to his room. He blamed this estate—it was an old, sprawling house, rumored to be built on a ley line of magic. Because of that, the Kitt mansion had a mind of its own. Doors opened and closed of their own volition, the curtains drew back at sunrise, and the floors shined themselves until they gleamed like ice. Sometimes when it rained, flowers would bloom in the most unexpected places—teacups and vases and even old shoes.

When Roman was fifteen—a year that he hated to remember—he had struggled with insomnia. Nearly every night, he would walk the dark corridors of the house, choking on heartache until he came across the kitchen. A candle would always be lit on the counter beside a warm glass of milk and a plate of his favorite biscuits. For that entire year, he thought the cook was the one leaving the meal out for him, until Roman realized it was the house, sensing his troubles and seeking to comfort him.

Roman now stared at Iris's letter on the floor.

"Still trying to amuse me?" he asked the wardrobe door. Of course, the house would not only seek to console him at his lowest but also be fond of mischief.

He had instantly known the letters were from Iris. She had given herself away not in name but in other ways. Her employment at the *Oath Gazette* was the primary one, and then her exquisite, visceral writing style was the other. At first Roman thought the letters were a prank. She had found a clever way to charm the house and get in his head, to unsettle him.

Which meant he would ignore them both. Iris and her letters. He had tossed that first letter of hers in his dustbin. It had sat there for a few hours while he typed at his desk, but by midnight, when he was exhausted and bleary-eyed and certainly not thinking straight, he retrieved the letter and stuck it in an old shoebox.

Forest must be her lover, off at war.

But then Roman soon realized, no. Forest was her older brother, and it tore something up in him to read how angry and sad and worried she was. How much she missed him. By the vulnerability in her letters, Roman knew Iris had no inkling her words had found their way into her rival's hands.

He had spent a full week pondering over this dilemma. He should let her know. Perhaps in person, one day at the office? But Roman lost the nerve every time he imagined it. So perhaps it was best by letter? He could write something along the lines of: *Hello, thank you for writing, but I believe you should be aware that your letters have somehow found their way to me. And this is Roman C. Kitt, by the way. Yes, the Roman C. Kitt at work. Your competitor.*

She would be mortified. He didn't want to embarrass her, nor did he want to suffer a slow, painful death at her hands.

He had decided he would say nothing, and simply pick up her letters when they arrived and put them in the shoebox. Eventually she would cease writing or Roman would at last move out of this room, and it would no longer be a problem.

Until the letter had arrived last night.

It wasn't addressed to Forest, which instantly hooked Roman's interest.

He had read it, like he had read all the others. Sometimes he read them multiple times. At first it was a "tactic," because she was his competition and he wanted to know as much about her as possible. But then he realized he was reading them because he was deeply moved by her writing and the memories she shared. Sometimes he studied the way she spun words and language, and it made him both envious and awed. She knew how to stir up feelings in a reader, which Roman found quite dangerous.

If he wasn't careful, she would beat him and win columnist.

It was time he wrote her back. It was time he got into her head for a change.

This isn't Forest was all he had typed last night, and a weight had slipped off his chest with the acknowledgment.

He had defied the logical side of his brain and slipped the words through his wardrobe door. *This is ridiculous. Why am I doing this?* he had thought, but when he checked his closet, the paper had vanished.

He was shocked but imagined Iris would be more so. To finally have someone write her back after three months. Someone who wasn't Forest.

Roman now bent to gather her letter. He read and felt the insult within it, particularly the *Do you make it a habit to read other people's post?* Scowling, he walked to his desk and fed a page into his typewriter. He wrote:

I've made a habit of picking up the stray pieces of paper that somehow appear in my room at random intervals. Would you pre-fer I leave them on the floor?

And then sent it back through the wardrobe.

He paced, impatient as he waited for her to reply. *I should tell her now,* he thought, dragging his hand through his hair. *I should tell her it's me. This is the point of no return. If I don't tell her now, I will never be able to.*

But the more he thought of it, it more he realized he didn't *want* to. If he told her, she would stop writing. He would lose his tactical advantage.

Her reply came at last. Roman was strangely relieved as he read:

You could always be a lamb and return my previous letters. I wouldn't want your floor to suffer. Or your dustbin.

It was like she *knew* he had tossed the first one in the trash. His face reddened as he sat at his desk. He pulled open one of the drawers, where the shoebox hid. Roman lifted its lid to stare at the host of letters within. Page after page. Words all written to Forest. Words he had read multiple times.

Roman should send them back to her.

And yet . . .

I'm afraid I'm unable to return them.

He sent the terse message. He paced again as he waited, and when Iris remained silent, Roman grimaced. This was it. She was done.

Until another page whispered over his floor.

You're welcome for the good laugh, then. I'm sure my letters were highly diverting while they lasted, but I won't bother you or distress your floor again.

Cheers!

Roman read it, three times. Here was his way out. No more annoying papers littering his floors. No more opportunities for Iris's writing to haunt him. This was good. This was brilliant. He had put a stop to it without having to embarrass her or reveal himself. He should be pleased.

Instead, he sat at his desk. He typed, allowing the words to spill out of him like a candlelit confession. And he sent his letter to her before he could think better of it.

By all means, don't stop on account of me or my floor. I claimed who I <u>wasn't</u>, and you then—quite naturally—asked who I am, but I think it's better this way. That we keep our identities secret and just rest in the fact that some old magic is at play here, connecting our doorways.

But just in case you were wondering ... I'll gladly read whatever you write.

5

Pity

I f any of you receive an offer like this, I want to know about it immediately," Zeb said the following morning, waving a piece of paper around the office. "It's sleazy, and I won't see any of you lost to some dangerous, feckless endeavor."

"What endeavor, sir?" Roman asked.

"Read it yourself and then pass it around," Zeb said, handing the sheet to him.

It took a minute for whatever it was to reach Iris at her desk. The paper was crinkled by then, and she felt Zeb hovering as she read:

WANTED IMMEDIATELY: War Correspondents

The *Inkridden Tribune* is looking to hire journalists who are willing to travel into the war zone to draft articles about the current state of the gods' war. The articles will be published in the *Inkridden Tribune*. Note that this is a neutral position, and as such will grant protection from both sides of the conflict, although there is still a measure of danger involved. If interested, please see Ms. Helena Hammond. The *Inkridden Tribune* will pay fifty bills per month for the position.

Fifty bills? That was twice the amount she made in a month here at the *Gazette*.

Iris must have taken too long to read it, because Zeb cleared his throat. She passed the paper to the desk behind her.

"*Inkridden Tribune* wants to sell more papers than us by *scaring* our readers," Zeb said. "This war is a problem for Western Borough and their chancellor to settle. They buried Dacre; let them deal with him and his anger accordingly, rather than drain *us* of our soldiers and resources."

"What of Enva, Mr. Autry?" Sarah asked.

Zeb looked stunned for a moment, that Sarah would voice such a thing. Iris was pleased by her friend's bravery, even as Sarah instantly hunched under the scrutiny, pushing her glasses farther up her nose as if she wanted to vanish.

"Yes, what of *Enva*?" Zeb continued, his face beet red. "She was ours to keep buried and tamed in the east, and we have done a poor job of it, haven't we?" He was quiet for a moment, and Iris braced herself. "While Enva and her music have convinced a few weak-minded individuals to enlist, most of us here want to focus on other matters. So don't let this war talk fool you. It'll all blow over soon. Keep up the good work and come to me at once if someone from the *Inkridden Tribune* approaches you about this."

Iris curled her hand into a fist under her desk until she could feel the bite of her fingernails.

Forest was the furthest thing from a *weak-minded individual*.

When Dacre had started attacking town after town last summer, the chancellor and residents of Western Borough had sent out a call for help. *He is overtaking us!* they had cried, the words traveling through crackling telephone wires. *He is killing us if we don't agree to bow to him, to fight for him. We need aid!*

Sometimes Iris still felt shame when she thought of how slow people in the east had been to answer that cry. But the ugly truth was the denizens of Oath hadn't believed it when the news broke of Dacre's return. Not until Enva's music began to trickle through the streets, woven with the revelation. It had been the Southern and Central Boroughs to respond first, assuming if they sent a few auxiliary forces, Dacre could be overcome before he razed the west to the ground.

They underestimated him. They underestimated the number of devout people who would choose to fight *for* Dacre.

That was the beginning of the war. It unfolded rapidly, ruthlessly. While Oath was sleeping, the west was burning. And yet despite the countless dark kilometers that stretched between the east and the west, Forest was one of the first to enlist.

Iris wondered where he was at that very moment. Sleeping in a cave, hiding in a trench, wounded in a hospital, shackled in the enemy's camp. All while she sat safely at her desk, typing up classifieds, obituaries, and articles.

She wondered if he was still breathing.

Zeb called her into his office an hour later.

"I'll give you three days, Winnow," he said, fingers steepled over his desk. "Three days to write an essay, topic of your choosing. If it's better than Kitt's, I'll publish it and seriously consider you for the column."

She could hardly believe him. An open assignment. He rarely gave those out. But then she remembered what he had said earlier, and she nearly spoke her mind.

I plan to write about those weak-minded individuals.

"Winnow?"

Iris realized she was frowning; her jaw was clenched. "Yes, thank you, sir."

She forced a smile and returned to her desk.

She couldn't afford to lose this promotion. Which meant she couldn't afford to upset Zeb with her essay. She needed to write something he would *want* to publish.

This open assignment suddenly felt very narrow indeed.

"There you are."

Roman's voice caught her on the way out of the lobby, just as dusk fell. Iris startled when he seamlessly fell into stride beside her.

"What do you want, Kitt?" she asked with a sigh.

"Are you hurt?"

"I'm sorry?"

"You've been limping all day."

She resisted the urge to glance down at her feet, at her mother's terrible pointed boots. "No, I'm fine. What do you want?" she repeated.

"To talk with you about Autry. He's giving you an open assignment, isn't he?" Roman asked, forging a path for them on the crowded pavement.

Iris thought it was only fair to let him know. "Yes. And it's not due to *special favors.*"

"Oh, isn't it?"

She halted, which inspired a flurry of curses as people had to walk around her and Roman. "And what's *that* supposed to mean?" she asked in a sharp tone.

"It means exactly as it sounds," Roman said. The streetlamps were beginning to flicker to life, illuminating his face with amber light. She hated how handsome he was. She hated how her heart softened when he looked at her. "Autry is giving you a special favor so he can promote you instead of me."

And that softness fled, leaving behind a bruise.

"*What?*" The word burst from her; it tasted like copper, and she realized the cut on her lip had reopened. "How dare you say that to me!"

Roman was frowning now. He shoved his hands into his coat pockets. "I was under the impression that this position would be fairly earned, and I don't—"

"What do you mean by this 'favor'?"

"He pities you!" Roman cried, exasperated.

Iris froze. His words struck her, deeply. She felt the frost in her chest, spreading outward to her hands. She was trembling, and she hoped he didn't notice.

"Autry *pities* me," she echoed. "Why? Because I'm a low-class girl who's out of her depth working for the press?"

"Winnow, I—"

"In your opinion, I should be washing dishes in a restaurant kitchen, shouldn't I? Or I should be cleaning houses, on my hands and knees, polishing floors for people like you to walk over."

His eyes flashed. "I never said you didn't deserve to be at the *Gazette*. You're a bloody good writer. But you dropped out of school in your final year and—"

"Why does that even matter?" she exclaimed. "Are you someone who likes to judge a person by their past? By what school they attended? Is that all you can look at?"

Roman was so still, so quiet that Iris thought she had charmed him into stone. "No," he finally said, but his voice sounded odd. "But you're becoming unreliable. You've been running late, missing assignments, and you're sloppy."

She took a step back. She didn't want him to sense how badly his words wounded her. "I see. Well, it's reassuring to know that if I get the position, it will only be due to pity. And if you get columnist, it will only be due to how much your rich father can bribe Autry to give it to you."

She spun and strode away, against the flow of traffic. The world blurred for a moment; she realized her eyes were burning with tears.

I hate him.

Over the noise of conversation and the bell of the tram and the jostle of strangers' shoulders, she could hear him calling to her.

"Now wait a minute, Winnow. Don't run from me!"

She melted into the crowd before Roman could catch up to her.

{ 6 }

Dinner with People You Love (or Don't)

Iris was still reeling from the things Roman had said to her when she dragged herself into the flat. She didn't notice that all the candles had been lit or the fragrance of dinner until her mother appeared wearing her best dress, hair curled and lips painted red.

"There you are, sweetheart. I was getting worried. You're home an hour late!"

Iris merely gaped for a moment, her eyes flickering from her mother to the dinner set on the kitchen table. "Are we expecting company?"

"No. It's just you and me tonight," Aster said, stepping forward to help Iris from her coat. "I thought we could have a special dinner. Like we used to, in the past."

When Forest was still with them.

Iris nodded, her stomach rumbling when she realized her mother had bought dinner from her favorite restaurant. A roast with vegetables sat on a platter, accompanied by rolls that gleamed with butter. Her mouth watered as she took her seat, Aster fixing her plate.

It had been a long time since her mother had cooked or bought dinner.

And while Iris wanted to be cautious, she was so hungry. For warm, nourishing food. For sober conversations with her mother. For the days of the past, before Forest had left and Aster had turned to the bottle.

"Tell me about work, sweetheart," her mother said, settling across the table from her.

Iris took a bite. How had her mother paid for such a feast? And then it hit her; the money from Nan's radio must have bought this meal—and alcohol, most likely—and the food suddenly tasted like ash.

"I've been working on obituaries lately," she confessed.

"That's lovely, darling."

Lovely was not how Iris would describe her obituary work, and she paused, studying Aster.

Her mother had always been beautiful in Iris's mind, with her heart-shaped face, russet-colored hair, and wide, charming smile. But there was a glaze in her eyes that night, as if she could look at things but not truly see them. Iris winced when she realized Aster wasn't sober.

"Tell me more about the *Tribune*," Aster said.

"It's actually the *Gazette*, Mum."

"Ah, that's right. The *Gazette*."

Iris proceeded to tell her bits and pieces, leaving Roman out of it. As if he didn't exist, but his words continued to haunt her. *You're sloppy.*

"Mum?" Iris began, hesitating when Aster glanced up at her. "Do you think you could help me curl my hair tonight?"

"I'd love to," her mother said, rising from the table. "In fact, I bought a new shampoo for my hair. We'll wash yours and set it with my rollers. Here, come into the lavatory."

Iris picked up one of the candles and followed her. It took a little bit of effort, but Aster was able to wash her hair over the side of the tub with the bucket of rainwater they had. And then it was back to her mother's bedroom, where Iris sat before the mirror.

She closed her eyes as Aster combed the tangles from her hair. For a moment, there were no blisters on her heels or heavy sorrows in her heart.

Forest would be home soon from the horology shop, and her mother would turn on the radio and they would listen to late-night talk shows and music.

"Is there someone you're interested in at work?" Aster asked, beginning to section Iris's long hair.

Iris's eyes flew open. "No. Why would you ask, Mum?"

Aster shrugged. "Just wondering why you want me to curl your hair."

"It's for *me,*" Iris replied. "I'm sick of looking like a slob."

"I've never thought of you as a slob, Iris. Not once." She began to clip the first roller into place. "Did a boy say that to you?"

Iris sighed, watching Aster's reflection in the speckled mirror.

"Perhaps," she finally confessed. "He's my competition. We both want the same position."

"Let me guess. He's young, handsome, suave, and knows you write better than him, so he's doing all he can to distract and worry you."

Iris nearly laughed. "How do you know that, Mum?"

"Mothers know everything, sweetheart," Aster said with a wink. "And I'm casting my bet on you."

Iris smiled, surprised by how much her mother's reassurance bolstered her.

"Now then. If your brother knew a boy said such a thing to you . . ." Aster clucked her tongue. "There would be no hope for him. Forest was always so protective over you."

Iris blinked back a surge of tears. Perhaps it was because this was the first true conversation she had had with her mother in a long time. Perhaps it was because Aster's fingers were gentle, coaxing memories to the surface. Perhaps it was because Iris finally had a full belly and clean hair. But she could almost see her brother again, as if the mirror had caught a flash of him.

Sometimes she relived the moment that had changed everything. The moment when Enva had stopped him on his walk home. A goddess in disguise. He had chosen to listen to her music, and that music welled in his heart, propelling him to enlist that night.

It had all happened so quickly. Iris had scarcely had the chance to catch her breath as Forest explained his rash decision. He had been packing, bright-eyed and feverish. She had never seen him so excited.

I have to go, Little Flower, he had said, touching her hair. *I need to answer the calling.*

And she had wanted to ask him, *What about me? What about Mum? How can you love this goddess more than us?* But she hadn't. She had been too scared to raise those questions to him.

"Mum?" Iris asked, tremulous. "Mum, do you think Forest is—"

"He's alive, sweetheart," Aster said, fixing the last roller. "I'm his mother. And I would know if he had left this realm."

Iris released a shaky breath. She met her mother's gaze in the mirror.

"It's going to be all right, Iris," Aster said, hands on her shoulders. "I'm going to be better too, from now on. I promise. And I'm sure Forest will return in the next month or so. Things will get better soon."

Iris nodded. Even though her mother's eyes were hazy from the alcohol that distorted her reality, she believed her.

Roman stormed home. He was so preoccupied with thinking about how horribly awry his conversation with Iris had gone that he didn't realize there was company in the drawing room. At least, not until he had slammed the front door and was striding through the foyer to the grand stairwell, and his mother's delicate voice called out to him.

"Roman? Roman, dear, please come say hello to our guests."

His foot froze on the step as he stifled a groan. Hopefully he could say hello to whoever it was and then retreat to his room and revise his essay on missing soldiers. *An assignment that* should *have gone to Iris,* he thought as he walked into the gilded drawing room.

His gaze went to his father first, as if all the gravity in the room was centered on him. Mr. Ronald Kitt had been handsome in his day, but years of grief, stress, cigars, and brandy had left their mark. He was tall but stooped, ruddy-faced with hard eyes that gleamed like blue gemstones. His raven hair was now streaked with thick lines of silver. His mouth was always pursed, as if nothing could ever please him or draw a smile.

Some days Roman was terrified he would turn into his father.

Mr. Kitt stood by the hearth, behind the chair Roman's mother was gracing. And while his father's presence was intimidating, his mother lent a gentleness to any room. In spite of that, she had become more and more distracted as the years passed, ever since Del had died. Conversations with her often didn't quite make sense, as if Mrs. Kitt belonged more with ghosts than the living.

Roman swallowed when he met his father's gaze.

"Roman, this is Dr. Herman Little, a chemist at Oath University, and his daughter, Elinor," Mr. Kitt introduced, extending his glass of brandy to his left.

Roman's eyes reluctantly traveled across the room, landing on an older gentleman with sandy brown hair and overly large spectacles on a small, crooked nose. Beside him on the divan was his daughter, a pale girl with blond hair crimped in a bob. Blue veins pulsed in her temples and on the backs of her clasped hands. She looked fragile, until Roman met her gaze and saw nothing but ice in her eyes.

"Dr. Little, Miss Elinor," Mr. Kitt continued. "This is my son, Roman Kitt. He's about to be promoted to columnist at the *Oath Gazette*."

"How splendid!" Dr. Little said with a yellow-toothed smile. "To be columnist at the most prestigious paper in Oath is a rare feat. You'll hold a great influence over your readers. Quite an achievement for one your age, which is . . ."

"I'm nineteen, sir," Roman replied. He must have sounded too brisk, because his father scowled. "It's a pleasure to meet you both, but if you'll excuse me, there is an article I need to wor—"

"Go and freshen up for dinner," Mr. Kitt interrupted. "Meet us in the dining room in half an hour. Don't be late, son."

No. Roman knew better than to be late for anything when his father was involved. His mother smiled at him as he turned and left.

In the safety of his room, Roman dropped his messenger bag and his façade of dutiful son. He raked his fingers through his hair and hurled his coat across the room. And it was strange how his gaze went to his wardrobe. There was no paper on the floor. No letter from Iris. But of course, she probably wasn't home yet. Roman had a terrible inkling that she didn't take the tram but walked to and from work, and that was why she was late sometimes.

It wasn't his problem, but he kept envisioning her limping. As if something was wrong with those godsawful boots she was wearing.

"Stop thinking about her!" he hissed, pinching the bridge of his nose.

He pushed Iris far from his thoughts. He washed and dressed in a black suit for dinner, descending to the dining hall. He was early by two minutes, but it didn't matter. His parents and the Littles were waiting on him. He unfortunately saw that he was to take the chair directly across from Elinor. Her cold stare pierced him the moment he sat down.

That was when Roman felt his first sense of dread.

This wasn't going to be a comfortable dinner.

His nan was also missing from the table, which meant his father was trying to control everything that was said tonight. Roman's nan lived in the east wing of the mansion. She had a temper and spoke her mind, and Roman fiercely wished she were present.

He was silent for the first two courses. So was Elinor. Their fathers did most of the talking, and they spoke of the cost of certain chemicals, the method of extraction, the rate and catalysts of reactions, why a certain element called praxin turned green when it was combined with a salt and how only a certain type of metal could safely store it.

Roman watched his father, who was nodding and acting like he knew exactly what Dr. Little was talking about. All too soon, the conversation turned to the railroad.

"My grandfather chartered the first railroad out of Oath," Mr. Kitt said. "Before that, it was horses and wagons and the stagecoach if you wanted to travel anywhere."

"What foresight your ancestors had," said Dr. Little.

Roman blocked out the rest of his father's story and Dr. Little's flattery, weary of hearing about how his family did this and that and made their fortune. None of it truly mattered when it came to the peers of Cambria, who were steeped in old wealth and often snubbed people like the Kitts, who were built from new, innovative money. Roman knew it bothered his father—how often their family was disregarded at social events—and Mr. Kitt was always plotting to change people's minds. One of those plans was Roman's gaining columnist instead of attending university and studying literature, as Roman wanted to do. Because if money couldn't seal the Kitts' prowess and respect in the city, then positions of power and esteem would.

Roman was hoping he could escape the table before the last course when his mother turned to Elinor.

"Your father says you are an accomplished pianist," Mrs. Kitt said. "Roman *loves* to listen to the piano."

He did? Roman had to bite back a retort.

Elinor didn't spare him a glance. "I was, but I prefer to spend my hours in my father's laboratory now. In fact, I don't play anymore."

"Oh. I'm sorry to hear of it."

"Don't be, Mrs. Kitt. Papa asked me to stop, since music is aligned with Enva these days," Elinor said. Her voice was monotone, as if she felt nothing.

Roman watched her push the food around her plate. He suddenly had a creeping suspicion that the Littles were Dacre sympathizers, and his stomach churned. Those who favored Dacre in the war tended to be people who were one of three things: zealously devout, ignorant of the mythology where Dacre's true and terrifying nature was depicted, or, like Zeb Autry, afraid of Enva's musical powers.

"Enva's music was never something to be afraid of," Roman said before he could stop himself. "In myths, she strummed her harp over the graves of mortals who died, and her songs guided souls from their bodies to the next realm, whether it was to live above with the Skywards or below with the Underlings. Her songs are woven with truth and knowledge."

The table had fallen deathly quiet. Roman didn't dare glance at his father, whose eyes were boring into him.

"Excuse my son," Mr. Kitt said with a nervous chuckle. "He read one too many myths as a boy."

"Why don't you tell us more of the *Gazette,* Roman?" Dr. Little suggested. "I've heard Chancellor Verlice has limited the newspapers in Oath on how much they can report on the war. Is this true?"

Roman froze. He wasn't sure—he was so focused on trying to outwrite Iris these days—but then he thought about how little he had written about the war, and how Zeb's assignments had drifted to other things. The fact that he was writing about missing soldiers was surprising, although perhaps even that was a ploy to turn people against Enva.

"I haven't heard of any restrictions," Roman replied. But it suddenly felt possible, and he could envision the chancellor of Oath—a tall, beady-eyed man with a stern countenance—quietly enforcing such a thing, to keep the east out of the war's destruction.

"When do you become columnist?" Dr. Little asked. "I'll be sure to purchase the paper that day."

"I'm not sure," Roman said. "I'm currently being evaluated for the position."

"But he *will* get it," Mr. Kitt insisted. "Even if I have to bribe the old bloke who runs the joint."

The men chuckled. Roman went rigid. Iris's words returned to him like a slap to the face. *If you get columnist, it will only be due to how much your rich father can bribe Autry to give it to you.*

He rose, bumping the table in his haste. The plates rattled, the candlelight trembled.

"If you'll pardon me," he began to say, but his father's voice overpowered his.

"Sit down, Roman. There's something important we need to discuss."

Slowly, Roman resumed his seat. The silence felt fraught. He wanted to melt through a crack in the floor.

"Oh, dearest," his mother exclaimed. "It'll be so exciting! To finally have something happy to celebrate."

Roman glanced at her, brow arched. "What are you speaking about, Mother?"

Mrs. Kitt looked at Elinor, who was staring down at her hands, expressionless.

"We've arranged a marriage between you and Miss Little," Mr. Kitt announced. "This joining of our families will not only be beneficial in our next endeavor but will also be just as your mother described: a joyous occasion. For too long, we have been in mourning. It's time to celebrate."

Roman exhaled through his teeth. It felt like he had fractured a rib as he struggled to fathom what his parents had done. Arranged marriages were still common in the upper class, amongst viscounts and countesses and anyone else still clinging to a dusty title. But the Kitts were not those sorts of people, no matter how determined his father was to elevate them into high society.

It also struck Roman as odd that his father was arranging a marriage with a *professor's* daughter, not the daughter of a lord. He sensed that something else lurked beneath the surface of this conversation, and Roman was simply a pawn in a game.

Calmly, he said, "I regret to inform you that I cannot——"

"Don't be a lad about this, Roman," Mr. Kitt said. "You will marry this lovely young woman and unite our families. That is your *duty* as my sole heir. Do you understand?"

Roman stared at his plate. The half-eaten meat and potatoes, now gone cold. He realized that everyone at the table had known but him. Even Elinor must have known, because she was watching him closely now, as if measuring his reaction to her.

He swallowed his emotions, hiding them deep in his bones. The things that he wanted, the simmering anger. The grief that was still tender, like a wound half healed. He thought of the small grave in the garden, a headstone he could hardly endure to visit. He thought of the past four years, how dark and cold and miserable they had been. And his guilt whispered to him. *Of course you must do this. You failed in your most paramount of duties once, and if this is for the good of your family, how could you not?*

"Yes, sir," he said in a flat tone.

"Excellent!" Dr. Little clapped his spindly hands. "Should we have a toast?"

Roman watched numbly as a servant filled a flute with champagne for him. His hand felt detached as he took hold of the glass; he was the last to raise it in a toast he didn't even hear because he felt a roaring panic cascade through him.

But just before he deigned to sip the wine, he met Elinor's eyes. He saw a flicker of fear in her, and he realized she was just as trapped as he was.

7

Skywards vs. Underlings

It was late by the time Roman returned to his room after dinner. Sweat was breaking out on his brow, lining his palms.

He was about to marry a stranger. A girl who looked at him with disdain.

He tore off his jacket, ripped away the bow tie at his throat. He kicked off his brogues and unbuttoned his shirt and then fell to his knees in the center of the floor, curling up as if he could ease the pain in his stomach.

He deserved this, though. It was his fault that he was his father's sole heir.

He deserved to be miserable.

His breaths were ragged. He closed his eyes and told himself to *inhale, exhale, inhale.*

He could hear his wristwatch ticking. Minutes were passing, one after the other. He could smell the rug beneath him. Musty wool and a faint trace of shoe polish.

When he opened his eyes again, he noticed the piece of paper on the floor.

Iris had written.

He crawled to it. His hands were trembling as he opened the folded paper, surprised to find a very short but intriguing message from her:

What do you know of Dacre & Enva?

For a moment, he was overwhelmed by her seemingly innocent question. But then his mind started racing through the myths he knew. The stories in the old volumes he had inherited from his grandfather.

It was a welcome distraction. He could lose himself in this; he could write her back because it was facts she wanted, nothing more.

Roman stood and whispered, "Please light the lamp."

The old estate answered, flickering his desk lamp on. The lightbulb cast his room in a soft golden glow as he approached his built-in bookshelves. He began to sift through his mythology tomes, handling them carefully as most of them were falling apart. He was trying to decide which myth to share with Iris when a few loose leaves fell out of one volume, drifting down to his feet.

Roman paused. Page after page, tinted caramel with age, and full of his grandfather's handwriting. He picked up the sheets and glanced through them, realizing it was a recording about Enva and Dacre. A myth that was rarely known these days.

His grandfather must have written it down and tucked the papers away in one of his books for safekeeping. He had often done that, forgetting where he had placed his writing. Roman had found everything from letters to stray ideas to random story chapters, years after his death.

And as Roman skimmed the handwritten myth, he knew this was the one he wanted to share with Iris.

He carried it to his desk and sat, working to transcribe it on the typewriter.

You're in luck. I happen to know a thing or two about Dacre and Enva. There's a myth I'm familiar with, and I'll share it with you. I found it tucked away in an old tome, handwritten and only half complete. So keep in mind that its latter part is missing, and I have yet to come across it.

———

There were two families that divided the gods of old: the Skywards and the Underlings. The Skywards ruled above, and the Underlings reigned below. Most of all, they hated each other—as immortals are prone to do—and often engaged in challenges, to prove who was more worthy to be feared or loved or worshiped among mortal kind.

Dacre Underling, hewn from white limestone with veins of blue-lit fire, decided he would capture one of his enemies because he was bored of living day after day, season after season, year after year. Such is the weight of immortality. As the god of vitality and healing, he craved a challenge, so he asked a human who lived below if they knew the name of the most beloved Skyward divine. A god or goddess whom mortals praised and loved.

"Oh yes, sire," said the denizen. "She plays music on a harp that would melt the coldest of hearts. She ferries mortal souls after they die, and there is none as fair as her above or below."

Dacre decided he must have this Skyward goddess.

Up through the earth he traveled, through kilometers of stone and the gnarled roots of trees and the bitter taste of soil. When he reached above, he was overwhelmed by the might of the sun, and he had to linger in a cave for three days and three nights, until his eyes could withstand the light of his enemies. Even then, he chose to wander at night, when the moon was gentler.

"Where is Enva?" he asked the mortals he came across. "Where can I find the fairest of Skywards?"

"She can be found in the last place you would think she'd be" was the reply he received.

And Dacre, who was too impatient and angry to overturn every stone for her, decided he would call up his hounds from below. Sinewy, fire-hearted beasts, with translucent skin and teeth that spawned nightmares in dreams, the hounds roamed the land that night, searching for beauty and devouring those who got in their way. For Dacre assumed Enva was lovely to behold. But when the sun rose, the hounds were forced to go below, back to the shadows, and they had not found the one Dacre sought.

So he summoned his eithrals from the deep caves of beneath. Great wyverns with filmed eyes and membranous wings and poisoned talons. They could withstand the sun, and they flew through the sky, searching for beauty and destroying whatever moved beneath them. But soon a storm came, and the eithrals' wings threatened to tear in the fierce winds. So Dacre sent them back below, even though they too had not found the one he sought.

It was only when he walked the land himself that he came upon a graveyard. And in the graveyard was a woman, ordinary by Dacre's standards, with long dark hair and green eyes. She was dressed in homespun; she was barefoot and slender, and he decided he would not waste his time asking her where to find Enva.

He passed her by without a second glance, but as he walked away... he heard the music of a harp, sweet and golden, even as the sky was gray and the breeze was cold. He heard the woman sing, and her voice pierced him. He was stunned by the beauty of her, beauty which could not be seen but felt, and he crawled back to her, over the graves of humans.

"Enva," he said. "Enva, come with me."

She did not stop her music for him. He had to wait while she sang over every grave, and he noticed the soil was richly turned, as if these humans had just been buried.

When she sang the last song, she turned to look at him. "Dacre Underling, god of below, why have you wrought such chaos among innocents?"

"What do you mean?"

She indicated the graves. "Your hounds and your eithrals have killed these people. With your power, you could have healed their wounds. But you did not, and now I must sing their souls into eternity, for your creatures took them before it was their appointed time."

Dacre at last found the strength to rise. When Enva looked at him, he felt insignificant and unworthy, and he wanted her to behold him with something else. Something much different than sorrow and anger.

"I did it to find you," he said.

"You could have found me on your own, had you taken the time to look for me."

"And now that I have found you, will you come below with me? Will you dwell where I live, breathe the air I inspire? Will you join me in ruling the world beneath?"

Enva was quiet. Dacre thought he would perish in that moment of uncertain silence.

"I am happy here," she said. "Why would I go below with you?"

"To forge peace between our two families," he answered, although peace was truly the last thing on his mind.

"I think not," she said, and she melted into the wind before Dacre could grasp the hem of her dress.

He burned with fury; she had slipped away. She had denied him. So he decided he would unleash the brunt of his wrath on innocents; he would refuse to heal them out of spite, knowing Enva would soon have no choice but to answer him and give herself up as an offering.

His hounds tore across the land. His eithrals haunted the skies. His anger made the ground shake, and he created new chasms and rifts.

But he was right. As soon as innocents began to suffer, Enva came to him.

"I will follow you into your realm below," she said. "I will live with you in the shadows on two conditions: you will uphold peace

and you will permit me to sing and play my instrument whenever
I desire."

Dacre, who was enchanted by her, readily agreed. He took Enva
below. But little did he know what her music would do once it was
strummed deep in the earth.

Roman finished typing. His shoulder blades ached; his gaze was bleary.
He glanced at his watch, so exhausted he struggled to read the time.

It looked to be half past two in the morning. He had to be up by six
thirty.

He closed his eyes for a moment, searching within himself. His soul was
quiet; he was no longer swarmed by that suffocating panic.

And he gathered the sheets of paper, folded them in perfect thirds, and
sent the myth to Iris.

8

A Sandwich with an Old Soul

Roman Kitt was late.

Not once in Iris's three months of working at the *Gazette* had he been late. She was suddenly keen to know why.

She took her time fixing a fresh cup of tea from the sideboard, expecting him to arrive any minute. When he failed to appear, Iris walked the route to her cubicle, passing Roman's on the way. She paused long enough to re-arrange his tin of pencils, his small globe, and the three dictionaries and two thesauruses on his desk, knowing it would irk him.

She returned to her station. Around her, the *Gazette* was coming to life. Lamps flickered on, cigarettes burned, tea was poured, calls were taken, paper was crumpled, typewriters clacked.

It felt like it was going to be a good day.

"I love your hair, Winnow," Sarah said as she came to a stop at Iris's desk. "You should wear it like that more often."

"Oh." Iris self-consciously touched the wild curls that framed her shoulders. "Thanks, Prindle. Did Kitt call in sick today?"

"No," Sarah replied. "But I just received this, which Mr. Kitt would like published in tomorrow's paper, front and center in the announcements column." She handed Iris a message sheet.

"Mr. Kitt?" Iris echoed.

"Roman's father."

"Ah. Wait a minute, is this a . . . ?"

"Yes," Sarah said. She leaned closer to add, "I hope it doesn't upset you, Winnow. I swear, I didn't know he was courting someone."

Iris tried to smile, but it failed to reach her eyes. "Why would this upset me, Prindle?"

"I always thought the two of you would make such a striking pair. A few of the editors—not *me,* of course—cast bets that you would end up together."

"Me and *Kitt?*"

Sarah nodded, biting her lip as if she feared Iris's reaction.

"Don't be silly," Iris said with a half-hearted laugh. But her face suddenly felt hot. "Kitt and I are like fire and ice. I think we'd probably kill each other if we had to be in the same room for too long. And besides, he's never looked at me in *that* way. You know what I mean?"

Gods, shut your mouth, Iris! she told herself, realizing she was rambling.

"What do you mean, Winnow? Once, I saw him—"Whatever Sarah was about to reveal was cut short when Zeb hollered for her. She cast a worried glance at Iris before she hurried away.

Iris sank deeper in her chair as she read:

Mr. & Mrs. Ronald M. Kitt are overjoyed to announce the engagement of their son, Roman C. Kitt, to Miss Elinor A. Little, the youngest daughter of Dr. Herman O. Little and Mrs. Thora L. Little. The wedding will take place one month from now, at the venerable Alva Cathedral in downtown Oath. More details and a photograph to come.

Iris covered her mouth, only to belatedly recall she was wearing lipstick. She wiped the red smudge off her palm and set the message down like it had scalded her.

Roman Coddled Kitt was engaged, then. Which was fine. People got engaged every day. Iris didn't care what he did with his life.

Perhaps he had been up late last night with his fiancée, and *she* had made him run late.

As soon as Iris imagined that, she recoiled from it with a grimace, returning to her typewriter.

Not five minutes later, Roman walked into the office. He was dressed impeccably as usual, in a freshly starched shirt, leather braces on his shoulders, and black trousers without a speck of lint on their pressed front. His dark hair was slicked back, but his countenance was pale.

Iris watched beneath her lashes as he set his messenger bag down with a heavy thud at his cubicle. She waited for it—for him to notice the disorder at his desk. To frown and cast a glare at her. Because she was the only one who took the time to annoy him in such a way.

She waited, but Roman made no response. He was staring at his desk, but his face was frozen. There was hardly any light in his eyes, and she knew that something was wrong. Even dressed to the nines and only a few minutes late, something was eating at him.

He walked to the sideboard, selecting one of the teapots—there were always at least five brewing at a time—and poured the biggest cup he could find, carrying it back to his chair. Once he sat, she could no longer see him, and even though the office was humming with noise, Iris knew Roman Kitt was sitting there, staring blankly at his typewriter. As if all the words had vanished within him.

She typed up her stack of announcements and classifieds by noon, setting them on the corner of Zeb's desk. And then she grabbed her bag and stopped at Roman's desk.

She noticed two things: First the paper tucked into his typewriter was woefully blank, even though his handwritten notes were scattered across his desk. Second, he was taking a sip of tea, scowling at that blank piece of paper as if it owned him.

"Congratulations, Kitt," said Iris.

Roman startled. The tea spewed from his mouth as he coughed, and then those blue eyes of his cut upward to where she stood, pinning her with a furious gleam. She watched as that anger burned away into shock. His gaze traced her long, wild hair. Down her body, although she was wearing her typical drab raiment. And then back up to her cherry-red mouth.

"Winnow," he said carefully. "Why are you congratulating me?"

"Your *engagement,* Kitt."

He winced, as if she had hit a bruise. "How do you know about that?"

"Your father wants it announced in the paper tomorrow," she replied. "Front and center."

Roman glanced away, back to his blank page. "Wonderful," he said drolly. "I cannot *wait.*"

This wasn't the reaction she was expecting from him. It only heightened her curiosity.

"Do you need help with your missing soldier article?" she asked on a whim. "Because I can give that to you."

"How?" He sounded suspicious.

"Because my brother is missing at war."

Roman blinked, as if he couldn't believe those words had come out of her mouth. She could hardly believe it either. She thought she would instantly regret telling him something so intimate, but she discovered the opposite. It was a relief to finally voice the words that constantly shadowed her.

"I know you hate sandwiches," she added, tucking a curl behind her ear. "But I'm going to a deli to buy two, to eat on the park bench. If you want my help, then you'll know where to find me. I'll try to resist eating the second sandwich, in case you decide to come, but I make no promises."

She began to stride to the door before the sentence had even cleared her mouth. It felt like a coal was smoldering in her chest as she waited for the slow-as-tar lift. She was halfway mortified until she felt the air stir at her elbow. Iris knew it was Roman without looking at him. She recognized his cologne—some heady mix of spice and evergreen.

"I don't *hate* sandwiches," he said, and he sounded more like his old self.

"You dislike them, though," Iris stated.

"I'm simply too busy for them. They're a distraction. And distractions can be dangerous."

The lift doors opened. Iris stepped inside, turning to look at him. A smile teased her lips.

"So I've heard, Kitt. Sandwiches are quite troublesome these days."

She suddenly had no idea *what* they were discussing—if it truly was about sandwiches or about her or about how he regarded her or about this tentative moment they were sharing.

He hesitated so long that her smile faded. Tension returned to her posture.

You're a fool, Iris, her mind railed. *He's engaged! He's in love with someone. He doesn't want to share lunch with you. He only wants your help with his article. Which . . . why on the gods' bloody earth are you helping him?*

She turned her attention to the switchboard, pressing the button repeatedly, as if the lift would hurry up and carry her away.

Roman joined her just before the doors closed.

"I thought you said this place had the best pickles," Roman said, twenty minutes later. He was sitting on a park bench beside Iris, unwrapping his sandwich from its newspaper. A thin, sad pickle rested on top of the bread.

"No, that's the *other* place," Iris said. "They make the best everything, but they're closed on Mir's Day."

Thinking of the gods and the days of the week made her mind stray to the letter, currently hiding in her bag, resting on the bench between her and Roman. She had been shocked when she had woken up to it. A literal pile of paper, full of a myth she was hungry to learn. A myth where the eithrals were mentioned.

She wondered who this correspondent was. How old were they? What gender were they? What time were they?

"Hmm." Roman set aside the pickle and took a bite of his sandwich.

"Well?" Iris prompted.

"Well what?"

"Is the sandwich to your liking?"

"It's good," Roman said, taking another bite. "It would be better if that sad excuse of a pickle hadn't made part of the bread soggy."

"That's high praise, coming from you."

"What exactly are you implying, Winnow?" he countered sharply.

"That you know exactly what you want. Which isn't a *bad* thing, Kitt."

They continued to eat, the silence awkward between them. Iris was beginning to regret inviting him until he broke the quiet with a shocking admission.

"All right," he said with a sigh. "I feel compelled to apologize for something I said a few months ago. When you stepped into the office for the first time, I let my prejudice get in the way, thinking that because you failed to graduate from school you would give me no trouble." Roman paused, opening his sandwich to rearrange the tomato and the cheese and to toss away the slice of red onion. Iris watched him with slight fascination. "I'm sorry for making assumptions about you. It was wrong of me."

She didn't know how to reply. She hadn't anticipated Roman Condescending Kitt ever apologizing to her. Although she supposed she never thought she'd be sitting beside him in the park, eating a sandwich with him either.

"Winnow?" He glanced at her, and for some strange reason, he sounded nervous.

"Were you trying to run me off?" she asked.

"At first, yes," he said, brushing imaginary crumbs off his lap. "And then when you nabbed the first assignment and I read your article . . . I realized you were far more than I had imagined. That my imagination was quite narrow. And you deserved to be promoted should you earn it."

"How old are you, Kitt?"

"How old do I look to you?"

She studied his face, the slight stubble on his chin. Now that she was sitting so close to him, she could see the cracks in his "perfect" appearance. He hadn't shaved that morning—she figured he had run out of time—and her eyes moved to his shock of sable hair. It was thick and wavy. She could also tell he had risen from bed and sprinted to work, which made her envision him in bed, and *why* was she thinking about that?

Her silence had taken too long.

Roman met her gaze, and she glanced away, unable to hold his stare.

"You're nineteen," she guessed. "But you have an old soul, don't you?"

He only laughed.

"I take it that I'm correct," Iris said, resisting the temptation to laugh with him. Because of course he would have one of *those* sorts of laughs. The ones you couldn't hear and not feel in your own chest. "So. Tell me about her."

"Who? My muse?"

"Your fiancée. Elinor A. Little," Iris said, although she was intrigued to know what, exactly, inspired him. "Unless she is your muse, and in that case, how utterly romantic."

Roman fell quiet, his half-eaten sandwich on his lap. "No, she's not. I've met her once. We exchanged polite pleasantries and sat across from each other at dinner with our families."

"You don't love her?"

He stared into the distance. Iris thought he wouldn't reply until he asked, "Is it possible to love a stranger?"

"Perhaps in time," Iris said, wondering why she was giving him hope. "Why are you marrying her, if not for love?"

"It's for the good of our families." His tone became cold. "Now. You've graciously offered to help me with my article. What sort of assistance would you like to give me, Winnow?"

Iris set her sandwich aside. "Can I see the notes you've gathered so far?"

Roman hesitated.

"Never mind," she said with a wave of her hand. "That's rude of me to ask. I would never show you my notes either."

He wordlessly reached into his bag and handed her his notepad.

Iris began to sift through the pages. He was methodical, organized. He had plenty of facts and numbers and dates. She read a few lines of his first draft, and she must have made a pained expression because Roman fidgeted.

"What is it?" he asked. "What have I done wrong?"

Iris closed the notepad. "You haven't done anything wrong *yet*."

"These notes are verbatim, Winnow. I asked the parents about their missing daughter. Those are their answers. I'm trying to express such in my writing."

"Yes, but there's no *feeling*. There's no emotion, Kitt," Iris said. "You asked the parents things like 'When was the last time you heard from your daughter?' 'How old is she?' 'Why did she want to fight for Enva?' And you have the facts, but you didn't ask them how they're doing or what advice they would give for someone experiencing a similar nightmare. Or even if there's something the paper or community can do for them." She handed him his notepad. "I think for this particular article, your words should be sharp as knives. You want the readers to feel this wound in their chest, even though they've never experienced a missing loved one."

Roman flipped his notepad open to a fresh page. He rummaged for a pen in his bag and then asked, "May I?"

Iris nodded. She watched as he wrote, his handwriting turning her words into elegant ink.

"You said that your brother is missing," he said. "Do you want to talk about it?"

"He enlisted five months ago," Iris said. "Forest and I were always very close. So when he promised to write to me, I knew he would. But week after week passed, and his letters never came. So then I waited for a letter from his commanding officer, which they send when soldiers are killed or go missing at the front. That never came either. So I'm left with this fragile thread of hope that Forest is safe but unable to communicate. Or perhaps he's engaged in a dangerous mission and can't risk contact. Those are the things I tell myself, at least."

"And what does that feel like?" Roman asked. "How would you describe it?"

Iris was quiet for a beat.

"You don't have to reply," he hurried to add.

"It feels like wearing shoes that are too small," she whispered. "With every step, you notice it. It feels like blisters on your heels. It feels like a lump of ice in your chest that never melts, and you can only sleep a few hours at a time, because you're always wondering where they are and those worries seep into your dreams. If they're alive, or wounded, or sick. Some days you wish that you could take their place, no matter the cost. Just so you can have the peace of knowing their fate."

She watched as Roman wrote everything down. He paused after a moment, staring at his script.

"Do you mind if I quote you for the article?"

"You can quote me, but I'd prefer to remain anonymous," Iris replied. "Autry knows my brother is fighting, but no one else at the *Gazette* does. I'd prefer to keep it that way."

Roman nodded. And then he said, "I'm sorry, Winnow. About your brother."

Two apologies from Roman Kitt in the span of an hour? This day had truly caught her by surprise.

As they began to pack up to return to work, a cold breeze blew through the park. Iris shivered in her trench coat, glancing up at the bare branches that creaked above her.

She wondered if she had just inadvertently given the promotion to Roman Kitt.

9

One Piece of Armor

Her mother was gone that evening.

Don't panic, Iris told herself as she stood in the quiet flat. Over and over, she thought those words. Like a record playing on a phonograph.

Aster would be home soon. Occasionally she stayed late at a club, drinking and dancing. But she always returned when the money ran out or the establishment closed at midnight. There was no need to panic. And she had promised Iris that she was going to be better. Perhaps she wasn't at a club at all but trying to get her old job back at the Revel Diner.

Yet the worry remained, pinching Iris's lungs every time she breathed.

She knew how to tamp down the anxious feelings that were boiling within her. It was currently hiding beneath her bed—the typewriter her Nan had once created poetry with. The typewriter Iris had inherited and had since been using to write to *This isn't Forest.*

She left the front door unlocked for her mother and carried a candle into her room, where she was surprised to find a piece of paper lying on her floor. Her mysterious pen pal had written again, even though she had yet to respond to their myth-filled letter.

She was beginning to wonder if they were from another time. Perhaps they had lived in this very room, long before her. Perhaps they were destined to live here, years from now. Perhaps their letters were somehow slipping through a fissure of time, but it was this *place* that was causing it.

Iris retrieved the paper and sat on the edge of her bed, reading:

Do you ever feel as if you wear armor, day after day? That when people look at you, they see only the shine of steel that you've so carefully encased yourself in? They see what they want to see in you—the warped reflection of their own face, or a piece of the sky, or a shadow cast between buildings. They see all the times you've made mistakes, all the times you've failed, all the times you've hurt them or disappointed them. As if that is all you will ever be in their eyes.

How do you change something like that? How do you make your life your own and not feel guilt over it?

While she was reading it a second time, soaking in their words and pondering how to respond to something that felt so intimate it could have been whispered from her own mouth, another letter came over the threshold. Iris stood to fetch it, and that was the first time she truly tried to envision who this person was. She tried, but they were nothing more than stars and smoke and words pressed on a page.

She knew absolutely nothing about them. But after reading something like this, as if they had bled themselves on the paper . . . she longed to know more.

She opened the second letter, which was a hasty:

I sincerely apologize for bothering you with such thoughts. I hope I didn't wake you. No need to reply to me. I think it helps to type things out.

Iris knelt and reached for her typewriter beneath the bed. She fed a fresh sheet of paper into the roller and then sat there, staring at its possibilities.

Slowly, she began to type, her fingers meeting the keys. Her thoughts began to strike across the page:

I think we all wear armor. I think those who don't are fools, risking the pain of being wounded by the sharp edges of the world, over and over again. But if I've learned anything from those fools, it's that to be vulnerable is a strength most of us fear. It takes courage to let down your armor, to welcome people to see you as you are. Sometimes I feel the same as you: I can't risk having people behold me as I truly am. But there's also a small voice in the back of my mind, a voice that tells me, "You will miss so much by being so guarded."

Perhaps it begins with one person. Someone you trust. You remove a piece of armor for them; you let the light stream in, even if it makes you wince. Perhaps that is how you learn to be soft yet strong, even in fear and uncertainty. One person, one piece of steel.

I say this to you knowing full well that I am riddled with contradictions. As you've read in my other letters, I love my brother's bravery, but I hate how he's abandoned me to fight for a god. I love my mother, but I hate what booze has done to her, as if it's drowning her and I don't know how to save her. I love the words I write until I soon realize how much I hate them, as if I am destined to always be at war within myself.

And yet I keep moving forward. On some days, I'm afraid, but most days, I simply want to achieve those things I dream of. A world where my brother is home safe, and my mother is well, and I write words that I don't despise half of the time. Words that will mean something to someone else, as if I've cast a line into the dark and felt a tug in the distance.

All right, now I've let the words spill out. I've given you a piece of armor, I suppose. But I don't think you'll mind.

She sent the letter over the threshold, telling herself not to expect a reply. At least, not for a little while.

Iris began to work on her essay, trying to sense the shape of it. But her attention was on her wardrobe door, on the shadows that lined the threshold and the stranger who dwelled beyond it.

She paused to check the time. It was half past ten at night. She considered leaving the flat to search for her mother. The worry was a nagging weight in her chest, but Iris wasn't sure where she should go. If it would be safe for her to walk alone this late at night.

She'll return soon. Just like she always does. When the clubs close at midnight.

A letter passed through the portal, bringing her back to the present.

Iris reached for it. The paper crinkled in her fingers as she read:

One person. One piece of armor. I'll strive for this.
    Thank you.

10

Station Nine

The office was overflowing with felicitations the following day.

Iris leaned against the tea sideboard, watching as Roman was greeted with grins and claps on the back.

"Congratulations, Kitt!"

"I hear Miss Little is beautiful and accomplished. What a catch."

"When's the wedding?"

Roman smiled and received it all graciously, dressed in starched clothes and polished leather shoes, his black hair combed out of his eyes and his face shaven. Another perfect appearance. If Iris didn't know better—if she hadn't sat on a park bench with him and heard him confess how reluctant he was to marry a stranger—she would have thought he was thrilled.

She wondered if she had dreamt that moment with him, when they had almost spoken to one another like old friends. When he had laughed, listened, and apologized. Because it suddenly felt like some feverish imagining.

The fuss was dying down at last. Roman dropped his messenger bag, but then he must have felt her stare. His gaze lifted and found her on the other side of the room, over the sea of desks and paper and conversations.

For a breath, Iris couldn't move. And whatever mask he had been wearing for everyone else—the smile and the merry eyes and the flushed cheeks—faded until she saw how exhausted and sad he was.

It struck a chord within her, music that she could feel deep in her bones, and she broke their stare first.

Iris was halfway through drafting an essay inspired by the myth she had received in the wardrobe when Sarah approached her desk with a scrap of paper.

"The constable just called this in," she said, setting it on Iris's desk. "Was hoping we could squeeze it into tomorrow's paper."

"What is it?" Iris asked, preoccupied with her writing.

"I'm not sure what to call it. But they found a body this morning, and they're hoping someone will be able to identify her. The description is there, written down. It's just dreadful, isn't it? Being killed like that."

Iris paused, hands in mid-type, to glance at the paper.

"Yes," she said in a hollow tone. "I'll take care of it. Thank you, Prindle."

She waited until Sarah strode away. Then she read it, and the words swam in her eyes, burned through her mind, until she felt as if she were trying to squeeze herself through a tight space. A long, narrow tunnel.

A woman was hit and killed by a tram last night around 10:45 PM. There was no identification on her, but she looks to be in her mid-forties, with light brown hair and fair skin. She was wearing a purple coat and was barefoot. If you think you may know her or be able to identify her, please see Constable Stratford at Station Nine.

Iris rose with the note, her knees shaking. The weight in her chest was overwhelming. She remembered to grab her tapestry bag, but she forgot her trench coat, draped over her chair. She left her desk lamp on and essay page curled in the typewriter and she simply quit the office without a word, hurrying out the glass doors.

She pushed the button for the lift, and then felt her gorge rising.

The elevator was taking too long. She rushed to the stairs, and she half ran, half tripped down them, trembling so violently that she barely made it out the lobby doors before she vomited into a potted plant on the marble steps.

Straightening, Iris wiped her mouth and began to walk to Station Nine, which wasn't far from her home.

It's not her, she told herself over and over, with each step that drew her closer. *It's not her.*

But Iris hadn't seen her mother in over twenty-four hours. She hadn't been sprawled on the sofa that morning, like she had been the dawn before. Iris had assumed she was in her bedroom with the door closed. She should have checked, to make sure. Because now this doubt was piercing her.

When Iris reached the station, she paused, as if not entering would keep the truth from happening. She must have stood on the front stairs for a while, because the shadows were long at her feet and she was shivering when an officer approached her.

"Miss? Miss, you can't stand on the stairs like this. You need to move."

"I'm here to identify a body," she rasped.

"Very well. Follow me, please."

The station corridors were a blur of cream-colored walls and crooked hardwood floors. The air was astringent and the light harsh when they made it to an examination room.

Iris came to an abrupt halt.

The coroner was standing with a clipboard, dressed in white clothes and a leather apron. Beside him was a metal table, and on the table was a body.

Aster looked like she was sleeping, save for the crooked way she rested beneath a sheet and the gash on her face. Iris stepped forward, as if taking her mother's hand would make her stir. She would feel her daughter's touch, and it would pull her back from whatever chasm that wanted her, from whatever nightmare they were trapped within.

"Miss?" the coroner was saying, and his nasal voice reverberated through her. "Can you identify this woman? Miss, can you hear me?"

Iris's hand froze in the air. Stars began to dance at the edges of her sight as she stared at her mother. Dead and pale and in a place so far away, Iris would never be able to reach her.

"Yes," she whispered before she collapsed, into the embrace of darkness.

{ 11 }

The Vast Divide

It was dark and cold and long past midnight when Iris walked home from the station, carrying a box of her mother's belongings. A mist spun in the air, turning lamplight into pools of gold. But Iris could hardly feel the chill. She could hardly feel the cobblestones beneath her feet.

Her hair and clothes were beaded with moisture by the time she stepped into her flat. Of course, it was full of quiet shadows. She should be used to it by now. And yet she still peered into the darkness for a glimpse of her mother—the spark of her cigarette and the slant of her smile. Iris strained against the roar of silence for any sound of life—a clink of a bottle or the hum of a favorite song.

There was nothing. Nothing but Iris's labored breaths and a box of belongings and the undertaker's bill to pay, to turn her mother's body into ashes.

She set down the box and wandered into Aster's room.

Iris sprawled on the rumpled bed. She could almost fool herself, remembering the time before the alcohol had set its claws into her mother. Before Forest left them. She could almost sink into the bliss of the past, when Aster had been full of laughter and stories, waitressing at the diner down the street.

Brushing Iris's long hair every night and asking her about school. What books she had been reading. What reports she was writing.

You'll be a famous writer someday, Iris, her mother had said, deft fingers braiding Iris's long brown hair. *Mark my words. You'll make me so proud, sweetheart.*

Iris let herself weep. She cried the memories into her mother's pillow until she was so exhausted the darkness pulled her under again.

She woke to the sound of persistent knocking on the front door.

Iris jolted upright in bed, her legs tangled in wine-stained sheets. Sunlight was streaming in through the window, and for a moment she was confused. What time was it? She had never slept this late . . .

She scrambled for the watch on her mother's bedside table, which read half past eleven in the morning.

Oh my gods, she thought, and rose from the bed on shaky legs. Why had she overslept? Why was she in her mother's bed?

It all came back to her in a rush. The message at the *Gazette,* Station Nine, her mother's cold, pale body beneath a sheet.

Iris staggered, tearing her fingers through her snarled hair.

The knocking came again, insistent. And then his voice—which was the *last* voice she wanted to hear—called through the wood: "Winnow? Winnow, are you there?"

Roman Kitt was at her flat, knocking on her door.

Her heart quickened as she strode into the living room, directly to the door so she could peer through the peephole. Yes, there he was, standing with her trench coat draped over his arm, his face marked with concern.

"Winnow? If you're there, please open the door."

She continued to stare at him, noticing when his concern turned into fear. She saw his hand stray to the doorknob. When the knob turned and the door began to open, she realized with a pang that she had forgotten to lock it last night.

Iris had only three seconds to scramble backward as the door swung open. She stood in a flood of sunshine, pulse hammering in her throat as Roman caught sight of her.

She must have looked exceptionally dreadful, because he startled. And then his breath left him in a rush as he stepped over the threshold.

"Are you all right?"

Iris froze as his eyes raced over her. For a split second, she was so relieved to see him that she could have wept. But then she realized two horrible things. The first was that her blouse was gaping open, the buttons undone halfway to her navel. She glanced down and saw the white lace of her bra, which Roman no doubt had also noticed by now, and she gasped, holding the fabric closed with a trembling hand.

"I hope I'm not interrupting anything," Roman said in a very strange voice. It took another two seconds for Iris to infer that he thought she had been *with* someone, and she blanched.

"No. I'm home alone," she croaked, but his eyes were drifting beyond her, as if he expected another person to emerge from the bedroom.

And that was when the second terrible revelation hit her. Roman Upper Class Kitt was standing in her home. Her rival was standing *in* her flat, beholding the disarray of her life. He could see the melted candles on the sideboard from all the nights she couldn't afford electricity, and the stray wine bottles that she had yet to gather and dispose of. How barren the living room was, and how the wallpaper was faded and falling apart.

Iris took a step away from him, pride burning in her bones. She couldn't bear for Roman to see her like this. She couldn't bear for him to see how messy things were in her life. For him to see her on her worst day.

"Winnow?" he said, taking a step closer, as if he felt the tug of her movements. "You're all right?"

"I'm fine, Kitt," she said, surprised by how rough-hewn her voice was, as if she hadn't spoken in years. "What are you doing here?"

"We're all very concerned," he replied. "You left work early yesterday, and you didn't show this morning. Is everything okay?"

She swallowed, torn between telling him the truth and concealing her pain. She stared at his chest, unable to meet his eyes. She realized if she told him about her mother, he would pity her even more than he already did. And that was the last thing she wanted.

"Yes, I'm sorry for leaving yesterday," she said. "I felt ill. And I overslept."

"Do you need me to send for a doctor?"

"*No!*" She cleared her throat. "No but thank you. I'm on the mend. Tell Autry I'll be in first thing tomorrow."

Roman nodded, but his eyes narrowed as he intently studied her, like he sensed her lie. "Can I get you anything else? Are you hungry? Should I fetch a sandwich or soup or whatever else you'd like?"

She gaped for a second, shocked by his offer. His gaze began to flicker around the room again, taking in the shambles she was so desperate to hide from him. Panic surged through her. "No! No, I don't need anything. You can go now, Kitt."

He frowned. The sunlight limned his body, but a shadow danced over his face.

"Of course. I'll leave, as you want. I brought your coat, by the way."

"Right. You, erm, you shouldn't have gone to so much trouble." She awkwardly accepted the coat, still holding her blouse shut. She avoided making eye contact.

"It was no trouble," he said.

She could feel him staring at her, as if daring her to meet his gaze.

She couldn't.

She would break if she did, and she waited for him to retrace his steps over the threshold.

"Will you lock the door behind me?" he asked.

Iris nodded, hugging the trench coat to her chest.

Roman finally shut the door.

She continued to stand in the empty flat. As if she had grown roots.

The minutes flowed, but she hardly sensed time. Everything felt distorted, like she was looking at her life through fractured glass. Dust motes spun in the air around her. A deep breath unspooled from her as she went to lock the door, and then she thought better of it, and looked through the peephole again.

He was still standing there, hands shoved into his coat pockets, his dark hair windblown. Waiting. Her annoyance flared until she bolted the door. As soon as he heard the locks slide, Roman Kitt turned and left.

A Shadow You Carry

Iris spent the rest of that day in a haze, trying to make sense of things. But it was like her life had shattered into a hundred pieces, and she wasn't sure how to make it fit back together. She thought that perhaps the ache she felt would never diminish, and she bit her nails to the quick as she wandered through the flat like a ghost.

Eventually she settled in her room, on the floor. She reached for her grandmother's typewriter and drew it out into the dusky light.

If she thought about it too hard, the words would become ice. And so Iris didn't think; she let the words pass through her heart to her mind, down her arms to her fingertips, and she wrote:

Sometimes I'm afraid to love other people.

Everyone I care about eventually leaves me, whether it's death or war or simply because they don't want me. They go places I can't find, places I can't reach. And I'm not afraid to be alone, but I'm tired of being the one left behind. I'm tired of having to rearrange my life after the people within it depart, as if I'm a puzzle and I'm now missing pieces and I will never feel that pure sense of completion again.

I lost someone close to me, yesterday. It doesn't feel real yet.

And I'm not sure who you are, where you are. If you are breathing the same hour, the same minute as me, or if you are decades before or years to come. I don't know what is connecting us—if it's magical thresholds or conquered god bones or something else we've yet to discover. Most of all, I don't know why I'm writing to you now. But here I am, reaching out to you. A stranger and yet a friend.

All those letters of mine you received for several months...I thought I was writing to Forest. I wrote with the unfaltering, teeth-clenched hope that they would reach him despite the kilometers between us. That my brother would read my words, even if they were minced with pain and fury, and he would come home and fill the void I feel and fix the messiness of my life.

But I realize that people are just people, and they carry their own set of fears, dreams, desires, pains, and mistakes. I can't expect someone else to make me feel complete; I must find it on my own. And I think I was always writing for myself, to sort through my loss and worry and tangled ambitions. Even now, I think about how effortless it is to lose oneself in words, and yet also find who you are.

I hope I'm making sense. I'm probably not, because I'm writing to you but I'm also writing for me. And I don't expect you to respond, but it helps to know someone is hearing me. Someone is reading what I pour onto a page.

It helps to know that I'm not alone tonight, even as I sit in quiet darkness.

She sat frozen for what could have been a minute or an hour, and eventually she roused enough courage to pull the sheet from the typewriter and fold it. To slip it over the threshold and into the portal. Because that was the hardest part—sharing the words she wrote. Words that could splinter steel, exposing the soft places she preferred to hide.

Night fell. She lit a candle. She paced the flat. She told herself to eat something, to drink something, but she wasn't hungry, even though she felt empty.

She thought she might be in shock, because she was numb and kept waiting for her mother to return home, to sweep in through the door.

Eventually, Iris stopped at the kitchen table. Her trench coat was draped over one of the chairs, and she gathered it into her arms, hiding her face in the worn fabric. She closed her eyes and breathed, realizing the coat smelled like spice and evergreen. It smelled like Roman Kitt, from when he had carried it all the way from the office to her home, to ensure she was all right.

She slipped it on and belted the coat tight at her waist, returning to her room.

A letter had arrived, the thickest one yet.

She lay on her bed and read by candlelight:

I rarely share this part of my life with others, but I want to tell it to you now. A piece of armor, because I trust you. A glint of falling steel, because I feel safe with you.

I had a little sister once.

My parents can hardly speak of her these days, but her name was Georgiana. I called her Del, because she liked her middle name Delaney best. I was eight when she was born, and I can still hear the rain that poured on the day she came into the world.

She grew up in a blink, as if the years were enchanted. I loved her fiercely. And while I had always been the obedient, reserved son who never needed discipline, she was full of curiosity and courage and whimsy, and my parents didn't know how to raise such a spirited child in society.

On her seventh birthday, she wanted to go swimming in a pond not far from our house. Just beyond the gardens and through a stretch of woods, hidden from the bustle and sounds of the city. Our parents said no; they had planned a dinner gala for her birthday, which Del couldn't care less about. So when she begged me to sneak out with her and go for a swim, with plenty of time to return before the party . . . I told her yes.

It was the heart of summer and sweltering hot. We stole from the house, barefooted and dew-eyed, and we ran through the gardens all the way to the pond. There was an old rope swing, fastened to an oak branch. We took turns, hurling ourselves out into the center of the pond, because that was where it was deepest, far from the rocks and sand of the shallows.

Eventually, I grew tired and waterlogged, and a storm was brewing overhead. "Let's go back," I told her, but Del begged me for a few minutes more. And I, weak brother that I was, couldn't deny her. I conceded to sit on the shore and dry off as she continued to swing and swim. I closed my eyes for a moment, it seemed. Just a moment, with the last of the sunlight on my face, lulling me to rest.

It was the silence that made me open my eyes.

Somewhere in the distance was the thunder and the wind and the rush of rain, but the pond had fallen still. Del was floating facedown on the water, her long dark hair streaming around her. At first I thought she was playing, but then the panic cut through me, cold and sharp as a blade. I swam to her and turned her over. I rushed her to the shore; I screamed her name and breathed into her mouth and pumped her chest, but she was gone.

I had closed my eyes for a breath, and she had slipped away.

I hardly remember carrying her back to my parents. But I will never forget the wail of my mother, the tears of my father. I will never forget feeling my life rend in two: with Del and without Del.

That was four years ago. And grief is a long, difficult process, especially when it is so racked by guilt. I still blame myself—I should have said no to the pond. I should have kept my eyes open. I should have never closed them while she swam, not even for a breath.

A month after I lost my sister, I had a dream where a goddess came to me and said, "I can take away the pain of your loss. I will cut out the shape of your grief, but I will have to also cull the memories of your sister. It will be as if Del had never been born, as if her life had never twined with yours for seven years. Would you choose that, to ease your suffering? To be able to draw a full breath again, to live a carefree life once more?"

I didn't even hesitate. I could barely look the goddess in the eye, but I firmly said, "No."

Not even for a moment would I trade my pain to erase Del's life.

This has gone longer than I anticipated, but I know what it feels like to lose someone you love. To feel as if you're left behind, or like your life is in shambles and there's no guidebook to tell you how to stitch it back together.

But time will slowly heal you, as it is doing for me. There are good days and there are difficult days. Your grief will never fully fade; it will always be with you—a shadow you carry in your soul—but it will become fainter as your life becomes brighter. You will learn to live outside of it again, as impossible as that may sound. Others who share your pain will also help you heal. Because you are not alone. Not in your fear or your grief or your hopes or your dreams.

You are not alone.

{ 13 }

An Unfair Advantage

It was strange returning to the office.

Nothing about it had changed; her desk was still covered in classifieds and obituaries, the five teapots were brewing, the smoke still danced from editors' fingertips, the typebars ticked like heartbeats. It was almost surreal to Iris, to return to something that felt outwardly so familiar when she felt inwardly so different.

Her life had been irrevocably altered, and she was still trying to adjust to what it would mean for her in the days to come. Living in that flat alone. Living without her mother. Living this new, unbalanced cycle, day in and day out.

Grief is a long, difficult process, especially when it is so racked by guilt.

She sat at her desk and prepared her typewriter, craving a distraction. Anything to keep her mind off of—

"You feeling better today, Winnow?" Sarah asked, stopping by on her way to Zeb's office.

Iris nodded but kept her eyes on her paper. "Much. Thanks for asking, Prindle."

She was relieved when Sarah moved on. Iris didn't think she could withstand speaking about her mother just yet, so she set her focus like iron and worked. But she knew the moment Roman walked into the office. She knew it like a cord was bound between the two of them, even though she refused to look at him.

He must have sensed she was ignoring him. He eventually walked to her cubicle and leaned on the wood, watching her type.

"You look well today, Winnow."

"Are you implying I looked ill before, Kitt?"

In the past, he would have returned her snark and left. But he continued to silently stand in her space, his eyes all but burning through her, and she knew he wanted her to look at him.

She cleared her throat, her attention riveted to her work. "You know, if you wanted to type up the classifieds so badly, you could just say so. You don't have to hover over me."

"Why didn't you say anything?" he asked, and she was surprised he sounded irritated, or angry, or perhaps a mix of both.

"What do you mean?"

"Why didn't you tell someone you were feeling ill the other day? You just . . . *left,* and none of us knew where you went or what had happened."

"It's really none of your business, Kitt."

"It *is,* because people here were worried about you, Winnow."

"Yes, they're quite worried about the classifieds not getting done on time."

"Now that isn't a fair statement, and you know it," he said, his voice dropping low.

Iris shut her eyes. Her composure was about to crack, and it had taken all of her will to even get up and dress herself that morning, to brush her hair and force some lipstick on, all so that she gave the appearance that she was *fine,* that she was not coming apart at the seams. She didn't want anyone to know what she was going through, because gods forbid they *pity* her—*he pities you!*—and she drew in a breath through her teeth.

"I don't see why you care, Kitt!" she whispered sharply, opening her eyes to meet his steady gaze. "If I'm not here, you finally get what you want."

He didn't answer, but his gaze held hers, and she thought she saw something flicker through him, like a star falling from the cosmos, or a coin underwater, reflecting the sun. Something fierce and vulnerable and very unexpected.

As soon as it came, it was gone, and he scowled at her.

She must have imagined it.

For once, Zeb had good timing.

"Winnow? In my office. Now," he called.

She stood from her desk and Roman had no choice but to ease away. She left him in the aisle, closing the door behind her as she stepped into Zeb's office.

He was pouring himself a drink. It crackled over ice cubes as she sat in the chair across from him, his desk a chaotic sprawl of paper and books and folders. She waited for him to speak first.

"I take it you have your essay ready for me?" he asked after taking a sip.

Her essay. *Her essay.*

Iris had forgotten about it. She laced her fingers together, hands shaking. Her knuckles drained white.

"No, sir," she said. "I'm sorry, but it's not ready."

Zeb only stared at her. "I'm disappointed in you, Winnow."

She wanted to weep. She swallowed the tears until they flooded her chest. She should tell him why the essay was late. She should tell him she had lost her mother, and her world had upended, and the last thing she was thinking about was becoming a columnist.

"Sir, my——"

"If you're going to lay out of work, you need to call it in, so your tasks for the day can be shifted to someone else," he said curtly. "Now, don't let it happen again."

Iris rose and left. She went directly to her desk and sat, pressing her cold fingers to her flaming face. She felt like a doormat. She had just let him walk all over her, because she was too afraid of crying in front of him.

Who was she becoming?

"Here are the obituaries for tomorrow's paper," Sarah said, seeming to appear out of thin air. She dropped a stack of notes on Iris's desk. "Are you all right, Winnow?"

"I'm fine," Iris said with a strained smile and a sniff. "I'll get these done."

"I can give them to Kitt."

"No. I have them. Thanks."

After that, everyone left her alone. Even Roman didn't glance her way again, and Iris was relieved.

She typed up the obituaries and then stared at her blank paper, wrestling with her feelings. She should type one for her mother. But it felt vastly different now. Being someone touched by the anguish of an obituary. Someone who felt the root of the words.

Iris began to write the first thing that came to mind, her fingers striking the keys with vehemence:

I have nothing. I have nothing. I have nothing. I have nothing. I have nothing. I have nothing. I have nothing. I have nothing. I have nothing. I have

She stopped herself, jaw clenched, even as the wound in her ached. If Zeb caught her wasting paper and ink ribbons, he would fire her. And so she ripped the paper from her typewriter, crumpled it, tossed it in her dustbin, and tried again.

Aster Winifred Winnow, age forty-two, passed away on Alva's Day, the fifth day of Norrow. She is survived by her son, Forest Winnow, and her daughter, Iris Winnow. She was born in Oath and loved the city best during autumn, when she felt as if magic could be tasted in the air. She attended school at Windy Grove, and later worked as a waitress at the Revel Diner. She was fond of poetry, classical music, and the color purple, although she would only ever call it "violet," and she loved to dance.

The words were blurring. Iris stopped typing and set her mother's obituary in the stack with all the others, to be delivered to Zeb's desk for tomorrow's paper.

She walked home after work. She removed her mother's too-small boots and Forest's trench coat and lay down in bed. She fell asleep to the rain.

She was an hour late to work.

She had overslept again, the grief pulling her into deep, dark slumber, and now she was full of frantic butterflies as she darted up the stairs to the fifth floor, drenched from the rain. Hopefully no one but Sarah would notice her walking in late. Sarah and Roman, most likely, since he obviously liked to keep tabs on her.

Iris stepped into the *Oath Gazette* only to discover Zeb was waiting beside her desk. His expression was stormy; she braced herself as she walked the aisle, her boots squishing.

He said nothing but inclined his head, turning to stride into his office.

Iris followed tentatively.

She was shocked to see Roman was present. There was an empty chair beside him, and Iris surrendered to it. She glanced sidelong at him, but Roman's eyes were dead set on something before them. His hands were on his thighs, his posture rigid.

For once, she wished he would look at her, because the longer she sat beside him, the more his tension coaxed her own, until she was cracking her knuckles and bouncing on the balls of her feet.

"All right," Zeb said, easing into his chair with a slight groan. "I'm sure you're aware why I've called the two of you in today. You're both bright, talented writers. And I've given you each an equal opportunity to prove yourselves worthy of columnist. I'm pleased to say I've made my decision."

He paused, and Iris tore her eyes from Roman to look at Zeb. He set down the morning's newspaper at the edge of his desk. It was folded in such a way to reveal the column. Roman's article. The one she had helped him write about missing soldiers. So Iris wasn't surprised by the words that came next. In fact, she felt nothing as Zeb announced, "Kitt, this is the best article you've ever written. The position is yours. You're reliable, industrious, and turn good pieces in on time. You'll officially start first thing tomorrow."

Roman didn't move. He didn't even seem to be breathing, and Iris's gaze flickered back to him as she wondered what thoughts were haunting his mind to make him so unresponsive. Wasn't this what he wanted?

Now Zeb was frowning, annoyed by Roman's lack of enthusiasm. "Did you hear me, Kitt?"

"Sir, would you consider giving us both more time before you made the decision?" Roman asked. "Give us each another chance to write an essay."

Zeb gaped at him. "More time? In what world would I do that?"

Iris's heart beat swift and hard within her chest. When Roman finally looked at her, time seemed to stall. His eyes were keen, as if he could see everything that dwelled in her—the light and the shadows. Her threads of ambition and desire and joy and grief. Never had a man looked at her in that way.

A shiver traced her bones.

"I've had an unfair advantage, sir," Roman said, directing his attention back to Zeb. "Winnow's mother passed away a few days ago. She's grieving, and she needs more time."

The room fell painfully silent.

Iris drew a tremulous breath. Her pulse was in her ears. And Zeb was saying something, but his voice was nothing more than a pesky drone as Iris met Roman's stare.

"How do you know that?" she whispered.

"I read your mother's obituary," he replied.

"But no one reads obituaries."

Roman was quiet but his face flushed, and she had the frightening inkling that while she made it a point to never read anything of his, he might be reading everything she touched. Including the dry classifieds and tragic obituaries. Perhaps he did it to see if she'd left a typo behind, to taunt her with after it went to print. Perhaps he did it because she was his competition and he wanted to know who, exactly, he was up against. She honestly couldn't think of a good enough reason, and she looked away from him.

"Winnow?" Zeb was barking. "Winnow, is this true?"

"Yes, sir."

"Why didn't you say something yesterday?"

Because I didn't want to cry in front of you. Because I don't want your pity. Because I'm holding myself together by a thread.

"I don't know," she said.

"Well," Zeb said curtly. "I can't help you if I don't know, can I?" He heaved a sigh and rubbed his brow. His voice softened, as if he realized how callous he was sounding. "I'm very sorry for your loss, Winnow. It's unfortunate. But I'm afraid my mind is made up. Kitt won the column, but if you need to take a few days off for bereavement . . . that would be fine."

Iris thought about taking time off. Which would mean she would be home, alone in that sad flat with the wine bottles and the melted candles and the torn wallpaper. She would be waiting for her mother to return, and she never would. And that was when it struck her. Iris didn't want time off, but neither did she want to be at the *Gazette*. The career she had dreamt of suddenly paled in comparison to other things in her life.

Her only family was in the west now, where the war raged.

She wanted to find her brother.

"No, sir. I'm turning in my resignation," she said, rising.

Roman shifted beside her. "What? No, Mr. Autry, I—"

Zeb ignored his newly appointed columnist, and sputtered, "Your *resignation*? You want to quit on me, Winnow? Just like that?"

She hated the way he made it sound. Like she was giving up. But now that she had voiced the words, a weight slipped off her shoulders.

She was going to find Forest.

"Yes, sir. It's time for me to move on," she said and pivoted to Roman, extending her hand to him. "Congratulations, Kitt."

He merely stared up at her, his blue eyes smoldering like flames.

She was awkwardly retracting her hand when his finally rose to meet it, and his grip was firm and warm. It sent a shock up her forearm, as if the two of them had created static, and she was relieved when he finally let her go.

"If you're quitting, then go ahead and leave, Winnow," Zeb said with a flick of his stubby fingers. "I don't need you anymore. But if you walk out that door, don't expect to ever be hired again."

"Listen, Mr. Autry." Roman's voice was brisk. "I don't think—"

Iris didn't hear the rest of what he said. She quit the office, found a wooden crate in the kitchen, and went to her desk to pack up her things.

She didn't have much. A small potted plant, a few of her favorite pencils and pens, a small figurine of a running horse, some grammar books, a tattered dictionary.

"Winnow." Sarah approached her with a worried expression. "You're not . . ."

"I'm resigning, Prindle."

"But why? Where will you go?"

"I'm not sure yet. But it's time for me to leave."

Sarah sagged, glasses flashing on her nose. "I'll miss you."

Iris found one last smile to give her. "I'll miss you too. Perhaps one day I'll find you at a museum?"

Sarah blushed but glanced down at her feet, as if that dream of hers was still too distant to grasp.

One by one, the desks around Iris fell quiet and still. One by one, she drew every eye in the room, until the *Oath Gazette* came to a halt.

Zeb was the one to break the silence. He walked to her with a cigarette clamped in his yellow teeth, a frown on his face, and a wad of bills in his hand.

"Your last paycheck," he said.

"Thank you." She accepted the money and tucked it into her inner coat pocket. She gathered up her crate, turned off her lamp, gently touched the keys of her typewriter one last time, and began to walk down the aisle.

Roman wasn't at his desk. Iris didn't know where he was until she glanced up at the glass doors and saw him standing before them like a barricade, his arms crossed over his chest.

"How kind of you to get the door for me on my way out," she said when she reached him. She was striving for a teasing tone, but her voice betrayed her and came out as a warble.

"I don't think you should go like this, Winnow," he whispered.

"No, Kitt? How, then, should I go?"

"You should stay."

"Stay and write obituaries?" She sighed. "I shouldn't have published it."

"The one for your mother? And then none of us would know you were hurting," he replied. "What would you do if you could take back the words you gave her? Continue to pretend that your life was fine while you were with us by day, even as you grieved by night? Would you even know yourself after a week had passed, a month, a year?"

"You know nothing about me," she hissed, and she hated how much she felt his words, as if she had breathed them in. How her eyes threatened tears again, if she dared to blink. "Now, please move, Kitt."

"Don't go, Iris," he said.

She had never heard him say her given name. It seeped through her like sunlight, warming her skin and her blood, and she had to glance away from him before he saw how much it affected her.

"Best of luck to you, Kitt," she said in a voice that was far colder and smoother than she felt.

He stepped aside.

She wondered if he would grow soft now, without her here to sharpen him. She wondered if he knew it too, and that was why he was so insistent she stay.

Iris opened the door and crossed the threshold.

She left the *Oath Gazette* and never looked back.

14

Farewell to Ghosts

I wanted to write and let you know that I'm leaving. I won't be staying in my current home after tomorrow, and I suppose the magic portal will no longer be accessible for us to communicate.

Iris paused in her typing. She stared at her wardrobe door, wondering why she was even writing to inform her mysterious correspondent. She wasn't obligated to, but she felt like she owed it to them—*him*, she had learned in his last letter, when he had shared the truth of his being an older brother.

She had left the *Oath Gazette* that morning and gone to the undertaker, to pay for her mother's cremation. He had given her a small jar full of ashes, and Iris decided she should go home, uncertain what else to do with them.

But she had a plan now. She was eager to leave Oath. There were too many memories, too many ghosts in these walls.

Tomorrow, she would go to the *Inkridden Tribune* and see if they would hire her as a war correspondent. And if they wouldn't, perhaps the war effort would, in whatever manner it needed her. She wasn't a fighter, but she could wash linens and cook and clean. She had two hands and she was a quick learner. Either way, she hoped it would bring her to Forest.

She returned to her typing:

Thank you for writing me back that day. For telling me about Del. I know we haven't been corresponding for very long (or, I have been to you, but you haven't been to me), but regardless of that... time feels different in a letter.

I'll carry the things you shared with me into my next adventure.

Farewell.

Iris sent it through the portal before she could change her mind. She chose her outfit for tomorrow—her best skirt and blouse—and prepared for bed, trying to distract herself from how empty the flat was and how deep the shadows felt.

She waited for him to write her back, even though she told herself he probably wouldn't. She drifted to sleep with her candle still burning. Late in the night, a loud noise woke her. Iris sat forward, heart in her throat until she realized it was someone leaving the flat below; they were laughing and guffawing and quite drunk.

It was one in the morning, and Iris blearily noticed there was a letter on her floor.

She picked it up, and she didn't know what she was expecting, but it wasn't a terse:

May I ask where you're going?

It struck her as odd.

They had both chosen to withhold their identities, and while they had never discussed any further boundaries of their correspondence, Iris had surmised location fell under the also-keep-this-secret part of their relationship.

She decided she wouldn't answer him, and she folded up his final letter and stuck it with the others she had kept, bound with a ribbon.

Her faithful candle extinguished at last, burning itself out.

Iris couldn't fall asleep in the dark.

She stared into its vastness, listening to the sounds of the city beyond her window, the creaks of the walls. It was strange to her—how close she could be to people and yet how far away and lonely she felt. How the night made things feel more poignant and desperate.

I should have gone looking for her. I shouldn't have just sat here at the flat, waiting. If I had found her, she would still be alive.

The guilt threatened to choke her. She had to sit forward and tell herself to breathe—*breathe*—because it felt like she was drowning.

She was up at first light, ready to wash the remorse from her eyes. She didn't think curled hair and lipstick would matter for a war correspondent, but she prepared herself the best she could, thinking she didn't want to leave anything to chance.

That was when another letter arrived over her threshold.

She stared at it a long moment, wondering if she should read it. She left it untouched as she packed her things in her mother's battered valise. She chose to take her favorite set of trousers, a summer dress, stockings, a few blouses, and a handkerchief for her hair. She also included the letters from her mystery correspondent, her grandmother's favorite volume of poetry, the jar with her mother's ashes, carefully sealed, and Forest's trench coat, since the days had finally become too warm for a jacket.

She was leaving far too many things behind, but Iris told herself that she should only carry that which had meaning to her. And even if she *did* achieve the impossible and was assigned to report on the war, would they let her carry so much?

She almost took the crinkled copy of the *Inkridden Tribune,* with the smeared eithral. But she decided to leave it on her desk, folded and face-down.

There was one more thing she wanted.

She walked into the living room, where she had left the box of her mother's things, untouched since the night she had brought them home. Iris sifted through them now, until she found the flash of gold. The chain and the locket that her mother had worn every day since Forest left.

Iris clasped it around her neck, tucking it beneath the fabric of her blouse. It was cold against her skin, and she laid her palm over it. She knew what hid within the locket: a small portrait of her, and a small portrait of Forest. She could care less about her own face, but her brother's . . . she prayed it would guide her to him, now. And Iris hadn't prayed in a very long time.

The last thing she needed was her typewriter.

She found its box in her wardrobe, carefully stepping around the letter that still sat on the floor, and she packed the typewriter and the remaining paper and ink ribbons she had. The box was a hard case, with two brass locks and a wooden handle. She carried it in one hand, her valise in the other, surveying her bedroom for the final time.

Her gaze caught on that letter again.

She was curious to know what he had written to her, but she had this strange feeling that if she read it, she would encounter nothing more than his insistence that she reply. And if he knew she was striking out to become a war correspondent, he would try to talk her out of it.

Iris had made up her mind; there was no changing it, and she was too tired to argue with him.

She quit the flat.

She left his letter lying in a pool of sunlight on the floor.

PART TWO

News
from
Afar

15

The Third Alouette

The *Oath Gazette* was quiet.

Roman sat at his desk, notes spread before him. He stared at the blank page curling from his typewriter. He should be thrilled. He had solidified himself as the new columnist. He no longer had to worry about the things on his desk being rearranged. He no longer had to race to the bulletin board for assignments. He no longer had to pretend he was too busy for sandwiches.

If this was the life he wanted, then why did it feel so hollow?

He rose to get another cup of tea, avoiding the temptation to glance at Iris's empty desk. But while he was spooning honey into his cup, one of the editors joined him at the sideboard.

"Feels strange here without her, doesn't it?" she asked.

Roman arched his brow. "Who?"

The editor only smiled, as if she knew something Roman didn't.

He was the last to leave the office that evening. He shrugged on his coat and turned off his lamp. He hadn't written a word, and he was irritated.

On the tram ride home, he considered his options. His fingers thrummed over his thigh, anxious as he thought about the best way to handle the dilemma he was caught within. If he didn't show any emotion, his father should hear him.

As soon as he reached home, he found Mr. Kitt in his study. On his desk was a strange crate, labeled with CAUTION and HANDLE WITH CARE.

"Roman," his father greeted him, glancing up from a ledger he was reading. A cigar was clamped in his teeth. "How was your first day as columnist?"

"I'm not marrying her, Father." The announcement rang in the air. Roman had never felt so relieved in his life until Mr. Kitt's eyes narrowed. He took his time crushing his cigar into an ashtray and stood, his tall frame casting a crooked shadow.

"Come again, Roman?"

"I'm not marrying Elinor Little," said Roman. He kept his inflection flat, his expression poised. As if he felt nothing and was merely stating a fact. "She and I are not a good match, but there are other ways I can serve the family. I would like to discuss them with you, if you have time tonight."

His father smiled. It gleamed like a scythe in the lamplight. "What's this really about, son?"

"It's about my freedom."

"Your *freedom*?"

Roman gritted his teeth. "Yes. I have already forgone one thing I wanted, based on your desires."

"And what was that, Roman? Oh wait. I remember," Mr. Kitt said with a chuckle. "You wanted to throw away *years* of your life studying *literature* at university. I've already told you once, but I suppose I should say it again: you can't do anything with such a degree. But being columnist at the *Oath Gazette*? That will carry you far, son. I only want the best for you, even if you can't see it now. And you'll thank me one day when you understand better."

It took everything within Roman to hold his temper in check. He ground the words he wanted to say between his molars and said, "I have gained columnist, as you wanted. At the very least, you should now agree that I have the right to choose who I want to marry, as you once chose Mother."

"This is about that lowborn girl at the *Gazette,* isn't it?" Mr. Kitt drawled. "She's caught your eye, against all reason."

Roman stiffened. He could feel the flush creep across his face, and he struggled to keep his voice calm, emotionless. "There's no other girl."

"Don't lie to me, son. I caught wind of you having lunch with her the other day. And it was a bloody good thing your engagement hadn't been announced yet, but what if the Littles had learned of it? What if they had *seen* you with *her,* the way you sat close beside her on a bench, sharing a sandwich, laughing at the things she said? How would you explain yourself?"

"It was strictly business," Roman snapped. "We were discussing an article. And I didn't pay for her lunch, just so you know."

Mr. Kitt suddenly looked amused. Roman hated himself, especially when he remembered watching Iris reach for the coins in her purse at the deli. She almost hadn't had enough, and she had chosen not to purchase a drink, as if she hadn't wanted one.

He had paid for his sandwich, but not hers. It had seemed like the right thing to do at the time, but now he loathed himself for it.

Roman bit the inside of his cheek. Did his father also know that he had gone to Iris's flat?

"I won't see my grandchildren's blood spoiled by the gutter," Mr. Kitt said.

Then yes. He also knew about that visit, however brief it was, but Roman wouldn't offer any explanations for it. Because no one had sent Roman but himself. Zeb Autry had been annoyed by Iris's absence, and Sarah worried, but Roman was the one to grab her trench coat and look up her address and do something about it.

"Your prejudices are quite profound, Father," he stated. "And you should stop having me followed."

"I'll call off my watch the moment you marry Miss Little," Mr. Kitt countered. "And then you can sleep with whoever you want as long as you are discreet. You can sleep with your freckle-faced girl from the *Gazette,* but my one stipulation is you must not have pups with her. She's far beneath you, son."

"*Enough,* Father!" The words exploded from Roman. "I'm not marrying Miss Little, and your comments about my colleague are unfounded and uncalled-for!"

Mr. Kitt sighed. "I'm disappointed in you, Roman."

Roman shut his eyes, suddenly drained. This conversation had taken a turn for the worse, and he didn't know how to salvage it.

"Do you know what this is, son?" Mr. Kitt asked. Roman opened his eyes to see his father touching the crate. "This right here is our future. It's going to save us in the war, because Dacre will one day reach us in Oath. And you breaking your commitment to Miss Little will jeopardize my plans to preserve our family."

Roman stared at the crate. "What's in it?"

Mr. Kitt lifted the lid. "Come take a look."

Roman edged a few steps closer. Close enough so he could catch a glimpse of what rested within. Slender metal canisters the length of his forearm, resting like silver bullets in the crate.

"What are those?" he asked, frowning. "Are those *bombs*?"

His father only smiled and shut the lid. "Perhaps you should ask your fiancée. She helped her father create them."

"This is evil," Roman said, his voice wavering. "These bombs or whatever they are . . . you can't return from something like this. They're going to kill innocent people. I won't—"

"No, this is ingenious," Mr. Kitt interrupted. "All of the lords and ladies of Oath who are bowing to Enva . . . where do you think their titles will go when Dacre takes the city? Who do you think he will reward?"

Roman stared at his father, eyes wide in horror. "Is *this* all you care about? Where you stand among high society? How you can take advantage of others?" He began to step away, his breath hissing through his teeth. "I won't be a part of this, Father."

"You will do *exactly* what I tell you to do, Roman," Mr. Kitt said. "Do you understand? If you won't do it to save your own hide, then at least think of your mother, who is still grieving over your recklessness."

Roman felt the blood drain from his face. The guilt over his sister's death burned like acid in his mouth, and he lost all desire to fight, to speak.

"This is your duty, son," his father said in a gentler voice. "I'm very proud of you for being promoted. You have a very bright future ahead of you.

Don't ruin it on a poor girl who no doubt wants to drain you of your inheritance."

Roman turned and left.

He hardly remembered striding into his room. The door closed and locked behind him with a sigh of magic. Roman looked at his wardrobe, where the floor was bare. No letters waited for him. He expected there wouldn't be any further correspondence with Iris from this point onward, since she had left to only the gods knew where. And he wasn't sure if she had read his last letter or not, but he decided he could take no chances.

There was a loose floorboard beneath his desk. Roman knelt and gently worked it up, exposing a perfect hiding place. Once he had stashed candy and money and a home run baseball he had caught at a game and newspaper clippings here. Now, he took the shoebox full of Iris's letters and he hid them, burying her words deep in the safety of darkness. He slid the floorboard back into place.

He couldn't protect Del when she had needed him most, but he would try his best to protect Iris now.

Because he wasn't sure how much his father truly knew about her. And Roman wasn't about to let him discover anything more.

The *Inkridden Tribune* was chaos.

To be fair, it was in the drafty basement of an ancient building downtown, in a room half the size of the *Oath Gazette*. Tables were haphazardly arranged as desks, exposed bulbs shed light from above, and it smelled like fresh-cut paper and mildew with a whirl of cigarette smoke. Editors were busy at their typewriters, and assistants moved back and forth as if they were on a track, delivering chipped cups of tea and strips of messages from the one telephone—which rang shrilly off its hook—to certain desks.

Iris stood at the foot of the stairs, staring into the hustle, waiting for someone to notice her.

No one did. There were only a handful of staff to do the same amount of work that the *Oath Gazette* did. And she couldn't deny that while the working conditions here were vastly different from her old employer, the air teemed with something electric. There was excitement and passion and that breathless feeling of creation, and Iris felt it catch in her lungs, as if she were falling ill to whatever fever was fueling these people.

She stepped deeper into the room and snagged the first assistant who passed by.

"Hi, I'm looking for Helena Hammond."

The assistant, a girl a few years older than Iris with short black hair, halted as if she had just stepped into a wall. "Oh, you must be here to apply as a war correspondent! Here, see that door over there? That's her office. She'll be thrilled to meet you."

Iris nodded her thanks and wove through the madness. Her breath felt shallow when she knocked on Helena Hammond's door.

"Enter," a gruff voice said.

Iris stepped into the office, surprised to see a trail of sunlight. There was a tiny square window high up on the wall, cracked to welcome fresh air and the distant sounds of the city. Helena Hammond, who couldn't have been taller than five feet, stood puffing on a cigarette, staring into that beam of light. She had auburn hair that was cut into a bob and a fringe that brushed her eyelashes every time she blinked. Her cheeks were freckled, and a long scar graced her jaw, tugging on the corner of her lips. She was dressed in a set of high-waisted trousers and a black silk shirt, and a silver ring gleamed on her thumb.

"Can I help you?" she asked, her voice pitched deep and scratchy. She kept her focus on the sunlight, breathing out a long curl of smoke.

"I'm here to apply as a war correspondent," Iris said. Her shoulders were aching from lugging around her typewriter and valise, but she stood as tall and elegant as possible. Because she could tell that the moment Helena looked at her, the woman would be able to see through her and weigh her mettle.

"Two in one day," Helena remarked, at last turning her face to Iris. "Whatever have they put in the water?"

Iris wasn't sure what she implied. But she held still as Helena walked around her desk to scrutinize her.

"Why do you want to be a correspondent, Miss . . . ?"

"Iris. Iris Winnow."

"Miss Iris Winnow," Helena said, flicking ash off the end of her cigarette. "Why are you here?"

Iris shifted her weight, ignoring the pain in her wrists. "Because my brother is fighting."

"Mm. That's not a good enough answer for me to send you, kid. Do you have any idea how difficult it'll be as a correspondent? Why should I send an innocent thing like you to see and digest and report such terrible things?"

A bead of sweat trickled down Iris's spine. "People in Oath think they're safe. They think that because the war is far away, it will never reach us here. But I believe it will come to the city one day, sooner than later, and when it does . . . there will be a lot of people unprepared. Your choice to report the news on the war front is going to help change that."

Helena was staring up at her, and a lopsided smile crept over her lips. "You still didn't answer why I should send *you,* Iris Winnow."

"Because I want to write about things that matter. I want my words to be like a line, cast out into the darkness."

"That's rather poetic of you," Helena said, eyes narrow. "What's your previous experience?"

"I worked three months at the *Oath Gazette,*" Iris replied, belatedly hoping that wouldn't dampen her chances.

"You worked for good ole Autry, did you? My, now *that's* a surprise." Helena chuckled, crushing her cigarette into an ashtray. "Why'd you leave such a splendid opportunity? Did he fire you for double spacing?"

"I resigned."

"I like you more already," Helena said. "When can you start?"

"Immediately," Iris replied.

Helena glanced at Iris's valise and her typewriter case. "You came prepared, didn't you? I like that in a person. Come, follow me." She walked out the door, and Iris had to scramble to catch up with her, weaving through the chaos again.

They ascended the stairs, leaving behind the chill of the basement for a small room on one of the upper floors. It was well lit and clean, with a table and two chairs.

"Have a seat, Iris," Helena said. "And fill this out for me. I'll be back in a moment." She set down a waiver and a pen before striding away, leaving Iris alone.

Iris glanced over it. The waiver was filled with things like *I agree to not hold the* Inkridden Tribune *responsible for anything which may befall me, including but not limited to: dismemberment, sickness, perforated and ruined organs, starvation, long-lasting disease of any kind, broken bones, and even death. I will take full responsibility for whatever happens to me—bodily and mentally and emotionally—while I am on the campaign to report.*

She read through the fine print; she signed where applicable, and she didn't think twice about it. But Forest came to mind. She wondered how many scars the war had given him.

"Here we go," Helena said, returning with an armload of supplies. She set down what looked to be a folded uniform and a narrow leather bag with a thick strap, to be carried across one's back. "Your jumpsuit. There's another one in the bag, for when you need to do laundry. Also socks, boots, menstrual supplies. I can't stress enough how vital it is you wear the jumpsuit, because of this little thing right here . . ." She snapped the jumpsuit so it would unfold. It was gray and plain, with buttons up the front. But Helena pointed to a white badge stitched with the words INKRIDDEN TRIBUNE PRESS, just over the right breast pocket. "If you get into a hairy situation—which gods willing you won't but we must prepare for anything—this proclaims you are neutral in the war—that you are only reporting what you see and should not be perceived as a threat. You understand?"

"Yes," Iris said, but her mind was whirling.

"Food rations are also in the bag," Helena said, tossing the jumpsuit onto the table again. "In case you need them, but you'll be assigned to a house, which will feed you and give you a safe place to sleep. Now, may I look at your typewriter?"

Iris unlatched the locks and lifted the lid to the case. And she didn't know what she expected, but it wasn't for Helena to go wide-eyed and let out a whistle.

"*This* is your typewriter?" she asked, inclining her head so her fringe would shift out of her eyes.

"Yes, ma'am."

"Where did you get it?"

"It was my grandmother's."

"May I touch it?"

Iris nodded, puzzled. But she watched as Helena reverently traced the lines of her old typewriter. Touching the keys, the carriage return, the roller knob. She let out another disbelieving whistle.

"An Alouette! Do you even know what you have here, kid?"

Iris held her tongue, uncertain how to answer.

"This typewriter is a very rare beast," Helena said, leaning closer to admire it. "Only three were made just like it. Haven't you heard the old story?"

"No."

"Then I should tell you, so you know exactly how precious this relic is. Decades ago, there was a rich man in the city named Richard Stone. He was a widower and had only one daughter, who was his pride and joy. Her name was Alouette, and she loved to write. Well, she fell sick with tuberculosis when she was only fifteen. Because of that, her two dearest friends could no longer visit her. Alouette was despondent. And Mr. Stone was driven to find a way for his daughter to communicate with her chums, and he found an old, cranky inventor who specialized in typewriters. Mr. Stone went into debt to allow three to be uniquely assembled. The legends claim the typewriters were constructed in a magical house on a magical street of Oath by a man with a magical monocle that could discern magical bonds—who soon vanished, by the way. But regardless . . . the typewriters were named after Alouette. She was given one, of course. And then her father gifted the other two to her friends. They sent letters and stories and poetry to each other for a full year, up until the night Alouette passed away. Shortly after that, Mr. Stone donated her typewriter to the museum, to be displayed with a few of her letters."

"And the other two typewriters?" Iris asked quietly.

Helena cocked her brow. "They remained with her two friends, of course." She lifted the typewriter and found the silver engraving. The one that Iris had spent years tracing and wondering about. "You said this belonged to your nan, correct? And were her initials by any chance D.E.W.?"

"They were," Iris said.

Daisy Elizabeth Winnow had been a reserved woman, but she had often told Iris stories her of childhood. The saga of her typewriter, however, had never been shared, and Iris was struck by the whimsy of it, imagining her nan being friends with two other girls. How the three of them had written to each other, through their separation and sadness and joy.

"It makes you wonder where the third one is, doesn't it?" Helena said, carefully setting the typewriter back down. "Or should I say, the *second* one, since this is technically the third."

Iris had an inkling. She said nothing, but her mind wandered to the letters that were hiding in her bag. Her heart quickened as she thought, *It isn't the wardrobes connecting us. It's our typewriters.*

"So, Iris," Helena said. "I have to ask this: are you sure you want to take your nan's typewriter to war? Because you could sell it to the museum. They would probably pay you a fortune and be downright giddy at the opportunity, displaying it with The First Alouette."

"I'm not selling it," Iris replied curtly. "And it goes wherever I go."

"I figured you'd say that," Helena replied. "But I digress. This is how your correspondence will work: you'll take the next train out of Oath, which leaves in half an hour. So we don't have much time. You're going to Avalon Bluff, a town six hundred kilometers west of here, close to the war front. Keep in mind you'll be under a new chancellor and their jurisdiction, and that the laws you once knew in Oath and the Eastern Borough might not apply in the west. Things also change drastically in war, so pay close attention to the rules of daily life, so you remain safe.

"Your contact is Marisol Torres. She runs a bed and breakfast, and she'll give you food and lodgings while you work. She doesn't know you're coming, but mention my name and she'll take good care of you.

"The train runs through Avalon every sixth day. I expect you to have your reports typed, edited, and ready for me to publish. I want *facts* and I want *stories*. It's the only way I'll be able to get around the chancellor's restriction on how much I can publish about the war—he can't deny us a soldier's story every now and then, nor the facts, all right? So make sure you cite your stuff so he can't claim it's propaganda. You'll then slip and *seal* your typed articles in the brown classified envelopes that you'll find in your bag, and you'll hand them directly to the conductor. Supplies will also come in on the train, so if you need something, let me know. Do you understand everything I've told you, Iris?"

"Yes Ms. Hammond," Iris said. But her mouth was dry, her palms sweaty. Was she really doing this?

"Good," Helena said. "Now, get dressed. You can't take your valise, only the approved leather bag and your typewriter. Meet me out front on the pavement in five minutes." She began to step out the door but tarried on the threshold. "Oh, what name are you writing under?"

Iris paused, uncertain. At the *Oath Gazette,* her articles had been published under Iris Winnow. She wondered if she should add her middle initial, like Roman did, but thought it sounded a bit pretentious. Roman *Cocky* Kitt.

As soon as she thought of him, her chest ached. The feeling surprised her because it was sharp and undeniable.

I miss him.

She missed irritating him by rearranging his desk. She missed stealing glances at his horribly handsome face, the rare sight of his smile and the fleeting sound of his laughter. She missed striking up banter with him, even if it was most often to see who could outsnark whom.

"Iris?" Helena prompted.

Iris shivered. That bewitching moment of longing for him faded as she set her resolve. She was about to go to the war front and she didn't have time to wallow in . . . whatever these feelings were.

"Iris Winnow is fine," she said, reaching for the jumpsuit.

"Just 'fine'?" Helena looked pensive for a second, her mouth twisting. And then she winked at Iris and said, "I bet I can come up with something better."

She slipped out the door before Iris could reply.

16

Attie

Six hundred kilometers feel like an eternity when you're waiting for the unexpected. An eternity made of golden fields and pine forests and mountains that look blue in the distance. An eternity made of things you've never seen, air you've never tasted, and a train that rocks and clatters like guilt.

I wonder if this is how it feels to be immortal. You're moving, but not really. You're existing, but time seems thin, flowing like a current through your fingers.

I try to close my eyes and rest, but I'm too tempted to watch the world pass by my window. A world that seems endless and sprawling. A world that makes me feel small and insignificant in the face of its wildness. And then that sense of distance tightens my chest as if my bones can feel these six hundred kilometers—I'm leaving the only home I've ever known—and I withdraw his letters from my bag, and I reread them. Sometimes I regret leaving his last letter on the floor. Sometimes I'm relieved that I did, because I don't think I'd be sitting here, pressing westward with nothing more than my courage, into a cloud of dust if I hadn't.

Sometimes I wonder what he looks like and if I'll ever write to him again.

Sometimes I—

The train lurched.

Iris stopped writing, glancing out the window. She watched as the train rumbled slower and slower, eventually coming to a complete, smoke-hissing stop. They were in the middle of a field in Central Borough. No towns or buildings were in sight.

Had they broken down?

She set her notepad aside, rising to peek out of the compartment. Most of the passengers had already disembarked at the previous stops. But farther down the corridor, Iris caught sight of another girl, speaking to one of the staff.

"We'll pick up speed once the sun sets, miss," the crew member said. "In about half an hour or so. Please, help yourself to a cup of tea in the meantime."

Iris ducked back into her compartment. They had purposefully stopped, and she wondered why they had to wait for darkness to continue. She was thinking about gathering her bags and seeking out the girl she had seen when a tap sounded on the sliding door.

"Is this seat taken?"

Iris glanced up, surprised to see the girl. She had brown skin and curly black hair, and she held a typewriter case in one hand, a cup of tea in the other. She was wearing the same drab jumpsuit as Iris, with the white INK-RIDDEN TRIBUNE PRESS badge over her heart, but she somehow made the garb look far more fashionable, with a belt cinched at her waist and the pants cuffed at her ankles, exposing red striped socks and dark boots. A pair of binoculars hung from her neck and a leather bag was slung over her shoulder.

Another war correspondent.

"No," Iris said with a smile. "It's yours if you want it."

The girl stepped into the compartment, nudging the door closed behind her. She set down her typewriter, then dropped her leather bag with a groan, taking the seat directly across from Iris's. She closed her eyes and took a sip of the tea, only to promptly cough, her nose crinkling.

"Tastes like burnt rubber," she said, and proceeded to open the window, dumping out the tea.

"Do you know why we've stopped?" Iris asked.

Her newfound companion shut the window, her attention drifting back to Iris. "I'm not exactly sure. The crew seemed hesitant to say anything, but I think it has to do with bombs."

"Bombs?"

"Mm. I think we've reached the boundary for Western Borough, and beyond it is an active zone, where the effects of the war can be felt. I don't know why, but they made it sound like it's safer for the train to travel by night from here on out." The girl crossed her legs at the ankles, studying Iris with an attentive eye. "I didn't realize I'd have a companion on this trip."

"I think I arrived at *Inkridden Tribune* right after you left," Iris said, still thinking about bombs.

"Helena ask you a hundred questions?"

"Yes. Thought she wasn't going to hire me."

"Oh, she'd have hired you," the girl said. "Even if you had arrived looking like you'd just danced at a club. Rumor has it they're desperate for correspondents. I'm Thea Attwood, by the way. But everyone calls me Attie."

"Iris Winnow. But most people call me by my last name."

"Then I'll call you by your first," said Attie. "So, Iris. Why are you doing this?"

Iris grimaced. She wasn't sure how much she wanted to reveal about her tragic past yet, so she settled for a simple "There's nothing for me in Oath. I needed a change. You?"

"Well, someone I once respected told me that I didn't have it in me to become published. My writing 'lacked originality and conviction,' he said." Attie snorted, as if those words still stung. "So I thought, what better way to prove myself? What could be a better teacher than having the constant threat of death, dismemberment, and whatever else *Inkridden Tribune* said in that waiver of theirs to sharpen your words? Regardless, I don't like attempting things that I think I'll fail at, so I have no choice but to write superb pieces and live to see them published, to my old professor's chagrin. In fact, I *paid* for him have a subscription, so the *Inkridden Tribune* will start showing up on his doorstep, and he'll see my name in print and eat his words."

"A fitting penance," Iris said, amused. "But I hope you realize that you didn't have to sign up to write about war to prove yourself to anyone, Attie."

"I do, but where's the sense of adventure in that? Living the same careful and monotonous routine, day in and day out?" Attie smiled, dimples flirting in her cheeks. The next words she said Iris felt in her chest, resounding like a second heartbeat. Words that were destined to bind them together as friends. "I don't want to wake up when I'm seventy-four only to realize I haven't lived."

17

Three Sirens

By the time the train chugged into the small station of Avalon Bluff, Iris and Attie were the only two passengers remaining, and it was half past ten o'clock at night. The moon hung like a fingernail, and the stars burned brighter than Iris had ever seen, as if they had fallen closer to earth. She gathered her things and followed Attie onto the platform, her legs sore from sitting most of the day, and drew a deep breath.

Avalon Bluff tasted like hay and meadow grass and chimney smoke and mud.

The girls walked through the abandoned station, which soon spilled them onto a dirt road. Helena had given them instructions on how to locate their lodgings: Marisol's B and B was on High Street, just through the station, third house on the left, with a green door that looked like it once belonged in a castle. Attie and Iris would need to go directly there while being wary of their surroundings, prepared to take shelter at any moment.

"I take it this is High Street?" Attie asked.

It was dark, but Iris squinted, studying the town that lay before them. The houses were old, two-storied and built from stone. A few even had thatched roofs and mullioned windows, as if they were constructed centuries ago. Fences were made of stacked rocks covered in moss, and it looked like there were a few gardens, but it was hard to discern things by the light of the moon.

There were no streetlamps to guide them along. Most houses were gloomy and cloaked in shadows, as if they were fueled by candlelight rather than electricity.

It was also very quiet and very empty.

Somewhere in the distance, a cow mooed, but there were no other sounds of life. No laughter, no voices, no music, no banging pots in a kitchen. No crickets or night birds. Even the wind was tamed.

"Why does this place feel dead?" Attie whispered.

The temperature had dropped, and a fog was settling. Iris stifled a shudder. "I think I see Marisol's," she said, eager to be off the haunted street.

Helena had been right; the B and B had an unmistakable door, arched as if the house had been built around it, with an iron knocker fashioned as a roaring lion's head. The building was quaint, with shutters that looked to be black in the starlight. Rosebushes crowded the front yard with scraggly limbs, still bare from winter, and ivy grew up the walls, reaching for the thatched roof.

But it was dark within, as if the old house was sleeping or under a spell. A sense of uneasiness washed through Iris as she knocked. The lion's head clanged far too loud, given how mum the town was.

"It doesn't look like she's home," said Attie before swearing under her breath. "Are the lower windows boarded up, or am I imagining it?"

Iris stared harder at the windows. Yes, they looked to be boarded up, but from the inside.

"What are we going to do if she doesn't answer?" Attie turned to survey the remainder of the town, which didn't look promising.

"Wait," Iris said. "I think I hear her."

The girls held their breath, and sure enough, there was the inner pattering of feet, and then a dulcet voice, drawn with an accent, spoke through the front door: "What do you want?"

Attie arched her brow, exchanging a dubious glance with Iris.

"Helena said she wasn't expecting us," Iris reminded her in a whisper, before replying, "We've been sent by Helena Hammond, of the *Inkridden Tribune.*"

There was a beat of silence, and then the sound of a lock turning. The green door creaked open a sliver, revealing a woman holding a candle. She had light brown skin and her black hair was bound in a thick braid, spilling over her shoulder. Her bold eyebrows slanted with a frown until she saw the girls, and her face softened instantly.

"Blessed Enva, there's two of you? And you look so young!" she said, full lips parted in shock. "Please, *please* come inside. I'm sorry, but you took me by surprise a moment ago. These days, you don't know who comes knocking at night."

"Yes, we noticed it's rather quiet here," Attie said, a bit dryly.

"It is, and there's a reason for it, which I'll explain in a moment," Marisol said, opening the door further in welcome.

Iris stepped inside. The foyer was spacious, with a cold floor of flagstones covered with vibrant rugs. The walls gleamed in the shadows, and Iris realized there was an array of gilded mirrors of all shapes and sizes hanging upon them, even all the way up the stairwell. She caught her dim reflection and felt as if she had stepped back in time.

"Have you two eaten?" Marisol asked, locking the door behind them.

"Train biscuits" was all Attie had to say.

"Then follow me into the kitchen." Marisol led them down a corridor and into the firelight.

The kitchen was large, rustic, and warm. The windows were covered with boards, though, as well as the double doors. As if Marisol needed to keep someone or something *out*.

Herbs and copper pots hung from the rafters above, and there was a table that could seat ten people. This was where both Attie and Iris collapsed, as if they hadn't just been sitting for nine hours.

Marisol was busy opening cupboards and a small fridge, which let Iris know there was electricity in the house, she was just simply opting not to use it to light the room.

"What can I fix you to drink? My specialty is hot cocoa, but I also have some milk and tea," Marisol said as she set an onion and a red pepper on the counter.

"Cocoa sounds heavenly," Attie said with a sigh, and Iris nodded her agreement. "Thank you."

Marisol smiled, rising up on her tiptoes to pull down one of the copper pots. "It was my grandmother's recipe. I think you'll both love it. And good gods! Forgive me, but I just realized I don't even know your names!"

Attie spoke first. "Thea Attwood, to be formal. Attie to friends."

"Nice to meet you, Attie," Marisol said, her doe eyes shifting to Iris next.

"Iris Winnow. You can call me by either one."

"Iris," Marisol echoed. "It's a pleasure to meet you both. I'm Marisol Torres and this is my bed and breakfast, but I think you already knew that, didn't you?"

"Yes, and your place is charming," Attie said, admiring the kitchen. "But if I may ask . . . why are you burning candles? Are you conserving electricity?"

"Ah," Marisol said, beginning to boil water on her cooker and chop up the onion. "I'm glad you asked. No, not really, although the past few months have taught me much about conservation. It's due to the war, and the front lines being so close to Avalon Bluff."

"How close?" Iris asked.

"About eighty kilometers away."

Iris looked at Attie. Attie was already gazing at her with an inscrutable expression. She wondered how long it would take before the war felt real to them. Before they felt how close it was, like a tremor in the ground beneath them.

"All right," Marisol said, wielding a knife. "How old are you two? Because I will chew Helena up one side and down another if she sent underage children to me."

"I'm eighteen," Iris said.

"Twenty," Attie replied. "By law, we're both legal adults who can drink and be formerly charged for murder, so Helena's safe for now."

"That's still too young to be reporting on the war."

Attie dared to ask, "And how old are you, Marisol?"

Marisol wasn't offended. "I'm thirty-three, but I know I look like I'm twenty-five."

"That's not a bad thing," Attie commented.

"I suppose," said Marisol with an arched brow. But a smile lit her face, and Iris thought she might be one of the loveliest people she had ever met. "All right. Tell me about you two while I cook."

"Do you need help?" Iris asked, rising.

"Absolutely not!" Marisol said. "Stay in that chair. No one cooks in my kitchen but me, unless they have my approval."

Iris quickly lowered herself back down. Attie was nearly shaking with laughter, and Iris shot her a stern look. Which only made Attie laugh, and gods, if she didn't have a contagious one, just like Roman Kitt.

The thought of him made Iris go cold.

She pushed him away, far from her mind, and was exceedingly glad when Attie began to talk about her life. She was the oldest of six kids—three boys, three girls—and Iris gaped at her, trying to imagine what that would be like. To live in a house overflowing with siblings.

"I love them more than anything," said Attie, turning her attention to Iris. "What about you? Any brothers or sisters?"

"I have an older brother," Iris said. "He's fighting in the war. For Enva."

That made Marisol pause. "That's very brave of him."

Iris only nodded, but her face flushed when she thought about all the times she had resented her brother for leaving. She absently touched her mother's locket, hidden beneath the jumpsuit.

"And you, Marisol?" Attie asked.

"I have two younger sisters," Marisol replied. "I would do anything for them."

Attie nodded, as if she understood perfectly. Iris struggled with a bout of jealousy until Marisol said, "They're not even my sisters by blood, but I choose them. And that sort of love is everlasting." She smiled and brought two mugs to the table.

Iris wrapped her fingers around hers, breathing in the rich, spicy steam. She took a sip and groaned. "This is delicious."

"Good." Marisol said, returning to the cooker, where onions and peppers and fried eggs were crackling in a skillet.

The kitchen fell quiet for a moment, but it was comfortable silence, and Iris felt herself truly relax for the first time in weeks. She drank the hot cocoa and felt a warmth in her chest as she enjoyed listening to Attie converse with Marisol. But in the back of her mind, she wondered why this place was so dark and quiet.

Marisol didn't explain until both girls were done eating the delicious meal she set down before them—plates full of rice, sautéed vegetables, and chopped herbs, topped by fried eggs.

"Now that I've fed you," she began, sitting in the chair across from Iris, "it's time for me to tell you why Avalon Bluff is the way it is, so you can also know how to respond."

"Respond?" Iris asked with a hint of worry.

"To the sirens, and what they foretell," Marisol said, tucking a wisp of hair behind her ear. A small red jewel in her lobe caught the light. "There are three different sirens, and they can sound at any time. No matter where you are in Avalon, whether it's the infirmary or the grocer or in the street, you need to always be prepared for them and respond accordingly.

"If a siren wails continuously during the night, you have exactly *three* minutes to extinguish all light, cover all windows, and lock yourself indoors before the hounds arrive."

"Hounds?" Attie echoed with a frown. "I thought they were just a myth."

"Not at all," Marisol replied. "I've never seen one, because I haven't dared to look out the window when they stalk the night, but a neighbor of mine caught a glimpse once and said the hounds are about the size of a wolf. They destroy anything in their path that lives."

"Have they ever killed someone here?" Iris asked. She remembered the myth her enigmatic correspondent had sent, about Dacre searching for Enva. How he had called up his hounds from the realm below.

"No," Marisol replied, but there was a trace of sadness in her tone. "But a flock of sheep was lost once, as well as some other livestock. You will most likely be here with me at night—Avalon has a curfew, because of this . . .

situation. Everyone is to be safely home by sunset. So if you are woken by this siren, make sure all candles are extinguished and lights are turned off instantly, cover your windows, and then come to my room. All right?"

Both Iris and Attie nodded.

"The second siren I want to tell you about," Marisol continued, "is the one that wails continuously during the day. If you hear that one, you have exactly *two* minutes to take cover before the eithrals arrive. They're wyverns, and Dacre uses them to carry bombs in their talons, which they will drop on anything that they see that moves below. If you are inside, then cover the windows and sit quietly until they pass by. If you happen to be out of doors when they fill the skies, then you must do what feels unthinkable— lie down exactly where you are and not move until they are gone. Do you both understand me?"

The girls nodded in unison once again.

"Is that why the train doesn't travel by day around here?" Iris asked. "We noticed that it stopped and delayed its course until nightfall at a certain point in the journey."

"Yes, that's exactly why," Marisol said. "The train has a better chance of outrunning the hounds at night than stopping in time if an eithral is spotted. And if the railway is bombed, it would be catastrophic for us. Which leads me to the third and last siren you may hear—the one that wails intermittently at any time. Day or night. We have yet to hear this one in Avalon Bluff, but with each day that passes, it becomes more and more of a possibility that we must prepare for.

"If you hear this siren, you need to evacuate to the east, immediately. It means that our soldiers on the western front lines are retreating and have given up ground and cannot defend us here. It means that the enemy is coming and will most likely take the town. I'll prepare dash-packs for you both, which I'll hang in the pantry for you to grab and run with. There'll be a matchbook, a flask of water, tins of beans, and other nonperishable items packed inside. Enough to hopefully last you to the next town.

"Now, I know this is more than you signed up for, and your heads must be swimming, but do you have any questions for me?"

Attie and Iris were silent for a full ten seconds. But then Attie cleared her throat and asked, "The sirens . . . where do they come from?"

"A town a few kilometers west of here, called Clover Hill. They have a great vantage point and a siren that once rang for foul weather and they agreed to alert us the moment they perceived any hounds or eithrals or enemy soldiers." Marisol began to gather up their empty plates. Iris noticed a slim golden band was on her left ring finger. She was married, then, although she had made no mention of a spouse. It seemed as if she lived alone here. "And it's late. Nearly midnight. Let me take you both upstairs. You can choose your rooms and then get a good night's sleep."

As long as a siren doesn't sound, Iris thought, and a spark of dread arced through her. She hoped it wouldn't happen, and then that it would, so she could go ahead and get the fright of experiencing one out of the way.

"Can we help you clean, Marisol?" Attie asked, rising from her chair.

"Not tonight," she replied. "I have a policy. Guests on their first night aren't expected to do anything but enjoy themselves. But tomorrow will be different. Breakfast will be at eight sharp, and then you both can help me prepare a meal to take to the infirmary, to feed the wounded soldiers. I thought it would be a good way for you to begin your research. Some of the soldiers won't want to talk about what they've seen and experienced, but others will."

"We'll be ready," Attie said, gathering her bags.

Iris reached for her leather bag, thoughts of Dacre running wild in her mind as she followed Marisol and Attie down the hall and up the stairs. Marisol carried a rushlight with her, the flame burning across multiple mirrors on the wall. She explained how most residents in Avalon Bluff had decided to forgo electricity—which was unapologetically bright and could be spotted from a distance—in the night and appoint themselves with candles that could be easily blown out in case of a hound or intermittent siren.

"Now," Marisol said when they reached the second floor, "this is the door to my room. There are four others, all empty and very charming. Choose whichever one speaks to you."

Attie stepped into one, Iris another. It felt like a crime to flip on the light switch after learning about the sirens.

The room Iris chose was decorated in shades of green. It had two windows that overlooked the back of the house, with a bed in one corner, a wardrobe carved into the wall that was similar to Iris's closet back home, and a desk, perfect for writing at.

"This room is one of my favorites," Marisol said from the threshold. "And you can use electricity, if you want. Or the candle."

"The candle will be fine," Iris said, just as Attie appeared.

"I want the room across from this one," she said. "It's red and suits me."

"Wonderful!" Marisol said, beaming. "I'll see you both in the morning. Spare blankets and towels are in the wardrobe there, if you need them. Oh, and the lavatory is down the hall."

"Thank you, Marisol," Iris whispered.

"Of course. Sleep well, my friend," Marisol said gently, just before she shut the door.

A Bloody Long Shot

I ris tried to fall asleep that night, in the cool darkness of her new room. But eventually, she became restless. The sorrow and guilt of her mother's death was climbing up her bones again, and she had no choice but to light her candle with a gasp.

She rubbed her eyes with the heel of her hand, her shoulders hunched. She was so exhausted; why couldn't she sleep?

When she opened her eyes, her gaze fixed on the narrow wardrobe door on the other side of her room. She wondered if this threshold would work just like the one in her bedroom. If she typed on Nan's typewriter, would her letters still reach the nameless boy she had been writing?

Iris wanted to find out how strong this magical bond was. If six hundred kilometers would break it. She slipped off her mattress and sat on the floor, opening her typewriter case.

This was familiar to her, even in a different place, surrounded by strangers who were becoming friends. This motion, her fingers striking words onto a blank page, cross-legged on a rug. It grounded her.

I know this is impossible.

I know this is a bloody long shot.

And yet here I am, writing to you again, sitting on the floor with a candle burning. Here I am reaching out to you and hoping you'll answer, even as I'm in a different house and nearly six hundred kilometers away from Oath. And yet I can't help but wonder if my words will still be able to reach you.

If so, I have a request.

I'm sure you remember the first true letter you wrote me. The one that detailed the myth of Dacre and Enva. It was only half complete, but do you think you could find the corresponding piece? I would like to know how it ends.

I should go. The last thing I want is for my typing to wake someone up, because this place is so quiet, so silent that I can hear my own heart, beating in my ears.

And I shouldn't hope. I shouldn't try to send this. I don't even know your name.

But I think there is a magical link between you and me. A bond that not even distance can break.

Iris gently removed the paper and folded it. She rose with a pop in her knees and approached the wardrobe door.

This will be wild if it works, she thought, proceeding to slip the letter beneath the door. She counted three breaths, and then opened the closet.

To her shock, the paper was gone.

It was wonderful and terrible, because now she had to wait. Perhaps he wouldn't write her back.

Iris paced her room, wrapping tendrils of hair around her fingers.

It took him two minutes to reply, the paper whispering over her floor. She caught it up and read:

SIX HUNDRED KILOMETERS FROM OATH?!!! Answer me, and I'll do my best to find the other half of the myth:

Did you go to war?

And before you ask, yes. I'm relieved to discover more paper of yours on my floor.

P.S.—Forgive my lack of manners. How are you these days?

She smiled.

She typed her reply and sent:

A war correspondent, actually. Don't worry—I've seen no battle. At least not yet.

The first thing I've learned is to expect the unexpected, and to always be prepared for anything. But I only just arrived, and I think it's going to take me some time to adjust to life this close to the front lines.

It's different. Like I said earlier, it feels quieter, in a strange way. You would think it would be loud and seething, full of gunpowder and explosions. But so far it's been shadows, and silence, and locked doors, and whispers.

As for how I'm doing these days…the grief is still heavy within me, and I think it would be dragging me into a pit if I wasn't so distracted. Some moments, I feel okay. And then the next, I'll be struck by a wave of sadness that makes it hard to breathe.

I'm learning how to navigate it, though. Just like you once said to me.

I should go now. I should also probably think more about conserving my paper and ink ribbons. But if you do find the myth, I'd love to read it. And you know where to find me.

He replied almost instantly:

I can't make you any promises that I'll be able to find the other half. I found the first portion on a whim, handwritten and tucked away in one of my grandfather's old books. But I'll scour the library for it. I'm certain Enva outwitted Dacre in the realm below, and men have since then read and hidden that portion of the myth with wounded pride.

In the meantime, I hope you will find your place, wherever you are. Even in the silence, I hope you will find the words you need to share.

Be safe. Be well.

I'll write soon.

19

Homesick Words

The infirmary was an old, converted school building, two-storied and shaped as a U with a courtyard garden. Most of the windows were curtained, blocking out the bright midday sun. Iris studied it as she helped unload the countless loaves of bread Marisol had baked that morning. Marisol's neighbor Peter had a rusted green lorry, and they had loaded up the back with basket after basket of bread and two massive pots of soup before driving across town to the infirmary.

Iris shivered as she carried a basket into the back of the building, where a few nurses were preparing lunch trays. Her palms were sweaty; she was nervous. She didn't know how to prepare for this—speaking to wounded soldiers.

She was also full of anxious hope. Perhaps Forest was here.

"Did you prepare questions ahead of time?" Attie whispered as they passed each other.

"No, but I've been thinking about them," Iris replied, walking the path back to the lorry to fetch another basket.

"I didn't either," Attie said as they passed again. "I suppose we'll both just do what feels right?"

Iris nodded, but her mouth went dry. If she was wounded and lying in an infirmary bed, in pain, would she want some stranger interviewing her? Probably not.

Marisol remained with the nurses in the kitchen, preparing lunches, but Attie and Iris were allowed to wander the ground floor. A few rooms were off-limits, but they were told most of the soldiers were in the great assembly hall, and that should be the focus of their task.

It was a wide room, lined with windows and beds. The floors were scuffed hardwood, creaking beneath Iris's steps as her gaze wandered. Immediately, she looked for Forest. She sought her brother in a sea of white sheets and slants of sunlight.

Some of the soldiers were missing limbs. Some of them had bandaged faces, burns, scars. Some of them were upright and talkative; some of them were lying down, sleeping.

Overcome, Iris was worried that she wouldn't recognize her brother, even if he was here. But she drew in a deep breath, because she knew these soldiers had been through more than she could even begin to imagine. The air tasted like cherry medicine syrup and lemon floor cleaner and cold stainless steel, all cloaking a hint of sickness. She closed her eyes and envisioned Forest, exactly as he had looked the day he departed.

I would know you anywhere.

When Iris opened her eyes, her attention caught on a particular soldier. The girl was sitting upright in her bed. She looked to be Iris's age, dealing a worn deck of playing cards on her quilt. Her hair was a soft shade of blond, like corn silk, and cut to her shoulders. Her skin was pallid, and her hands were shaking as she continued to set out cards. But her eyes were warm and brown and fierce, and the moment they met Iris's gaze, Iris found herself walking toward her.

"You play?" the girl asked. Her voice was brittle.

"Only when I can find a good partner," Iris replied.

"Then pull up that stool and join me."

Iris obliged. She sat at the girl's bedside and watched as she reshuffled the cards with her quaking hands. Her fingers were long, like a pianist's.

"I'm Prairie," the girl said, glancing at Iris. "Like the grass."

"I'm Iris. Like an eyeball."

That coaxed a small smile from Prairie. "I haven't seen you in here before, Iris Like an Eyeball."

"I only arrived yesterday," Iris replied, taking the cards Prairie dealt to her.

"Reporter, hmm?"

Iris nodded, uncertain what more to say. If it would even be right for her to ask Prairie if she could—

"I don't speak to reporters," Prairie said, clearing her throat. Her voice remained hoarse and weak. "But I'm always looking for someone to beat me in cards. Here, you go first."

Well, that settles that, Iris thought. At least Prairie's candid bluntness dimmed her nerves and expectations, and Iris could merely enjoy a hand of cards.

The girls were quiet as they played. Prairie was competitive, but Iris was close to matching her. They ended up playing two more rounds, until the nurses delivered lunch.

"I suppose I should let you eat in peace," said Iris, rising from the stool.

Prairie dipped her spoon into her bowl of soup. It helplessly clattered with her shaky movements. "You might as well stay. Those who would talk to you will be eating right now."

Iris glanced around to find Attie, who was seated with a soldier farther down the room. A young handsome soldier who was smiling at her, and Attie had her notepad out, writing down the things he was saying.

"I do have a question for you," Iris said, easing back down onto the stool. "If I wanted to find out where a certain soldier is stationed, who would I write to?"

"You could write to the command center in Mundy, but chances are you won't get a reply. They don't like to reveal where soldiers are stationed. It's a security measure. Things are also a bit chaotic right now. The mail isn't very reliable."

Iris nodded, trying to hide her despair. "If a soldier is wounded, is there a way for me to find that out?"

Prairie met Iris's gaze. "Do you know the name of their platoon or company?"

Iris shook her head.

"What about their battalion?"

"No, I don't know any of that information. Just their first and last name."

Prairie grimaced. "Then it'll be very difficult to find out any information or updates. Sorry to tell you that."

"It's all right. I was just wondering," Iris said with a weak smile.

Her disappointment must have been evident, because Prairie set down her spoon and said, "I don't speak to reporters, but perhaps there is something you could do?"

"What's that?"

"Would you write out a letter for me?"

Iris blinked.

The hope in Prairie's eyes shuttered with the moment of awkward silence, and she looked down. "Never mind."

"*Yes*," Iris said, recovering from her moment of shock. She reached for her back pocket, where her notepad and pen were stashed. "Yes, I would love to." She flipped it open to a fresh page, waiting, pen poised.

Prairie stared down at her half-eaten meal. "It's for my sister."

"Whenever you're ready."

It took Prairie a moment, as if she had fallen shy, but then she began to speak soft wistful words, and Iris wrote them all down.

She went soldier to soldier after that, offering to write a letter for each of them. She didn't ask for details about the war, or why they had chosen to fight, or how they had sustained their injuries, or if they knew of a private named Forest Winnow. All of them had someone to write home to, and Iris tried not to think of her brother as she scribed letter after letter, as her notepad soon brimmed with homesick words and memories and encouragement and hope.

But a cold flicker of dread went through her.

Why hadn't Forest ever written to her? He had made that promise, and her brother had never been one to break vows.

Iris was beginning to believe he might be dead.

To Whom It May Concern,

I am writing to you with the fervent hope that you will be able to tell me the current whereabouts or station of one private Forest Merle Winnow, who was recruited by Enva in the city of Oath, in Eastern Borough, Cambria, almost six months ago. His date of birth is the seventh day of Vyn, year 1892. His height is 182 cm, and he has chestnut brown hair and hazel eyes.

I am his only remaining blood relative and have been seeking to reach him by letter. I was never informed of his battalion or company, but neither have I received any news from a captain that he has perished in conflict. If you can assist me in obtaining this knowledge or pass on my letter to one who is able to, I would be eternally grateful.

Thank you for your time.

Sincerely,
Iris Winnow

20

The Music Below

That evening, Iris sat at the desk in her room, watching the sunlight fade over a distant field, and she began to type all the letters she had written down at the infirmary. She felt like a vessel, being filled up by the stories and questions and reassurances the soldiers had shared with her. Typing to people she didn't know. Nans and paps and mums and dads and sisters and brothers and friends and lovers. People she would never see but was all the same linked to in this moment.

One after the other after the other. With each word she typed, the sun sank a little farther until the clouds bled gold. A breath later, the light surrendered to night. The stars smoldered in the darkness, and Iris took dinner in her room and continued to work by the flame of a candle.

She was drawing the final page from the typewriter when she heard the unmistakable rush of paper on the floor.

He had written her.

Iris smiled and rose, picking up the letter. She read:

I have good news, my friend. I found the latter half of the myth you want. Don't ask me where and how I managed this great feat, but let's just say I had to bribe someone over tea and biscuits. That someone just so happens to be my nan, who is renowned for her temper and likes to point out my flaws every time I see her. This time it was that I "slouch," and that I "woefully" have my father's pointed chin (as if it might have changed since the last time I saw her), and that my "hair has grown exceedingly long. You could be a rogue or a knight errant on second glance." I will be frank with you: I do slouch from time to time, mainly when I'm in her presence, but my hair is fine. Alas, I cannot do anything about my chin.

But why am I rambling? Forgive me. Here's the second half, picking up where we last left off. When Enva agreed to go below with Dacre on her terms:

———

Enva, who loved the sky and the taste of the wind, was not happy in the realm below. Even though it was made of a different sort of beauty—whirls of mica and veins of copper, and stalactites that dripped into deep, mesmerizing pools.

Dacre served her in the beginning, eager to make her happy. But he knew that she was a Skyward, and she would never truly belong in the heart of the earth. There would always be a sense of restlessness within her, and he caught it from time to time, in the sheen of her green eyes and in the line of her lips, which he could never coax a smile from.

Desperate, he said to her, "Why don't you play and sing for me and my court?" Because he knew her music would not only give him pleasure, but her as well. He remembered how transcendent she had looked, upon playing for the fallen. And she had yet to sing beneath.

Enva agreed.

A great assembly was called in Dacre's firelit hall. His minions, his hounds, his eithrals, his human servants, and his ugly horde of brothers. Enva brought forth her harp. She sat in the center of the cave, surrounded by Underlings. And because her heart was laden with sorrow, she sang a lament.

The music of her instruments trickled through the cold, damp air. Her voice, pure and sweet, rose and reverberated through the rock. She watched, astonished, as Dacre and his court began to weep. Even the creatures keened in sadness.

She decided to sing a joyful song next. And once again, she watched as her music influenced all who could hear. Dacre smiled, his face still shining from his previous tears. Soon, hands were clapping and feet stomping and Enva worried their boisterous merriment would bring the rock down on their heads.

Lastly, she sang a lullaby. One by one, Dacre and his court began to descend into deep sleep. Enva watched as eyes were closed, chins dipped down to chests, and creatures curled into themselves. Soon her music was woven with the sound of hundreds of snores, and she stood alone in the hall, the only one still awake. She wondered how long they would sleep. How long would her music hold them ensorcelled?

She left the hall and decided to wait and see. And while she waited, she roamed Dacre's underground fortress, those old ley lines of magic, memorizing its twists and bends and its many secret doorways to above. Three days and three nights later, Dacre finally awoke, closely followed by his brothers, and then the remainder of his court. His mind was foggy; his hands felt numb. He lumbered to his feet, uncertain what had happened, but the fires in the hall had burned down, and it was dark.

"Enva?" he called to her. His voice carried through the rock to find her. "Enva!" He feared she had gone, but she emerged into the hall, carrying a torch. "What happened?" he demanded, but Enva was poised and calm.

"I'm not certain," she replied with a yawn. "I only just woke, a minute before you."

Dacre was disconcerted, but in that moment, he thought Enva

beautiful, and he trusted her. Not a week passed before he was hungry for her music again, and he called another assembly in the hall, so she could entertain them.

She played for sorrow. For joy. And then for sleep. This time, she sang her lullaby twice as long, and Dacre and his court slept for six days and six nights. By the time Dacre stirred awake, cold and stiff, when he called to Enva through the stone there was no answer. He reached to feel her presence, which was like a thread of sunlight in his fortress, but there was only darkness.

Enraged, he realized she had gone above. He rallied his creatures and his servants to fight, but when they emerged through the secret doorways into the world above, Enva and a Skyward host were awaiting them. The battle was bloody and long, and many of the Underlings fled, deep into the earth. Dacre was wounded by Enva's own arrow; she shot him in the shoulder, and he had no choice but to retreat, down into the bowels of his fortress. He blocked every passageway so no one and nothing from above could trespass below. He descended to the fire of the earth, and there he plotted his revenge.

But Dacre was never victorious. He could not best the Skywards, and so he chose to terrorize the mortals above. He never realized that Enva had learned all the passages of his realm while he slept beneath her charm. And when she decided to step into his hall again, two centuries later, she carried her harp with a vow lodged in her heart. To make him and his court sleep for a hundred years.

Some say she was successful, because there was a time of peace, and life was pleasant and golden for the mortals above. But others say she was unable to sing that long without diminishing her power, to hold Dacre and his court asleep for such a stretch of time. All of this to say—it is never wise to offend a musician. And choose your lovers wisely.

Iris fell pensive with the ending of the myth. She wondered if history was wrong; all this time, she had been taught of her kind's victory over the five surviving gods—Dacre, Enva, Alva, Mir, and Luz—who had been fooled into drinking a poisonous draught to make them sleep beneath the loam. But perhaps it had been Enva and her harp all along, which meant there had only ever been four gods slumbering, with the fifth still roaming in secret.

The more Iris dwelled on it, the more it rang true. Enva had never been buried in an eastern grave; she must have struck a deal with the mortals long ago. *She* had been the one to sing the other four divines to enchanted sleep in deep, dark graves. It suddenly wasn't so difficult to fathom why Dacre would wake with such vengeance in his blood. Why he would tear through town after town, hell-bent upon drawing Enva to him.

Iris shivered at the thought, and wrote her correspondent back:

I'm <u>thrilled</u> by **your** ability to find this second part and am eternally grateful for how you sacrificed yourself with tea and biscuits and reprimands from your nan, who sounds like someone I'd probably like.

I almost hesitate now to ask anything more of you, but there is something else...

I went to the infirmary ~~here at Aval~~ where I'm stationed. It gave me the chance to meet with soldiers who have been wounded. Some are recovering well, and yet some of them will die, and I find that truth difficult to swallow. They've been torn open and mangled, shot and stabbed and splintered. Their lives have been irrevocably altered, and yet none of them regret their choice to fight the evil that is stealing across the land. None of them are full of regrets save for one thing: they want to mail a letter home to loved ones.

I'm sending you a bundle of these letters. The addresses are typed at each footer, and I wanted to see if you would you be willing to place them in envelopes, address and stamp them, and drop the letters in the post for me? I promise to repay you for the postage. If you're unable to, please don't worry. Just send them back over the portal to me and I'll mail them with the next train. P.S. Do you happen to have a typewriter that looks ordinary upon first glance but has a few quirks that makes it unique? For instance, its ribbon spools might sometimes chime like a musical note, the space bar might gleam in a certain slant of light, and there should be a silver plaque on the underside. Can you tell me what's engraved there?

She gathered the soldiers' letters and sent them over the portal. She paced the room while she waited for his reply, which came sooner than she anticipated:

Of course, I'm more than happy to do this for you. I'll drop the letters in the post first thing tomorrow morning. No need to repay me for postage.

And yes, my typewriter has a few quirks. It was my nan's. She granted it to me on my tenth birthday, in the hopes I would become an author someday, like my grandfather.

Before your letter, I never thought to check the underside. I'm shocked to find the silver plaque you described. The engraving is as follows: THE SECOND ALOUETTE / MADE ESPECIALLY FOR H.M.A. Which are my nan's initials.

I'll have to ask her more about this, but I take it your typewriter is also an Alouette? Do you think this is how we're connected? Our rare typewriters?

Warmth welled in her chest, as if she had breathed in the firelight. Her theory was confirmed, and she quickly began to reply:

Yes! I just recently learned the legend of these Alouette typewriters, which I'll tell you in a moment because I think you will find it quite intriguing. But my nan, who was a solemn woman full of poetry, gave me hers on my

The haunting wail of a siren stopped her mid-sentence.

Iris's fingers froze above the keys, but her heart was suddenly pounding. That was a hound siren.

She had three minutes before they reached Avalon Bluff, which was plenty of time to prepare herself, but it felt as if Dacre's wild hounds would leap from the shadows any moment.

With a tremble in her hands, she hastily wrote:

I haver to go! Sorryy. More latwr.

She wrenched the paper from the typewriter. The bottom half of the page tore, but she managed to fold it and send it over the portal.

Quickly, she thought. *Cover the window, blow out the light, go to Marisol's room.*

Iris strode to the window, the siren continuing to wail. It made goose-flesh rise on her arms, to hear the keen of it. To know what was coming. She stared through the glass panes, into the dark pitch of night. The stars continued to wink as if nothing was amiss; the moon continued to shed light with its waxing. Iris squinted and could just discern the sheen of the neighbor's windows and roof and the field beyond them, where a gust raked over the long grass. Her bedroom faced the east, so chances were the hounds would come from the other direction.

She yanked the curtains closed and blew out her candle. Darkness flooded around her.

Should she grab anything else? She began to reach for her typewriter, fingertips tracing its cold metal in the dark. The thought of leaving it behind made her feel like the wind had been knocked from her.

Everything is going to be fine, she told herself in a firm voice, forcing her hands to leave the typewriter on her desk.

Iris took a step toward the door and proceeded to trip on the rug. She should've waited to blow out her candle until she was with Marisol. But she made it into the hallway and nearly collided with Attie.

"Where's Marisol?" Iris asked.

"I'm here."

The girls turned to see her ascend the stairs, holding a rushlight. "The downstairs is prepared. Come, to my room, the two of you. You'll spend the night here with me."

Attie and Iris followed her into a spacious chamber. There was a large canopied bed, a settee, a desk, and a bookshelf. Marisol set down her light and proceeded to shift the heaviest piece of furniture against the door. Attie rushed to help her, and Iris hurried to close the window curtains.

It was suddenly very quiet. Iris didn't know what was worse: the siren, or the silence that came after it.

"Make yourselves comfortable on the bed," Marisol said. "It might be a long night."

The girls sat against the headboard, cross-legged. Attie finally blew out her candle, but Marisol still had her rushlight lit. She opened her wardrobe, and Iris could see her shoving aside dresses and blouses to find a flashlight and small revolver.

She loaded the gun and extended the flashlight to Iris.

"If the hounds manage to get inside, which they shouldn't but there's always a possibility . . . I want you to shine the light on them so I can see them."

So she can shoot them, Iris realized, but she nodded and studied the flashlight, finding its switch with her thumb.

Marisol eased onto the edge of the bed, between the girls and the door, and she blew out her rushlight.

The darkness returned.

Iris began to count her breaths, to keep them deep and even. To keep her mind distracted.

One . . . two . . . three . . .

She heard the first hound on her fourteenth inspiration. It howled in the distance, a sound so chilling it made Iris's jaw clench. But then the sound grew closer, joined by another. And another, until there was no telling how many of them had reached Avalon Bluff.

Twenty-four . . . twenty-five . . . twenty-six . . .

They were snarling in the street, just below Marisol's window. The house seemed to shudder; it sounded like one of them was raking its claws on the front door. There was a bang.

Iris jumped.

Her breaths were frantic now, but she gripped the flashlight like a weapon, prepared for anything. She felt Attie take her other hand, and they held on to each other. And even though she couldn't see, Iris knew Marisol was directly in front of them, sitting like a statue in the darkness, a gun resting in her lap.

The shrieks faded. They returned. The house shook again, as if they were living in a loop.

Iris was exhaling her seven hundred and fifty-second breath when the silence returned. But it was just as Marisol had foretold.

It ended up being a very long night.

21

Knight Errant or Rogue

Are you safe? Are you well? What happened?
Please write to me, whenever you can.

Roman sent the message through his wardrobe not long after Iris sent her abrupt one. He knew something unexpected and terrible must have happened, for her to misspell three different words. He paced late into the night, his eyes straying to the closet, to the clean-swept floor before it. Hour after hour passed, dark and cold, and she didn't write.

What was happening? He was desperate to know. Eventually he was so exhausted that he sat on the edge of his bed, overwhelmed with misgivings.

Perhaps the town she was stationed in had come under attack. He imagined Iris having to take shelter while bombs cascaded, exploding in a blazing array of sparks and destruction. He imagined Iris wounded. He imagined Dacre's soldiers swarming in victory, taking her prisoner.

Roman couldn't bear to sit.

He stood and paced again, wearing a trench into the rug.

If something befell her . . . how would he learn of it?

"Iris," he spoke into the lamplight. "*Iris,* write to me."

It was three in the morning when he withdrew her old letters from their hiding place. He sat on the floor and reread them, and while he had always been moved by her words to Forest, he realized that he felt pierced by all the words she had written to *him.* They made him ache, and he didn't know why.

He left his room to walk the mansion's dark corridors. He took the route that he had walked night after night in the wake of Del's death, when sleep evaded him. When he had been fifteen years old and so broken that he felt like his grief would bury him.

Down the stairs he went, quiet as a wraith. Through cold rooms and winding passages. Eventually he was drawn to faint light spilling from the kitchen. He expected to step into the chamber and discover the house had set out warm milk and biscuits for him, sensing his distress. Roman startled on the threshold when he saw it was his nan, sitting at the counter with a candle and cup of tea.

"Roman," she said in her typical brusque tone.

"N-Nan," he replied. "Sorry, I didn't mean to . . . I'll be going now."

"Don't be ridiculous," Nan said. "The kettle's still warm if you want a cup of tea, although I know you prefer coffee."

It was an invitation to talk. Roman swallowed; he was haggard as he slowly entered the kitchen, reaching for a cup. He poured himself some tea and sat on the stool across from his nan, fearful to make eye contact with her at first. She had a knack for reading minds.

"What has you up at such an hour?" she asked, her shrewd gaze boring into him.

"I'm awaiting a letter."

"A letter in the dead of the night?"

His face flushed. "Yes."

Nan continued to stare at him. She had smiled only maybe three times in her entire life, and so Roman was shocked when he saw her pursed lips curve in a grin.

"You're finally putting my typewriter to good use, then," she said. "I take it you're writing to Daisy Winnow's granddaughter?"

Roman hesitated but conceded to nod. "How did you know?"

"A mere hunch," she replied. "Considering that Daisy and I were both determined to keep our typewriters in the family rather than surrender them to that pitiful excuse of a museum."

Roman thought about the letter Iris had been writing to him before she was interrupted by whatever it was that was currently happening, kilometers away. She had figured out the connection between their typewriters, and he was keen to know what exactly was binding them together.

"You were friends with Daisy Winnow?" he dared to ask, knowing his grandmother was reluctant to talk about the past.

"That surprises you, Roman?"

"Well . . . yes, Nan," he replied with a hint of exasperation. "Our family is—"

"Upper-class snobs built on new money?" she supplied. "Yes, I know. Hence why I loved Daisy so much. She was a dreamer, innovative, and openhearted. Alouette and I never cared about her social status." She paused. Roman was quiet, waiting. He held his breath as his grandmother began to tell the story about her friendship with Alouette Stone and Daisy Winnow, and the typewriters that had once kept them connected.

He was stunned at first. He drank his lukewarm tea and listened, and he began to see the invisible threads that drew him to Iris. It didn't feel like fate; Roman didn't quite believe in such fancies. But it certainly felt like *something*. Something that was now stealing his sleep and making his chest ache with each breath.

"What's she like?" Nan asked. "Daisy's granddaughter?"

Roman stared at his tea dregs. "I'm not sure. I don't know her that well."

"In case you forgot, I can tell when you lie, Roman. You squint."

He only laughed, because hadn't Iris said the very thing to him last week? "Very well, Nan. I would say she's like her grandmother, then. Given your descriptions of Daisy."

"Is that so?" Nan fell quiet, pensive. "Hmm. Is that why you wanted the other half of my myth? To send it to . . . ?"

"Iris," he whispered.

His grandmother only arched her brow. But then she said, "*Iris,*" and the sound was so gentle it made Roman shiver.

"Yes." He thought it was time to leave, before she said anything else that made him uncomfortable. He was rising from the stool when his grandmother drawled, "And you're going to let her slip away, then?"

He froze. How was he to answer that?

He said, "I don't think I have much of a choice, Nan."

Nan puffed and swatted his hand. "There is always a choice. Are you going to let your father write your story, or will you?"

He was silent as she rose with a slight grunt. Nan walked to the threshold but paused, and Roman tensed, uncertain what she was about to say.

"I am seventy-five years old, Roman," she began. "I've seen endless things throughout my life, and I can tell you right now that this world is about to change. The days to come will only grow darker. And when you find something good? You hold on to it. You don't waste time worrying about things that won't even matter in the end. Rather, you take a risk for that light. Do you understand what I'm telling you?"

He nodded, although his heart was racing.

"Good," his nan said. "Now wash those cups, or else Cook will fuss about the mess."

And then she was gone. The kitchen shadows felt deeper without her as Roman carried the pot and cups to the sink, realizing that he had never once in his life washed any dishes.

He did his best, setting the porcelain back into the cupboard before he retreated to his room, where he glanced at the wardrobe. Still no letter.

He slid down to the floor and dozed at last. When he stirred at first light, he saw she had finally written to him. Roman scrambled over the rug, his pulse hammering in his throat as he unfolded her letter and read:

I'm safe and well. Don't worry! I apologize for having to abruptly leave last night.

I don't have time to write a long letter this morning as I need to go. It's back to the infirmary today, but I'll write you soon.

P.S. I'm hoping to send you more soldier letters this evening or the next, to mail in the post, if you don't mind.

He shuddered in relief, even as he knew whatever had happened last night hadn't been good. But she was safe and well, and Roman sighed, leaning his head against the floor.

The reassurance was like a warm blanket, and he suddenly realized how sore and weary he was. He wanted to fall asleep with Iris on his mind but resisted her taunting draw.

His wristwatch was ticking, nagging him.

Roman groaned as he checked the time. He rose in a hurry, gathering Iris's letters, returning them to their hiding place. Quickly, he dressed. There was no time to shave, no time to polish his shoes or even comb his hair.

He grabbed his messenger bag and flew down the stairs.

He was late to work.

"Come, the last of the frost has passed and the garden needs some care," Marisol said that afternoon. "I could use both of your help. We'll till today and plant tomorrow."

Iris was relieved to be given a task, even if it was the difficult one of breaking hard ground with a shovel, which she had never done before, growing up on the stone and pavement of Oath. The three of them worked in the B and B's backyard, where a garden plot lay dormant from winter, covered in weeds and withered old stalks.

"It looks like someone was here before us," Attie remarked, crouching to trace deep gouge marks in the soil.

"That would be the hounds," Marisol said as she worked with a hand trowel. "That's the trouble with planting a garden in Avalon Bluff. The hounds like to trample everything when they stalk the town at night. Sometimes we go months without seeing them, but sometimes Dacre sends them every night."

Iris and Attie stared at the gouges, which they now could recognize as claw marks. A shudder went through Iris, and she returned her attention to shoveling up the dirt.

"You plant a garden every year, Marisol?" she asked, noticing the raised beds off in the corner, where flowers, lettuce, and other cold weather crops flourished.

"Yes, but only because of Keegan," Marisol replied.

"Who's Keegan?"

"My wife."

"Where is she?" Attie asked. Iris recognized the careful, respectful tone; neither of them were sure if Marisol's spouse was alive. She had made no mention of her, although she wore a wedding band.

"She travels for work," Marisol replied. "There's no way for me to know when exactly she'll be back home. But soon, I hope."

"A saleswoman?" Iris asked.

"Something like that."

"How did you two meet?"

"Well, Keegan was traveling through the bluff one summer day, and she rented a room here," Marisol began, wiping dirt from her hands. "She said the house was charming and the food was delicious and the hospitality was perfect, but my garden was in a sad state. I didn't like that comment so much, as you might imagine, but the truth was, this place was my aunt's, and she was an excellent gardener and grew most of our produce that we cooked with. And while I had inherited the place from her, I woefully didn't acquire her skill with plants.

"After I fumed at Keegan for her bluntness, she decided to stay long enough to help me with the garden. I think she might have felt bad at first, because my aunt had passed away a year before and I was missing her fiercely. And while I wanted to refuse her help . . . Keegan told the most amazing stories in the evenings, and I decided if she wanted to help restore my aunt's garden for free, who was I to turn that away?

"The garden came back together, slowly but surely, with both of us working side by side. Sometimes we argued, but most of the time we were laughing and enjoying each other's company and stories. When she eventually left, I told myself not to hope. I thought she wouldn't return for a long while. She had always been a roaming sort of soul, never prone to stay in one place too long. But she came back not a week later, and she chose to stay with me, and I knew she was the one, as silly as that might sound."

Attie was smiling, dimples flaring as she leaned on her shovel. "Not silly at all. Although I cannot even *imagine* you saying a cross word, Marisol. You're like a saint."

Marisol laughed. "Oh, trust me. I have a temper."

"I can believe it," Iris teased, to which Marisol tossed a weed at her in playful reproach.

They returned to their work, Iris watching the ground soften and crumble beneath her efforts. She spoke before she could stop herself. "I hope we get to meet Keegan soon."

"As do I, Iris. She will love you both," Marisol said, but her voice was suddenly tremulous, as if she were swallowing tears.

And Iris realized Keegan must have been gone for quite some time now, if the garden had fallen into this much disarray again.

Iris, full of nerves, wrote to him that night:

Would you ever want to meet me?

He replied, swiftly:

YES.
But you're also six hundred kilometers away from me.

Iris countered:

If I had wings, I would fly home for a day. Since I don't, it'll have to be whenever I return to Oath.

He asked:

You're returning? When? Do you know, or will you wait for the
end of the war?
P.S. You truly don't have wings? I'm shocked.

She paused, uncertain how to respond. It suddenly felt as if she had a
host of butterflies within her, and she typed:

I'll return most likely when the war is over.
    I want to see you. I want to hear your voice.
P.S. I most certainly don't have wings.

She sent that confession over the portal, and her mind added, *I want to
touch you.* It took him a minute to answer, which had her biting her nails and
fervently wishing she had kept those things to herself.
Until he wrote:

I want the same.
    Perhaps we could go irritate the librarians of Oath with our
quest for missing myths, or I could take you to meet my nan
over tea and biscuits. I think she would take a shine to you. You
could also settle the debate about my chin being too pointy and
sharp, and if I look more like a knight errant or a rogue. Or
maybe we could even just walk the park together. Anything you
would like, I would too.
    I'll be here, waiting for whenever you're ready to see me.

She read it twice before hiding her smile in the crease of the paper.

———

Dear Ms. Winnow,
    We have on record that one private Forest M. Winnow of Oath

enlisted for Enva's cause on the first day of Shiloh, nearly six months prior to your query. He was sorted into Second E Battalion, Fifth Landover Company, under Captain Rena G. Griss. We are unable to provide you with any further information at this time but advise you to write to the E Brigade C.O., stationed in Halethorpe. Please be advised that mail running through Southern Borough has been unreliable, and hence could be the reason why you have not received word from Private Winnow or his C.O.

Best,

William L. Sorrel

Second Asst. to Brigadier-General Frank B. Bumgardener

22

To Make Iridescent

A war with the gods is not what you expect it to be.

You expect what history tells you of mortal affairs, which are battles that rage for days and nights, sieges, heavy casualties, food rations, ruthless tactics and generals, secret missions that lead to surprising success, and a white flag of surrender. You expect numbers and heavily guarded maps and a sea of uniforms.

But it's also a town that must lock itself up during the night, to hide its light from stalking hounds. A town that must be vigilant even more so during the day, prepared for earth-shattering consequences provoked by something as gentle and ordinary as walking the street you grew up on.

It's a school-turned-infirmary filled with wounded bodies and souls and lives, and yet they are people so full of bravery and hope and determination it makes you hold a mirror to your own self when you're alone. To find and name what lurks within you. Relief, shame, admiration, sadness, hope, encouragement, dread, faith. And why such things are there in your bones, when you've yet to give yourself up to something so selfless.

It's wondering what tomorrow will bring. What the next hour will bring. What the next minute will bring. Time suddenly feels sharper than a knife grazing your skin, capable of cutting you at any moment.

Iris stopped typing.

She stared at the jar on her desk—her mother's ashes. Her breath felt shallow, and a knot formed in her chest. She was still debating where to spread them. If she should do it soon or wait.

What would you like, Mum?

It was quiet. There was no answer. Her eyes drifted back to the page as she sorted through the tangle of emotions she was feeling.

She still hadn't seen the front lines. She still hadn't experienced any sort of battle or catastrophe or hunger or injury. But she had felt loss, and she sought to see the war through that lens. A few minutes passed, and Iris sighed.

I don't know how to write about war.

As if sensing her debate, Attie knocked on her door.

"How's your article coming along?" she asked.

"Harder than I expected," Iris confessed with a sad smile.

"Same with mine. Let's take a walk."

The girls left via the B and B's back doors, through the freshly tilled garden and down the next street over, into the golden field that Iris could see from her bedroom window. The grass was long, touching their knees as they walked side by side. They were far enough away from the town that they could speak freely, but close enough that they could easily make it to shelter if a siren went off.

To Iris's surprise, Attie didn't ask for details on what she was writing about, or why it was coming so slowly and arduously. She asked, "Where do you think Marisol's wife is?"

"Keegan? Marisol said she was traveling, didn't she?" Iris replied, fingers tracing wispy seed heads. "I assume she's in Oath, or perhaps another city up north."

Attie was quiet for a moment, squinting against the late afternoon sun. "Maybe. I just have this strange feeling Marisol is lying to us."

That gave Iris pause. "Why would she need to lie to us about that?"

"Maybe *lie* is the wrong word. *Mislead* is better suited, because she's trying to protect herself and her wife."

"Protect them from what?"

"I don't know," Attie said. "But something feels odd."

"I feel like Marisol would tell us if it was important," Iris replied.

"Yes. I think she would too. Perhaps I'm only imagining it."

They strode farther down the field, and just the movement of walking after sitting crunched at her desk most of the day lifted Iris's demeanor. There was nothing but the sound of grass whispering against their legs, and a few starlings trilling overhead. No matter how long she lived here, she didn't think she would ever get used to how quiet it was.

"Do you think it's possible to fall in love with a stranger?" Iris asked.

"Like love at first sight?"

"Not exactly. More like loving someone you've never met. Someone whose name you don't even know but who you have a connection with."

Attie was quiet for a beat. "I'm not sure. Maybe? But only because I'm a romantic at heart." And she cast a wry smile Iris's way. "Why do you ask? Has a stranger caught your eye at the infirmary?"

"No. It's just something I'm currently thinking about."

Attie glanced up to the sky, as if the answers hid above them, high up in the clouds. The words she said next lingered with Iris for hours afterward.

"These days, I think anything is possible, Iris."

Things I know about you:

1. You slouch sometimes.
2. You have your father's chin.
3. Your hair is perfect, somewhere between rogue and knight errant.
4. You have a nan, who is full of myths.

5. You're Del's older brother.

6. You live in Oath.

7. You're 19 (I think? I added up your age from a previous letter).

8. Your writing is impeccable and often makes me laugh.

Things I don't know about you:

1. Your name.

Iris folded the paper and sent it over the portal that night. She waited, expecting him to reply swiftly, as he was prone to do. But when the minutes continued to stretch long and quiet, her stomach began to ache and she paced her room, full of worry. She had thought they were ready to exchange names at last. But perhaps she had somehow misinterpreted their communication.

An hour later, he replied.

Iris snatched the paper off the floor and read:

Then you already know all the important facets of me. I don't feel as if my name is worthy to note, but you can call me Carver. That's what Del used to call me, and I miss it some days.

—C.

Carver. Iris let his name wash through her before she whispered it into the shadows of her bedroom.

"Carver."

A name that was hard and unforgiving, cutting the air with its sound. A name she never would have thought belonged to him.

She typed:

Hi, Carver. I'm Iris.

He sent a message back:

"Little flower." I see it now. The name suits you.
P.S. Hi, Iris.

Iris chuckled, uncertain what to make of him. Gods, she wanted to know what he looked like. She wanted to know the cadence of his voice. What sort of facial expressions did he make when he typed his postscripts?

Dear Carver (I confess, it's so nice to finally be able to address my letters to you!),

Most people instantly think of an eyeball when they learn my name. It bothered me so greatly when I was younger in school. Some boys relentlessly teased me, so that's why Forest nicknamed me "Little Flower."

Even then, I disliked my name, and asked my mother (whose name was Aster, by the way) why she didn't name me something fashionable, like Alexandra or Victoria.

"The women in our family have always been named after flowers," Mum said. "Be proud of your name."

Alas, I'm still striving to be.

—Iris

He replied:

Dear Iris,

I have to say that an eyeball is the furthest image from my mind. Even the fierce flower that inspired your mother to name you wasn't the first thing I thought of. Rather:

iris: transitive verb: to make iridescent.

Let us make our names exactly what we want them to be.

—C.

Dear Commanding Officer of the E Brigade,

My name is Iris Winnow, and I am currently seeking the

whereabouts of my brother, Private Forest M. Winnow. I was informed by the Brigadier-General's second assistant that my brother was sorted into Second E Battalion, Fifth Landover Company, under Captain Rena G. Griss.

I haven't heard from Forest since the day he enlisted nearly six months ago, and I am concerned about his well-being. If you could provide me with an update on the Fifth Landover Company, or an address that I may write to, I would be deeply grateful.

Sincerely,

Iris Winnow

War correspondent for the Inkridden Tribune

Stationed at Avalon Bluff, Western Borough, Cambria

23

Champagne & Blood

Roman had told Iris his middle name, and he winced every time he thought about it. He thought about it as he rode the lift to the *Gazette*. He thought about it as he prepared his tea at the sideboard, wishing it were coffee. He thought about it when he sat at his desk and turned his dictionaries paper side out, as she had often done to irk him.

He was thinking about her far too much, and he knew this was going to doom him.

But the truth was he was anxious. Because whenever he saw her again, he would have to tell her he was Carver. He worried she would feel like he had been lying to her, although he had only ever granted her truth, even if it had been in roundabout ways.

I want her to know it's me, he thought, staring at his typewriter. He wanted her to know today, and yet it would be foolish to impart such a load by letter. No, it needed to be done in person. Face-to-face, where he could explain himself.

"You look hard at work," said a familiar voice.

Roman stiffened, turning to look up at the last person he expected to see in the *Gazette*. He set down his teacup and rose. "Father."

Mr. Kitt's eyes roamed the office. It took Roman a moment to realize his father was looking for *her*. For Iris.

"She's not here," Roman said in a cold voice.

Mr. Kitt's gaze returned to his. "Oh? And where is she?"

"I don't know. I haven't seen her since I was promoted."

An awkward silence came between them. Roman could feel Sarah's glance as she passed by, granting Mr. Kitt a wide berth. A few of the editors had also halted, watching through swirls of cigarette smoke.

Roman cleared his throat. "Why are you—"

"I made lunch reservations for you and Miss Little," Mr. Kitt said tersely. "Today. One o'clock sharp at Monahan's. You'll be marrying her in three weeks, and your mother thought it would be nice if the two of you spent some time together."

Roman forced himself to swallow a retort. This was the *last* thing he wanted to do today. But he nodded, even as he felt the life drain from him. "Yes. Thank you, Father."

Mr. Kitt gave Roman an appraising glance, as if he were surprised that Roman had given in so easily.

"Good, son. I'll see you tonight for supper."

Roman watched his father leave.

He sank back to his chair and stared at the blank page in his typewriter. The dictionaries he had turned paper side out. He forced his fingers to rest on the keys but he couldn't write a word. All he could hear was Iris's voice, as if she were reading her letter aloud to him.

You remove a piece of armor for them; you let the light stream in, even if it makes you wince. Perhaps that is how you learn to be soft yet strong, even in fear and uncertainty. One person, one piece of steel.

Roman sighed. He didn't want to be vulnerable with Elinor Little. But perhaps he should take Iris's advice.

Slowly, he began to find words to give to the page.

The sun was at its zenith when a huge lorry rumbled into town. Iris was walking with Marisol down High Street, carrying baskets of goods they had just bartered for at the grocer, when the truck arrived without warning. Iris didn't know what to think of it—its massive tires were coated in mud, its metal body dinged by bullets.

It rolled in from the western road, which Iris knew led to the war front.

"Oh my gods," Marisol said with a gasp. She dropped her basket and ran, following the lorry as it drove down another road.

Iris had no choice but to set down her basket and follow her. "Marisol! Marisol, what's happening?"

If Marisol heard her, she didn't slow. Her black hair was like a pennant as she raced, as everyone around them followed suit, until a huge crowd gathered around the lorry. It parked at the infirmary, and that was when Iris, sore for breath with a stitch in her side, realized what this was.

The lorry had brought a load of wounded soldiers.

"Quickly, get the stretchers!"

"Easy, now. *Easy.*"

"Where's a nurse? We need a nurse, please!"

It was madness as the lorry's back doors were opened and the wounded were carefully unloaded. Iris wanted to help. She wanted to step forward and do something—*Do something!* her mind screamed—but she could only stand there, frozen to the road, watching.

The soldiers were dirty, smeared in grime and blood. One of them was weeping, his right leg blown off at the knee. Another was missing an arm, moaning. Their countenances were blanched in shock, creased in agony. Some were unconscious, with battered faces and ripped uniforms.

Iris felt the world tilt.

But no one paid her any attention as she turned and vomited.

Get a grip on yourself, she thought, hands on her knees, eyes closed. *This is war. This is what you signed up for. Don't look away from it.*

She straightened and wiped her mouth with the back of her hand. She turned, envisioning her brother. If Forest were in that lorry, she would go to him with confidence. She would be calm and collected and helpful.

She wove through the crowd and helped a soldier down from the lorry bed. Iris noticed the girl could hardly stand upright; she had a gut wound.

The blood on her dark green uniform was sticky—it smeared onto Iris's hand and jumpsuit, crimson as a rose—and the girl groaned as Iris eased her inside the infirmary.

There weren't enough beds.

A nurse at the door motioned for Iris to take the girl down the right-hand corridor after looking at her wounds.

"Find any place you can where she'll be comfortable," the nurse had said, and Iris was now searching for a spot. But there was only the floor—even all the chairs were taken—and Iris could feel the girl slowly losing consciousness.

"You're all right," Iris said to her when she whimpered. "You're safe now."

"Just . . . put me down . . . on the . . . floor."

Iris did, gently, leaning her against the wall. The girl closed her eyes, hands pressed to her stomach.

Overwhelmed, Iris found the closest nurse, who was rushing by with a bucket of bloody water and rags.

"Please, there's a soldier over there who needs attention. I'm not sure what to do to help her."

The nurse, haggard, glanced over Iris's shoulder. He studied the girl sitting on the floor and then whispered to Iris, "I'm sorry, but she's not going to make it. We can't heal a wound like that. Just make her as comfortable as you can. There are spare blankets in that wardrobe over there."

Dazed, Iris turned to fetch a blanket. She brought it back to the soldier and draped it over her, the girl's eyes remaining shut, her face tense with pain.

"Thank you," she whispered before drifting unconscious.

Iris remained beside her, uncertain what to do, until she heard Marisol call for her down the hall.

"Iris? We need your help," Marisol said, taking Iris's hand to draw her out of the tumult through a side door. "All the beds here are full. Will you come with me and Attie and help me gather the mattresses from the B and B? And some spare linens, which we can tear into bandages?"

"Yes, of course," Iris said, but her voice sounded tinny.

Peter had agreed to drive his lorry so they could easily transport the mattresses, and he helped Marisol, Attie, and Iris drag the feather-stuffed pallets from the B and B bedrooms down the stairs and out the front door. They even gave their own mattresses, leaving behind nothing but bed frames and quilts.

By the time they returned to the infirmary, all of the wounded had been unloaded and a middle-aged man dressed in a threadbare officer's uniform was standing in the street, speaking to one of the doctors.

Iris could hear them arguing as she climbed out of the back of Peter's truck.

"You keep bringing me soldiers that I can't heal," the doctor was saying, her voice tinged in frustration. "There's not much I can do for them."

"All I ask is they have some dignity in death," the officer replied. "I refuse to leave them vulnerable on the battlefield."

The doctor's frown faded. Her exhaustion was nearly tangible as she said, "Of course, Captain. But I won't be able to save many of these soldiers."

"You and your staff providing them a safe and comfortable place to expire is more helpful than you could ever know," the captain said. "Thank you, Dr. Morgan."

He turned to open the door of the lorry, which was now loaded down with supplies that the town had provided, when his gaze snagged on Iris. The captain froze and then immediately approached her.

"You're a war correspondent?" he asked, noticing her badge. "When did you arrive?"

"Last week, sir," Iris replied.

"We both did, Captain." Attie spoke up from behind her.

"I can take one of you with me to the front now, if the infirmary can spare you," he said. "And I can bring you back on the next transport, which would be in seven days, if all goes smoothly."

Iris turned to face Attie, heart thundering in her chest. This was unexpected.

"Should we flip a coin for it, Iris?" Attie whispered.

Iris nodded. From the corner of her eye, she could just discern Marisol, pausing to watch what would happen.

Attie reached into her pocket and procured a coin. She held it up to the light and asked, "Mountain or castle?"

Iris licked her lips. She felt parched. She didn't know what she wanted, and the indecision felt like a knife in her side. Perspiration began to prickle her palms. "Castle."

Attie nodded and flicked the coin, high into the air. She caught the tumbling copper in her hands and opened her palm, extending it so Iris could see.

It was the mountain side of the coin.

Attie would go, then.

Roman stepped into Monahan's at ten till one, hoping to be the first to arrive. To his shock, Elinor Little was already sitting at their table, waiting on him.

"Roman," she greeted him in a cool voice. Her blond hair was crimped, her lips painted blood red. She was dressed in a navy dress with a fringed shawl, and her blue eyes were cold as she watched him take the chair across from hers.

"Elinor," he replied.

This was one of the finest restaurants in Oath, where Roman's parents had fallen in love over a long candlelit dinner. The setting was dim and romantic, with black and white floors, vases of roses on every table, marble statues in the corners, and velvet-draped windows.

Roman had never been more uncomfortable in his life, and he cleared his throat as he glanced over the menu. Elinor seemed uninclined to talk, and he had no idea what to say to her. Thankfully, a waiter emerged to pour them each a flute of champagne and to take the order for their first course.

But then it was back to a stilted silence, and Roman glanced around the restaurant, his eyes eventually landing on two marble statues in the nearest corner. Lovers, entwined together, and so magnificently carved that Roman could imagine they were real. The wrinkles in their raiment, the give of their skin as they clung to each other, the flow of their breaths . . .

"So," Elinor finally said, and Roman returned his gaze to her. "Here we are."

"Here we are," he echoed, and when she held out her flute, he clinked his glass to hers. They drank to this strange arrangement, and Roman's palms were slick with perspiration when he looked at his fiancée. "Tell me more about you."

Elinor snorted. "You don't have to pretend, Roman. I know you don't want to marry me any more than I want to wed you. We can eat in silence, appease our parents, and then return to our separate lives."

He blinked. He didn't know what to make of her statement—whether she was performing or if she *truly* felt that uninterested in him. He was marrying her in three weeks, and she was an utter stranger to him. He knew nothing about her other than her name and that she had once played the piano. And that she assisted her father in his laboratory, creating bombs.

The first course arrived.

Roman decided he would keep quiet, as she wanted, and see how long the two of them could eat in complete silence. He made it through three courses before he couldn't stand it. He raked his fingers through his hair and set his eyes on her. She had scarcely looked at him the entire lunch, as if he didn't exist.

"Why are we doing this?" he asked bluntly.

Elinor's sharp gaze almost cut through him when she glanced up. "It's for the good of both of our families."

"Is it good when it's to our own detriment?" he countered.

Elinor held his stare. "There are things happening beyond us, Roman. Things that are bound to unfold. And we must prepare for them."

"Like what?" he asked a bit loudly. "Dacre coming to Oath?"

"Hush!" she whispered, but her eyes blazed. "You shouldn't speak of such things in the open."

"Such as how you're helping your father build bombs to send to the war front on my father's railroad," he said in an icy tone. "To allow Dacre to destroy innocent people." He inevitably remembered the night he had paced, worried sick about Iris. His hands curled into fists beneath the table.

Elinor froze. Her cheeks flushed, but she recovered swiftly, granting him a smile that didn't reach her eyes. "Bombs? Don't be ridiculous."

"I saw them, Elinor. A huge crate of them in my father's office."

She took a sip of champagne. He was amazed by how callous she was.

"They aren't *bombs*, Roman," she said at last in a condescending tone. "They're something else. Don't judge or speak of things you don't understand."

Now he was the one to flush, embarrassed. "Then what are they?"

"You'll find out once we're married." She drained her champagne and gathered her shawl closer about her shoulders. She was ready to leave before the last course had arrived, and Roman watched her rise.

"You're in love with someone else," he stated, which made her pause. He could see her swallow, and he knew she was working to hide her emotions. "You should be with them, not me. Don't you see it, Elinor? You and I will be miserable together."

"We can keep to our separate rooms, until we need an heir," she murmured.

Roman was quiet as the weight of her words unfolded. His fiancée was suggesting they would take their own lovers, then. Their marriage would be in title only. A sad binding with hollow vows.

You deserve this, a voice whispered to him. The voice of his guilt, which still flared brightly even four years after Del's death. *You don't deserve to be happy or loved.*

"As you want, then," he said.

Elinor met his gaze for a brief, unguarded moment. She was relieved he had agreed to it, and it only deepened his despair.

She strode away, her heels clicking on the checkered floors. But Roman remained seated at the table as the dessert arrived. He stared at it for a long moment before his gaze wandered back to the statues, entwined in the corner.

He would soon be married to a girl who had no interest in knowing him. Her heart belonged elsewhere, and he'd never know what it would feel like to be loved by her.

It's what I deserve, he thought again as he drank the rest of the champagne.

He left the restaurant and began the walk back to the *Gazette,* hands shoved into his pockets and a scowl on his face. There was a crowd on one street corner, and Roman began to divert his path until he realized it was gathered around the newsstand.

Quickly, he changed course, getting in line to purchase whatever paper it was that had stirred up a frenzy in the people. Of course, it wasn't the *Gazette.* It was the *Inkridden Tribune,* and Roman paid for a copy.

He walked a few paces away, told himself to quickly glance over the front page and then toss it in the nearest rubbish bin. Zeb Autry would fire him on the spot if he knew his newly appointed columnist was entertaining the competition. Roman could skim and walk, and he snapped the creases from the paper as he read the headline.

He came to an abrupt halt.

His heart was suddenly thrumming, pounding in his ears.

In bold type, the headline raced across the page:

THE UNEXPECTED FACE OF WAR by INKRIDDEN IRIS

Roman stood in the sunshine and read every word of her article. He forgot where he was, where he was standing. Where he was going. Where he had just come from. He forgot everything when he read her words, and a smile crept over his face when he reached the end.

Damn, he was proud of her.

There was no possible way this paper was going into the rubbish bin. Roman carefully folded it, hiding it in his jacket. As he hurried back to the *Gazette,* he couldn't think of anything else save for Iris and her words.

He thought of her as he waited for the lift. It was broken. So he took to the stairs, and his heart continued to race long after he had returned to his desk, and he didn't know why.

It was that ache again. The one that tasted like salt and smoke. A longing he feared would only grow stronger with each passing year. A regret in the making.

He shifted, listening to the paper crinkle in his jacket. A paper inked with her words.

She was writing brave, bold things.

And it had taken him a while, but he was ready now.

He was ready to write his own story.

Iris remained with Marisol at the infirmary that night. After all the mattresses had been laid down, the two of them had helped in the kitchen, preparing soup and bread. Then they had washed plates and linens and scrubbed blood off the floors and prepared bodies for burial.

The soldier Iris had helped off the lorry was one of them.

It was almost midnight now, and Iris and Marisol were sitting on a stack of empty crates in a corner, shredding bedsheets into bandages. Attie had been gone for hours, and Iris couldn't help but wonder where she was, if she had reached the war front yet. How much danger she would be in.

"She'll be safe," Marisol said gently, as if she had read Iris's mind. "I know it feels futile to say this, but try not to worry."

Iris nodded, but her thoughts ran in a tight circle. She kept seeing the moment the lorry doors were opened, revealing the wounded soldiers.

"Marisol?"

"Hmm?"

Iris was quiet, watching her shred the sheets with precision.

"Is Keegan fighting in the war?"

Marisol froze. But she met Iris's gaze, and there was a hint of fear within her. "Why do you think that, Iris?"

"My brother is fighting for Enva, and I recognize the same gleam in you that dwells in me. The worry and the hope and the dread."

Marisol sighed, her hands dropping to her lap. "I was going to tell you and Attie eventually. I was just waiting."

"What were you waiting for?" Iris asked.

"I didn't want it to interfere with your work," she replied. "Helena has no idea my wife is fighting. I don't know if she would even send correspondents to my door if she knew. You are, after all, supposed to be writing from a neutral perspective."

"She knows my brother is fighting, and she still hired me," Iris said. "I don't think you should have to hide the fact that your wife is brave and selfless."

Marisol was silent, her long fingers tracing the bandages on her lap. "She's been gone seven months now. The day word broke out that Dacre had taken the town of Sparrow, she enlisted. In the beginning, I asked her—I *begged* her—not to go. But then I realized I couldn't hold her in a cage. And if she felt so passionately about fighting Dacre, then I needed to support her. I told myself I would do whatever it took at home to help, whether that was making food for the infirmary or agreeing to house war correspondents, or even giving up my groceries to send to the soldiers on the front."

"Does she ever write to you?" Iris whispered.

"Yes, whenever she can, which isn't often. They were on the move for a while, and now the army must prioritize transporting only the most essential of things, and letters often get overlooked." Marisol paused before asking, "Have you heard from your brother, Iris?"

"No."

"I'm sure you will soon."

"I hope so," Iris said, although her heart was heavy. She hadn't received a reply from the E Brigade's C.O. yet, and she worried she never would.

An hour later, Marisol told her to rest. Iris lay on the infirmary floor and closed her eyes, exhausted to the bone.

She dreamt of Forest.

Dear Carver,

I'm sorry I haven't written to you in a while. The days have been long and hard here. And they've made me realize that I don't think I'm brave enough or strong enough for this. I don't think my words will ever be able to describe how I feel right now. I don't think my words will ever be able to describe the things I've seen. The people I've met. The way the war creeps like a shadow.

How am I supposed to write articles about this when my

words and my experience are so terribly inadequate? When I myself feel so terribly inadequate?

Love,

Iris

Dear Iris,

I don't think you realize how strong you are, because sometimes strength isn't swords and steel and fire, as we are so often
made to believe. Sometimes it's found in quiet, gentle places. The
way you hold someone's hand as they grieve. The way you listen
to others. The way you show up, day after day, even when you
are weary or afraid or simply uncertain.

That is strength, and I see it in you.

As for your bravery... I can honestly tell you I don't know
anyone of your mettle. Who else packs up everything and leaves
the comfort of their home to become a war correspondent? Not
many. I admire you, in more ways than one.

Keep writing. You will find the words you need to share. They
are already within you, even in the shadows, hiding like jewels.

Yours,

—C.

24

Dangerous Instruments

She's back," Marisol said.

Iris paused on the threshold of the B and B, eyes wide with surprise. She had just walked home from the infirmary in the dark, breaking curfew, and had expected Marisol to greet her with a reprimand.

"Attie?" Iris breathed.

Marisol nodded, shutting the door behind her. "She's in her room."

Iris bounded up the stairs and knocked on Attie's door. When there was no answer, her heart skipped in dread, and she cracked the door open.

"Attie?"

The room was empty, but the window was open. A night breeze played with the curtains as Iris stepped deeper into the room, leaning out the window to catch a glimpse of her friend sitting on the roof, binoculars raised to her face as she gazed up at the stars.

"Come join me, Iris," Attie said.

"You don't think Marisol will kill us for sitting on the roof?"

"Maybe. But at least she'd do it *after* the war."

Iris, who had never been fond of heights, carefully edged her way onto the roof, crawling over to sit beside Attie. They sat in silence for a few moments, until Iris gently asked, "How was the front?"

"Grueling," Attie replied, her attention still focused on the stars.

Iris gnawed on her lip, thoughts racing. *I'm so happy you're back! I was worried about you. It didn't feel right, being here without you . . .*

"Do you want to talk about it?" Iris asked tentatively.

Attie was quiet for a beat. "Yes, but not now. I need to still process it." She lowered the binoculars from her eyes. "Here, take a look, Iris."

Iris did, and at first it was blurry and dark until Attie taught her how to bring the binoculars into focus, and suddenly the world exploded with hundreds of stars. Breathless, Iris studied the clusters, and a smile crept over her face.

"It's beautiful," she said.

"My mother's an astronomy professor at Oath University," Attie said. "She taught me and my brothers and sisters the names of the stars."

Iris spent a few more seconds studying the sky before she handed the binoculars back to Attie. "I've always admired them, but I'm terrible at naming the constellations."

"The trick is to find the northern star first." Attie pointed upward. "Once you find it, the others are easier to name."

The girls fell silent again, staring up at the constellations. Attie eventually broke the quiet with a whisper.

"I have a secret, Iris. And I'm debating if I should tell you."

Iris glanced at her, surprised by Attie's confession. "Then that makes two of us," she replied. "Because I have a secret too. And I'll tell you mine if you tell me yours."

Attie snorted. "Fine. You've convinced me. But you must go first."

Iris proceeded to share about her enchanted typewriter and her letters to Carver.

Attie listened, mouth agape, which soon turned into a wily smile. "*That's* why you asked me about falling in love with a stranger."

Iris chuckled, slightly embarrassed. "I know, it sounds . . ."

"Like something out of a novel?" Attie offered wryly.

"He could be horrid in real life."

"True. But his letters suggest otherwise, I imagine?"

Iris sighed. "Yes. I'm growing fond of him. I've told him things that I've never said to anyone else."

"That's wild." Attie shifted on the roof. "I wonder who he is."

"A boy named Carver. That's really all I know." She paused, gazing up at the stars again. "All right. Now tell me your secret."

"It's not nearly as dashing as yours," Attie said. "But my father is a musician. Years ago, he taught me how to play the violin."

At once, Iris thought of the current restriction on stringed instruments in the city. All due to fear of Enva's recruitment.

"I once thought I could earn a place with the symphony," Attie began. "I practiced hours a day, sometimes until my fingertips were bloody. I wanted it more than anything. But of course, things changed last year, when the war broke out. When suddenly everyone was afraid of falling prey to Enva's songs, and Oath began to shed its musicians like we were a sickness. The constable actually came to our house, to confiscate anything with strings. You can imagine how many of them we probably had in our house. I told you I'm the oldest of six, and my father was keen on seeing all his children learn to play at least one instrument.

"But Papa had planned for this. He surrendered all his strings save for one violin, which he hid in a secret compartment in the wall. He did it for me, because he knew how much I loved it. And he told me that I could still play, but not nearly as much. I would have to go down to the basement and play during the day when my siblings were at class, when the city was loud beyond the walls. And no one, not even my younger brothers and sisters, could know about it.

"So that's what I did. In between my classes at university, I came home and I played in the basement. My father was my only audience, and while it seemed like our lives had been put on hold, he told me to keep my chin up. To not lose hope or let fear steal my joy."

Iris was quiet, soaking in Attie's story.

"There were some evenings I would feel so angry," Attie continued.

"That a goddess like Enva had interrupted our lives and stolen so many of our people, compelling them to fight in a war hundreds of kilometers away. I was angry that I could no longer play my violin in the light. That my symphony dreams were dashed. And I know I told you about my stuffy professor claiming my writing was 'unpublishable,' but another reason why I signed up to be a correspondent was simply because I wanted to know the truth about the war. In Oath, there's this undercurrent of fear and half-hearted preparations, but I feel like no one truly knows what's happening. And I wanted to see it with my own eyes.

"So here I am. Freshly returned from the front. And now I understand."

Iris's heart was beating in her throat. She watched Attie in the starlight, unable to take her gaze from her friend. "What, Attie?" she asked. "What do you understand?"

"Why Enva sang to our people. Why she filled their hearts with knowledge of the war. Because that's what her music did and still does: it shows us the truth. And the truth is the people in the west were being trampled by Dacre's wrath. They *needed* us, and they still do. Without soldiers coming from Oath, without us joining in this fight . . . it would already be over and Dacre would reign."

Attie fell quiet, lifting her binoculars back up to her eyes. To study the stars again.

"Do you think we'll lose?" Iris whispered, wondering what the world would be like if the gods rose again to rule.

"I hope not, Iris. But what I do know is we need more people to join this war in order to win. And with music being treated like a sin in Oath, how will people learn the truth?"

Iris was pensive. But then she whispered, "You and I, Attie. We'll have to write it."

Dear Iris,

I have good news and <u>slightly</u> not good news. All right, it's bad news. But I've always been an advocate for giving the best first, so here it is:

I found a snippet of a myth I think you'll enjoy. It's about Enva's instrument and is as follows:

"Enva's harp, the only one of its kind, was first born in the clouds. Her mother goddess loved to hear Enva sing and decided to fashion an inimitable harp for her. Its frame is made of dragon bone, salvaged from the wasteland beyond sunset. Its strings are made of hair, stolen from one of the fiercest harpies in the skies. Its frame is held together by the very wind itself. They say the harp is heavy to mortals, and it would refuse to let such fingers play it without screeching. Only Enva's hands can make it truly sing."

Now, onto the news you won't like: I'm going to be away for a while. I'm uncertain how long at the moment, and I won't be able to write to you. That's not to say I won't be thinking of you often. So please know that, even in the silence that must come between us for a little while.

I'll write to you whenever I'm able. Promise me you'll remain safe and well.

Yours,

—C.

Dear Carver,

Let me first say thank you for the myth snippet. I enjoyed it, immensely. I wonder if you are perhaps a wizard, for how you're able to find missing myths the way you do. As if by magic.

But I also can't help but wonder ... where are you going? Are you leaving Oath?

Love,

Iris

She waited for him to write a reply. And when it never came, she hated how her heart sank into the silence.

25

Collision

Dear Carver,

I don't know why I'm writing this. You just told me last night you were going away, and yet here I am. Writing to you. As I've been doing so compulsively the past few months.

Or maybe I'm truly writing for myself today, under the guise of your name. Perhaps it's a good thing you're gone. Perhaps now I can fully lower my armor and look at myself, which I've resisted doing since my mum died.

You know what? I need to completely restart this letter ~~to you~~ to me.

Dear Iris,

You don't know what's coming in the days ahead, but you're doing just fine. You are so much stronger than you think, than you feel. Don't be afraid. Keep going.

Write the things you need to read. Write what you know to be true.

—I.

"We need to get the seeds in the ground," Marisol said with a sigh. They still hadn't planted the garden yet, despite the fact that it was tilled and ready. "I'm afraid I won't have time to do it today, though. I'm needed in the infirmary kitchen."

"Iris and I can plant them," Attie offered, finishing her breakfast tea.

Iris nodded in agreement. "Just show us how to do it and we can get everything planted."

Half an hour later, Iris and Attie were on their knees in the garden, dirt beneath their nails as they created mounded rows and planted the seeds. It caught Iris by surprise—this weighted sense of peace she felt as she gave the earth seed after seed, knowing they would soon rise. It quieted her fears and her worries, to let the soil pass through her fingers, to smell the loam and listen to the birdsong in the trees above. To let something go with the reassurance it would return, transformed.

Attie was quiet at her side, but Iris sensed her friend was feeling the same.

They were nearly done when a distant siren began to wail. Instantly, the warmth and security Iris had been experiencing bled away, and her body tensed, one hand in the soil, the other cupping the last of the cucumber seeds.

On instinct, her eyes lifted.

The sky was bright and blue above them, streaked with thin clouds. The sun continued to burn near its midday point, and the wind blew gently from the south. It seemed impossible that a day this lovely could turn sour so quickly.

"Hurry, Iris," Attie said as she rose. "Let's go inside." She sounded calm, but Iris could hear the apprehension in her friend's voice as the siren continued to blare.

Two minutes.

They had two minutes before the eithrals reached Avalon Bluff.

Iris began to inwardly count in her mind as she rushed after Attie, through the back doors of the B and B. Their boots tracked dirt along the floor and rugs as the girls began to pull the curtains, covering the windows as Marisol had once instructed them to do.

"I'll take the ground-floor windows," Attie suggested. "You go on upstairs. I'll meet you there."

Iris nodded and bounded up the steps. She went to her room first and was just about to snap the curtains over one of the windows when something in the distance caught her eye. Over the neighbor's thatched roof and garden plot and into the expanse of the golden field, Iris saw a figure moving. Someone was walking toward Avalon Bluff through the long grass.

Who was that? Their foolish persistence in walking during a siren was threatening the entire town. They should be lying down where they were, because the eithrals would soon haunt the skies, and if the winged creatures dropped a bomb that close . . . would it obliterate Marisol's house? Would the blast level Avalon Bluff to the ground?

Iris squinted against the sun, but the distance was too great; she couldn't discern any details of the moving figure, other than they seemed to be briskly walking in defiance of the siren, and she hurried into Attie's bedroom, finding her binoculars on the desk. Iris returned to her window with them, palms sweating profusely, and she looked through the lenses.

It was blurry at first, a world of amber and green and shadows. Iris drew a long, calming breath and brought the binoculars into focus. She searched the field for the lone individual, at last finding them after what felt like a year.

A tall, broad-shouldered body dressed in a gray jumpsuit was striding through the grass. They carried a typewriter case in one hand, a leather bag in the other. There was a badge over their chest—another war correspondent, Iris realized. She didn't know if she was relieved or annoyed as she dragged her eyes upward to their face. A sharp jaw, a scowling brow, and thick hair the color of ink, slicked back.

Her mouth fell open with a gasp. She felt her pulse in her ears, swallowing all sound but that of her heart, pounding heavy and swift within her. She stared at the boy in the field; she stared at him as if she were dreaming. But then the truth shivered through her.

She would know that handsome face anywhere.

It was Roman Confounded Kitt.

Her hands went cold. She couldn't move as the seconds continued to pass and she realized he was *this* close to her and yet so far away, walking in a field. His ignorance was going to draw a bomb. He was destined to be blown apart and killed, and Iris tried to envision what her life would be like with him dead.

No.

She set down the binoculars. Her mind whirled as she turned and ran from her room, passing Attie on the stairs.

"Iris? *Iris!*" Attie cried, reaching out to snag her arm. "Where are you going?"

There was no time to explain; Iris evaded her friend and bolted down the hallway, out the back doors and through the garden they had just been kneeling and planting in mere minutes ago. She leapt over the low stone wall and dashed across the street, winding through the neighbor's yard. Her lungs felt as if they had caught fire, and her heart was thrumming at the base of her throat.

She finally reached the field.

Iris sprinted, feeling the jolt in her knees, the wind dragging through her loose hair. She could see him now; he was no longer an unfamiliar shadow in a sea of gold. She could see his face, and the scowl lifted from his brow as he saw her. Recognized her.

He finally sensed her terror. He set down his typewriter case and leather bag and broke into a run to meet her.

Iris had lost count in her mind. Over the hammering of her pulse and the roar of her adrenaline, she realized the siren had gone silent. The temptation to look at the sky was nearly overwhelming, but she resisted. She kept her eyes on Roman as the distance began to wane between them, and she pushed herself to run faster, *faster,* until it felt like her bones might melt from the exertion.

"Kitt!" she tried to shout, but her voice was nothing more than a wisp.

Kitt, get down! she thought, but of course he didn't understand what was happening. He didn't know the cause of the siren, and he continued to run to her.

In the moment before they collided, Iris clearly saw his face, as if time had frozen. The fear that lit his eyes, the confused furrow in his expression, the way his lips parted to either heave air or say her name. His hands reached for her as she reached for him, and the stillness broke when they touched, as if they had cracked the world.

She took hold of his jumpsuit and used all of her momentum to push him to the ground. He wasn't expecting it and she easily unbalanced him. The impact was jarring; Iris bit her tongue as they tangled together in the long grass, his body warm and firm beneath hers. His hands splayed against her back, holding her to him.

"Winnow?" he gasped, his face only a fraction of a centimeter away from hers. He was staring at her as if she had just fallen from the clouds and attacked him. "*Winnow,* what is hap——?"

"Don't move, Kitt!" she whispered, her chest pumping like a bellows against his. "Don't speak, don't *move.*"

For once in his life, he listened to her without arguing. He froze against her, and she closed her eyes and fought to quiet her breaths, waiting.

It didn't take long for the temperature to drop, for the wind to die. Shadows spilled over her and Roman as the eithrals circled high overhead, their wings blocking the sun. Iris knew the moment Roman saw them; she felt the tension coil in his body, felt his sharp inhale as if terror had pierced his chest.

Please . . . please don't move, Kitt.

She kept her eyes clenched shut, tasting blood in her mouth. Tendrils of hair dangled against her face, and she suddenly had the fierce urge to scratch her nose, to wipe the perspiration that began to drip from her jaw. The adrenaline that had fueled her across the field was ebbing, leaving behind a tremor in her bones. She wondered if Roman could feel it, how she was quaking against him, and when his hand pressed harder into her back, she knew he could.

Wings flapped steadily above them. Shadows and cold air continued to trickle over their bodies. A chorus of screeches split the clouds, reminiscent of nails on a chalkboard.

Iris chose to focus on the musty scent of the grass around her, broken from their fall. The way Roman breathed as a counterpoint to her—when his chest rose, hers was collapsing, as if they were sharing the same breath, passing it back and forth. How his warmth seeped into her, greater than the sun.

She could smell his cologne. Spice and evergreen. It ushered her back in time to moments they had spent together in the lift and in the office. And now her body was draped across his and she couldn't deny how good it felt, as if the two of them fit together. A flicker of desire warmed her blood, but the sparks swiftly dimmed when she thought of Carver.

Carver.

The guilt nearly crushed her. She kept him at the forefront of her mind until a shiver spun through her, and she felt a strange prompting to open her eyes.

She dared to do so, only to discover Roman was intently studying her face. Her hair lay tangled across his mouth, and her sweat was dripping onto his neck, and yet he didn't move, just as she had ordered. He stared at her and she stared back, and they waited for the end to come.

It felt as if spring had blossomed into midsummer by the time the eithrals retreated. The shadows fled, the air warmed, the light brightened, the wind returned, and the grass sighed against Iris's shoulders and legs. Somewhere in the distance, she could hear shouting as life slowly returned to Avalon Bluff. It took her a few more moments to quell her fear, to be confident enough to move again, to trust that the threat was gone.

She winced as she pushed upward, her wrists and shoulders numb from holding herself frozen. A slight groan escaped her as she sat back on Roman's waist, her hands tingling with pins and needles. The pain was good; it reminded her of how furious she was at him, for arriving unannounced in the middle of a siren. How his utter foolishness had nearly killed them both.

Iris glared down at him. He was still watching her attentively, as if waiting for her to lift the command over him, and a smirk played across his lips.

"What the *hell* are you doing here, Kitt?" she demanded, shoving his chest. "Have you lost your mind?"

She felt his hands slide down her back, resting on the curve of her hips. If she wasn't so exhausted and stiff from the harrowing encounter they had miraculously survived, she would have knocked away his touch. She would have slapped him. She might have kissed him.

He only smiled as if he had read her mind, and said, "It's good to see you again too, Winnow."

Outshine

What was she supposed to do with him?

Iris had no idea, but her stomach was in knots as she pushed away from Roman's lithe body, standing with a wobble. She crossed her arms and watched as he rose with a slight groan. It felt like she had swallowed sunlight—there was a warm humming in her body that intensified the longer she regarded Roman—and she realized that she was actually *pleased* to see him. But her pride remained in place like a shield; she would never let him know such a thing.

"Do I need to ask you again, Kitt?" she asked.

He took his time brushing stray grass and dirt from his jumpsuit before he glanced up at her. "Perhaps. Profanity is quite becoming on you."

She gritted her teeth but managed to hold back another curse, cracking her neck instead. "Do you have any idea how much danger we were in? Because you decided to walk across a field during a siren?"

That sobered him and he gazed at her. A cloud passed over the sun. Shadows fell again, and Iris flinched, as if an eithral's wings were the cause.

"Those were eithrals, weren't they?" Roman's voice was thick.

Iris nodded. "You're familiar with the old myths?"

"A few. I slept through most of my mythology classes."

She had a hard time imagining that. Roman Competitive Kitt, who wanted to be the best at everything.

"I take it the siren warns of their approach?" he asked.

"Yes, among other things," she answered.

He stared at her for a long, heady moment. The wind gusted between them, cool and sweetened from the crushed grass. "I didn't know, Winnow. I heard the siren and thought it meant to hurry into town. You shouldn't have risked yourself for me, running into the open like that."

"They would have dropped a *bomb* on you, Kitt. It would have most likely leveled the town."

He sighed and ran his hand through his dark hair. "Again, I'm sorry. Is there anything else I should know?"

"There are other sirens and protocols, but I'll let Marisol tell you about them."

"Marisol? She's my contact." He began to look around for the luggage he had dropped. He retraced his steps and retrieved his typewriter case and leather bag, returning to where Iris stood waiting for him like a statue. "Do you mind introducing me to her?"

"I'm not doing *anything* until you answer my question," Iris said. "Why are you here?"

"What does it look like, Winnow? I'm here to write about the war, same as you."

He wasn't squinting, but she still struggled to believe him. Her heart continued to pound. She couldn't tell if it was from the close brush with death or the fact that Roman was here, standing before her and looking just as good in a jumpsuit as he did in his pressed shirt and trousers.

"In case you forgot . . . you *beat* me, Kitt," she said. "*You* won columnist, just as you always wanted. And then you decide it's not good enough for you and your highbrow tastes, and you decide to hound me here as well?"

"Last I checked, they needed more war correspondents," Roman countered, a dangerous gleam in his eyes.

"They couldn't send you to another town?"

"No."

"Being columnist too much pressure for you?"

"No, but Zeb Autry was. I didn't want to work for him anymore."

Iris thought about the last conversation she had had with Zeb. She stifled a shudder, but Roman noticed. She could hardly believe her audacity, but she had to know . . .

"What about your fiancée, Kitt? She's fine with you reporting this close to the front?"

His frown deepened. "I broke the engagement."

"You what?"

"I'm not marrying her. So I suppose you could say I'm here to escape the death wish my father had for me upon realizing I'd vastly disappointed him and disgraced the family name."

That took the fun out of vexing him. Iris suddenly felt cold, and she rubbed her arms. "Oh. I'm sorry to hear that. I'm sure your father will be worried about you."

Roman smiled, but it was skewed, as if he was trying to hide his pain. "Perhaps, but not likely."

Iris turned, glancing at the town. "Well, come on, then. I'll take you to Marisol's." She led the way through the field, Roman following close behind her.

Attie was pacing the kitchen, a furious expression on her face when Iris opened the back doors.

"Don't you *ever* do that to me again, Iris Winnow!" she cried. "Or else I'll kill you myself, do you hear me?"

"Attie," Iris said calmly, stepping over the threshold. "I need to introduce you to someone." She moved aside so Attie could get a clear view of Roman, entering the B and B for the first time.

Attie's jaw dropped. But she quickly recovered from her surprise, her eyes narrowing with slight suspicion. "Did the eithrals drop a boy from the sky, then?"

"Another correspondent," Iris said, at which Roman glanced at her. "This is Roman Kitt. Kitt, this is my friend and fellow writer, Att—"

"Thea Attwood," he finished, and he set down his typewriter case to extend his hand to Attie, reveling in her renewed shock. "It's an honor to finally meet you."

Iris was confused, glancing between the two of them. But Attie's own surprise melted and suddenly she was grinning.

She shook Roman's hand and asked, "Do you have a copy with you?"

Roman slid the leather bag from his shoulder. He untethered it and procured a newspaper, wound tight to ward off wrinkles. He gave it to Attie, and she viciously unfurled it, her eyes racing across the headlines.

"Gods below," she murmured, breathless. "Look at this, Iris!"

Iris moved to stand at Attie's side, only to stifle her own gasp. Attie's war article was on the front page of the *Inkridden Tribune*. A major headline.

THE PATH OF DACRE'S DESTRUCTION by THEA ATTWOOD

Iris read the first few lines over Attie's shoulder, awe and excitement coursing through her.

"If you'll both excuse me, there's a letter I need to write," Attie said abruptly.

Iris watched her bolt down the hallway, knowing she was probably going to wax vengefully poetic to the professor who had once dismissed her writing. Iris's smile lingered, thinking about Attie's words on the front page and how many people in Oath had most likely read them.

From the corner of her eye, she saw Roman reaching into his bag again. There was another crinkle of paper, and she resisted looking at him until he spoke.

"Did you think I wouldn't bring one for you, Winnow?"

"What do you mean?" she asked, a touch defensively. She finally glanced at him to see he was extending another rolled newspaper to her.

"Read it for yourself," he said.

She accepted the paper, slowly unrolling it.

Another edition of the *Inkridden Tribune,* from a different day. But this time, it was Iris's article on the front page.

THE UNEXPECTED FACE OF WAR by INKRIDDEN IRIS

Her eyes passed over the familiar words—*A war with the gods is not what you expect it to be*—and her vision blurred for a moment as she gathered her composure. She swallowed and rolled the paper back up, extending it to Roman, who was watching her with an arched brow.

"*Inkridden Iris,*" he said, his rich drawl making her sound like a legend. "Oh, Autry fumed for days when he saw it, and Prindle cheered, and suddenly the city of Oath is reading about a not-so-distant war and realizing it is only a matter of time before it reaches them." He paused, refusing to take the paper she continued to hold in the space between them. "What made you want to come here, Winnow? Why did you choose to write about war?"

"My brother," she replied. "After I lost my mum, I realized my career really didn't matter to me as much as family did. I'm hoping to find Forest, and in the meantime make myself useful."

Roman's eyes softened. She didn't want his pity, and she was steeling herself for it as his mouth parted, but whatever he planned to say never came, because the front door opened and slammed.

"Girls? *Girls,* are you all right?" Marisol's frantic voice called through the house, her footsteps rushing to the kitchen. She appeared in the archway, black hair escaping her braided crown, her face flushed as if she had just sprinted from the infirmary. Her eyes traced Iris with relief, but then they shifted to the stranger standing in her kitchen. Marisol's hand slipped away from her chest as she straightened and blinked at Roman. "And who might you be?"

"Kitt. Roman Kitt," he said smoothly, granting her a bow as if they dwelled in medieval ages, and Iris almost rolled her eyes. "It's a pleasure to make your acquaintance, Ms. Torres."

"Marisol, please," Marisol said with a smile, charmed. "You must be another war correspondent?"

"Indeed. Helena Hammond just sent me," Roman replied, lacing his fingers behind his back. "I was supposed to arrive on tomorrow's train, but it broke down a few kilometers away, and so I walked. I apologize that my arrival has been unexpected."

"Don't apologize," Marisol said with a wave of her hand. "Helena never gives me notice. The train broke down, you said?"

"Yes, ma'am."

"Then I'm glad you were able to reach us safely."

Iris's eyes slid to Roman. He was already looking at her, and in that shared moment, they were both remembering the sway of a golden field and their mingled breaths and the shadow of wings that had rippled over them.

"Do you two know each other?" Marisol asked, her voice suddenly smug.

"No," Iris said quickly, in the same instant that Roman replied, "Yes."

An awkward pause. And then Marisol said, "Which one is it, then?"

"Yes, actually," Iris amended, flustered. "We're acquaintances."

Roman cleared his throat. "Winnow and I worked together at the *Oath Gazette*. She was my greatest competition, if I must confess."

"But we really didn't know each other all that well," Iris rambled on, as if that mattered. And why was Marisol pressing her lips together, as if she were concealing a smile?

"Well, that is lovely," Marisol remarked. "We're happy to have you join us, Roman. I'm afraid I gave the infirmary all of the B and B mattresses, so you'll be sleeping on the floor, like the rest of us. But you'll have your own private room, and if you'll follow me up the stairs, I can show it to you."

"That would be wonderful," Roman said, gathering his bags. "Thank you, Marisol."

"Of course," she said, turning. "Come this way, please."

He made to pass by Iris, and she realized she was still holding the newspaper with her headline.

"Here," she whispered. "Thank you for showing me."

He glanced down at the paper, at her white-knuckled hand that was holding it, before his gaze shifted to hers.

"Keep it, Iris."

She watched him disappear down the hall. But her thoughts were tangled.

Why is he here?

She feared that she knew the answer.

Roman was the sort of person who thrived in competition. And he had come to Avalon Bluff to outshine her, once again.

That night, Iris lay on her pallet in a tangle of blankets. She stared up at the ceiling and watched the shadows dance to candlelight. It had been a long, strange day. Her grief sat like a rock in her chest.

It was at moments like these, when she was too exhausted to sleep, that Iris inevitably thought of her mother. Sometimes all she could see was Aster's body beneath the coroner's sheet. Sometimes Iris would weep into the darkness, desperate for swift, dreamless sleep so she wouldn't have to remember the last time she saw her mother.

A cold, pale, broken body.

Iris resisted the urge to glance at her desk, where the jar of ashes sat beside her typewriter. A jar of ashes, waiting to be spread somewhere.

Are you proud of me, Mum? Do you see me in this place? Can you guide me to Forest?

Iris wiped the tears from her eyes, sniffing. She reached for her mother's locket, an anchor about her neck. The gold was smooth and cool.

She soaked in old memories—the good ones—until she realized she could hear through the thin walls as Roman clacked on his typewriter. She could hear his occasional sigh and the chair creak beneath him when he moved.

Of course, he would be in the room next to hers.

She closed her eyes.

She thought of Carver, but she fell asleep to the metallic song of Roman Kitt's typing.

Seven Minutes Late

He was late for breakfast.

Iris drank her amusement along with her tea as Marisol huffed, watching the porridge grow cold on the table.

"I told him eight sharp, didn't I?" she said.

"You did," Attie confirmed, forgoing manners to reach for a scone. "Perhaps he overslept?"

"Perhaps." Marisol's gaze flickered across the table. "Iris? Will you go knock on Roman's door and see if he's awake?"

Iris nodded, setting her teacup down. She hurried up the shadowed stairs, her reflection spilling across mirror after mirror. She approached Roman's bedroom door and knocked loudly, pressing her nose to the wood.

"Get up, lazybones. We're waiting to eat breakfast because of you."

Her words fell on silence. She frowned, knocking again.

"Kitt? Are you awake?"

Again, there was no answer. She couldn't describe why her chest constricted or why her stomach suddenly dropped.

"Answer me, Kitt." Iris reached for the door, only to find it was locked.

Her fears rose, until she told herself she was being ridiculous and to shake them off.

She returned to the heat of the kitchen, both Marisol and Attie glancing at her with expectation.

"He didn't answer," Iris said, sliding into her chair. "And his door was locked."

Marisol paled. "Do you think I need to climb the roof and look through his window, to ensure he's all right?"

"You will leave all roof climbing to me," Attie stated, pouring herself a third cup of tea. "But don't you have a skeleton key, Marisol?"

That was when the back doors swung open and Roman burst into the kitchen, bright-eyed and windblown. Marisol screeched, Attie spilled tea all over her plate, and Iris jumped so hard she banged her knee against the table leg.

"Forgive me," Roman panted. "I lost track of the hour. I hope the three of you weren't waiting on me."

Iris glowered. "Yes, of course we were, Kitt."

"My apologies," he said, closing the twin doors behind him. "I'll see that it doesn't happen again."

Marisol's hand was clamped over her mouth, but it gradually lowered to her neck as she said, "Please, have a seat, Roman."

He took the chair across from Iris's. She couldn't help but study him beneath her lashes. His face was flushed as if the wind had kissed him, his eyes gleamed like dew, and his hair was tangled as if fingers had been raked through it. He looked half wild and smelled like morning air and mist and sweat, and Iris couldn't keep her mouth shut a moment longer.

"Where were you, Kitt?"

He glanced up at her. "I was on a run."

"A run?"

"Yes. I like to run several kilometers every morning." He shoveled a spoonful of sugar into his tea. "Why? Is that acceptable to you, Winnow?"

"It is, so long as we don't expire from hunger waiting for you every sunrise," Iris quipped, and she thought she saw a smile tease his lips, but perhaps she imagined it.

"Again, I'm sorry," he said, glancing at Marisol.

"There's no need to apologize." Marisol handed him the pitcher of cream. "But all I ask is you refrain from running when it's dark, due to the first siren I told you about."

He paused. "The hounds, yes. I waited until first light before I left this morning. I'll see to it that I'm back on time tomorrow." And he winked at Iris.

She was so flustered by it she spilled her tea.

Dear Carver,

It's only been five days since you last wrote, and yet it feels like five weeks for me. I didn't realize how much your letters were grounding me, and while I feel far too vulnerable confessing this . . . I miss them. I miss you and your words.

I was wondering when

A knock on her door interrupted her.

Iris paused, her fingertips slipping off the keys. It was late. Her candle had burned half of its life away, and she left her sentence dangling on the paper as she rose to answer the door.

She was shocked to find Roman.

"Do you need something?" she asked. Sometimes she forgot how tall he was, until she was standing toe to toe with him.

"I see you're working on more front-page war essays." His gaze flickered beyond her to the typewriter on her desk. "Or perhaps you're writing to someone?"

"I'm sorry, is my nocturnal typing keeping you up?" Iris said. "I suppose we'll have to ask Marisol to move you to a different roo—"

"I wanted to see if you would like to run with me," he said. Somehow he made the possibility sound sophisticated, even as they stood facing each other in wrinkled jumpsuits at ten o'clock at night.

Iris's brow raised. "I'm sorry?"

"Run. Two feet on and off the ground, pushing forward. Tomorrow morning."

"I fear I don't *run*, Kitt."

"I beg to disagree. You were like wildfire in the field yesterday afternoon."

"Yes, well, that was a special circumstance," she said, leaning on the door.

"And perhaps another occasion like that will arise again soon," he countered, and Iris had nothing to say, because he was right. "I thought I'd ask, just in case you're interested. If so, meet me tomorrow morning in the garden at first light."

"I'll consider it, Kitt, but right now I'm tired and need to finish this letter that you interrupted. Good night."

She gently shut the door in his face, but not before she noticed how his eyes flashed, widening as if he wanted to say something more but he lost the chance.

Iris returned to her desk and sat. She stared at her letter and tried to pick up where she had left off, but she no longer had the desire to write to Carver.

He was to write her first. Whenever he was able or cared to.

She needed to wait. She shouldn't sound so desperate to a boy she hadn't even met.

She pulled the paper from the typewriter and tossed it in the dustbin.

She really didn't want to exercise with Roman. But the more she remembered the sight of him returning from his run—all vigor and fire, as if he had drunk from the sky, untamed and unburdened and *alive*—the more she wanted to feel that herself.

It also helped that she conveniently woke just before dawn.

Iris lay on her pallet, listening to him move in his room. She listened as he quietly opened his door and walked past hers on gentle tread, down the stairs. She imagined him standing in the garden, waiting for her.

She decided she would go, thinking it wouldn't be a bad idea to get in better shape before she was summoned to the front lines.

Iris dressed in her clean jumpsuit, rushing to don her socks and lace her boots in the dark. She braided her hair on the way downstairs, and then had a stab of worry. Perhaps he wouldn't be waiting for her. Perhaps she had taken too long, and he had left her.

She opened the twin doors and found him there, pacing the edges of the garden. He stopped when he saw her, his breath hitching as if he hadn't believed she would come.

"Worried I would stand you up, Kitt?" she asked, walking to him.

He smiled, but it could have passed for a wince in the shadows. "Not in the slightest."

"What made you so confident?"

"You're not one to let a challenge slip away, Winnow."

"For being a mere acquaintance and office rival, you seem to know a lot about me," Iris mused, standing before him.

Roman studied her. A few stars burned above them, extinguishing one by one as day broke. The first rays of sun illuminated the tree boughs overhead, the ivy and mossy stones of the B and B, and the flittering of birds. Light limned Iris's arms and the length of her braid, Roman's angular face and tousled dark hair.

It felt like she had woken in another world.

"I may have said you were a *rival,*" he countered. "But I never said you were an *acquaintance.*"

Before Iris could scrounge up a retort—was that a good thing or a bad thing?—Roman was striding to the gate, stepping onto the street.

"Tell me, Winnow," he said. "Have you ever run a kilometer before?"

"No." She began to keenly regret her decision to join him; she realized he was bound to run her ragged, to gloat with his stamina. She could already taste the dust he would kick up in her face, leaving her far behind. Perhaps this was some sort of twisted payback, for making him work to become columnist when the position would have been given to him on a silver platter if she hadn't been at the *Gazette.* A column that he surrendered almost as swiftly as he had earned it, which continued to puzzle her.

"Good," he said as she followed him through the gate. "We'll start simple and work our way up every morning."

"*Every* morning?" she cried.

"We need to be consistent if you want to make any sort of progress," he said, beginning a brisk walk up the street. "Is there a problem with that?"

Iris sighed, keeping pace with him. "No. But if you're a sorry coach, then don't expect me to return tomorrow morning."

"Fair enough."

They walked for several minutes, Roman keeping an eye on his wristwatch. The silence was soft between them, the chilled morning air sharp as a blade down her throat. Soon, Iris felt her blood warm, and when Roman said it was time to run, she fell into a slow jog at his side.

"We'll run for a minute, walk for two, and repeat that cycle until we need to return to Marisol's," he explained.

"Are you some sort of professional at this?" She couldn't resist asking.

"I ran track at school, a few years back."

Iris tried to imagine that—him dashing around a circular track in very short trousers. She laughed, partly embarrassed by her train of thought, which drew his attention.

"That's hilarious to you?" he asked.

"No, but I'm wondering why you're going so slow for me when you could run laps around this town."

Roman checked his watch. She didn't think he was going to respond until he said, "And now we walk." He slowed, and she mirrored him. "I often run alone. But sometimes it's nice to have company." He looked at her. Iris quickly glanced away from him, distracting herself with details of the street.

They fell into a dance side by side, running for one minute, walking for two. At first, it felt easy to her, until they reached the hilly side of the bluff, and she suddenly felt like she might expire.

"Are you trying to kill me, Kitt?" she panted, struggling up the slope.

"Now, *that* would be a bestselling headline," he said cheerfully, not at all winded. "INKRIDDEN IRIS AND THE HILL THAT BESTED HER."

She smacked his arm, pressing a smile between her lips. "How much . . . longer . . . until we walk?"

He checked his watch. "Forty more seconds." And he wouldn't be Roman Kitt if he didn't show off.

He turned to face her, running backward and slightly ahead, so he could keep his gaze on her as she labored up the hill.

"That's it. You're doing great, Winnow."

"Shut up, Kitt."

"Absolutely. Whatever you want."

She glared at him—the flush of his cheeks, the mirth in his eyes. He was quite distracting, and she panted, "Are you trying . . . to tempt me to . . . press onward, like you're some . . . metaphorical carrot?"

He laughed. The sound went through her like static, down to her toes. "If only I were. Do we need to stop?"

Yes. "No."

"Good. You have twenty more seconds. Deep breaths through your belly, Winnow. Not your chest."

She bared her teeth against the discomfort and strove to breathe as he had instructed. It was difficult when her lungs were heaving beyond her control. *I am not doing this torture tomorrow,* she thought over and over. A chant to carry her up the rest of the hill. *I am not—*

"Tell me what you think of this place," he said, not two seconds later. "Do you like Avalon Bluff?"

"I can't run *and* chat, Kitt!"

"When I'm done training you, you'll be able to."

"Who says . . . I'm doing this . . . tomorrow?" Gods, she felt like she was about to die.

"This does," he said, at last turning around to lead her the rest of the way up the hill.

"Your backside?" she growled, helplessly studying it.

"No, Winnow," he tossed over his shoulder. "This view." He came to a stop on the crest of the hill.

Iris watched the sun gild his body. The light hit her two breaths later, when she reached the top at his side. Hands on her knees, she fought to calm her heart, sweat dripping down her back. But when she could stand upright, she reveled in the view. The fog was melting in the valleys. A river meandered through a field. The dew glittered like gemstones on the grass. The land seemed to roll on and on forever, idyllic as a dream, and Iris shielded her eyes, wondering where the road would take them if they kept running.

"It's beautiful," she whispered. And how strange to know this view had been here all along, and she had failed to see it.

Roman was quiet at her side, and they stood like that for a few moments. Soon, her heart was steady and her lungs calm. Her legs felt a bit shaky, and she knew she'd be sore tomorrow.

"Winnow?" he said, glancing at his watch with a frown.

"What's wrong, Kitt?"

"We have exactly five minutes to get back to Marisol's."

"What?"

"We'll have to run the whole way to make it by eight, but it's mostly downhill."

"Kitt!"

He began to jog the route they had come, and Iris had no choice but to chase after him, ankles sore as her boots hit the cobblestones.

Oh, she was going to kill him.

They were late by seven minutes.

{ 28 }

A Divine Rival

Dear Iris,

Last night, I had a dream. I was standing in the middle of Broad Street in Oath, and it was raining. You walked past me; I knew it was you the moment your shoulder brushed mine. But when I tried to call your name, no sound emerged. When I hurried to follow you, you quickened your steps. Soon, the rain fell harder, and you slipped away from me.

I never saw your face, but I knew it was you.

It was only a dream, but it has unquieted me.

Write to me and tell me how you are.

Yours,

—C.

P.S. Yes, hello. I'm able to write again, so expect my letters to flood your floor.

Dear Carver,

I can't even begin to describe how happy I was to discover your letter had arrived. I hope everything is well with you in

Oath, as well as whatever required your attention the past week. Dare I say I missed you?

An odd dream, indeed. But there's no need to worry. I'm quite well. I think I would like to see you in a dream, although I still try to imagine your appearance by day and often fail. Perhaps you can grant me a few more hints?

Oh, I have news to share with you!

My rival from a previous employment has shown up as a fellow correspondent, just like a weed. I'm not sure why he's here, although I think it's to try and prove that his writing is far superior to mine. All of this to say... his arrival has caused a stir, and I'm not sure what to do with him being next door.

Also, I have more letters transcribed for soldiers. I'm sending them to you—there are more than usual, given that we just recently had an influx of wounded brought into the infirmary—and I'm hoping you can drop them in the post. Thank you in advance for doing this for me!

In the meantime, tell me how you are. How is your nan? I just realized that I have no inkling what you do for a living, or even for fun. Are you a student at university? Are you working somewhere?

Tell me something about you.

Love,

Iris

They had planted the garden but had completely forgotten to water it. Marisol grimaced when she realized this.

"I don't even want to know what Keegan will think of me," she said, hand on her forehead as she stared at the crooked rows Iris and Attie had made. "My wife is fighting on the front lines and I can't even do something as simple as water a garden."

"Keegan will be impressed that you instructed two city girls who have never tilled or planted or tended a garden to help you. And the seeds will be fine," Attie said, but then quietly added, "won't they?"

"Yes, but they won't germinate without water. The soil needs to say wet for about two weeks. This is going to be a late summer garden, I suppose. If the hounds don't trample it."

"Do you have a watering can?" Iris asked, thinking of sirens in the daylight and rivals arriving unexpectedly and wounded soldiers returning to the front. How did any of them remember to eat, let alone water a garden?

"Yes, two, actually," Marisol said, pointing. "In the shed there."

Iris and Attie exchanged a knowing look. Five minutes later, Marisol had retreated to the kitchen to continue baking for the soldiers, and the girls had the metal cans full, watering the dirt mounds.

"Six mornings," Attie said with a smirk. "*Six* mornings you've been late to breakfast, Iris. All due to *running* with that Roman Kitt."

"*Four* mornings, actually. We've been on time two mornings in a row, now," Iris replied, but her cheeks warmed. She turned to water a second row before Attie noticed. "It's because he underestimates how slow I am. We wouldn't be late if I were in better shape. Or if he chose a shorter circuit." But she loved the view of the countryside on the hill that seemed destined to best her, even though Iris would never confess as much to Roman.

"Hmm."

"You want to join us, Attie?"

"Not in the slightest."

"Then why are you smiling at me like that?"

"He's an old friend of yours, isn't he?"

Iris huffed. "He's a former competitor, and he's only here to outperform me once again." The words had no sooner left her lips than a triangularly folded piece of paper crashed into the soil, right in front of her. Iris gaped at it before lifting her eyes to the ivy-laden house. Roman was leaning on the open sill of his second-story window, watching her with a smile.

"Can't you see some of us are trying to work?" she shouted.

"Indeed," he called back smoothly, as if he was well versed in arguing from a window. "But I need your assistance."

"With what?"

"Open the message."

"I'm busy, Kitt."

Attie snatched the paper up before Iris could ruin it with water. She unfolded it and cleared her throat, reading aloud, "'Alas, what is a synonym for *sublime?*'" Attie paused as if sorely disappointed, glancing up at Roman. "That's it? *That's* the message?"

"Yes. Any suggestions?"

"I seem to recall that you used to have three dictionaries and two thesauruses on your desk, Kitt," Iris said, resuming her watering.

"Yes, which *someone* liked to frequently turn upside down and page-side out. But that's beside the point. I wouldn't be bothering you if I had my thesaurus handy," he replied. "Please, Winnow. Give me a word, and I'll leave you—"

"What about *transcendent?*" Attie offered. "Sounds like you're writing about the gods. The Skywards?"

"Something along those lines," said Roman. "And you, Winnow? Just one word."

She glanced up in time to watch him rake his hand through his hair, as if he were anxious. And she had rarely seen Roman Kitt anxious. There was even a smudge of ink on his chin.

"I personally like *divine,*" she said. "Although I'm not sure I would attribute that to the gods these days."

"Thank you both," Roman said, ducking back into his room. He left the window open, and Iris could hear his typewriter clacking as he started to write.

The garden fell suspiciously quiet.

Iris looked at Attie to see her friend was biting her lip, as if to hide a grin.

"All right, Attie. What is it?"

Attie shrugged nonchalantly, draining her watering can. "I wasn't too sure about this Roman Kitt at first. But he sure does bring the fire out in you."

"You give him far too much credit," Iris said, lowering her voice. "You would be the same if your old enemy showed up to challenge you again."

"Is that why he's here?"

Iris hesitated, and then fiddled with her watering can. "Do you need a refill?" She took Attie's empty pail and was retreating to the well when she realized Marisol was standing in the open doorway to the kitchen, regarding them. How long had she been there?

"Marisol?" Iris asked, reading her tense posture. "What's wrong?"

"Nothing's wrong," Marisol replied with a smile that didn't reach her eyes. "The captain is here and would like to take one of you with him to the front."

Roman had just finished typing his letter to Iris and slipped it through his wardrobe when he heard the knock on the front door. It sent a shiver through the house, and he stood in his room, listening. He could faintly hear Iris and Attie's conversation, drifting up from the garden through his window. But he could also hear Marisol as she answered the door.

A man had arrived and was speaking, his voice a muffle through the walls.

Roman couldn't catch the words. He eased his bedroom door open, straining to hear more.

". . . to the front. You have two correspondents here, correct?"

"Three, Captain. And yes, come in. I'll gather them to speak with you."

Roman drew in a deep breath and quietly hurried down the stairs. All he could think was that he had to be the one chosen. Not Attie and certainly not Iris. And yet as he moved down the corridor, his heart clenched, stung by fear. He came to a pause in the doorframe, gazing into the kitchen.

Iris was walking in from the garden, dirt on her knees. She had been wearing her hair loose these days, and it never ceased to shock him—to see how long and wavy it was. She came to a stop beside Attie, her hands anxiously fidgeting. Roman couldn't take his eyes from her. Not even when the captain began speaking.

"I have one seat available in my lorry," he said in a clipped tone. "Which one of you would like to go?"

"I will, sir," Iris said before Roman could so much as flinch. "It's my turn."

"Very good. Go and fetch your bag. Only bring the essentials."

She nodded and turned toward the hall. That was when she saw Roman standing in her way.

He didn't know what sort of expression was on his face, but he watched her surprise descend into something else. It looked like worry and then annoyance. Like she knew the words that were about to come from his mouth, before he even spoke them.

"Captain?" he said. "If she goes, I would like to go with her, sir."

The captain spun to look at him, brow cocked. "I said I only have *one* seat in the lorry."

"Then I'll ride on the side step, sir," Roman said.

"*Kitt,*" Iris hissed at him.

"I don't want you to go without me, Winnow."

"I'll be perfectly fine. You should stay here and—"

"I'm going with you," he insisted. "Will that be acceptable, Captain?"

The captain sighed, tossing up his hand. "The two of you . . . go pack. You have five minutes to meet me out front by the lorry."

Roman turned and hurried up the stairs. That was when it hit him: he had just sent Iris a very *important* letter, and now was an immensely bad moment for her to read it. He was wondering whether he had enough time to sneak into her room and sweep it up off the floor when he heard her pursuing him.

"Kitt!" she called. "Kitt, why are you doing this?"

He was at the top of the staircase and had no choice but to glance back at her. She was hurrying after him, an indignant blush staining her cheeks.

All opportunities of recovering his bumbling letter were gone, unless he wanted to spill the news to her this instant, with the space closing between them as she climbed the stairs. With a lorry parked out front, waiting to carry them west.

They might be killed on this venture. And she would never know who he was and how he felt about her. But when he opened his mouth, his courage completely crumbled, and different words emerged instead.

"They might as well let both of us come," he said, gruffly. He was trying to hide how his heart was striking against his breast. How his hands were shaking. He was terrified to go, and terrified that something would befall her if he didn't, but he couldn't let her know that. "Two writers, twice the articles, am I right?"

She was glaring at him now. That fire in her eyes could have brought him to his knees, and he loathed the façade he was wearing. He rushed along his way to pack before he said anything else that would further demolish his chances with her.

Iris was fuming as she slipped into her room. She didn't want Roman going to the front. She wanted him here, where he would be safe.

She groaned.

Focus, Iris.

Her leather bag was tucked away in the wardrobe, and she stepped on a stack of paper as she reached for the door handle. She paused, glancing down at the heap of typed letters. The letters she had transcribed for the soldiers.

Dread pierced Iris's chest as she knelt and gathered the papers. Had a draft pushed them back into her room? She had sent them to Carver that morning, and she wondered if the magic between them had broken at last.

She opened the folded sheet that was on top of the pile, relieved to find it was a letter from him. She stood in a slant of afternoon sunshine, finger-tips tracing her lips as she quickly read:

Dear Iris,

Your rival? Who is this bloke? If he's competing with you, then he must be an utter fool. I have no doubt you will best him in every way.

Now for a confession: I'm not in Oath. Or else I would put these letters in the post this afternoon. I'm sorry to cause you any delay and inconvenience, but I'm sending them back to you, as

I feel like it's the best option. Again, I apologize I can't be of more assistance to you, as I fervently wish to be.

As for your other inquiries, my nan is fine, albeit quite put out with me at the moment—I'll tell you why when I finally see you. She sometimes asks if

"Winnow?" Roman called to her through the door, softly knocking. "Winnow, are you ready?"

She crumpled Carver's half-read letter into her pocket. She didn't have time to wonder at the oddness of his words—*I'm not in Oath*—as she took the soldiers' letters and set them on the desk, tucking their edges under her typewriter.

It hit her like a brick to her stomach.

She was about to go to the front lines.

She was about to be gone for *days,* and she had no time to write Carver and explain to him the reason for her impending silence. What would he think of her suddenly going quiet?

"Winnow?" Roman spoke again, urgent. "The captain's waiting."

"I'm coming," Iris said, her voice thin and strange, like ice crackling over warm water. She stole one last second of peace, touching the jar that held her mother's ashes. It sat on her desk, next to the Alouette.

"I'll return soon, Mum," Iris whispered.

She turned and took inventory—blanket, notepad, three pens, a tin of beans, canteen, extra socks—and hastily packed her bag, slinging it over her shoulder. When she opened the door, Roman was waiting for her in the dim hallway, his own leather bag hanging from his back.

He said nothing, but his eyes were bright, almost feverish, when he looked at her.

She wondered if he was afraid as he followed her down the stairs.

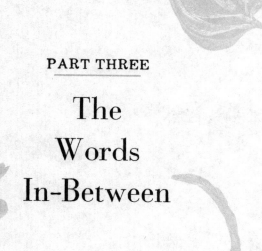

PART THREE

The
Words
In-Between

The Sycamore Platoon

She unfortunately had to sit on Roman Kitt's lap, nearly all the way to the front lines.

The lorry was packed to the brim with food and medicine and other resources, leaving one seat available in the cab. Just as the captain had forewarned. One seat for Iris and Roman to fight over.

Iris hesitated, wondering how to handle this strange situation, but Roman seamlessly opened the passenger door for her, as if it were a vehicle in Oath and not a massive truck, rusted by war. She avoided eye contact as well as his offered hand and hauled herself up the metal side step into the dusty cab.

It reeked of sweat and petrol. The leather seat was beaten and worn beneath her. There looked to be an old streak of blood across it, and the dash was freckled with mud. *Pray it doesn't rain,* Attie had said to her before kissing her cheeks in farewell, and Iris cleared her throat and slipped her bag onto the floorboard between her legs. It must be something about rain and the trenches, Iris surmised, although Attie still hadn't spoken much of her experience on the front lines.

"All set?" Roman asked.

Iris decided it would be best to tackle this . . . unpleasantness head on. She turned to address him—*you really don't need to come, Kitt*—but he had already shut the door, perching on the side step as he had promised to do.

Iris got a good eyeful of his chest, which was blocking her window. But she could see he was holding on to the rickety metal of the side mirror—which looked like it might come off any moment—as well as the door handle. A strong gust might blow him away, but she held her tongue as the captain turned the engine.

They rolled out of Avalon Bluff, heading along the western road. Iris had never ridden in a lorry; it was surprisingly bumpy and slow, and she watched as the captain shifted the gear stick. She could feel the purr of the engine through the soles of her feet, and she couldn't help but keep an eye on Roman with every pothole they hit. And there were quite a few of them.

"These roads haven't been cared for in a while," the captain explained when Iris nearly bounced off her seat. "Not since the war broke out in this borough. I hope your friend there can hold tight. It's only going to get worse."

Iris winced, shielding her eyes from a sudden flood of sunlight. "How long will this ride be?"

"Three hours, if the weather permits."

Half an hour later, they stopped at the neighboring town of Clover Hill so the captain could load one last round of resources in the back. Iris rolled down her window and prodded Roman in the chest.

"It won't do us any good if you break your neck on the way to the front," she said. "I don't mind sharing the seat. That is, if you don't mind me sitting on your—"

"I don't mind," he said.

He stepped down, his hair snarled from the wind.

Iris opened the door and stood, cramped in the cab, as Roman ascended, sliding into the seat. He wedged his bag next to hers and then reached for her hips, guiding her back to sit on his lap.

She was rigid as a board, settled on his thighs.

This was bad. This was very, very bad.

"Iris," he whispered, and she stiffened. "You'll go through the windshield if you don't lean back."

"I'm fine."

He sighed, exasperated, as his hands fell away from her.

Her determination lasted all of ten minutes. The captain was right; the roads got bumpier, rutted from weeks of rain, and she had no choice but to relax, aligning her spine with Roman's chest. His arm slid around her waist, and she rested in the warmth of his hand, knowing he was keeping her from bashing her head against the windshield.

At least he got mouthfuls of her hair in return, she thought. There was no doubt in her mind that he was as uncomfortable as she was. Especially when she heard him groan after a particularly deep set of ruts in the road, which seemed to knock their thoughts sideways.

"Am I hurting you?" Iris asked him.

"No."

"Are you squinting, Kitt?" she teased.

She could feel his breath in her hair as he murmured, "Do you want to turn and see for yourself, Winnow?"

She didn't dare, thinking it would place her mouth far too close to his. At the very least, he was calling her Winnow again. That was familiar ground for them; she knew what she could expect from him in those moments. The word spars and the snark and the frowns. When he addressed her as Iris . . . it was like completely new territory and it scared her sometimes. As if she were stepping up to the edge of a great cliff.

They reached the front late that afternoon.

A small town had been vacated by the residents, every building given over to the cause. The lorry parked in front of what looked to have been a city hall, and soldiers began to swiftly unload the crates of vegetables and bullets and fresh uniforms. Iris stood in the bustle, Roman behind her. She wasn't sure where she should go or what she should be doing, and her heart was beating in her throat.

"Correspondents?" a middle-aged woman with a deep voice asked, stopping before them. Her uniform was an olive green with brass buckles, and a golden star was pinned over her breast. A cap covered her short black hair.

"Yes," Iris said. "Where should we—"

"You'll be shadowing Dawn Company. I'm Captain Speer, and my soldiers are just finishing up their time in reserves and will be heading to the trenches at sundown. Here, come this way."

Iris and Roman fell into pace with her as she strode down the dirt street, soldiers sidestepping and casting curious glances at the correspondents as they passed. Iris had the brief, wild hope that she might encounter Forest. But she soon realized that she couldn't afford to be distracted, letting her eyes roam over the many faces around her.

"Our companies serve on twelve-hour rotations," the woman said. "Sunrise to sunset, whether that be watching the front, tending the communication trenches, or resting in reserve. This town is the reserve base. If you need to refill your canteens or grab a hot meal, you'll go there, to the mess hall. If you need to wash, you'll go to the old hotel on the street corner. If you need a doctor, you'll go to that house, although do be forewarned that the infirmary is overflowing at the moment and we are low on laudanum. And if you look ahead, you'll notice this road leads into the woods. That is where you will march with Dawn Company to the communication trenches, which can be found on the other side of the forest. You'll stay there for the night, and then be ready to move to the front at sunrise. Any questions?"

Iris's mind was whirling, trying to sort through all the new information. Her hand reached for her mother's locket, hidden beneath the linen of her jumpsuit.

"Is there a chance we'll see action?" Roman asked.

"Yes," Captain Speer said. "Wear a helmet, obey orders, and stay down at all times." Her gaze snagged on a soldier passing by. "Lieutenant Lark! See to it that the correspondents are given instruction and equipment for their time here. They'll shadow your platoon for the next several days."

A fresh-faced soldier stood at attention before his eyes rested on Roman and Iris. Captain Speer was halfway across the road before Lark said, "First time, is it?"

Iris resisted the urge to glance at Roman. To see if he was feeling the same dread and excitement that was coursing through her.

"Indeed," Roman said, extending his hand. "Roman Kitt. And this is—"

"Iris Winnow," Iris said before he could introduce her. The lieutenant smiled as he shook her hand. A scar cut through his mouth; it tugged the right corner of his lips down, but his eyes were crinkled at the edges, as if he had smiled and laughed often in the time before the war. Iris wondered how long he had been fighting. He looked so young.

"We're happy to have you both here," Lark said. "Come, I'm just heading to the mess hall to eat my last hot meal for a few days. It'd be good to grab a bite yourselves, and I'll explain more about what you can expect."

Lark began to lead the way to the city-hall-turned-mess, and Iris moved to walk on the other side of him, so that the lieutenant was between her and Roman. Roman noticed; he granted Iris a slight glance before turning his attention to what lay before them.

"I have a confession, Lieutenant," she began. "I'm not familiar with how the army is divided. Captain Speer said we'll be accompanying your *platoon*?"

"Yes," Lark replied. "There are four companies per battalion. Two hundred men and women per company, and four platoons in each company. I oversee roughly fifty men and women in mine, with Sergeant Duncan as my second. You'll soon learn we've been dubbed the Sycamore Platoon."

She should have had her notepad at the ready, but she tucked away the names and numbers to record as soon as she could. "The Sycamore Platoon? Why is that?"

"A long story, Miss Winnow. And one I'd like to share with you when the time's right."

"Very well, Lieutenant. Another question, if you don't mind," Iris said. "I was curious as to how a soldier is organized into their company. For instance, if a soldier is from Oath but enlists, who decides where they are to serve?"

"A good question, as we have quite a few soldiers from Oath, and Eastern Borough still has yet to declare war on Dacre and join the fight," Lark said with a sad smile. "When someone from Oath enlists, they are added to an auxiliary company. They are still considered residents of Eastern Borough, but are added to a branch of our military, as if they were one of our own."

Iris envisioned her brother. She wanted to ask about the whereabouts of the Second E Battalion, Fifth Landover Company, but another question emerged instead. "Is there anything we *shouldn't* report on?"

Lark tilted his head to the side, as if considering. "Well, of course. No strategies, should you overhear them. No messages that we pass in the communication trenches. No locations or intel that would grant Dacre an advantage should he catch wind of the paper." The lieutenant paused so he could open the door for Iris. A waft of air washed over them, smelling of onions and meatloaf. "I hear that you're to be *neutral* reporters, but I also don't think that's quite possible, if I'm frank. I highly doubt you'll be welcomed over to Dacre's side, let alone return whole from it. I think the best piece of advice, Miss Winnow, is to write what you see happening and what you feel and who we are and why it's vital that the people in Oath and the cities beyond join our effort. Is that something you think is possible?"

Iris paused, meeting the lieutenant's hopeful eyes.

"Yes," she said, in almost a whisper.

But the truth was . . . she felt in over her head. As if a rock were tied to her ankles and she had just been dropped into the ocean.

At five sharp, they marched.

Iris and Roman had been granted helmets and some food for their packs, and they followed the two hundred strong Dawn Company through the winding, shadowed forest road. Lark had informed them it would be a four-kilometer march at a brisk pace, utterly silent save for the sound of their boots hitting the earth, and Iris was suddenly very thankful for those early morning runs with Roman.

Her calves were burning and she was short of breath by the time the woods began to thin, the sunset spilling orange veins across the sky. The road now ran parallel to the front, with stations erected in the cover of the forest as far as she could see. The outposts were built of stones and thatch, with soldiers coming in and out of them. Communication checkpoints, perhaps?

Her thoughts were pruned short by Lark, who suddenly emerged from the river of olive-brown uniforms to speak to her and Roman again.

"We are about to enter the communication trenches here at Station Fourteen," he explained in a low voice. "We're still a few kilometers from the front lines, but it's paramount that you remain low and aware of your surroundings, even if you are at rest in the allotment of 'safe' trenches. You'll also notice there will be bunkers. These are reserved for attacks, whether from Dacre's soldiers or his hounds."

Iris licked her lips. "Yes, I wanted to ask you about the hounds, Lieutenant Lark. What should we do if they are loosed in the night?"

"You'll go directly to a bunker, Miss Winnow," he replied. "With Mr. Kitt, of course."

"And the eithrals?" Roman asked. "What is the protocol for them?"

"Eithrals are rarely seen at the front, as they cannot differentiate between Dacre's soldiers and ours from above. The beasts would drop a bomb on their own forces if they were moving below. They're a weapon Dacre likes to reserve for civilian towns and the railroad, I'm afraid."

Iris couldn't hide her shiver. Lark noticed, and his voice mellowed.

"Now then, the company will soon divide in the trenches, but you'll trail my platoon. When we come to a stop, you may both also find a place to rest for the night. I'll ensure you're up before dawn, to move to the front. Of course, keep quiet and stay low and alert. Those are your imperatives. Should we be bombarded and Dacre's forces overtake our trenches, I want the two of you to retreat to the town instantly. You may be deemed 'neutral' in this conflict, but I wouldn't put it past the enemy to kill you both on sight."

Iris nodded. Roman murmured his agreement.

She followed Lieutenant Lark's Sycamore Platoon down into the trenches, Roman close behind her. So close, she could hear his breath, and the way it skipped, as if he were nervous and struggling to conceal it. A few times, he inadvertently stepped on her heel, jarring her.

"Sorry," he whispered with a fleeting touch to her back.

It's all right, she wanted to say, but the words caught in her throat.

She didn't really know what she had expected, but the trenches were well constructed, with wood planks laid on the ground to ward off mud. They were wide enough for two people to walk shoulder to shoulder comfortably. Sticks were woven along the walls, which curved like the path of a snake. Winding left and then right, and then splitting into two pathways before splitting yet again. She passed artillery stations, where huge cannons sat on the grass like sleeping beasts. A few low points had sandbags piled up, to provide additional coverage, and the deeper she went into the channels, the more she began to see the bunkers Lark had mentioned. Stone shelters were hollowed out of the earth, with dark, open doorways. There was nothing inviting about them, almost as if they were frozen maws, waiting to swallow soldiers, and Iris hoped she didn't have to shelter in one.

Cool air touched her face. It smelled of dank soil with a touch of rot from the decaying wood. A few times, Iris caught the stench of refuse and piss, all threaded with cigarette smoke. She imagined she saw the scurrying of a rat or two, but perhaps the shadows were teasing her.

Her shoulders sagged in relief when the Sycamore Platoon came to a halt for the night, in a stretch of trench that was relatively dry and clean.

Iris let her bag slip from her shoulders, choosing a spot beneath a small, hanging lantern. Roman mirrored her, sitting across the path from her, his long legs crossed. Lark came by to check on them just as the stars began to dust the sky overhead. He smiled with a cigarette clamped in his teeth, settling down not too far from them, just within Iris's sight.

The silence felt thick and strange. She was almost afraid to breathe too deeply, welcoming that heavy, chilled air into her lungs. The same air that the enemy was drawing and exhaling, mere kilometers away.

It was a silence to drown in.

She untethered her bag and found her flannel blanket, draping it across her knees as the night deepened. Next, she procured her notepad and a pen, and she began to write down highlights of the day while they were still fresh in her mind.

The darkness continued to unspool.

Iris reached for an orange in her bag, setting her notepad aside to eat. She hadn't glanced up at Roman one time, but she knew he was also writing. She could hear the faint scratch of his pen marking the paper.

She shifted, only to feel something crinkle in her pocket.

Carver's letter.

In the furor of the day, she had forgotten about it, still half read. But remembering it now as she was sitting in a trench, hungry and cold and anxious . . . his letter felt like an embrace. Like reaching for a friend in the darkness and finding their hand.

She studied Roman as he wrote, his brow furrowed. A second later, his gaze snapped up to hers, as if he had felt her eyes on him, and she glanced away, preoccupied with her orange.

She would have to wait for him to fall asleep before she retrieved the letter. The last thing in the world she wanted was for Roman Chafing Kitt to know she was magically corresponding with a boy she had never met but felt sparks for.

An hour passed. It felt like three hours, but time followed its own whim in the trenches, whether that be stalling or flowing.

Iris leaned her head back against the woven birch branches, her helmet clinking against the wood. She closed her eyes, feigning sleep. And she waited, staving off her own exhaustion. When she looked at him beneath her lashes ten minutes later, Roman's face was slack. His eyes were shut, his breaths deep, as his chest rose and fell, his notepad precariously balanced on his knees. He looked younger, she thought. Softer. For some reason, it made her ache, and she had to push those alarming feelings aside.

But she wondered how much the two of them would change in this war. What marks would it leave on them, shining like scars that never faded?

Slowly, Iris retrieved the letter from her pocket.

Of course, it crinkled loudly in the silence of the trench. When Lark glanced at her, she grimaced, wondering if Dacre could hear such an innocent sound over the expanse of dead man's zone.

She froze, the paper halfway from her pocket. She mouthed an apology to Lark, who realized what she was doing and winked at her. She imagined letters were sacred on the front.

Her eyes then flickered to Roman. He hadn't budged. The three-hour lorry ride with her sitting on his lap must have truly worn him down.

Iris eased Carver's letter the rest of the way free, feeling like she could finally take a deep inhale as it unfolded in her grubby hands.

She found the place where she had left off. Something about his nan, and she read:

—my nan is fine, albeit quite put out with me at the moment—I'll tell you why when I finally see you. She sometimes asks if I've written my own novel on the typewriter she gave me years ago—the typewriter that connects me to you—and I always hate to disappoint her. But sometimes I feel as if my words are mundane and dull. There doesn't seem to be a story hiding in my bones these days, as she believes. And I don't have the heart to tell her that I'm not who she thinks I am.

But tell me more about you. One of your favorite memories, or a place you long to go one day, or a book that changed your life and the way you perceive the world. Do you drink coffee or tea? Do you prefer salt or sugar? Do you revel in sunrises or sunsets? What is your favorite season?

I want to know everything about you, Iris.

I want to know your hopes and your dreams. I want to know

Her reading was interrupted by a crumpled ball of paper, flying across the trench to hit her in the face.

Iris winced, shocked until she looked up to see Roman staring at her.

She glared at him until he motioned for her to open the wad he had just thrown at her.

She did, only to read his scrawl of *What's that you're reading, Winnow?*

She picked up her pen and wrote her reply: *What does it look like, Kitt?* She recrumpled and hurled it at him.

Her attention was divided now, between him and Carver's letter. She longed for a moment in private, to savor the words she had been reading. Words that were turning her molten. But Roman was not to be trusted. He was smoothing the paper out and writing a reply, and Iris had no desire to be smacked in the face again.

She caught it when he tossed it to her, and read, *A love letter, I presume?*

Iris rolled her eyes in response, but she could feel the warmth flood her face. She hoped the shadows cast from the lantern were hiding her blush.

It's none of your business, but if you would be so kind as to allow me to finish reading it in peace . . . I would be eternally grateful, she wrote, returning the paper to him.

Roman scribbled and sent back, *So it is a love letter. From whom, Winnow?*

She narrowed her eyes at him. *I'm not telling you, Kitt.*

Their piece of paper was wrinkled beyond saving at this point. He carefully tore a new page from his notebook and sent *You should take advantage of me. I can give you advice.*

And why did her gaze hang on that first sentence of his? She shook her head, lamenting the day she had met Roman Kitt, and responded, *I don't need your advice although I thank you for the offer.*

She thought surely that would settle it. She began to reread Carver's letter, her eyes hungry to finish that confession of his . . .

Another paper wad sailed across the trench, striking her on the collar this time.

She was tempted to ignore it. He might persist and send another, but paper was valuable here, and they were both being foolish to waste it. As if he had read her mind, Roman bumped her boot with his own, and she looked at him. His face was haggard in the lantern light, as if he were half wild.

She swallowed and opened the wad to read:

Let me guess: he's pouring his heart out onto the page, claiming how inadequate he feels because what he truly craves is affirmation from you. And he probably threw something in there about his family: a mum or his sister or his nan. Because he knows you'll melt at the thought of the other women in his life, the ones who have shaped him. And if he knows you well enough . . . then he'll mention something about books or newspaper articles, because surely by now he knows your writing is exquisite, and above all he knows that he doesn't deserve you and your words and he never will.

Iris was stunned. She stared at him, uncertain how to respond. When Roman held her gaze, as if challenging her, she dropped her eyes to the letter. She would have to wait to finish it. She carefully folded and slipped it back in her pocket.

But nor would she let her old rival have the last word.

She penned and sent: *You're overthinking it. Go to sleep, Roman Kitt.*

He sighed and leaned his head back. She realized his face was flushed. She watched as his eyes grew heavy. Perhaps that was all she needed to do to make him heed her: call him Roman. But she fell asleep before she could think further on it. And she dreamt of a cold city with streets that never ended and a heavy mist and a boy with dark hair who ran ahead of her, just beyond her reach.

{ 30 }

Notes from the Trenches

Rules for a Civilian in the Trenches:

1. Stay down. Resist the temptation to crawl up one of the ladders to catch a glimpse of the land above, which you previously took for granted before you descended. The ladders are to be used by the lookouts and their peri-scopes, or for snipers, or when the barrage* (see footnote #1) happens.

2. Become comfortable with a home of open sky and damp dirt walls, but never trust them. The sky is always a threat, and while the earth is your greatest shield when the hounds prowl and the mortar strikes, it can also be dangerous* (see footnote #2).

3. Pray against rain. Daily. Or else prepare to live in flooded conditions* (see footnote #3).

4. Ignore the rats. Yes, this is extremely difficult when they roam the trench at night and crawl over your legs and chew through your bag. Also, ignore the lice.

5. Eat and drink just enough to keep yourself fueled and hydrated. You'll always feel the faint (or intense) gnaw of hunger as you live off of dried

meat and tins of beans. But on a very good day, you might get an egg banjo* (see footnote #4), which tastes utterly divine.

6. *Lanterns are allowed to burn low in the communication trenches, but no fire is permitted at night on the front lines. Not even a spark to light a cigarette* (see footnote #5).*

7. *There is no privacy. Not even when you need the loo.*

Footnotes:

1. *A "barrage" can be defined as a "concentrated artillery bombardment over a wide area." Lieutenant Lark has informed me this tactic is used when one side wants to cross the "dead man's zone," which is the plot of ground between the two forces' trenches. Heavy casualties occur in this zone, which often means a stalemate can occur and nothing might happen for days in the trenches, each side waiting for the other to strike. But a "fire, cover, and move" approach can occur when heavy artillery is fired, which causes smoke to rise and conceal the soldiers who crawl across the zone to take their opponent's trenches. There's a soldier in each company who is tasked with measuring which way the wind is blowing for the day. Sometimes that alone is a good indicator as to when it's best to make a strike, so the smoke blows with you in the direction you plan to attack. Or it could be a sign as to when your enemy plans to strike.*

2. *Sergeant Duncan informed me of an instance when soldiers retreated to one of the bunkers for shelter during an artillery bombardment, only for the bomb to hit the ground directly above it. The bunker collapsed and the soldiers were buried alive within it.*

3. *Thank whatever gods care about mortal affairs that it hasn't rained while I've been here, but I believe it rained quite a bit when Attie was in the trenches. She might be able to provide an honest opinion on how miserable and morale-breaking it is.*

4. *Recipe for an egg banjo, as cooked by one Private Marcy Gould: Fry an egg over the fire in your cast-iron skillet. Make sure the yolk is bright and runny. Take two thick slices of buttered bread and put the egg between*

them. You'll undoubtedly be asked by your fellow soldiers if you are going
to eat all of it. Don't worry; you'll eat every last crumb.

5. *Lieutenant Lark informed me of a private who lit a cigarette while on*
post on the front lines. Two breaths later, heavy artillery was fired, and
half of the private's platoon was killed.

Three days came and went. It was a strange rhythm to adjust to: nights in the communication trenches and rigid days at the front lines. The Sycamores were rotating with another platoon and would do so for seven days before they returned to base to rest and recover for seven.

And all the while, Iris filled up her notepad.

She never wrote during the day, when she was hunkered down beside Roman at the front, terrified to do something as innocent as scratch her nose. But at night when they were in reserves, the Sycamore Platoon began to warm to her, and she often played cards with them by lantern light, remembering how friendly competition was an effective way to gain access to a deeper, more intimate story.

She asked the privates about their lives back home and the families that loved them. She asked what had made them want to join the war. She asked about past battles—losses and victories—and soaked in the stories of courage and loyalty and pain they shared. The soldiers called one another brother and sister, as if the war had forged bonds that were deeper than blood.

It made her feel incredibly fulfilled one moment and deeply sad the next.

She missed her mother. She missed Forest. She missed Attie and Marisol. She missed writing to Carver.

Sometimes she tried to mentally trace the path that had brought her to this place, but it was too difficult to relive. It stirred up half-buried feelings in her, too dangerous to unearth at the moment.

Even so . . . the blood was humming in her veins.

On the fourth night, Iris was writing her notes for the day when she was struck by a wave of exhaustion.

She paused, her hand cramping.

Roman sat in his customary place across the trench from her, eating from a tin of beans. His black hair hung tangled in his eyes and his beard was growing, shadowing the lower half of his face. His cheekbones were more pronounced, as if he had lost weight. His knuckles were bright with scabs, his fingernails crowded with dirt, and his jumpsuit had a hole in one knee. He honestly looked nothing like she remembered. When they were working at the *Oath Gazette,* he was always groomed and richly dressed, walking around with a pompous air.

Why is he here? she wondered for the hundredth time. She had once thought he would be easy to understand, but with each day that passed, she was beginning to realize that Roman Kitt was a mystery. A mystery she was tempted to solve.

Iris didn't study him for long, for fear of drawing his attention. She glanced back down to her notepad and she suddenly felt empty and tired, as if she had aged years in a night.

She closed her eyes and leaned her head back.

She surrendered to slumber before she knew it.

Iris walked the trenches at night.

She was alone with only the moon for company, full and bright above her, swollen with silver light. She paused, listening to the wind that descended. Where was everyone? Where was she supposed to be?

Where was Roman, her pesky shadow?

In the distance, she heard howls. *The hounds.* Her heart spiked as she rushed to the closest bunker, feeling exposed and frightened.

There was a light burning within the darkness.

The moment Iris stepped into the bunker, drawn to the fire, she realized it was a room. Her old living room in the flat. The place she had shared with her mother and Forest. As her eyes traced over the familiarity—the threadbare rug, the wallpaper that was hanging in strips, the sideboard with Nan's radio—they caught on one person she never thought she'd see again.

"Little Flower," her mother said, perched on the sofa. A cigarette was smoking in her fingertips. "Where have you been, sweetheart?"

"Mum?" Iris's voice felt rusted. "Mum, what are you doing here?"

"I'm here because you're here, Iris."

"Where are we?"

"Home for now. Did you think I'd ever leave you?"

Iris's breath caught. She felt confused, trying to remember something that was slipping from her memory.

"I'm writing again, Mum," she said, her throat narrow. "On Nan's type-writer."

"I know, my love," Aster said with a smile. The smile that had thrived before the wine and the addiction. The smile that Iris loved most. "You'll be a famous writer someday. Mark my words. You'll make me so proud."

Iris tilted her head. "You've said that to me before, haven't you, Mum? Why can't I remember?"

"Because this is a dream and I wanted to see you again," Aster said, smile fading. Her wide-set eyes—hazel eyes that Forest and Iris had both stolen from her—were bright with piercing sadness. "It's been so long since I looked at you and truly *saw* you, Iris. And I realize how much I missed. I'm sorry, sweetheart, but I see you now."

The words cleaved Iris's chest in two.

She was doubling over from the pain, the rawness, and she realized she was weeping, as if her tears could wash away what had happened. Because her mother was dead.

"Iris."

A familiar voice began to melt the edges of the room. The bunker. The tendril of darkness.

"Iris, wake up."

It was the voice of a boy who had arrived at her flat on the worst day of her life. Who had brought her abandoned coat to her, as if he were worried she would catch cold. The voice of a boy who had followed her to war and thrown paper wads at her face and set a newspaper in her hands with her article on the front page and challenged her to run up a hill to see the view beyond it.

The dream broke. Iris was curled into herself, quietly weeping.

Roman sat beside her. The moonlight was bright, and his hand was on her shoulder. She could feel the heat of his palm through her jumpsuit.

"It's all right," he whispered.

She covered her face, to hide her emotion. But terrible sounds slipped through her fingers, and she shuddered, trying to swallow everything down to where she had once kept it hidden in her bones. She could deal with this *later.* She was mortified that she was sobbing in a trench, and the Sycamores were no doubt listening to it, and they must think she was so weak and pathetic and—

Roman gently removed her helmet. He caressed her hair; it was matted and gross and she longed for a proper shower and yet his touch was comforting.

She drew a resolved breath, pressing her fingertips to her throbbing eyes. Roman's hand drifted from her hair, his arm coming to rest around her shoulders. She sank into his side, into his warmth.

"I'm sorry," Iris whispered. "I dreamt of my mum."

"You have nothing to be sorry about."

"I'm embarrassed that I—"

"No one heard you but me," he said. "It's not uncommon to wake up with tears in your eyes here."

Iris raised her head, a crick pulling in her neck. Snot flowed from her nose, and she was about to reluctantly wipe it on her sleeve when a handkerchief appeared, as if from thin air. She blinked and realized Roman was handing her one.

"Of course, you would bring a handkerchief to the front lines," she said, half a grumble.

"They didn't include it in your 'things to bring to war' list, Winnow?" he quipped.

Iris blew her nose. "Shut up, Kitt."

He only answered with a chuckle, setting the helmet back onto her head. But he remained close at her side, keeping her warm through the darkest hours before dawn.

31

Western Wind

That afternoon, the temperature rose to a sweltering level. Spring had at last arrived with its warm sun and lengthening days, and huge clouds were building in the sky overhead. Roman watched them brew, knowing they would soon break with a storm.

Sweat dripped down his back, tickling the nape of his neck. His jumpsuit was drenched, sticking to his skin. Shade was scarce in the trenches at this time of day, and he tried to mentally prepare himself to soon be wet and muddy, wading through ankle-deep puddles. His bag, at least, was made of oiled leather, so everything within it should be protected. Because that was all that really mattered to him. The things in his bag and Iris, sitting across from him. Very soon, they would return to Avalon Bluff, and he could finally draw a full breath. He could finally have a moment to relax.

She caught him staring at her.

He was suddenly grateful that speaking was forbidden in this part of the trenches. Or else Iris might have made a comment about the frequency of his gazes.

The wind began to blow.

It whistled over the trenches, but a few threads of air spun downward, and Roman was thankful for the coolness.

That was what he was absently thinking about—his gratitude for the wind, Iris, his future articles, Iris, how much longer until sundown, *Iris*— when the blasts came, rupturing the quiet, blue-skyed afternoon. The shells screeched in rapid fire, earsplitting, shaking the earth. Roman's heart shot into his throat as Iris fell off her stool, reflexively cowering on the ground.

This was it.

This was his absolute worst nightmare coming to life.

He lunged across the distance, covering her with his body.

The mortars continued to howl and explode. One after the next after the next. The blasts seemed everlasting, and Roman clenched his eyes shut as clods of soil and splinters of wood began to rain down on him. Iris didn't move beneath him, and he was worried that he was crushing her when she whimpered.

"It's all right," he said, unsure if she could hear him over the din. "Stay down, breathe."

At last, there came a lull, but the air steamed and the earth seemed to weep.

Roman shifted his weight, easing Iris upright.

She was trembling.

Her eyes were wide and wild as she stared at him. He could lose himself in those hazel eyes, in wanting to calm the fear that blazed within her. But he had never felt so terrified or powerless himself, and he wasn't sure if he was going to be able to get them both out safely.

Soldiers began to flow around them like a current, preparing rifles and screaming orders. Yet there was such stillness between him and Iris. As if time was stopping.

"Get your bag, Iris," he said. Calmly, as if they had experienced this together before.

She grabbed the strap of her leather bag. It took her a moment to slip it over her back, her hands were quivering so violently.

Roman thought about her notes. All of the soldiers' stories she had gathered over the past few days. The horror and the pride and the pain and the sacrifice and the victories.

She had to carry those words back home. She had to live through this so she could type it out. So her words could be carried by train six hundred kilometers to the *Inkridden Tribune* in the glib city of Oath.

She has to survive this, Roman thought. He didn't want to live in a world without her and her words.

He exhaled—his breath shook, like the bones in his body—and he looked up to the sky. A wall of smoke was rising, blowing on the western wind. It would soon cover them, and Roman could taste the salt and the metal and the soil in his mouth.

Fire, cover, and move.

"Are they coming?" Iris asked.

She was answered by another heavy round of artillery. She jumped again as the screaming shells exploded closer now, pounding deep into the ground. Before she could cower, Roman was pressing her upright against the wall of the trench, covering her with his body. If anything hurt her, it would have to come through him first. But his mind was racing.

Behind them was the dead man's zone, which suddenly felt more perilous than he had ever imagined. Roman realized Dacre's soldiers could be creeping closer to their trenches, using the cover of smoke. They could be creeping like shadows across the scorched grass, rifles in their hands, mere meters away from them.

He envisioned a battle coming to a head; he envisioned fighting. Would Iris run if he ordered her to? Should he let her out of his sight? He envisioned hiding her in a bunker, fleeing through the trenches with her, fueled by white hot fear.

He waited for the bombardment to cease, his hand cupping the back of her neck, keeping her close. His fingers were lost in her hair.

Lieutenant Lark was suddenly shaking sense into him, grabbing Roman's shoulder.

The artillery continued to scream, cascade, and explode, and he had to shout so they could hear him.

"You both need to retreat to the town! That's a direct order."

Roman nodded, relieved to be given a command, and he pulled Iris away from the wall. His fingers wove with hers as he began to lead her through the chaos of the trenches. Over riven wood and mounds of earth and kneeling soldiers. It took Roman a moment to realize some of them were wounded, bowed over in pain. Blood was splattered along the floor planks. Odd pieces of metal flared in the sun.

She began to pull back. "Kitt. *Kitt!*"

Roman whirled to look at her. His panic was rushing through him like hot oil. "We have to run, Iris."

"We can't just leave them like this!" She was screaming, but he could hardly hear her. His ears felt full of wax. His throat felt raw.

"We were given an order," Roman replied. "You and I . . . we're not soldiers, Winnow."

But he knew the exact emotion she was experiencing. It felt wrong to run. To flee when others were hunkering down, preparing to fight. When men and women were on the ground, moaning in pain. Torn apart by mortar shells, waiting to die with the splintered shine of their bones and the bright red sheen of their blood.

Roman hesitated.

That was when he saw the small round object arcing through the air. At first he thought it was a mere clot of dirt until it landed right behind Iris in the trench with a plink. It spun on the wood for a moment, and Roman stared at it, realizing . . . realizing it was a . . .

"*Shit!*"

He grasped the collar of Iris's jumpsuit, picking her up as if she were weightless. He spun them around until he had come between her and the hand grenade. The terror tasted sour in his mouth and he realized he was about to heave the peaches and toast he had eaten for breakfast that morning.

How many seconds did they have before that grenade exploded?

Roman propelled Iris forward, one hand on the small of her back, urging her faster, *faster around the next bend.* They had almost reached it, the place where the trench took a sharp, protective turn. She tripped over one of the planks jutting up from the ground. He took hold of her waist, drawing her up before him, into the smoke and the fading light and the perpetual snap of guns.

There was a click . . . click . . . ping behind them as she turned the corner first.

"*Iris,*" Roman whispered, desperate.

His grip on her tightened just before the explosion blew them apart.

32

Smoke in Her Eyes

Iris stirred. Her face was pressed against churned earth and her mouth tasted like warm metal.

She pushed herself up slowly, her helmet crooked on her head.

Soldiers were running past her. Smoke writhed in the golden light. There was an incessant popping that made her pulse constantly jump, her body wince. But she sat forward and she spit the dirt and blood from her mouth, rushing her hands over her legs, her torso, her arms. She had a few scrapes on her fingers and knees and one long cut on her chest, but she was largely unscathed, even as shards of metal glittered on the ground.

Kitt.

She had cleared the corner before the grenade had exploded, but she wasn't sure if he had.

"Kitt!" she screamed. "*Kitt!*"

She wobbled to her feet, her eyes searching the haze. She found him sprawled a few paces away. He was on his back, and his eyes were open as if he could see through the smoke, up to the clouds.

Iris swallowed a sob, falling to her knees beside him. Was he dead? Her heart wrenched at the thought. She couldn't bear it, she realized as her hands raced over his face, his chest. She couldn't bear to live in a world without him.

"Kitt?" she called to him, resting her palm over his heart. He was breathing, and the relief nearly melted her bones. "*Kitt,* can you see me?"

"Iris," he rasped. His voice sounded so far away, and she realized it was her ears, ringing. "Iris . . . in my bag . . ."

"Yes, Kitt," she said, smiling when he blinked up at her. He was dazed, and she began to assess the rest of his body. Down his stomach, his sides, and then she saw it. His right leg had pieces of shrapnel lodged in it. The destruction looked mainly concentrated around the outside of his thigh and calf, and around his knee, but his wounds were steadily bleeding. It was impossible to tell how much blood he had already lost. The splatters on the ground could be his or spilled from others who had been hurt. Iris took a deep breath, willing herself to be calm.

"All right, Kitt," she said, meeting his gaze again. "You're injured. It looks like it's primarily your right leg, but we need to get you to a doctor. Do you think—"

"Iris, my bag," he said, his hands futilely searching for it. "I need you . . . need to get my bag. There's something . . . I want you—"

"Yes, don't worry about your bag, Kitt. I need to get you out of here first," Iris said, squatting. "Here, if I help you, can you stand on your left foot?"

He nodded.

Iris worked to haul him up and balance him. But he was so much taller and far heavier than she expected. They took a few stilted steps before Roman slowly sank to the ground again.

"Iris," he said, "I need to tell you something."

She went rigid, dread crackling through her. "You can tell me later," she insisted. But she began to worry he had lost far more blood than she realized. He looked so pale; the agony in his eyes stole her breath. "You can tell me when we're back at Marisol's, all right?"

"I don't think . . ." he began, half a whisper, half a moan. "You should take my bag and go. Leave me here."

"Like hell I am!" she shouted. Everything within her was fracturing under the weight of her fear. She had no idea how she was going to get Roman to safety, but in that split second of desperation, she clearly beheld what she wanted.

She and Roman would survive this war. They would have the chance to grow old together, year by year. They would be friends until they both finally acknowledged the truth. And they would have everything that other couples had—the arguments and the hand-holding in the market and the gradual exploration of their bodies and the birthday celebrations and the journeys to new cities and the living as one and sharing a bed and the gradual sense of melting into each other. Their names would be entwined—*Roman and Iris* or *Winnow and Kitt* because could you truly have one without the other?—and they would write on their typewriters and ruthlessly edit each other's pieces and read books by candlelight at night.

She wanted him. Leaving him behind in the trenches wasn't even a possibility.

"Here, let's try again," she said, softening her voice in the hopes it would encourage him to try. "Kitt?"

Roman was unresponsive, angling his head against the wall of the trench.

Iris touched his face. Her fingertips left a trail of blood on his jaw. "Look at me, Roman."

He did so, his eyes wide and glazed.

"If you die in this trench," Iris said, "then I die with you. Do you understand? If you choose to simply sit here, I'll have no choice but to drag you until Dacre arrives. Now, come on."

Roman struggled to rise with her help. He leaned against the wall, and they took a few laborious steps before he stopped.

"Did you get my bag . . . my *bag*, Iris?"

Why was he so worried about his bloody bag? She exhaled and looked for it, her body burning with the strain of bearing his weight. *I can't carry him alone,* she thought just as her eyes fell on a soldier who was about to pass them, his rifle slung across his back.

"Hey!" Iris shouted, intercepting him. "Yes, you, Private. Help me carry this correspondent to Station Fourteen. Please, I need your help."

The soldier didn't even hesitate. He looped Roman's other arm over his shoulders. "We need to hurry. They've taken the front trenches."

His words sent a bolt of fear through Iris's stomach, but she nodded and shifted beneath Roman's other arm, so that he was between her and the soldier. They moved faster than Iris had anticipated, winding through the trenches. There were more wounded sprawled on the ground. She had no choice but to step around them, and her eyes were smarting, and her nose running, and her ears continued to ring but she was breathing and alive and she was going to get Roman out of here and to a doctor, and she—

The private turned a corner and abruptly stopped.

They were almost to the end of the trenches. They were almost to the woods and Station Fourteen and the road that would lead them to town, but Iris had no choice but to follow the private's lead, Roman groaning between them at the jolt. She recognized the captain who had brought her and Roman to the front moving through the confusion. Blood was splattered across his face and his teeth gleamed in the light as he grimaced. Wounded soldiers lined the trenches around him; there was no way that Iris was going to be able to get past them, and she panicked as the private began to lower Roman down to the ground.

"Wait, *wait!*" she cried, but the captain caught sight of her. He called out a few more orders before he approached, and Iris watched as the wounded were carried away on stretchers, up and out of the trenches.

"Miss Winnow," the captain said, glancing down at Roman. "Is he breathing?"

"Yes, only wounded. Shrapnel, right leg. Captain, can we—"

"I'll have him carried out on a stretcher and loaded into the lorry for transport. Are you wounded?"

"No, Captain."

"Then I need you. I'm short of hands, and we need to get as many wounded to this point as possible before Dacre takes them. Here, go with

Private Stanley and use this stretcher to bring back as many as possible. You only have as long as the guns fire. Now go!"

Iris was stunned as the captain turned and began calling out more orders. She was a correspondent, not a soldier, but Private Stanley was now staring at her, holding one end of a bloodied and vomit-stained stretcher, and time suddenly felt heavy on her skin.

Did it matter what she was?

Iris knelt before Roman. "Kitt? Can you look at me?"

His eyes cracked open. "Iris."

"I'm needed elsewhere, but I'll find you, Kitt. When this is over, I'll find you, all right?"

"Don't leave," he whispered, and his hand flailed, reaching for her. "You and I . . . we need to stay together. We're better this way."

A lump lodged in her throat when she saw the panic in his eyes. She laced their fingers together, holding him steady. "You have to stay strong for me. Once you're healed, I need you to write an article about all of this. I need you to steal the front page from me like you normally do, all right?" She smiled, but her eyes were burning. It was all the smoke, drifting closer from the barrage. "I'll find you," she whispered and kissed his knuckles. He tasted like salt and blood.

The pain in her chest swelled when she had to shake his hand away, taking the other end of the stretcher. When she had no choice but to turn and leave him, following the steady trot of Private Stanley.

They picked up one wounded soldier, carrying her back to the place Iris had left Roman. As she helped Stanley carefully slide the private off the stretcher, Iris's eyes skimmed the others and saw Roman was still waiting, but closer in line to be carried up to the lorry.

They left again, scurrying just like the rats did through the trenches. They carried another soldier with a mangled leg back to Station Fourteen. This time, Roman was gone, and Iris was both relieved and anxious. He must have been loaded and be currently in transit to an infirmary. But that meant she wasn't there to curse at him, to insist he keep his eyes open, to hold his hand and ensure he was all right.

She swallowed, her mouth dry and full of ash. She blinked away her tears.

It was just smoke in her eyes. Smoke in her eyes, burning her up from within.

"I think we can retrieve one more," Stanley said. "As long as there's gunfire, we have time. Can you do that?"

Iris nodded, listening to the pop of the guns in the distance. But her shoulders were sore, her breaths were uneven. Her heart pounded a painful song in her chest as she ran behind Stanley, the stretcher banging against her sore thighs.

They went deeper into the trenches this time. Iris's legs were trembling as she realized the gunfire was beginning to ease. Did that mean Dacre's soldiers had killed everyone at the front? Did that mean they would soon press closer? Would they kill her if they found her, stranded in the thick of the trenches? Did they take prisoners?

Before Dacre takes them. The captain's words echoed through her, making her shiver.

Distracted, Iris tripped over something.

It brought her to her knees, and she felt stray pieces of shrapnel bite into her skin.

Stanley paused, glancing over his shoulder to look at her. "Get up," he said, and he suddenly sounded afraid, because the gunfire was waning.

But Iris was scarcely listening to him, or the way the world was becoming eerily silent again. Because there on the ground was a leather bag that looked just like the one she was carrying. Scuffed and freckled with blood and trampled by countless boots.

Roman's bag.

Iris slipped it onto her shoulder. It rested beside her own bag, and she felt the weight settle on her back as she rose to her feet once more.

"What are you still doing here, correspondent?" Captain Speer shouted at Iris. "Get in the lorry! You should have evacuated an hour ago!"

Iris startled. She was standing in Station Fourteen, uncertain what she should be doing. All she knew was there was blood dried on her hands and jumpsuit, and the scrape on her chest was burning, and her pulse was frantic, wondering where Roman was.

"Go!" the captain screamed when Iris remained standing blankly.

Iris nodded and stumbled through the dusky light to the back of the lorry. Soldiers were being loaded, and she waited, not wanting to push her way through. Eventually, one of the privates saw her and hefted her up into the crowded bed without a word.

She sprawled on top of someone groaning in pain.

Iris shifted her weight, unbalanced by the two bags on her back. "Oh, I'm so sorry!"

"Miss Winnow?"

She studied the bloodied soldier beneath her. "Lieutenant Lark? Oh my gods, are you all right?"

It was a ridiculous thing for her to ask. Of course, he wasn't all right—none of them were *all right*—but she suddenly didn't know what to do, what to say. She gently moved to sit beside him, wedged between his body and another soldier. The lorry jerked and rumbled forward, jostling everyone in the back.

Lark grimaced. In the faint light she could see the dirt and blood on his face, the shock haunting his eyes.

"Lieutenant Lark?" Iris glanced down at his hand. His fingers were splayed over his stomach, coated in bright blood. As if he were holding himself together.

"Miss Winnow, I told you to retreat. Why are you still here? Why are you in this last lorry with me?"

The last lorry? Iris swallowed the acid that rose in her throat. There had been so many other wounded soldiers at Station Fourteen. She shouldn't have taken a seat. She shouldn't be here.

"I wanted to help," she said. Her voice sounded rough and strange. Like it belonged to someone else, and not her. "Here, what can I do to make you more comfortable, Lieutenant?"

"Just sit here with me, Miss Winnow. Everyone . . . they're gone. All of them."

It took her a moment to understand what he meant. That "everyone" was his platoon. The Sycamores.

She closed her eyes for a moment, to center herself. To tamp down her rising panic and tears. She was sitting in the covered back of a lorry, surrounded by wounded soldiers. They were driving east, to where Avalon Bluff lay, kilometers away. They were safe; they would reach the infirmary in time.

The cut on her chest flared.

Iris lifted her hand and pressed her palm over it. That was when she realized something was missing. Her mother's golden locket.

She swore under her breath, searching around her. But she knew the necklace was long gone. The chain must have broken when the grenade's blast hurled her forward along the ground. The remnant of her mother was most likely still there, in the place that had blown her and Roman apart. She could see it in her mind's eye—the locket now trampled into the mud of the trench. A small glimmer, a faint trace of gold among shrapnel and blood.

Iris sighed, lowering her hand.

"Are you well, Miss Winnow?" Lark asked, bringing her back to the present.

"Yes, Lieutenant. Just thinking of something."

"Where is Mr. Kitt?"

"He was wounded earlier. He's already in transport."

"Good," Lark said, nodding. He clenched his eyes shut. Iris watched the blood continue to pool through his fingers. She could feel it slowly seep into the leg of her jumpsuit. "Good. I'm glad . . . I'm glad he's safe."

"Would you like to hear a story, Lieutenant Lark?" Iris asked quietly, not sure where the question came from. "Would you like to hear how Enva played Dacre for a fool with her harp beneath the earth?"

"Yes. I would like that, Miss Winnow."

Her mouth was so dry. Her throat felt splintered and her head was throbbing, but she began to spin the myth. She had read it so many times in Carver's letters; she had his words memorized.

When the soldiers in the lorry around her fell quiet, listening, she wondered if perhaps she should have chosen a different myth. Here she was, talking about Dacre, the author of their wounds and pain and losses and heartaches. But then she realized that there was power in this story; it proved that Dacre could be tamed and bested, that Dacre was not nearly as strong and shrewd as he liked to be perceived.

"I owe you a story in return," Lark said after Iris had finished. "You once asked me about the Sycamore Platoon. Where our name came from."

"Yes," Iris whispered.

"I want to tell you now. We all grew up in the same town, you see," Lark began. His voice was low and raspy. Iris had to bend closer to catch his words. "It's a place north of here, hard to find on a map. We're farmers; we toil under rain and sun, we know everything about the loam, and we count our lives by seasons more than years. When the war broke out . . . we decided we should join the fight. There was a group of us that could form our own platoon. And we thought that if we joined, the conflict would end sooner." He snorted. "How wrong we were."

Lark quieted, his eyes closing. The lorry hit a pothole, and Iris watched as his face grooved in pain.

"Before we left home," he continued, even fainter now, "we decided to carve our initials into the great sycamore tree that overlooked one of the fields. The tree was on a hill, like a sentry. It had been struck by lightning twice but had yet to split and fall. And so we believed there was magic in that tree, that its roots gave nutrients to the soil we tilled and planted and harvested. That its boughs watched over our valley.

"We carved our initials into its bark. It was a prayer for the magic of home to watch over us, even as the kilometers came between us. A prayer and a promise that we would all return someday."

"That's beautiful, Lieutenant," Iris said, touching his arm.

He smiled, opening his eyes to look upward. Blood bubbled between his teeth.

"I didn't even want to be lieutenant," he confessed. "I didn't *want* to lead us. But that's how the cards fell, and I carried that weight. Carried the worry that some of us might not return home. That I would have to go to these mothers and fathers and brothers and sisters and wives and husbands. People I had known all my life. People who were like family. And say . . . I'm sorry. I'm sorry for your loss. I'm sorry I couldn't stop it. I'm sorry I couldn't do more to protect them."

Iris was silent. She wondered if he was about to slip into unconsciousness. If the pain of his wounds was too great. She wondered if she should keep him talking, keep him awake.

She reached for his hand.

Lark said, "I'll have to say it over and over and over, now. If I live, I'll be full of nothing but regrets and apologies, because I'm the last one. The Sycamore Platoon is gone, Miss Winnow. We woke up this morning to one world, and now the sun is setting on another."

When he closed his eyes again, Iris remained quiet. She held his hand, and the last of the light waned. Eventide was giving way to the night, and once she would have been terrified of Dacre's hounds and the possibility of their attack. But now there was nothing to fear. There was only grief, raw and sharp.

She was still holding Lieutenant Lark's hand an hour later when he died.

There was smoke in her hair, smoke in her lungs, smoke in her eyes, burning her up from within.

And Iris covered her face and wept.

33

The Snow in Kitt's Bag

They rolled into Avalon Bluff in the middle of the night. The air was cool and dark and the stars blistered the sky as Iris climbed down from the lorry on shaky legs.

She was suddenly surrounded by nurses, doctors, townspeople. She was swept up and away into the light of the infirmary, so exhausted she could hardly speak—*I'm fine, don't waste your efforts on me.* Before she could protest, a nurse had her inside the hall, cleaning her scrapes and cuts with antiseptic.

"Are you injured anywhere else?" the nurse asked.

Iris blinked. She felt like she was seeing double for a moment. She couldn't remember the last time she had drunk or eaten something, the last time she had slept.

"No," she said, her tongue sticking to her teeth.

The nurse reached for a cup of water and dissolved something in it. "Here, drink this. Marisol is just down the hall. I know she'll want to see you."

"*Iris!*" Attie's voice cut through the clamor.

Iris jumped and frantically looked around, finding Attie weaving through the crowd. She set down the cup of water and launched herself into her friend's arms. She drew a deep breath and told herself to be calm, but the next moment she was sobbing into Attie's neck.

"You're all right, you're all right," Attie whispered, holding her tightly. "Here, let me get a good look at you." She angled herself back, and Iris dashed the tears from her eyes.

"I'm sorry," Iris said, sniffing.

"Don't apologize," Attie said firmly. "I've been worried *sick* about you, ever since the first lorry pulled up hours ago. I've literally looked at everyone who arrived, hoping to find you."

Iris's heart stalled. She felt the color drain from her face. "Kitt. Is he here? Did you see him? Is he all right?"

Attie grinned. "Yes, he's here. Don't worry. He just got out of surgery on the upper floor, I believe. Here, I'll take you to him, but grab your water first."

Iris reached for her cup. She didn't realize how badly she was shaking until she tried to take a sip and spilled half of it on her chest. Attie noticed but said nothing, leading her to the lift. They ascended to the second floor. It was quieter on the upper story; the corridors smelled like iodine and soap. Iris's throat narrowed as Attie led her farther down the hallway, around a corner and into a dimly lit room.

There were multiple beds, each partitioned off by cloth walls for meager privacy. Iris's eyes found him instantly.

Roman was in the first bay, lying on a narrow cot. He was sleeping, his mouth slack and his chest rising and falling slowly, as if he were in the throes of a deep dream. He looked so thin in a hospital gown. He looked so pale in the lamplight. He looked like the slightest thing might break him.

She took a step closer, uncertain if she was supposed to be in there. But a nurse nodded at her, and Iris tentatively continued her path to Roman's bedside. His injured leg was swathed in linens, propped up on a spare pillow, and intravenous fluids were being fed into a vein in his right hand.

She stopped, gazing down at him. He had taken multiple wounds for her. He had put himself in harm's way to keep her safe, and she wondered if she would be standing here in this moment with minor scrapes without him or if she would be shredded by shrapnel, dead in the shadows of a trench. If he hadn't come with her . . . if he hadn't been so stubborn, so *insistent* that he follow her . . .

She couldn't breathe, and she dared to reach out and trace his hand, the nicks and cuts on his knuckles.

Why did you come here, Kitt?

She returned her gaze to his face, half expecting to find his eyes open and his mouth upturned in a cocky smile. As if he felt the same dangerous spark she did when their skin touched. But Roman continued to sleep, lost to her in the moment.

She swallowed.

Why did you take the wounds that should have been mine?

Her fingertips traced up his arm, across his collar and the slope of his jaw to the thick shock of his hair. She brushed away a lock from his brow, daring him to wake up to her caress.

He didn't, of course.

She was partly relieved, partly disappointed. She was still rife with worry over him, and she felt as if the ice in her stomach wouldn't fully melt until she spoke with him. Until she heard his voice again and felt his gaze on her.

"We removed twelve pieces of shrapnel from his leg," the nurse said quietly. "He's very fortunate it was only his leg, and all of his arteries were missed."

Iris's hand dropped from Roman's dark hair. She glanced over her shoulder to see the nurse standing at the foot of his bed.

"Yes. I was with him when it happened," Iris whispered, beginning to back away. She could see Attie at the corner of her eye, waiting in the doorway.

"Then he must be here because of you," the nurse said, moving closer to take his pulse. "I'm sure he'll want to see and personally thank you tomorrow."

"No," Iris said. "I'm here because of him." And that was all the lump in her throat would allow her to say.

She turned and left the room, her breaths turning shallow and quick, and she thought she might faint in the corridor until she glanced up and saw someone striding toward her with purpose. Long black hair was escaping a braid. Blood was splattered on her skirts and fire shone in her brown eyes.

Marisol.

"*There* you are!" Marisol cried, and Iris worried she was in trouble until she realized that that Marisol was *crying.* Tears shone on her cheeks. "My gods, I have been praying every day for you!"

One moment, Iris was standing uncertain, trembling in the hall. The next, Marisol had embraced her, weeping into her matted hair. Iris sighed— she was safe, *she was safe,* she could let down her guard and *breathe*—and she held to Marisol, struggling to hide the tears that surged.

She didn't think she could cry anymore, but when Marisol leaned back and framed her face, Iris let her tears fall.

"When's the last time you ate, Iris?" Marisol asked, tenderly wiping her tears away. "Come, I'm taking you home and feeding you. And then you can take a shower and rest."

She reached for Attie's hand, holding both girls close.

Marisol led them home.

Iris wanted a shower first.

While Marisol and Attie prepared hot cocoa and a late-night meal in the kitchen, Iris trudged upstairs to the lavatory. The adrenaline that had kept her going since that afternoon—a day that felt like years ago, a day when the sky was blue and the storm clouds were building and the trenches were full of heavy silence and the Sycamore Platoon was alive—was utterly gone. She could suddenly feel the keen edge of her exhaustion.

She carried a candle into her bedroom. She dropped the bags from her back to the floor, where they lay like two heaps on the rug. She stripped, shivering as the bloodstained linen peeled off her skin.

A quick shower, Marisol had told her. Because it was the middle of the night, and they must always be ready for the hounds to come.

Iris washed by candlelight. It was dark and warm, the steam curling up from the tiles, and she stood in the shower, her eyes closed and her skin burning as she scrubbed. She scrubbed as if she could wash it all away.

Her ears still held a faint ring; she wondered if it would ever fade.

She knocked something off the soap ledge. The clang made her jump, her heart faltering. She almost cowered, but slowly told herself she was fine. She was in the shower, and it was just a metal tin of Marisol's lavender shampoo.

When Iris was certain she had washed away the dirt and the sweat and the blood, she shut off the valve and dried herself. She didn't even want to look at her body, the marks on her skin. Bruises and cuts to remind her what she had experienced.

She thought of Roman as she drew on her nightgown. He lingered in her mind as she worked the tangles from her damp hair. When would he wake? When should she return to him?

"Iris?" Marisol called. "Breakfast!"

Breakfast, in the middle of the night.

Iris set her comb aside and carried her candle down the stairs, into the kitchen. At the smell of the food, her stomach clenched. She was so hungry, but she wasn't sure if she would be able to eat.

"Here, start with the cocoa," Attie said, offering a steaming cup to Iris.

Iris took it gratefully, sinking into her usual chair. Marisol continued to set down plates on the table. She had made some sort of cheesy hash, full of comforting ingredients, and gradually, Iris was able to begin taking a few bites. The warmth trickled through her; she sighed and felt herself slowly returning to her body.

Attie and Marisol sat and ate with her, but they were quiet. And Iris was thankful. She didn't think she could speak of it yet. Just having them close beside her was all she needed.

"Can I help you clean, Marisol?" Attie asked, rising to gather the dishes when they were done.

"No, I've got this. Why don't you help Iris to her room?" Marisol said.

Iris's eyes were heavy. Her feet felt like iron as she rose, and Attie took hold of her arm. She hardly remembered ascending the stairs, or Attie opening her door and guiding her inside.

"Do you want me to stay with you tonight, Iris?"

Iris sank to her pallet on the floor. The blankets were cold.

"No, I'm so tired I don't think sleeping will be an issue. But wake me if a siren sounds."

She hardly remembered falling asleep.

Iris woke with a start.

She didn't know where she was at first. Sunlight was streaming in through the window, and the house was silent. She sat forward, her body stiff and sore. The B and B. She was at Marisol's, and it looked to be late morning.

The events of the past few days returned to her in a rush.

Roman. She needed to go to the infirmary. She wanted to see him, touch him. Surely he was awake by now.

Iris stood with a groan. She had fallen asleep with wet hair, and it was a snarled mess now. She was reaching for her comb when she saw her bag on the floor nearby, Roman's directly next to it. Both were scuffed and streaked with dirt. And then her gaze roamed to her jumpsuit, discarded by her desk where her typewriter sat, gleaming in the light.

Carver.

His name whispered through her, and she eagerly glanced at her wardrobe, expecting to find letter after letter on the floor.

There was nothing. The floor was bare. He hadn't written to her at all while she was away, and her heart sank.

Iris closed her eyes, her thoughts swimming. She remembered his final letter to her. The one she had shoved in her pocket and tried to read before Roman interrupted her *twice.*

She dove for her jumpsuit, searching the pockets. She half expected the paper to be gone, just like her mother's locket, as if the battle had also torn it away from her. But the letter was still there. A few specks of blood had dried on one of the corners. Iris's hands trembled as she smoothed the page out.

Where had she left off? He was asking her questions. He wanted to know more about her, as if he felt the same hunger she did. Because she wanted to know him too.

She found the place. She had almost been at the end when Roman had rudely tossed that paper wad at her.

Iris bit her lip. Her eyes rushed along the words:

I want to know everything about you, Iris.

I want to know your hopes and your dreams. I want to know what irritates you and what makes you smile and what makes you laugh and what you long for most in this world.

But perhaps even more than that...I want you to know who I am.

If you could see me right now as I type this...you would smile. No, you'd probably laugh. To see how badly my hands are shaking, because I want to get this right. I've wanted to get it right for weeks now, but the truth is I didn't know how and I'm worried what you might think.

It's odd, how quickly life can change, isn't it? How one little thing like typing a letter can open a door you never saw. A transcendent connection. A divine threshold. But if there's anything I can should say in this moment—when my heart is beating wildly in my chest and I would beg you to come and tame it—is this: your letters have been a light for me to follow. Your words? A sublime feast that fed me on days when I was starving.

I love you, Iris.

And I want you to see me. I want you to know me. Through the smoke and the firelight and kilometers that once dwelled between us.

Do you see me?

—C.

She lowered the letter but continued to stare at Carver's inked words.

What is a synonym for sublime? Roman had once asked her from his second-story window. As if he were a prince, trapped in a castle.

Divine, she had grumbled from below, where she had been watering the garden. *Transcendent,* Attie had offered, assuming he was writing about the gods.

Iris's heart pounded. She read through Carver's letter again——*I love you, Iris*——until the words began to melt into each other, and her eyes were blinking back a sudden flood of tears.

"No," she whispered. "No, it can't be. This is a mere coincidence."

But she had never been one to believe in such things. Her gaze snagged on Roman's bag, lying in the center of the floor. He had been so insistent that she grab his bag after he had been injured. She could still hear his voice, vividly.

Iris . . . my bag . . . I need you . . . need to get my bag. There's something . . . I want you——

The world stopped.

The roaring in her ears returned, as if she had just crouched through an hour of artillery fire.

Carver's letter slipped from her fingers as she walked to Roman's bag. She bent down and retrieved it, dried dirt cascading in clumps from the leather. It took her a minute to get the front untethered. Her fingers were icy, fumbling. But at last it was open and she turned it upside down.

All his possessions began to spill out.

A wool blanket, a few tins of vegetables and pickled fruits. His notepad, full of his handwriting. Pens. A spare set of socks. And then the paper. So many loose pages, fluttering like snow down to the floor. Page after page, crinkled and folded and marked by type.

Iris stared at the paper that gathered at her feet.

She knew what this was. She knew as she dropped Roman's bag, as she knelt to retrieve the pages.

They were her letters.

Her words.

First typed to Forest, and then to someone she had known as Carver.

Her emotions were a tangled mess as she began to reread them. Her words stung as if she had never once typed them sitting on the floor of her old bedroom, lonely and worried and angry.

I wish you would be a coward for me, for Mum. I wish you would set down your

gun and rend your allegiance to the goddess who has claimed you. I wish you would
return to us.

She had thought that Carver had thrown away the very first of her letters. She had asked him to send them back to her, and he had said it wasn't
possible.

Well, now she knew he was lying. Because they were here. They were *all*
here, wrinkled as if they had been read numerous times.

Iris stopped reading. Her eyes were smarting.

Roman Kitt was Carver.

He had been Carver all along, and this realization struck her so hard she
had to sit down on the floor. She was overwhelmed by a startling rush of
relief. It was *him*. She had been writing to him, falling for him, all this time.

But then the questions began to swarm, nipping at that solace.

Had he been playing her? Was this a game to him? Why hadn't he told
her sooner?

She covered her face, and her palms absorbed the heat of her cheeks.

"*Gods,*" she whispered through her fingers, and when she opened her
eyes again, her sight had sharpened. She stared at her letters, spread around
her. And she began to gather them up, one by one.

{ 34 }

C.

Iris walked into the infirmary ten minutes later, wearing a fresh jumpsuit and a tightly cinched belt. Her hair remained a tangled, hopeless mess around her shoulders, but she had more important things on her mind. All her letters were folded and in hand as she rode the lift to the upper level.

The doors chimed.

She stepped into the corridor, passing a few nurses and one of the doctors, none of whom paid her any attention, and she was glad for it. She wasn't sure what, exactly, was about to unfold, but her blood was thrumming.

Her face was flushed by the time she approached Roman's room.

He was in the same curtained bay and bed. His hand was still hooked to an intravenous tube, and his right leg was freshly bandaged, but he was sitting upright, his attention focused on the bowl of soup he was eating.

Iris stood on the threshold and watched him, her heart softening to see him awake. He wasn't as pale as he had been the day before. She was relieved that he looked much better, and he swallowed a spoonful of soup, his eyes closing briefly as if savoring the food.

Iris felt the perspiration begin to bead on her palms, soaking into her letters. She hid them behind her back and walked to him, coming to a stop at the foot of his bed.

Roman glanced up and startled at the sight of her. He dropped his spoon with a clatter, rushing to set the bowl on his side table.

"Iris."

She heard the joy in his voice. His eyes drank her in, and when he made to move—was he truly trying to rise and come to her on one leg?—she cleared her throat.

"Stay where you are, Kitt."

He froze. A frown creased his brow.

She had rehearsed what she wanted to say to him. How to begin this strange conversation. She had pounded it into her mind the entire walk here. But now that she was looking at him . . . the words vanished within her.

She held up her handful of letters. And she said, *"You."*

Roman was silent for a beat. He drew a deep breath and whispered, "Me."

Iris smiled, a shield for how mortified she was. She felt like laughing and crying, but she forced them both down. Her head began to ache. "All this time, you were receiving my letters?"

"Yes," Roman replied.

"I just . . . I can't believe this, Kitt!"

"Why? What's so hard to believe, Iris?"

"All this time it was *you.*" She blinked away her tears and tossed one of the letters onto Roman's bed. It was satisfying, to hear the paper crinkle, a distraction from her embarrassment. She dropped another page, and then another. The letters fell onto his lap.

"Stop it, Iris," Roman said, gathering them up as they drifted. As she carelessly crinkled them. "I understand why you're angry at me, but let me expl—"

"How long have you known?" she asked tersely. "When did you know it was me?"

Roman paused, his jaw clenched. He continued to gently gather her letters. "I knew from the beginning."

"The beginning?"

"From the first letter you sent," he amended. "You didn't mention your name, but you talked about your job at the *Gazette,* the columnist position."

Iris froze in horror, listening to him. He had known all this time? *He had known all this time!*

"I honestly thought it was a prank at first," he rambled on. "That you were doing it to get in my head. Until I read the other letters—"

"Why didn't you *say* something to me, Kitt?"

"I wanted to. But I was worried you would stop writing."

"So you thought it best to play me for a fool?"

His eyes smoldered with offense. "I never once played you for a fool, Iris. Nor did I ever think that of you."

"Were you humoring me, then?" she asked. She hated how her voice trembled. "Was this all some joke to play on the poor low-class girl at work?"

She hit a nerve. Roman's face crumpled, as if she had just struck him.

"*No.* I would never do any of those things to you, and if you think that I would, then you don't—"

"You *lied* to me, Kitt!" she cried.

"I didn't lie to you. All the things I told you . . . none of them were lies. *None* of them, do you hear me?"

Iris stared at Roman. He was red-faced and holding her letters to his chest, and she suddenly had to add new layers to him. All the Carver details. She thought of Del, realizing that Roman had been an older brother; he had lost his sister. He had pulled her from the waters after she had drowned on her seventh birthday. He had carried her body home to his parents.

A lump rose in her throat. Iris closed her eyes.

Roman sighed. "Iris? Will you come here? Sit beside me for a while, and we can talk more."

She needed a moment to herself. To process this snarl of feelings within her.

"I need to go, Kitt. Here. Take your letters. I don't want them."

"What do you mean, you don't want them? They're mine."

"Yes! And that's the other thing you lied to me about!" she said, pointing.

"I asked you to send my old letters back. The ones I wrote to Forest. And you said you couldn't."

"I said I couldn't, because I didn't *want* to," said Roman. "Did you finish reading my last letter? Although by the looks of it . . . I don't think you can even begin to understand what your words mean to me. Even if they were addressed to Forest in the beginning. You were a sister writing to her missing older brother. And I *felt* that pain as a brother who had lost the only sibling he ever had."

Iris didn't know what to do. With her pain or with his and how they were suddenly fused. A warning flashed in her mind; she was dancing too close to the fire, about to get burned. Her armor had been stripped away, and she felt naked.

"Here," she said, handing him the last of the letters. "I need to go."

"Iris? *Iris,*" he whispered, but when he reached for her hand, she evaded him. "Please stay."

She took a step back. "There are things . . . things I need to do so I need to . . . I need to leave."

"I'm sorry," he said. "I'm sorry if I've hurt you, but that was never my intention, Iris. Why do you think I'm here?"

She was almost to the door. She paused but avoided meeting his gaze. She stared at her letters, clutched fiercely in his hands.

"You're here to outshine me again," she said in a detached tone. "You're here to prove your writing is far superior to mine, just like you did at the *Gazette.*"

She turned to flee but hadn't made it two steps when she heard a clatter—the sound of a cot creaking and a grunt of pain. Iris glanced over her shoulder, eyes widening when she saw it was Roman, standing on one foot and ripping the intravenous needle from his hand.

"Get back in bed, Kitt," she scolded.

"Don't run from me, Iris," Roman said as he began to hobble toward her. "Don't run from me, not after what we've just lived through. Not without granting me one final request."

Iris winced as he struggled to reach her on one foot. She moved forward, hands ready to catch him, but he took hold of the doorframe and found his balance, his blue eyes piercing hers. There was only a slender amount of space between their bodies, and Iris almost backed away, fighting the taunting pull she felt toward him.

"What is this request, then?" she asked coldly, but it was only to hide how her heart ached. "What is so important to you that you had to act like a *fool* and yank a needle from your vein, and possibly tear your stitches, and——"

"I never lied to you," Roman said. His expression softened but his eyes remained keen, and he whispered, "You asked me this once, months ago, and I refused to answer. But I want you to ask me again, Iris. Ask me what my middle name is."

She gritted her teeth, but she held his stare. Her memory began to roll like a phonograph, and she heard her past voice, snide and amused and full of curiosity.

Roman Cheeky Kitt. Roman Cantankerous Kitt. Roman Conceited Kitt . . .

Her breath caught.

"The C is for Carver," Roman said, leaning closer to her. "My name is Roman *Carver* Kitt."

He wove his fingers into her hair and brought his mouth down to hers. Iris felt the shock ripple through her the moment their lips met. His kiss was hungry, as if he had longed to taste her for some time, and at first she couldn't breathe. But then the shock melted, and she felt a thrill warm her blood.

She opened her mouth against his, returning the kiss. She felt him shiver as her hands raced up his arms, clinging to him. When he shifted their bodies, Iris sensed they were falling and she was utterly helpless to it until she felt the wall at her back. Roman pressed against her, his lean body blazing as if he had caught fire. His heat seeped into her skin, settled into her bones, and she couldn't stop the moan that escaped her.

Roman cradled her face in his hands. Yes, he had wanted her for a long time. She could feel it in the way he touched her, in the way his lips claimed hers. As if he had endlessly imagined this moment happening.

Iris hardly knew the hour or the day or where they stood. They were both caught in a storm of their own making and she didn't know what would happen when it broke. She only knew that something ached within her chest. Something that Roman must need, because his mouth and his breath and his caresses were trying to draw it from her.

Someone cleared their throat.

Iris suddenly returned to herself, feeling the cool, astringent air of the infirmary. The lightbulbs, shining overhead. The metallic sounds of bedpans and lunch trays being moved.

She broke away from Roman, panting. She stared up at him and his swollen mouth, the way his eyes brimmed with dangerous light as he continued to stare at her.

"I'm going to have to restrict your visiting hours if snogging is bound to happen again, Mr. Kitt," said a tired voice. Iris glanced around Roman to see a nurse was holding the intravenous needle and tube he had torn away from his hand. "You need to be in bed. *Resting.*"

"It won't happen again," Iris promised, face flaming.

The nurse only arched her brow. Roman, on the other hand, exhaled as if Iris had punched him.

What am I doing? Iris thought and slipped under Roman's arm. *This is foolish. This is . . .*

She paused on the threshold, glancing back at him.

Roman continued to lean against the wall. But his gaze was wholly consumed by her, even as the nurse moved to help him.

Iris left him with the tingling memory of her kiss and her letters scattered across his bed.

Dear Iris,

~~What were you thinking?~~
~~How could you let your heart cloud your mind?~~
~~You should have known!!!~~

How did you miss this? How could you let him get the best of you? Roman "C.-is-for-Carver" Kitt has played you.

Kitt: 2 (1 point for columnist, 1 point for elaborate deception)

Winnow: 0

I just...I don't even know what to think anymore. I'm embarrassed, I'm angry. I'm sad and strangely relieved. Attie and Marisol keep inviting me to the infirmary, but if I see Kitt right now I don't know how I'd react to him. I made an idiot of myself this morning, so I think it's best I stay away. I'm volunteering to dig graves in the field instead. I dig, hour after hour. I give all my anger and helplessness and sadness to the ground. And I help the people of Avalon Bluff take the names of soldiers before we bury them.

It's backbreaking work. The blisters have burst on my hands, but I don't even feel them. So many have died, and I'm just so tired and sad and angry, and I don't know what to do about Kitt.

I reread all his letters last night. And I don't think he tried to play me. At least, maybe he did at the very beginning, but not anymore. I also don't know how to fully describe how I'm feeling. Perhaps there are no words to explain such a thing, but...

Sometimes I still feel his hand in mine, drawing me through the smoke and terror of the trenches. Sometimes I still feel him lifting me up as if I were weightless, spinning me around as if we were dancing. Or how he came between me and the grenade, and I still can't breathe. Sometimes I remember how my heart stopped when I saw him sprawled on his back, staring up at the sky as if he were dead. When I saw him walking through the field during the eithral siren. When we collided in the golden grass. When his lips touched mine.

I am coming to love him, in two different ways. Face to face, and word to word. If I'm honest, there were moments when I longed for Carver, and moments when I longed for Roman, and now I don't know how to bring the two together. Or if I even should.

He was trying to tell me. And I was too distracted to put the pieces together. It's my own fault; my pride is simply wounded, and I need to let it go and continue with my life, with or without him.

I'm just ~~furious mortified upset seething~~ afraid.

I'm afraid he's going to hurt me. I'm afraid to lose someone I love again. I'm afraid to let go. To acknowledge what I feel for him. And yet he has proven himself to me. Over and over. He found me on my darkest day. He followed me to war, to the front lines. He came between me and Death, taking wounds that were supposed to be mine.

There is something electric within me. Something that is <u>begging</u> me to remove the last of my armor and let him see me as I am. To choose him. And yet here I sit, alone, typing word after word as I seek to make sense of myself. I watch the candlelight flicker and all I can think is...

<u>I am so afraid</u>. And yet how I long to be vulnerable and brave when it comes to my own heart.

35

The Hill That Almost Bested Iris

I ris knelt in the garden, watering the soil. In the days that she had been away at the front, a few green tendrils had started to break the ground, and the sight of their fragile unfurling made her heart soften. She imagined Keegan returning from the war soon, and the joy she would feel upon realizing that Marisol had ensured the garden was planted. It wasn't the most beautiful or orderly garden, but it was slowly awakening.

I grew something living in a season of death.

The words echoed through Iris as she gently traced the closest stem with her fingertip. Her watering can was empty, but she remained kneeling, and the dampness of the soil bled into the knees of her jumpsuit.

She felt so tired and heavy. They had finished burying all the deceased the day before.

"Thought I might find you here," Attie said.

Iris glanced over her shoulder to see her friend standing on the back terrace, shielding her eyes from the afternoon sunlight.

"Does Marisol need me?" Iris asked.

"No, actually." Attie hesitated, kicking a pebble with the toe of her boot.

"What is it, Attie? You're worrying me."

"Roman just returned from the infirmary," Attie said, clearing her throat. "He's resting in his bedroom."

"Oh." Iris returned her attention to the soil, but her heart was suddenly pounding. It had been two days since she had gone to him, letters in hand. Two days since she had seen or spoken with him. Two days since they had kissed like they were each starving for the other. Two days that she had spent sorting through her feelings, trying to decide what to do. "That's good to hear, I suppose."

"I think you should go visit him, Iris."

"Why?" She needed a distraction. There, a weed to pull. Iris made quick work of it, suddenly craving another task for her hands.

"I'm not sure what has come between the two of you, and I won't ask," Attie said. "All I know is that he doesn't look well."

The words chilled Iris to the bone.

"Doesn't *look* well?"

"I mean . . . it looks like his spirit's broken. And you know what they say about injured soldiers in low spirits."

"Kitt's a correspondent," Iris argued, but there was a splinter in her voice. She couldn't help but glance at Roman's second-story window, remembering the day he had leaned on the sill, tossing a message to her.

His window was shut now, the curtains drawn over the glass panes.

Attie was silent. The lull eventually drew Iris's gaze back to hers.

"Will you please visit him?" Attie asked. "I'll take over the watering for you."

Before Iris could scrounge up an excuse, Attie had scooped up the metal pail and was heading to the well.

Iris bit her lip but rose, knocking the dirt from her jumpsuit. She saw how filthy her hands were and stopped to scrub them in Marisol's wash bin, only to give up with a sigh. Roman had already seen her at her dirtiest. Her messiest.

The house was full of quiet shadows as Iris ascended the stairs. Her heart quickened when she saw Roman's bedroom door, closed to the world. She paused before the wood, listening to the ebb and flow of her breath, and then she scolded herself for being cowardly.

I won't know what I want to do until I see him again.

She knocked, three times fast.

There was no answer. Frowning, she knocked again, harder and deliberate. But Roman was unresponsive.

"Kitt?" she called to him through the wood. "Kitt, will you please answer me?"

At last he replied in a flat voice, "What do you want, Winnow?"

"May I come in?"

Roman was silent for a beat, and then drawled, "Why not."

Iris opened the door and stepped into his room. It was the first time she had been in his quarters, but her gaze went directly to him in the dusky light, where he was lying on his makeshift pallet on the floor. His eyes were closed, his fingers laced over his chest. He was dressed in a clean jumpsuit, his dark hair damp across his brow. She could smell the soap on his skin, which was uncommonly pallid. His face was shaved and his sharp cheekbones were sunken, as if he had become hollow.

And she was right; she knew exactly what she wanted to choose.

"What do you want?" he repeated, but his voice was a rasp.

"Good afternoon to you too," Iris countered happily. "How are you feeling?"

"Peachy."

A smile flirted with the corner of his lips, and the pit in her stomach began to ease. But his eyes remained shut. She suddenly longed for him to look at her.

"Ah, there's the Second Alouette," she said, her gaze fixing on his typewriter. Her heart warmed to see it. "Although it's far too dim in here, Kitt! You should let the light in."

"I don't want the light," he grumbled, but Iris had already parted the window curtains. He raised his hands to shield his face against the stream of sunshine. "Why have you come to torture me, Winnow?"

"If this is my torture, I would hate to see what my pleasure would be."

Roman made no reply, his hands remaining splayed over his face. As if the last thing he wanted was to look at her.

She walked to the side of his pallet, her shadow spilling across his lean body. "Will you look at me, Kitt?"

He didn't move. "You shouldn't feel obligated to visit me. I know you hate me right now."

"Obligated?"

"By Attie. I know she told you to come. It's all right; you can return to whatever important task you were busy with."

"I wouldn't be here if I didn't want to see you," Iris said, and her chest tightened, as if a thread was wound about each of her ribs. "In fact, I came to ask you a question."

He was quiet, but she could hear the curiosity in his voice as he said, "Go on, then."

"Would you like to go on a walk with me?"

Roman's hands slid away from his disbelieving face. "A *walk?*"

"Erm, maybe not a walk, exactly. If your leg . . . if you don't feel like it. But we could go outside."

"Where to?"

Now that his eyes had locked with hers, Iris felt seen, down to her bones. She could hardly breathe and she glanced at her dirty fingernails. "I was thinking we could go to our hill."

"*Our* hill?"

"Or your hill," she rushed to amend. "The hill that nearly bested me. Unless you think it's destined to get the best of you now. If so, I think it can make the headlines by tomorrow."

Roman was quiet, staring up at her. Iris couldn't deny it a moment longer. She met his gaze and tentatively smiled, extending her hands to him.

"Come on, Kitt. Come outside with me. The sun and fresh air will do you good."

Slowly, he lifted his fingers and wove them with hers—fingers that had typed letter after letter to her. And she raised him to his feet.

He was insistent on walking, and he used a crutch to avoid putting weight on his right leg. At first he moved with a strong rhythm, swinging himself forward. But then he began to tire, and their pace slowed. Fifteen minutes down the cobbled street, perspiration shone on Roman's face from the heat and the effort. Iris instantly wished she had thought better of her offer.

"We don't have to go *all* the way to the hill," she said, glancing sidelong at him. "We can turn around halfway."

He huffed a smile. "I'm not going to break, Winnow."

"Yes, but your leg is still—"

"My leg is fine. I'd like to see the view again, anyways."

She nodded but fiddled with the end of her braid, anxious about over-working him.

They turned onto the street that would gradually build to the crest. For the first time since she had met him, Iris didn't know what to say. In the office at the *Gazette,* she always had a retort ready for him. Even when she was writing to him as Carver, the words had spilled out of her onto the page. But now she felt uncommonly shy, and the words were like honey on her tongue. She desperately wanted to say the right things to him.

Iris waited for him to speak, hoping perhaps he would break this strange silence between them, but his breaths became labored as the street steepened. She dwelled on that last letter of his, and suddenly Iris knew exactly what to say to Roman Carver Kitt.

She turned to face him, walking backward. He noticed, giving her an arched brow.

"Salty," she said.

He chuckled, glancing down to the cobblestones as he crutched forward. "I know, I'm sweating."

"No," Iris said, drawing his eyes back to hers. "I prefer salty over sweet. I prefer sunsets over sunrises, but only because I love to watch the constellations begin to burn. My favorite season is autumn, because my mum and I both believed that's the only time when magic can be tasted in the air. I am a devout tea lover and can drink my weight in it."

A smile flickered over Roman's face. She was answering the questions he had asked in his last letter to her.

"Now," she said. "Tell me yours."

"I have the worst sweet tooth imaginable," Roman began. "I prefer sunrises, but only because I like the possibilities a new dawn brings. My favorite season is spring, because baseball returns. I prefer coffee, although I'll drink whatever is placed in front of me."

Iris grinned. Laughter slipped out of her, and she hurried to continue walking ahead of him, just out of his reach should he try to grab her. Because he had a hungry gleam in his eye, as if she were indeed a metaphorical carrot.

"You find my answers surprising, Winnow?"

"Not really, Kitt. I always knew you were my opposite. A nemesis usually is."

"I prefer *former rival*." His gaze dropped to her lips. "Tell me something more about you."

"More? Such as what?"

"Anything."

"Very well. I had a pet snail when I was seven."

"A snail?"

Iris nodded. "His name was Morgie. I kept him in a serving dish with a little tray of water and some rocks and a few wilted flowers. I told him all of my secrets."

"And whatever happened to Morgie?"

"He slinked away one day when I was at school. I came home to discover him gone, and he was nowhere to be found. I cried for a fortnight."

"I can imagine that was devastating," Roman said, at which Iris playfully batted him.

"Don't poke fun at me, Kitt."

"I'm not, Iris." He effortlessly caught her hand in his, and they both came to a halt in the middle of the street. "Tell me more."

"More?" she breathed, and while her hand felt hot as kindling, she didn't pull away from him. "If I tell you anything else today, you'll grow tired of me."

"Impossible," he whispered.

She felt that shyness creeping over her again. What was happening right now, and why did it feel like wings were beating in her stomach?

"What's your middle name?" Roman asked suddenly.

Iris arched her brow, amused. "You *might* have to earn that morsel of information."

"Oh, come now. Could you at least give me the initial? It would only be fair."

"I suppose I can't argue with that," she said. "My middle name begins with an *E.*"

Roman smiled, his eyes crinkling at the corners. "And whatever could it be? Iris *Enchanting* Winnow? Iris *Ethereal* Winnow? Iris *Exquisite* Winnow?"

"My gods, Kitt," she said, blushing. "Let me save us both from this torture. It's Elizabeth."

"Iris Elizabeth Winnow," Roman echoed, and she shivered to hear her name in his mouth.

Iris held his stare until the mirth faded from his eyes. He was looking at her the way he had in Zeb's office. As if he could see all of her, and Iris swallowed, telling her heart to calm, to slow.

"I need to say something to you," Roman said, tracing her knuckles with his thumb. "You mentioned the other day that you think I'm only here to 'outshine' you. But that's the furthest thing from the truth. I broke my engagement, quit my job, and traveled six hundred kilometers into war-torn land to be with you, Iris."

Iris squirmed. This didn't feel real. The way he was looking at her, holding her hand. This must be a dream on the verge of dashing. "Kitt, I—"

"Please, let me finish."

She nodded, but she inwardly braced herself.

"I don't really care to write about the war," he said. "Of course, I'll do it because the *Inkridden Tribune* is paying me to, but I would much rather that your articles live on the front page. I would much rather read what you write. Even if they aren't letters to me." He paused, rolling his lips together as if he was uncertain. "That first day you were gone. My first day as columnist. It was horrible. I realized I was becoming someone I didn't want to be, and it woke me up, to see your desk empty. My father has had my life planned for me, ever since I could remember. It was my 'duty' to follow his will, and I tried to adhere to it, even if it was killing me. Even if it meant I couldn't buy your sandwich at lunch, which I still think about to this day and despise myself for."

"Kitt," Iris whispered. She tightened her hold on his hand.

"But the moment you walked away," Roman rushed on, "I knew I felt something for you, which I had been denying for *weeks*. The moment you wrote me and said you were six hundred kilometers away from Oath . . . I thought my heart had stopped. To know that you would still want to write to me, but also that you were so far away. And as our letters progressed, I finally acknowledged that I was in love with you, and I wanted you to know who I was. That's when I decided I would follow you. I didn't want the life my father had planned for me—a life where I could never be with you."

Iris opened her mouth, but she was so full and overwhelmed that she said nothing at all. Roman intently watched her, his cheeks red and his eyes wide, as if he was waiting to hit the ground and shatter.

"Are you . . ." she began, blinking. "Are you saying you want a life with me?"

"Yes," he said.

And because her heart was melting, Iris smiled and teased, "Is this a proposal?"

He continued to hold their stare, deadly serious. "If I asked you, would you say yes?"

Iris was quiet, but her mind was racing, full of golden thoughts.

Once, not long ago, in her life *before* the front lines, she would have thought this was ridiculous. She would have said *no, I have other plans right now*. But that was *before,* a time that was gilded by a different slant of light, and this present moment was now limned in the blue tinge of *after*. She had seen the fragility of life. How one could wake to a sunrise and die by sunset. She had run through the smoke and the fire and the agony with Roman, his hand in hers. They had both tasted Death, brushed shoulders with it. They had scars on their skin and on their souls from that fractured moment, and now Iris saw more than she had before. She saw the light, but she also saw the shadows.

Time was precious here. If she wanted this with Roman, then why shouldn't she grasp it, claim it with both hands?

"I suppose you'll have to ask me and find out," she said.

And just when she thought she couldn't be surprised by anything else, Roman began to kneel. Right there in the center of the street, halfway up the hill. He was about to ask her. He was truly about to ask her to be his wife, and Iris gasped.

He winced as his knee found the cobblestones, a glint of pain in his eyes.

Iris glanced down, beyond their linked hands. Blood was seeping through the right leg of his jumpsuit.

"Kitt!" she cried, urging him to stand again. "You're bleeding!"

"It's nothing, Winnow," he said, but he was beginning to look pale. "I must have pulled a stitch."

"Here, sit down."

"In the road?"

"No, over here on this crate." Iris guided him to the closest front yard. It must have been the O'Briens' property, because there were multiple cats sunbathing on the dead grass, and she remembered Marisol talking about how most of Avalon Bluff worried those felines would get them all bombed one day.

"I must have failed to mention that I'm allergic to cats," Roman said, frowning as Iris forced him to sit on the overturned milk crate. "And I'm more than capable of walking back to Marisol's."

"No, you're not," Iris argued. "The cats will leave you alone, I'm sure. Wait here for me, Kitt. Don't you dare move." She began to step away, but he snagged her hand, dragging her back to him.

"You're leaving me here?" He made it sound as if she were abandoning him. Her heart rose in her throat when she recalled how she had left him in the trenches. She wondered if that day haunted him the way it did her. Every night when she lay in the dark, remembering.

You and I . . . we need to stay together. We're better this way.

"Only for a moment," Iris said, squeezing his fingers. "I'll run and fetch Peter. He has a lorry, and he can give us a ride to the infirmary, so a doctor can look at your—"

"I'm not going back to the infirmary, Iris," Roman stated. "They're overworked and there's no room for me with something as minor as a pulled stitch. I can fix it myself, if Marisol has a needle and thread."

Iris sighed. "All right. I'll take you to the B and B, so long as you don't move while I'm gone."

Roman relented with a nod. He relinquished her hand, albeit slowly, and Iris broke into a run, flying down the street and around the bend at a breakneck pace. She thankfully found Peter at home, next door to the B and B, and he agreed to drive up the bluff to give Roman a lift.

Iris stood in the back of the lorry beside a hay bale, holding on to the wooden side panel as the truck rumbled through the streets. She didn't understand why her breath continued to skip, as if her heart believed she was still running. She didn't understand why her blood was coursing, and why she was suddenly afraid.

She half expected for them to ascend the hill only to find Roman was gone. It felt like she was caught up in the pages of a strange fairy tale, and she shouldn't be foolish but shrewd, preparing for something horrible to thwart her. Because good things never lasted for long in her life. She thought about all the people who had been close to her, the threads of their lives weaving with hers—Nan, Forest, her mother—and how they had all left, either by choice or by fate.

He was about to ask me, Iris told herself, closing her eyes as they began to lurch up the hill. *Roman Kitt wants to marry me.*

She remembered the words she had written to herself, nights ago. She reminded herself that even though she had been left, time and time again, by the people she loved, Roman had come *to* her.

He was choosing her.

The lorry began to slow as Peter downshifted. There was a pop of backfire, and Iris jumped. It sounded so much like a gun firing, and her pulse spiked. She winced, fighting the urge to cower, choosing instead to open her eyes.

Roman was sitting on the milk crate just as she left him, with a scowl on his face. And a cat curled up in his lap.

Dear Kitt,

Now that your stitches are set and you've recovered from your encounter with the cat, it's time to settle two very pressing matters between us, as they both keep me up at night. Don't you agree?

—I.W.

Dear Winnow,

I have an inkling as to one of the matters, which was rudely interrupted by my damn stitches. But the other ... I want to make sure I know precisely what is stealing your sleep.

Alas, enlighten me.

Your Kitt

P.S. Is it odd we're next door to each other and still choosing to send letters through our wardrobes?

Dear Kitt,

I'm surprised you don't recall in vivid detail the previous debate you once shared with me. I was supposed to settle it once I saw you.

I think your nan will be happy with my choice.

My answer is firmly this: Knight Errant.

—I.W.

P.S. Yes, it's odd, but so much more efficient, wouldn't you agree?

Dearest Winnow,

I'm flattered. It must be the pointy chin. But as to the other matter? It must be done in person.

Your Kitt

P.S. Agreed. Although I wouldn't mind seeing you at the moment...

My Dear Kitt,

You'll have to wait to see me until tomorrow, when I plan to drag you out to the garden. No more cats and no more walks for the time being, however. Not until you heal. Then we can race to the hill, and I might beat you for once (but don't go easy on me).

And you can officially ask me tomorrow.

Love,

Iris

P.S. If you see me too much, you're bound to tire of my sad snail stories.

Dear Iris,

The garden it is.

Your Kitt

P.S. Impossible.

36

In the Garden

Iris wanted him to ask her in the garden. But there was something she needed to ask him first, and she waited to get him settled on a chair in the shade. Roman watched as she knelt in the dirt, pulling up weeds and watering row after row.

"I was thinking about something last night, Kitt," she said.

"Oh? What's that, Winnow?"

She glanced up at him. Patches of sunlight danced over his shoulders, over the striking features of his face. His dark hair almost looked blue. "I was thinking about how much time I've squandered in the past."

Roman's brow arched, but his eyes gleamed with interest. "You don't strike me as one who would 'squander' anything."

"I did a few days ago. When I came to see you in the infirmary. When I brought my letters to you." She couldn't bear to look at him as she spoke, so she created a weed to pull. "The truth is I have my pride, and I feared my feelings. And so I left you with many things unsaid, and then I put what I thought was a cushion of days between us. Time to protect myself, to put all my armor on again. But then I realized that I'm not guaranteed anything. I should know this well by now, after being in the trenches. I'm not promised this evening, let alone tomorrow. A bomb could fall from the sky any moment, and I wouldn't have had the chance to get to do this."

Roman was quiet, soaking in her rambling confession. Gently, he asked, "And what is *this* you speak of?"

She felt the irresistible draw of his gaze, and she glanced up to meet it. "Are you sure you want me to tell you?"

"*Yes,*" he said.

She wiped the dirt from her palms and stood, walking down the row to stand before him. Her hand dipped into her pocket, where a folded piece of paper waited.

"You see, Kitt," she began. "I'm quite fond of Carver. His words carried me through some of the darkest moments of my life. He was a friend I desperately needed, someone who listened and encouraged me. I have never been so vulnerable with another person. I was falling in love with him. And yet my feelings became conflicted when you arrived at Avalon, because I realized that I halfway liked you."

Roman was trying not to smile. And failing. "Is there a way to make up that difference?"

"There is, in fact." She pulled the letter from her pocket. Bloodstained and dirty. "I know you as Carver. And I know you as Roman Kitt. I want to bring the two of you together, as you should be. And there's only one way I know how to do that."

She held the letter out to him.

He accepted it, his smile waning when he realized which letter this was. As he began to retrace his words.

"Are you asking me to——"

"Read your letter aloud to me?" she finished with a grin. "Yes, Kitt. I am."

"But this letter . . ." He chuckled, raking his hand through his hair. "I say quite a few things in this particular letter."

"You do, and I want to hear you say them to me."

Roman stared at her, his eyes inscrutable. She suddenly felt the heat on her skin. A slight breeze toyed with her loose hair. And she thought, *I've asked for too much. Of course he won't do this for me.*

"Very well," he conceded. "But since we aren't guaranteed tonight, what is my reward for reading this horribly dramatic letter to you?"

"Read it first, and then perhaps we'll see."

Roman glanced back down to his words, chewing on his lip.

"If it helps," she began in a singsong voice, dropping to her knees to weed the next row. "I won't look at you as you read. You can pretend I'm not even here."

"Impossible, Iris."

"How come, Kitt?"

"Because you're highly distracting."

"Then I won't move."

"So you'll just kneel there in the dirt?"

"You're stalling, aren't you?" Iris said, looking at him again. His eyes were already on her, as if he had never looked away. Her pulse was beating like a drum, but she drew a deep breath and whispered, "Read to me, Roman."

Whatever emotion was lurking within him—fear or worry or embarrassment—faded away. He cleared his throat and dropped his eyes to the letter. His lips had already parted to read the first word when he paused, glancing back up at her.

"You're still looking at me, Iris."

"Sorry." She wasn't the least bit sorry as she directed her attention to the soil, tugging a weed loose.

"All right, here we go," Roman said. "*Dear Iris. Your rival? Who is this bloke? If he's competing with you, then he must be an utter fool. I have no doubt you will best him in every way.* I'm inserting a personal note to say: I enjoyed writing that far more than I should have."

"Yes, quite clever of you, Kitt," said Iris. "I should have known right then and there it was you."

"I actually thought you would realize it was me on the next line, the part where I say: *Now for a confession: I'm not in Oath.*"

"Need I remind you that the first time I tried to read this letter, you interrupted me because we were going to the front," she explained. "The second time I tried to read this letter, you threw paper wads at my face."

Roman laid his hand over his heart. "In my defense, Iris, I knew you were reading this here letter in the trenches and I thought it wasn't the *best* of times for my blundering confession."

"Understandable. Now, please continue."

"Gods, where was I before I interrupted myself?"

"You're only six lines in, Kitt."

He found his place and continued to read, and Iris savored the sound of his voice. She closed her eyes, his rich baritone turning the once silent words into living, breathing images. She had always wondered what Carver looked like, and now she saw him. Long fingers dancing over the keys, eyes blue as a midsummer sky, black tousled hair, a pointed chin, a teasing smile.

Roman's voice faltered. Iris opened her eyes, gazing into the sultry haze of late morning. Slowly, he continued, "*I've wanted to get it right for weeks now, but the truth is I didn't know how and I'm worried what you might think. It's odd, how quickly life can change, isn't it? How one little thing like typing a letter can open a door you never saw. A transcendent connection. A divine threshold. But if there's anything I should say in this moment—when my heart is beating wildly in my chest and I would beg you to come and tame it . . .*"

He paused.

Iris looked at him. His eyes were still fastened to his typed words until she rose from the dirt, drawing his gaze.

"*Is this,*" he whispered as she closed the distance between them. "*Your letters have been a light for me to follow. Your words? A sublime feast that fed me on days when I was starving. I love you, Iris.*"

Iris took the paper from him, folding it back into her pocket. She knew what she wanted, and yet if she thought about it too much, she might ruin everything. The fear that this might shatter was nearly overwhelming.

As if sensing her thoughts, Roman reached out, guiding her to straddle his lap.

She was wonderfully, unbearably close to him. Their faces were level, their gazes aligned. His heat seeped into her and she shifted on his thighs.

She gripped his sleeves, as if the world was spinning around them. He made a sound—a slip of breath—that made her heart race.

"I'll hurt you, Kitt!" She started to lean back, but he touched her hips, holding her steady.

"You're not going to hurt my leg," he said with a smile. "Don't worry about hurting me." He drew her closer, closer until she gasped. "Now, before we can proceed with anything else, I have a very important question for you."

"Go on," Iris said. This must be *the* moment. He was about to propose again.

Mirth shone in his eyes. "Were you serious when you told the nurse that you wouldn't snog me again?"

Iris gaped, and then she laughed. "Is *that* what you're most worried about?"

Roman's hands tightened on her hips. "I fear that once you taste something like that . . . you don't forget it, Iris. And now I must see if your words from three days ago hold, or if you will rewrite them with me here, in this moment."

She was quiet, full of heady thoughts as Roman's statement sank in. She had never wanted someone so fiercely—it nearly felt like she was falling ill—and she caressed his hair. The black strands were soft between her fingers, and Roman shut his eyes, wholly captive to her touch. She took that moment to study his face, the slant of his mouth as his breaths skipped.

"I suppose I can be persuaded to rewrite those words," she whispered in a teasing cadence, and he opened his eyes to regard her. His pupils were large and dark, like new moons. Iris could nearly see herself within them. "But only with you, Kitt."

"Because I excel at writing?" he countered.

Iris smiled. "That, among *other* things."

She kissed him—a light brushing of her lips against his—and he was still, as if she had enchanted him. But soon his mouth eagerly opened beneath hers, his hands tracing the curve of her spine. It sent a shiver through her, to feel his fingertips memorize her, to feel his teeth nip at her bottom lip as they began to explore each other.

She touched him in return, learning the broad slope of his shoulders and the dip of his collarbone and the sharp cut of his jaw. She felt like she was drowning; she felt like she had run up the bluff. There was a pleasant ache within her—bright and vibrant and molten—and she realized that she wanted to feel his skin against hers.

He broke their kiss, his eyes glazed as they briefly met hers. He pressed his mouth to her neck, as if drinking in the scent of her skin. His fingers were splayed over her back, holding her close against him, and his breath was warm on her throat.

"Marry me, Iris Elizabeth Winnow," Roman whispered, drawing back to look at her. "I want to spend all my days and all my nights with you. *Marry me.*"

Iris, heart full of fire, framed his face with her hands. She had never been this close to someone, but she felt safe with Roman. And she had not felt such safety in a long time.

"Iris . . . Iris, say something," he begged.

"Yes, I'll marry you, Roman Carver Kitt."

Roman's confidence returned, a flicker of a smile. She watched it in his eyes, like stars burning at eventide; she felt it in his body as the tension melted. He wove his fingers into her long, unruly hair and said, "I thought you'd never say yes, Winnow."

It had only been a matter of seconds.

She laughed again.

His mouth found hers, swallowing the sound.

When her blood was coursing, she ended their kiss to ask, "When are we getting married?"

"This afternoon," Roman replied without hesitation. "You said it earlier: at any moment, a bomb could drop. We don't know what tomorrow might bring."

She nodded, agreeing. But her thoughts bent to dusk. If they exchanged vows today, they would be sharing a bed together tonight. And while she had imagined being with him before . . . she was a virgin.

"Kitt, I've never slept with anyone before."

"Neither have I." He tucked a loose tendril of hair behind her ear. "But if that's something you're not ready for, then we can wait."

She could hardly speak as she caressed his face. "I don't want to wait. I want to experience this with you."

She leaned down to kiss him again.

"Do you think I need to ask Marisol for permission to marry you?" he eventually asked against her lips.

Iris smiled. "I don't know. Should you?"

"I think so. I also need Attie's approval."

They were really doing this, then. As soon as Marisol and Attie returned from the infirmary, she was going to marry Roman. She was about to say something more when the tree boughs rustled overhead. She heard the yard gate swing open, its rusty hinges whining. She heard the chimes Marisol had hanging at the terrace, a tangle of silver notes.

Iris knew it was the western wind, a surprising burst of power, blowing from the front lines.

A sense of unease came over her. It almost felt as if she and Roman were being watched, and Iris frowned, glancing around the garden.

"What is it?" Roman asked, and she heard a thread of worry in his voice.

"I just have a lot on my mind," she said, her attention returning to him. "There's so much happening right now. And I haven't even begun to work on my article."

Roman laughed. She loved the sound of it and nearly stole it from his mouth but resisted, playfully scowling at him.

"What's so funny, Kitt?"

"You and your work ethic, Winnow."

"If I remember correctly, you were one of the last people to leave the *Gazette* almost every single night."

"So I was. And you've just given me an idea."

"I have?"

He nodded. "Why don't we open the twin doors and bring our typewriters down to the kitchen? We can write at the table and enjoy this warm air while we wait for Marisol and Attie to return."

Iris narrowed her eyes. "Are you saying what I think you're saying, Kitt?"

"Yes." Roman traced the corner of her mouth with his fingertip. "Let's work together."

37

The Crime of Joy

They sat across from each other at the kitchen table, their typewriters nearly touching. Their notepads were open, stray papers with thoughts and outlines and snippets spread over the wood. It was harder than Iris had anticipated, looking over the notes she had gathered at the front. The stories of soldiers she knew were now dead.

"Any ideas on where to start?" Roman asked, as if he was feeling the same reluctance as her.

Sometimes she still dreamt of that afternoon. Sometimes she dreamt she was endlessly running through the trenches, unable to find her way out, her mouth full of blood.

Iris cleared her throat, flipping to the next page. "No."

"I suppose we could tackle this in two different ways," he said, dropping his notepad on the table. "We could write about our experiences and the timeline of the attack. Or we could edit the stories we gathered about individual soldiers."

Iris was pensive, but she felt like Roman was right. "Do you remember much, Kitt? After the grenade went off?"

Roman raked his hand through his hair, mussing it even more than it already was. "A bit, yes. I think the pain had me quite dazed, but I vividly remember you, Iris."

"So you remember how stubborn you were, then? How you insisted I grab your bag and leave you."

"I remember feeling like I was about to die, and I wanted you to know who I was," he said, meeting her gaze.

Iris fell silent, pulling a loose thread from her sleeve. "I wasn't about to let you die."

"I know," Roman said, and a smile broke over his face. "And yes. Stubborn is my middle name. Don't you know it by now?"

"I believe that name is already taken, *Carver*."

"Do you know what Carver would like right about now? Some tea."

"Make your own tea, lazybones," Iris said, but she was already rising from her chair, thankful that he had given her something to do. A moment to step away from the memories that were flooding her.

By the time she had prepared two cups, Roman had started to transcribe soldier stories. Iris decided it would be best for her to write about the actual attack, since she had been lucid the entire time.

She fed a fresh page into her typewriter and stared at its crisp blankness for a long moment, sipping her tea. It was strangely comforting to hear Roman type. She almost laughed when she remembered how it had once irked her, to know his words were flowing while she worked on classifieds and obituaries.

She needed to break this ice.

Her fingers touched the keys, tentatively at first. As if remembering their purpose.

She began to write, and the words felt slow and thick at first. But she fell into a rhythm with Roman, and soon her keys were rising and falling, the accompaniment to his, as if they were creating a metallic song together.

She caught him smiling a few times, as if he had been waiting to hear her words strike.

Their tea went cold.

Iris stopped to freshen up their cups. She noticed that the wind was still blowing. Every now and then, a tendril would sneak into the kitchen, fluttering the papers on the table. The breeze smelled like warm soil and moss and freshly cut grass, and she watched as the garden beyond danced with it.

She continued with her article, cutting up her memories and setting them back down on paper. She made it to the moment when the grenade went off and she paused, glancing up at Roman. He tended to scowl while he wrote, and there was deep furrow between his brows. But his eyes were alight, and his lips were pressed into a line, and he tilted his head to the side, so his hair would drift out of his eyes.

"See something you like?" he asked, not missing a beat. His gaze remained on his paper, his fingertips flying over the keys.

Iris frowned. "You're distracting me, Kitt."

"I'm pleased to hear it. Now you know how I've felt all this bloody time, Iris."

"If I was distracting you for such a long period of time . . . you should have done something about it."

Without another word, Roman reached for a piece of paper and crumpled it into a ball, hurling it across the table at her. Iris blocked it, eyes flashing.

"And to think I made you *two* perfect cups of tea!" she cried, crumpling her own sheet to fire back at him.

Roman caught it like it was a baseball, his eyes still on his work as one hand continued to type. "Is there any chance of a third, do you think?"

"Perhaps. But it'll come with a fee."

"I'll pay whatever you want." He stopped typing to look at her. "Tell me your price."

Iris bit her lip, wondering what she should ask for. "Are you sure about that, Kitt? What if I want you to wash my laundry for the rest of the war? What if I want you to massage my feet every night? What if I want you to make me a cup of tea every hour?"

"I can do all of that and more if you like," he said, deadly serious. "Simply tell me what you want."

She breathed, slow and deep, trying to dim the fire that seemed so eager to burn within her. That blue-hearted fire that Roman sparked. He was watching, waiting, and she dropped her eyes to where she had left her sentence hanging on the page.

The explosion. His hand being ripped from hers. The smoke that rose. Why had *she* been unscathed, when so many others hadn't? Men and women who had given so much more than her, who would never get to return home to their families, their lovers. Who would never see their next birthday, or kiss the person they least expected, or grow old and wise, watching flowers bloom in their garden.

"I don't deserve this," she whispered. She felt like she was betraying her brother. Lieutenant Lark. The Sycamore Platoon. "I don't deserve to be this happy. Not when there's so much pain and terror and loss in the world."

"Why would you say that?" Roman replied, his voice gentle but urgent. "Do you think we could live in a world made only of those things? Death and pain and horror? Loss and agony? It's not a crime to feel joy, even when things seem hopeless. Iris, look at me. You deserve all the happiness in the world. And I intend to see that you have it."

She wanted to believe him, but her fear cast a shadow. He could be killed. He could be wounded again. He could choose to leave her, like Forest. She wasn't prepared for another blow like that.

She blinked away her tears, hoping Roman couldn't see them. She cleared her throat and said, "That seems like quite a bit of trouble, doesn't it?"

"Iris," said Roman, "you are worthy of love. You are worthy to feel joy right now, even in the darkness. And just in case you're wondering . . . I'm not going anywhere, unless you tell me to leave, and even then, we might need to negotiate."

She nodded. She needed to *trust* him. She had doubted him before, and he had proven her wrong. Again and again.

Iris gave him a hint of a smile. Her chest felt heavy, but she wanted this. She wanted to be with him.

"A cup of tea," she said. "That's my fee for today."

Roman returned her smile, rising from the table. "A cup every hour, I suppose?"

"That depends on how proficient you are at brewing tea."

"Challenge accepted, Winnow."

She watched him limp to the cooker, filling the kettle at the faucet. He didn't like to use his crutch in the house, but it looked like he still needed it. She held her tongue, admiring the way the light limned him and the graceful movement of his hands.

Roman was just pouring her a cup of perfectly brewed tea when the siren sounded. Iris stiffened, listening as the distant wail rose and fell, rose and fell. Over and over, like a creature in the throes of death.

"Eithrals?" Roman asked, setting the kettle down with a clang.

"No," Iris said, standing. Her gaze was on the garden, on the breeze that raked over it. "No, this is the evacuate siren."

She had never heard it before, but she had often thought of it happening. Her feet froze to the floor as the siren continued to wail.

"Iris?" Roman's voice brought her back into the moment. He was standing beside her, intently watching her face.

"Kitt." She reached for his hand as the floor began to shake beneath her. She wondered if it was the aftershocks of a distant bomb, but the rumbling only intensified, as if something was drawing closer.

There was a loud pop, and Iris instantly cowered, teeth clenched. Roman pulled her back up, holding her against his chest. His voice was warm in her hair as he whispered, "It's just a lorry. It's just backfire. We're safe here. You're safe with me."

She closed her eyes, but she listened to the beat of his heart and the sounds encircling them. He was right; the rumbling she felt was from a lorry driving by the house. The icy sweat still prickled on her palms and at the nape of her neck, but she was able to steady herself in his arms.

Multiple lorries must be driving by. Because the siren continued to wail, and the ground continued to shake.

She opened her eyes, feeling the sudden urge to look at him. "Kitt, you don't think . . . ?"

Roman only gazed down at her, but there was a haunted gleam in his eyes.

You don't think this is Dacre's soldiers? You don't think that this is the end, do you?

He didn't know, she realized as he caressed her face. He touched her the same way he always had, as if he wanted to savor it. As if it could be the last time.

The front door blew open with a bang.

Iris startled again, but Roman kept his arms around her. Someone was in the house, striding down the corridor with a heavy tread. And then came a voice, unfamiliar yet piercing.

"Marisol!"

A woman appeared in the kitchen. A tall soldier, dressed in an olive-green blood-splattered uniform. A rifle was strapped to her back, grenades to her belt. A golden star was pinned above her heart, revealing her status as a captain. Her blond hair was cut short, but a few tendrils shone in the light beneath her helmet. Her face was gaunt as if she hadn't eaten properly over the past few months, but her brown eyes were keen, cutting across the kitchen to where Iris and Roman stood, embracing.

At once, Iris knew her. She had been kneeling in this woman's garden, preparing it for her return. "Keegan?"

"Yes. Where's my wife?" Keegan demanded. She hardly gave Iris the chance to respond before she turned on her heel, disappearing down the hallway. "Mari? *Marisol!*"

Iris slipped from Roman's arms, hurrying after her. "She's not here."

Keegan pivoted in the foyer. "Where is she?"

"At the infirmary. What's happening? Do we need to evacuate?"

"Yes." Keegan's gaze flickered beyond her, to where Roman had limped into the hallway, following them. "One of you needs to get the dash-packs ready. The other, come with me." She stepped back into the brightness of the front yard, and Iris turned to Roman.

"Marisol has the dash-packs in the pantry," she explained. "There should be four of them, one for each of us. If you'll gather them together, I'll meet you back here in a few minutes."

"Iris, *Iris,* wait." He snagged her sleeve and drew her to him, and she thought he was about to argue until his mouth crashed against hers.

She was still breathless from his kiss a full minute later, when she was chasing Keegan through the chaotic streets. There were lorries parked everywhere, and soldiers were spilling out of them, preparing for battle.

"Keegan?" Iris called, hurrying to keep pace with Marisol's wife. "What's happened?"

"Dacre is about to assault Clover Hill," Keegan replied, stepping around a man who was running home with three goats on a leash and a basket full of produce in his arms. "That's a small town only a few kilometers from here. I don't think we'll be able to hold it for long, so we expect Dacre will strike the Bluff next, within a day or so."

The words went through Iris like bullets. She felt a flash of pain in her chest, but then she went numb with shock. *This can't be happening,* she thought, even as she saw how the residents of Avalon Bluff were rushing out of their homes with suitcases and dash-packs, heeding the orders of soldiers who were telling them to load up into the lorries and evacuate.

There was one family who had dragged a huge framed portrait out of the house and into their yard. A soldier was shaking his head, saying, "No, only the essentials. Leave everything else behind."

"The residents are being evacuated by lorry?" Iris asked.

"Yes," Keegan replied, her eyes set dead ahead of them as they continued to wind through the crowded street. "They'll be driven to the next town east of here. But I'm asking for any residents who want to fight and defend the town to stay behind and assist. Hopefully, there'll be a few who volunteer."

Iris swallowed. Her mouth felt dry, and her pulse was beating hard in her throat. She wanted to stay and help, but she knew in that moment that she and Roman should evacuate.

"I never got your name," Keegan said, glancing at her.

"Iris Winnow."

Keegan's eyes widened. She tripped over a loose cobblestone, but her reaction to Iris's name was quickly stifled, which made Iris wonder if she had merely imagined it. Although she was haunted by an unspoken question . . .

Has Keegan heard of me before?

The infirmary at last came into view. Iris noticed how Keegan's strides lengthened until she was almost running. The yard was teeming with nurses and doctors assisting wounded patients into the trucks.

What should I do? Should I stay or go? Iris's thoughts helplessly rolled, just like the siren that continued to wail.

Keegan fought the flow of traffic into the infirmary hall, Iris in her shadow. Most of the cots were empty by now. Footsteps rang hollow off the high ceilings. Sunlight continued to faithfully pour into the windows, illuminating the scuffs on the floor.

The air smelled like salt and iodine and spilled onion soup. Keegan came to an abrupt halt, as if she had stepped into a wall. Iris looked beyond her to behold Marisol, a few paces away. The sun gilded her as she bent down to lift a basket of blankets, Attie at her side.

Iris held her breath, waiting. Because Keegan was like a statue, frozen to the spot, watching her wife.

At last, Marisol glanced up. Her mouth went slack, the basket tumbling from her hands. She ran to Keegan with a shriek, weeping and laughing, leaping into her arms.

Iris felt her vision blur as she watched them reunite. She dashed her tears away, but not before she met Attie's gaze.

Keegan? Attie mouthed with a grin.

Iris smiled and nodded.

And she thought, *Even when the world seems to stop, threatening to crumble, and the hour feels dark as the siren rings . . . it isn't a crime to feel joy.*

"I want you to evacuate, Mari. You'll go with one of my sergeants, and they'll take good care of you."

"No. *No,* absolutely not!"

"Marisol, darling, listen to me——"

"No, Keegan. *You* listen to *me*. I'm not leaving you. I'm not leaving our home."

Iris and Attie stood in the infirmary yard, awkwardly listening as Marisol and Keegan argued between kisses.

Keegan glanced at Iris and Attie, waving a hand toward them. "And what of your girls, Mari? Your correspondents?"

Marisol paused. A stricken expression overcame her face when she looked at Iris and Attie.

"I want to stay," Attie said. "I can help in any way I'm needed."

Iris hesitated. "I also want to stay, but with Kitt's injury . . ."

"You should evacuate with him," Marisol said gently. "Keep him safe."

Iris nodded, torn. She didn't want to leave Attie and Marisol. She wanted to stay and help them fight, defending the place that had become a beloved home to her. But she couldn't bear to leave Roman.

Keegan broke the tense moment by drawling to her wife, "So you can want Iris and her Kitt to be safe, but the same can't be said for me over *you*?"

"I'm old, Keegan," Marisol argued. "They're still young."

"Marisol!" Attie cried. "You're only thirty-three!"

Marisol sighed. She stared up at Keegan and said firmly, "I'm not leaving. My girls can do whatever they feel is best."

"Very well," Keegan conceded, rubbing her brow. "I know better than to argue with you."

Marisol only smiled.

"I suppose Kitt and I should catch a ride on one of the lorries?" Iris said, the words thick in her mouth. Her guilt flared as she glanced down at her hands, lined with garden dirt and smudged by ink ribbons.

"Yes," Keegan said, her tone grave. "But before you go, I have something for you."

Iris watched, spellbound, as the captain reached into her pocket, withdrawing what looked to be a letter. Keegan extended the envelope to her, and for a moment, all Iris could do was stare at it. A letter, addressed to her, wrinkled from war.

"What is this?" Iris faintly asked. But her heart knew, and it pounded in dread. This was the answer she had been waiting for. An update on her brother.

"It got sorted with my post," Keegan explained. "I think because your address is Avalon Bluff. I was going to mail it along with my letter to Marisol, but then we were on the move and I'm sorry I wasn't able to send it to you sooner."

Numb, Iris accepted the letter. She stared at it—her name scrawled in dark ink over the envelope. It wasn't Forest's handwriting, and Iris suddenly thought she might be sick.

She turned away from her friends, uncertain if she should read it in their presence or go find a private place. She took four steps away and then thought her knees might give out, so she halted. Her hands were icy, even as she squinted against the brunt of the sun, and she finally opened the envelope.

She read:

Dear Iris,

Your brother was indeed fighting in the Second E Battalion, Fifth Landover Company, under Captain Rena G. Griss. He was unfortunately wounded in the Battle of Lucia River and was taken via transport to an infirmary in the town of Meriah. As his captain was one of the casualties, this news failed to reach you.

A fortnight later, Meriah came under fire, but Private Winnow was evacuated in time. As his injuries were sustained some months ago and his entire company perished at Lucia River, he was incorporated into a new auxiliary force and is fighting bravely for Enva's cause. If any further news of his current station reaches my desk, I will pass it onto you.

Lt. Ralph Fowler
Assistant to the Commanding Officer of the E Brigade

"Iris?"

She pivoted, blinking away her tears as Marisol touched her shoulder.

"My brother," Iris whispered, overcome with hope. "He was wounded, but he's *alive*, Marisol. That's why I never heard from him, all these months."

Marisol gasped, drawing Iris into an embrace. Iris clung to her, battling the sob of relief that threatened to split her chest.

"Good news?" Keegan asked.

Iris nodded, slipping from Marisol's arms. "How far away is Meriah?" she asked Keegan.

A shadow passed over the captain's face. She must be remembering the battles, the bloodshed. How many soldiers had died.

"About eighty kilometers," Keegan replied. "Southwest of here."

"So not that far," Iris whispered, tracing the bow of her lips. Forest was fighting with another company. One that might be near Avalon Bluff.

"Iris?" Attie said, breaking her reverie. "Does this mean you're staying?"

Iris opened her mouth to respond, but the words hung in her throat. She glanced from Attie to Keegan to Marisol, and then blurted, "I need to speak to Kitt."

"You'd best hurry," Keegan said. "The last evacuee lorry will be leaving soon."

Her announcement sent a shock wave through Iris. She nodded and turned, sprinting down the street. The town still felt frantic, but lorries of residents were beginning to drive away, pressing east. Iris jumped over a discarded suitcase, over a sack of dropped potatoes, over a crate of tinned vegetables.

High Street was surprisingly quiet. Most of the residents here had already been transported, but as Iris drew closer to the B and B, she saw that the front door was wide open.

"That should do it, Kitt. Thank you, son."

Iris slowed to a walk, her eyes following the voice. It was Peter, the next-door neighbor. He and Roman were loading possessions into the back of his small lorry.

"Happy to help, sir," Roman was saying, securing the crate. As Iris approached, she could see his jumpsuit was dampened with sweat. She reflexively looked at his right leg, worried she would find blood seeping through the fabric again.

"Kitt," she said, and he turned. She watched the tension in his posture ease at the sight of her, and he reached for her hand, pulling her closer.

"Is everything all right?" he asked.

"Yes." But the words seemed to crumble, and she quietly handed Roman the letter.

He frowned, confused until he began to read. When he looked at Iris again, his eyes glistened with tears.

"Iris."

"I know," she said, smiling. "Forest is alive, and he's with another company." Iris swallowed. She couldn't believe she was about to say these words. She couldn't believe that she was standing in such a moment, one that could seal her fate. "I was planning to evacuate with you. But after this letter, I need to stay here. The whole reason why I became a correspondent was for Forest. He is the last of my family, and I traveled west in the hopes that my path would cross with his. And now that I know he could be heading this way, preparing to defend Avalon Bluff against Dacre . . . I have to stay and help."

Roman's arm tightened around her as he listened. His eyes were so blue they pierced her to the bone, and she wondered what sort of expression was on her face. She wondered what he saw in her, if she looked determined or frightened or worried or brave.

"I won't ask you to remain here with me," Iris continued, her voice wavering. "In fact, I know it's best if you go, because you're still recovering, and most of all, I want you to be safe."

"I came here for you, Iris," Roman said. "If you stay behind, then so will I. I'm not leaving you."

She sighed, surprised by the relief she felt to hear his decision—he wasn't going to abandon her, no matter what the next day brought—and she wrapped her arms around his waist. And yet she couldn't help but glance down at his leg again.

"Can I give you two a lift?" Peter asked. "My wife will be in the cab, but if you want to sit in the back, there's room."

"No, but thank you, Mr. Peter," Roman replied. "We're staying put to help."

Iris watched as Peter and his wife drove away with a cloud of exhaust. She felt a pit in her stomach, and she wondered if she was making a huge mistake, if she would come to regret this decision to stay. To resist flying to the east with Roman when she still had the chance.

The street fell quiet and still, save for a few soldiers marching by. A newspaper fluttered over the cobblestones. A bird trilled from the hedges.

Iris began to walk back to Marisol's, her hand in Roman's. She thought about the wedding they had been so close to having. How they had been mere hours from weaving their lives together. How everything had just changed, as if the world had turned inside out.

But Forest is alive.

She clung to the hope of seeing him, of their paths crossing. Even if it seemed improbable in the chaos that was bound to unfold.

Quietly, Iris and Roman returned to the kitchen. Their typewriters sat on the table, and the twin doors leading to the terrace remained open just as they had left them. A breeze had stolen into the room and blown a few loose papers onto the floor.

Iris, uncertain what else she should be doing while she waited for Keegan and Marisol and Attie, knelt and began to clean up the mess. Roman was saying something, but her attention was snared by one of the papers on the floor. There was a muddy boot print on it.

She held the paper up to the light, studying the mark.

"What's wrong, Winnow?" Roman asked.

"Did you walk over these papers with dirty boots, Kitt?"

"No. The papers were on the table when I left to help Peter. Here, let me see that."

She handed the page to him and realized there was another sheet on the floor with a boot mark. Iris stood, her eyes straying to the open doors. She followed the light to the terrace and stood on the threshold, studying the backyard.

The gate was open, creaking in the wind. The tree boughs groaned. The chimes sang. And there were boot marks, marring the garden. Someone had tromped directly through it, over the carefully tended rows and sprouting plants.

Iris clenched her jaw, staring at the path. All that hard work and devotion and toil. Someone had stridden through it without a second thought.

She felt Roman's warmth as he stood close behind her. She felt his breath stir her hair as he saw the trail.

"Someone came into the house," he murmured.

She didn't know what to say, what to think. It had been tumultuous when the infantry arrived in the lorries. Residents had been given only a handful of minutes to evacuate. It could have been anyone in the backyard.

Iris knelt and quickly began to smooth over the tracks, fixing the garden before Keegan returned. She wanted it to be perfect for her. She wanted to make Marisol proud.

The siren at Clover Hill finally fell silent.

38

The Eve of Enva's Day

Where are the other dash-packs?" Marisol asked. They were the first thing she looked for when she returned to the B and B with Attie and Keegan. She picked up the two burlap bags that were sitting on the kitchen counter, eventually glancing to where Iris and Roman were cleaning off the table.

Roman paused. "They should all be there, Marisol. I laid out four of them."

"That's odd," Marisol said with a frown. "Because there are only two."

Iris watched as Marisol searched the rest of the kitchen, her pulse dropping. "Marisol? I think someone must have stolen them."

"Stolen them?" Marisol echoed, as if the thought of stealing in Avalon Bluff was unheard of. "What makes you think that, Iris?"

"Because there were footprints in the garden, leading into the house."

"Garden?" Keegan said, glancing at her wife. "Did you actually plant one, Mari?"

"Of course I did! I told you I would. But it wouldn't have happened with quite a bit of help."

"Show me."

Attie was closest to the doors; she led the way into the afternoon light.

It was strange, how quiet the world felt now. Even the wind had abated, Iris noticed as she followed the others out onto the terrace.

Keegan let out a low whistle. "It looks nice. You remembered to water it this time, Marisol."

Marisol playfully nudged Keegan's arm. "Yes, well, it wouldn't have happened without Iris and Attie."

"Indeed. And I see what you were talking about, Iris." Keegan walked to one of the rows, crouching down to trace the lump in the soil. "You covered up their trail?"

"Yes, because I wanted the garden to look nice for you," Iris explained in a rush. "But I have a perfect imprint of the boot." She brought the dirt-marked paper to Keegan.

Keegan studied it with a frown. "A soldier's boot, then. They must have come into the house during the evacuation and taken two of the dash-packs. I'm surprised. My company knows better. They never steal from civilians."

"It's fine," Marisol said. "Whoever it was must have needed resources, and I'm glad to have given to someone in need. I can easily make three more bags. In fact, I'll do that right now."

"Three more?" Keegan said, gently grasping Marisol's arm to stop her. "You only need to make two, darling."

"Yes, and one for you as well," Marisol replied with a smile. "Since you're here with us now."

"Of course." Keegan loosened her grip and Marisol retreated to the kitchen. But Iris saw the sadness that flickered through the captain's eyes as she glanced at the garden again. As if she sensed this might be the last time she would enjoy it.

Everything was changing.

Iris could taste it in the air, as if the season had crumbled like an ancient page, skipping summer and autumn to usher in the creeping chill of winter. Soldiers were stationed everywhere in their olive-green uniforms and helmets, preparing the town for the imminent battle. Barricades now sat in the streets, made of sandbags, mismatched furniture salvaged from residents' homes, and anything else that could grant coverage.

The town no longer felt like a haven but like a snare, as if they were waiting to catch a monster.

As if Dacre himself might walk into the Bluff.

And what if he did? What did his face look like? Would Iris know him if their paths crossed?

She thought of Enva and her harp. The power of her music, deep in the earth.

Enva, where are you? Will you help us?

Iris made herself useful to Marisol, who was in the kitchen preparing meals for the platoons, and assisted with Keegan's quest to create as many strategic barricades as possible in the streets, but there was a quiet moment when Iris remembered her mother and her ashes that were held in a jar upstairs on her desk.

If I die tomorrow, my mother's ashes will never have found a resting place.

The words were serrated, making every passing minute feel dire. More than anything, Iris wanted to see her mother set free.

She took the jar and approached Keegan, because her soldiers had set up a watch around the town and no one could get in or out without special permission.

"How much longer do we have?" Iris asked the captain. "Before Dacre arrives?"

Keegan was quiet, staring into the west. "He'll take the rest of today to fully sack Clover Hill. I predict he'll march for the Bluff by tomorrow morning."

Iris released a tremulous breath. One final day to do the things she wanted, she needed, she *longed* to accomplish. It was wild to imagine it— the remaining span of golden hours. She decided she would do everything she could, filling this last day to the brim.

Surprised by the lapse into silence, Keegan at last glanced at Iris, noticing the jar she held in her hands. "Why do you ask, Iris?"

"I would like to spread my mother's ashes before then."

"Then you should do so, now. But take your boy with you," Keegan said.

Iris asked Roman and Attie to accompany her to the golden field.

A slight breeze stirred, blowing from the east.

Iris closed her eyes.

Not so long ago, she had arrived at this place, full of grief and guilt and fear. And while those things still dwelled in her, they were not as sharp as they had been.

I hope you see me, Mum. I hope you're proud of me.

She opened the lid and overturned the jar.

She watched as her mother's ashes were carried by the wind, into the golden dance of the grass.

"Do either of you know how to drive a lorry?" Keegan asked half an hour later.

Iris and Attie exchanged a dubious look. They had just finished carrying a table from Peter's house out into the street.

"No," Iris said, wiping sweat from her brow.

"All right, well, come on then. I'm going to teach you both."

Iris glanced over her shoulder at the B and B, where Marisol was still cooking in the kitchen. Roman had been assigned to help her, and Iris was grateful, knowing Marisol had him peeling potatoes at the kitchen table.

He probably was stewing about it, but he needed to rest his leg.

Iris followed Attie and Keegan around the barricades to the eastern edge of the town, where lorry after lorry was parked. Keegan chose a truck that was situated at the front of the lot, with a clear path to the eastern road.

"Who wants to go first?" Keegan asked, opening the driver's door.

"I will," Attie said, before Iris could even draw a breath. She climbed up into the driver's seat while Iris and Keegan crammed into the other side of the cab. A few soldiers stationed on this side of town had to open a make-shift gate, but then there was nothing but wide-open road before them.

"Turn on the ignition," Keegan said.

Iris watched as Attie cranked the engine. The lorry roared to life.

"Now, do you know how a clutch operates?"

"Yes." Attie sounded a bit hesitant, but her hands were on the steering wheel and her eyes were taking quick inventory of the dash and the levers.

"Good. Put your foot on that pedal. Push it in."

Iris watched as Attie heeded Keegan's instructions. Soon they were bouncing along the road, Avalon Bluff nothing more than a cloud of dust behind them. First, second, third gear. Attie was able to shift seamlessly between them, and when they were traveling so fast that Iris's teeth were rattling, Attie let out a triumphant whoop.

"Very good. Now gear back down to neutral and park it," Keegan said.

Attie did so, and then it was Iris's turn.

Her palms were damp as she took the steering wheel. Her foot could barely reach the gas pedal, let alone the clutch she had to push to the floorboard.

It was . . . disastrous.

She nearly ran the lorry off the road twice, killed the engine at least four times, and was spouting off a stream of curses by the time Keegan took over.

"A little more practice, and you'll be fine," the captain said. "You get the general idea, and that's all that matters."

Iris slid into the passenger seat with Attie, and they were quiet as Keegan drove them back into town. The makeshift gate closed behind them, and soon the lorry was parked where it had been before, its nose pointing to the east.

Keegan turned off the engine, but she didn't move. She stared out the dust-streaked windshield and said, "If things go badly here, I want to the two of you to take Marisol and that Kitt of yours and flee in this lorry. If you have to drive through this gate to get out, don't hesitate to run over it. And you don't stop for anything. You drive east until you're safe." She paused, setting her dark gaze on the girls. "Marisol has a sister who lives in a small town called River Down, about fifty kilometers west of Oath. Go there first. You stay together and you prepare for the worst. But you have to get Marisol out of here for me. Do you swear it?"

Iris's mouth was suddenly dry. She stared at the captain—at the hard edges of her face and the scars on her hands—and she hated this war. She hated that it was dragging good people early to their graves, that it was tearing people's lives and dreams apart.

But she nodded and spoke in unison with Attie.

"I swear it."

They were delegated as runners after that.

Attie and Iris ran through the winding streets of Avalon Bluff, delivering meals and messages and anything else that either Marisol or Keegan needed. Iris had come to know this town like the lines on her palm, and she often ran the same routes she had with Roman when he had been training her. When they had run with the dawn. She was pleased to discover how much her stamina had improved since that first jog.

She only wished he could run beside her now.

The platoon stationed on the bluff needed a meal, and Iris and Attie ran to deliver it to them. Afternoon clouds were beginning to swell, blocking the sunlight, and Iris could smell a hint of smoke on the wind. She knew why when she reached the crest of the summit.

In the distance, Clover Hill was burning.

She delivered the baskets of food to the soldiers, studying each of their faces just in case Forest was among them. He wasn't, but her hope remained like iron within her, even when she stood and watched the smoke rise in the distance. She wondered if there had been any survivors in Clover Hill, or if Dacre had slaughtered them all.

"How much longer until Dacre comes for us, do you think?" Attie asked, coming to a stop beside her. The land that sprawled between them and Clover Hill was peaceful, idyllic. Its innocence was deceiving.

"Keegan said he would come tomorrow morning," Iris replied. They still had four hours of sunlight remaining in the day, and then night would come. Beyond that, Iris could only imagine.

In some ways, this quiet stretch of waiting was more difficult to bear. Hour after hour of wondering and preparing and anticipating. Who would die? Who would live? Would they be able to successfully hold the town? Would Dacre burn it to the ground, like Clover Hill?

"If things go bad and we have to uphold our vow to Keegan," Attie began. "I'll grab Marisol. You grab Roman. We'll meet at the lorry."

"How do we know when things are bad *enough*?" Iris asked, licking her lips. She could taste the salt of her sweat. "At what point do we know *when* to flee?" She had wanted to pose this question to Keegan but had swiftly swallowed it, worried that the captain would think it unnecessary. *Shouldn't you know when things are bad enough?*

"I'm not sure, Iris," Attie replied grimly. "But I think in the moment . . . we'll just *know*."

Iris felt something brush her ankle. She startled as she heard a sorrowful meow, and she glanced down to see a calico cat rubbing against her legs.

"Why, look here!" Attie cried, delightedly scooping up the cat. "A good luck charm!"

"I didn't realize cats brought favor," Iris said, but she smiled as she watched Attie coo over the feline.

"Who do you think she belongs to?" Attie asked. "A stray, do you think?"

"I think she's one of the O'Briens' cats. They had about seven. I'm guessing this one was left behind when they evacuated." It looked suspiciously like the very cat that had been curled up in Roman's lap the day before. Iris reached out and scratched behind its ears, craving to touch something soft and gentle.

"Well, she's coming home with me. Aren't you, Lilac?" Attie began to walk down the hill, purring cat in her arms.

"Lilac?" Iris echoed, following. She passed the O'Briens' yard. The crate where she had appointed Roman to wait for her was long gone, harvested for the barricades. It felt so strange, to realize how much could change in a day.

"Yes. My favorite flower," Attie said, glancing back at Iris. "Second only to an iris, of course."

Iris smiled, shaking her head. But her happiness dimmed as she continued along the path back to the B and B, around barricades and chains of soldiers. As she watched Attie speak affectionately to the cat.

It was just one more thing they would need to grab if things fell apart.

"You brought a *cat* back with you?" Roman exclaimed. He was sitting at the kitchen table, peeling a mountain of potatoes. His eyes flickered from Attie to the cat to finally rest on Iris, his gaze rushing up and down her body, as if he was searching for a new scratch on her.

Iris flushed when she realized she was doing the same to him—searching his every bend and line to ensure he was all right. She felt heat crackle through her when their gazes united.

"Yes," Attie said, her embrace tightening around Lilac. The cat emitted a plaintive meow. "The poor thing was on the hill all alone."

"In case you didn't know, I'm allergic to cats," Roman drawled.

"I'll keep Lilac in my room. I promise."

"And if her fur gets on your jumpsuit, I'll wash it for you," Iris offered. If cats truly were good luck charms, they were going to need it.

"Then I'd have *nothing* to wear," Roman said, returning his attention to the potato in his hand. "Because my second jumpsuit is missing."

"What?" Iris breathed. "What do you mean, Kitt?"

"I mean it was hanging in my wardrobe this morning, and now it's gone."

She continued to study him, realizing his dark hair was damp, slicked back like in the old days at the office. His face was freshly shaven, his nails scrubbed clean. She could smell a faint trace of his cologne, and her heart quickened.

"Did you just take a *shower,* Kitt?" It was the most ridiculous thing she could've asked, but it felt so strange to her. That he would wash in the middle of the day, when things were about to collapse. Although perhaps it shouldn't take her by surprise. He had always liked to look his best. Why should the end of the world change that?

Roman met her gaze. He didn't say anything, but a flush was creeping across his cheeks, and before Iris could say anything further about it, Marisol strode through the kitchen and set a heavy basket of carrots in her hands. "Peel and chop these for me, please, Iris."

That ended the deliveries and building barricades and running through the streets and imagining Roman Kitt in the shower. As the sun began to set, they all worked together to make several pots of vegetable soup and fresh bread for the soldiers.

Iris's stomach was growling by the time Marisol said, "Attie? Why don't you see if Iris can help you with that particular matter upstairs."

"Right," Attie said, jumping up from her chair. "Come on, Iris."

Iris frowned but rose. "What do you need my help with?"

"It's hard to explain, so just follow me," Attie said, waving her hands. But she glanced over Iris's shoulder and widened her eyes, and Iris turned just in time to see Roman drop his gaze.

"What's going on, Attie?" Iris asked, trailing her up the stairs. It was almost dusk.

"In here," Attie said, stepping into the lavatory.

Iris stood on the threshold, confounded, as Attie turned on the faucet. "Why don't you shower while I go and find—"

"*Shower?*" Iris demanded. "Why would I shower at a time like this?"

"Because you've been running up and down a hill all day and cutting up carrots and parsnips and onions and your jumpsuit smells like lorry exhaust," Attie said. "Trust me, Iris. Use the fresh shampoo there, in that tin."

She shut the door, leaving Iris in the steamy room.

Iris shed her jumpsuit and stepped into the shower. She would go quickly, because there was still so much left to do. But then she studied the dirt beneath her nails and thought of Roman. A curious feeling stole over her, inspiring a shiver.

She took her time washing, until every trace of onion and exhaust and sweat and dirt was gone, and she smelled like gardenias with a hint of lavender. She was drying her hair when Attie knocked.

"I have a clean jumpsuit for you."

Iris opened the door to find Attie standing with a pressed jumpsuit in one hand, a crown of flowers in the other.

"All right," Iris said, her gaze hanging on the flowers. "What's going on?"

"Here, get dressed. I need to braid your hair." Attie stepped into the lavatory, shutting the door behind her.

Iris intended to protest until Attie arched her brow. Iris meekly drew on the jumpsuit and fastened the buttons up the front. She sat on a stool so Attie could tame her hair into two thick braids, which she clipped up to crown her head with pearl-tipped pins. It was similar to how Marisol wore her hair, and Iris thought she looked older when she caught her reflection in the mirror.

"Now for the best part," Attie said, gathering the flowers. They were freshly cut, woven together. Daisies and dandelions and violets. Flowers that grew wild in the garden.

Iris held her breath as Attie set the flowers over her braids.

"There. You look beautiful, Iris."

"Attie, *what's* happening?"

Attie smiled, squeezing Iris's hands. "He asked for my approval. At first I said I wasn't sure if I could grant it, because you were falling in love with a boy named Carver who wrote you enchanting, soul-stirring letters, and how on earth could Kitt even compare to that? Upon which he informed me that he *is* Carver and showed me proof. And what else could I say but yes, you have my approval, a hundred times over."

Iris breathed, slow and deep. But her heart was dancing, stirring a heady song in her blood.

"When?" she panted. "When did he ask you?"

"When we were delivering food earlier today. You ran out ahead of me at one point, remember? And yes, he's already asked for Marisol's permission. Even Keegan's. He's very thorough, that Kitt of yours."

Iris closed her eyes, hardly able to believe it. "You don't think this is foolish, do you? With Dacre on his way? For me to be celebrating when death is coming?"

"Iris," Attie said, "it only makes this all the more beautiful. The two of you have found each other against great odds. And if this is your one and only night with him, then savor it."

Iris met Attie's gaze. "Are you telling me . . ."

Attie smiled, tugging on her hand. "I'm telling you that Roman Carver Kitt is in the garden, waiting to marry you."

39

Vows in the Dark

Roman stood with Keegan and Marisol at the edge of the garden, watching the light fade. The vows would have to be quick, Keegan had warned him earlier, which sounded perfectly fine to him. He had been shocked by how supportive and excited everyone had been about his plans. He thought for sure one of them would say, *No, there are more important things at hand, Roman. Look around you! There's no time for a wedding.*

He had been met by the opposite, as if Attie and Marisol and Keegan were eager for something to lift the heaviness of their spirits.

He continued to wait for Iris, and he didn't know what to expect, but the moment he saw her walk through the doors with her hair swept up, adorned with flowers . . . he felt a rush of pride. Of immense joy, so deep there was no end to it, nor a way to measure it. He felt it break across his face in a wide smile, create a skip in his breath.

Attie brought her to him over the stone pathway, and there was a brightness in Iris's eyes he had never seen before. It seemed like he waited hours for her, and yet it only felt like a breath had passed when Iris reached for his hand.

She was warm, flushed from her shower. Her palm was like silk in his.

Roman studied her face. He wanted to memorize it, the way she looked in the dusk. *We are really doing this,* he thought with a shiver. They were getting married in their jumpsuits on the eve of battle, six hundred kilometers away from home.

He didn't know why she suddenly began to blur. Why her edges melted before him, as if she were a vision. A dream about to fade. Not until he blinked and tears slipped down his face.

He hadn't cried in years. He hadn't cried since Del. He had kept his feelings tightly locked away since then, as if it were wrong to set them free. As if they were a weakness, bound to ruin him.

But now that his tears were falling, it was like a dam had been breached. A small crack, and those old feelings of guilt flowed forth. He wanted to let them go; he didn't want to bring all this baggage into his marriage with Iris. But he didn't know how to be free of it, and he realized she would simply have to take him as he was.

"Roman," Iris whispered tenderly. She rose on her toes and framed his face. She wiped his tears, and he let them fall until he could see her again, vividly.

And he thought, *What have you done to me?*

"Are we ready?" Keegan asked.

He had nearly forgotten about Keegan with her little book of vows, and Marisol with the two rings, and Attie with her basket of flowers.

But the stars were emerging overhead. The sun had retreated behind the hill; the clouds bled gold. It was almost dark.

"Yes," he whispered, never taking his eyes from Iris.

"Take each other's hands," Keegan said. "And repeat after me."

Iris let her hands slip back into his. Her fingers were damp from his tears.

The vows they spoke to each other were ancient. Words once carved in stone during a time when all the gods lived and roamed the earth.

"I pray that my days will be long at your side. Let me fill and satisfy every longing in your soul. May your hand be in mine, by sun and by night. Let our breaths twine and our blood become one, until our bones return to dust. Even then, may I find your soul still sworn to mine."

"Beautiful," Keegan said, turning to her wife. "Now for the rings."

Marisol had found these rings in her jewelry box. She had told Roman that the silver band that had once been her aunt's would fit Iris. And the copper ring was for him, to wear on his smallest finger. Just until he could get them proper matching bands.

Iris's brows raised in surprise when Marisol gave her the copper ring. She obviously hadn't expected they would still get married this day, let alone have rings to exchange, and she slipped it on his pinkie. Roman quickly returned the favor, sliding the silver onto her finger. It was a bit loose, but it would do for now.

He liked to see it on her hand, gleaming in the light.

"And now to conclude our service," Keegan said, shutting the book, "seal your vows with a kiss."

"*At last,*" Roman said, despite the fact their vows had taken only half a minute.

Iris laughed. Gods, he loved the sound, and he drew her closer. He kissed her thoroughly; his tongue brushed against hers, and he reveled in the slight gasp she gave him.

His blood was pounding, but they still had to eat dinner. Marisol had insisted on it. And so he broke the kiss.

Attie cheered, tossing flowers over them. Roman watched the petals cascade like snow, catching in their hair. Iris smiled, weaving her fingers with his.

He thought about who he had been before he had met her. Before she had stepped into the *Gazette*. Before her letter had crossed his wardrobe door. He thought about who he wanted to be now that her hand was in his.

He would always be grateful for his decision that night, not so long ago. The night when he decided to write her back.

Marisol sat them down, side by side, at the table. Iris was hungry, but she was also so excited and nervous that she wasn't sure how much she'd be able to eat.

"Soup and bread tonight," Marisol said, setting two bowls down before them. "Simple fare, but it should be enough, I hope?"

"This is perfect, Marisol," Iris said. "Thank you."

Not long after that, soldiers began to file in, partaking in a quick meal before they returned to their stations. The B and B was soon hot and crowded, brimming with candlelight and low murmurs. Iris continued to sit close beside Roman, her hand in his, resting on his thigh.

"I hear someone got married tonight," one of the soldiers said with a smile.

Iris blushed when Roman held up his hand. "I'm the lucky one."

That set off a round of cheers and claps, and Iris was amazed to find this felt normal, like any other night. And yet tomorrow was Enva's Day, the end of the week. Anything could happen, and Iris tried to bury her worries. She wanted to simply enjoy the present. *This* was the life she wanted—slow and easy and vibrant, surrounded by people she loved.

If only she could bottle this moment. If only she could drink from it in the days to come, to remember this feeling of warmth and wholeness and joy. As if all of her pieces had come back together, far stronger than they had been before she had broken.

She realized this was her family now. That there were bonds that ran deeper than blood.

All too soon, the B and B fell quiet.

The soldiers had come and gone. The last of the soup and bread had been devoured, and the dishes were sitting in the wash bin. Candles burned on the kitchen table; the light flickered over Roman's face as he leaned closer to Iris, whispering in her ear, "Are you ready for bed?"

"Yes," she said, and her heart pounded. "But perhaps we should wash the dishes first?"

"You'll do no such thing!" Marisol cried, aghast. "The two of you will go on to bed and enjoy your night."

"But, Marisol," Iris was beginning to protest when Roman stood, tugging her upward.

"I won't hear of it, Iris," Marisol insisted.

"Nor will I," Attie said, crossing her arms. "And besides, Roman's room is ready for you both."

"What?" Iris panted.

Attie only winked before turning to the wash bin. Marisol shooed them into the hall, where they passed Keegan returning from a quick errand.

The captain gave them a nod and a smirk, and Iris was suddenly sweating as she began to ascend the stairs with Roman.

"Sorry, I'm quite slow," he said, wincing as he took another step.

Iris held his hand, waiting for him to catch up.

"Do your wounds still hurt?" she asked.

"Not too much," he replied. "I just don't want to pull another stitch."

His response worried her. She had an inkling he was hiding how much his leg bothered him, and she decided that they would have to be careful that night.

They reached Roman's room. Iris braced herself, uncertain what she would encounter. She stepped inside and gasped.

A host of candles were lit, filling the room with romantic light. Stray flowers had been dropped along the floor and on the bed, which was still a pallet since the mattress was at the infirmary. But it looked like Attie had added a few more blankets to the pile, creating a soft place for them to sleep.

"It's beautiful," Iris whispered.

"And much appreciated," Roman said, shutting the door. "I sadly can take no credit for this. It was all Attie."

"Then I'll have to thank her tomorrow," Iris said, turning to glance at Roman.

His gaze was already fixed on her.

Iris swallowed, feeling awkward. She didn't know if she should go ahead and undress, or maybe he wanted to undress her. Sometimes his face was hard to read, as if he wore a mask, and before she could reach for the top button of her jumpsuit, he spoke.

"I have a request, Winnow."

"Gods, Kitt," she said before she could stop herself. "What now?"

The corner of his mouth lifted, amused. "Come and sit next to me on our bed." He walked past her and knelt on the pile of blankets, careful of his leg as he situated himself with his back against the wall.

Iris followed but chose to unlace and remove her boots before she stepped on the blankets. She helped Roman with his, and so that was the first article of clothing removed between them. Their shoes.

She settled beside him. His heat began to seep into her side, and she realized how brilliant this was going to be, sleeping next to him every night. She would never get cold again.

"All right, Kitt," she said. "What is your request?"

"I would like you to read something to me."

"Oh? And what is this *something*?"

"One of your letters."

That caught her by surprise. She cracked her knuckles but thought it was only fair of her to return the favor to him. "Yes, all right. But only one. So choose wisely."

He smiled down at her, his hand reaching to the floor beside the pallet.

"You keep my letters at your bedside?" she asked.

"I reread most of them every night."

"You do?"

"Yes. Here it is. This is the one," he said, handing her a very wrinkled piece of paper.

She smoothed the creases from the letter, skimming a few lines. Ah yes. *This* one. Iris cleared her throat, but she glanced up at Roman before she began. He was intently watching her.

"There's one stipulation, Kitt."

"I can't look at you while you read," he surmised, remembering his own dilemma.

Iris nodded and he shut his eyes, leaning his head against the wall.

She returned her gaze to the paper. She began to read, and her voice was deep and smoky, as if she were pulling the words from her past. From a night when she had been sitting on the floor of her room.

"I think we all wear armor. I think those who don't are fools, risking the pain of being wounded by the sharp edges of the world, over and over again. But if I've learned anything from those fools, it is that to be vulnerable is a strength most of us fear. It takes courage to let down your armor, to welcome people to see you as you are.

Sometimes I feel the same as you: I can't risk having people behold me as I truly am. But there's also a small voice in the back of my mind, a voice that tells me, 'You will miss so much by being so guarded.'"

She paused, emotion rising in her throat. She didn't dare look at Roman. She didn't know if his eyes were open or still shut as she continued, reaching the end.

"All right, now I've let the words spill out. I've given you a piece of armor, I suppose. But I don't think you'll mind," she finished, folding the letter back up. "There. Does that satisfy you, Kitt?"

He took the letter back. "Yes. Although there is another one I'd like you to read. Where did I put it . . . ?"

"Another one? At this rate, you'll have to read a second letter to me, then."

"I accept those terms. This one is quite short, and it might be my favorite." He found it, holding the paper between them.

She was curious. She accepted it and was just about to glance over this letter when a firm knock rattled the door, startling them both. Her stomach dropped when she imagined all the reasons why someone might be interrupting them. *Dacre has been spotted. It's time to retreat. It's the beginning of the end.*

She met Roman's gaze. She saw the same dread in his countenance. That their time had been cut short. They had managed to speak their vows but never had the chance to fulfill them.

"Roman? Iris?" Marisol's voice called through the wood. "I'm so sorry to interrupt, but Keegan has issued a blackout for the town. No electricity and no candlelight for the rest of the night, I'm afraid."

Roman was frozen for a second. And then he said, "Yes, of course! Not a problem, Marisol."

Iris scrambled to her feet, blowing out the countless candles Attie had lit for them. The flames died, one by one, until only one candle remained burning, held in Roman's hand.

Iris returned to their bed. She sat facing him this time, the letter still in her fingers.

"Read it to me quickly, Iris," he said.

A shiver coursed through her. She felt like sugar melting in tea. She dropped her gaze to the letter and softly read, "*I'll return most likely when the war is over. I want to see you. I want to hear your voice.*"

She looked at Roman again. Their gazes held while he blew out the candle. The darkness rushed in, surrounding them. And yet Iris had never seen so many things before.

She whispered, "I want to touch you."

"Now *that* wasn't in the letter," he said wryly. "I would have framed it on the wall had it been."

"Alas," she countered. "I wanted to write it to you then. I didn't, though, because I was afraid."

He was quiet for a beat. "What were you afraid of?"

"My feelings for you. The things I wanted."

"And now?"

She reached out and found his ankle. Slowly, her fingers drifted up to his knee. She could feel the bandages beneath his jumpsuit; she could see his wounds in her mind, the way they would scar. She said, "I think you've made me brave, Kitt."

His breath escaped him, a tenuous unspooling, as if he had been holding it in years for her. "My Iris," he said, "there is no question that you are the brave one, all on your own. You were writing to me for *weeks* before I roused the courage to write you back. You walked into the *Gazette* and took me and my ego on without a blink. You were the one who came to the front lines, unafraid to look into the ugly face of war long before I did. I don't know who I would be without you, but you have made me in all ways better than I ever was or could have ever hoped to be."

"I think you and I are simply better together, Kitt," she said, and her hand traveled to his thigh.

"You took the words right from my mouth," he replied with a slight gasp. She felt him shift; the blankets pulled at her knees. She thought he was retreating from her until he said, "Come closer, Iris."

She moved forward, reaching for him. His hands found her at last, touching her face, the slope of her shoulders. He drew her to him, and after momentarily getting her foot caught in one of the blankets, she straddled his lap.

Kissing him in the dark was entirely different from kissing him in the light. When the sun had gilded them hours ago, they had been eager and clumsy and hungry. But now, in the shadows of night, they were languid and thorough and curious.

She was bold in the darkness. She drew her lips across his jaw; she pressed her mouth to his throat, to the wild beat of his pulse. She drank the scent of his skin; she slid her tongue along his, tasting his sighs. She noticed how he touched her in return—reverently, mindfully. His hands would come to rest on the front of her ribs, his fingers splayed as if yearning for more, and yet they didn't rise any higher or slide any lower.

Iris *wanted* his touch. She didn't know why he was hesitating until she felt his fingers find the top button of her jumpsuit, and he whispered, "May I?"

"Yes, Kitt," she said, shivering as he began to unbutton them, one by one, in the dark. She felt the cool air wash over her as he slid her jumpsuit down, off her shoulders. The fabric gathered at her waist, and she waited. She waited for him to touch her, and he took his time, tracing the dip of her collarbone, the curve of her bare back, the straps of her bra. His hands came to rest on her ribs again. She was trembling with the anticipation.

"Is this all right, Iris?" he asked.

"Yes," she said, and she closed her eyes as his hands began to learn the shape of her.

No one had ever worshipped her like this. She felt his breath on her skin, his lips hovering above her heart. He kissed her once, twice, softly and then roughly, and she reached up, to remove the flowers, the pearls, and the braids from her hair. It fell free in long waves down her back, still damp and fragrant, and Roman's fingers instantly wove within it.

"You're beautiful, Iris," he said.

She began to unfasten his jumpsuit, desperate to feel his skin against hers. One of the buttons tore loose, tumbling to the blankets at their knees.

Roman chuckled. "Careful. This is the only jumpsuit I have."

"I'll repair it tomorrow," Iris promised, even though she didn't know what would come at sunrise. She cast those worries aside, though, as she undressed Roman.

They were both anxious to be free of the garments that had held them through countless troubles. Once liberated, they tossed their raiment across the room with hushed laughter. And the world melted into something new and molten.

Iris couldn't see him with her eyes, but she did with her hands. With her fingertips and her lips. She explored every dip and hollow of his body, claiming it as her own.

He is mine, she thought, the words a pleasant shock to her soul. *I am his.*

Iris laid him down beneath her, mindful of his leg, even if he swore his wounds weren't hurting him. She didn't know what to fully expect—nor did he—and it was awkward for a moment until Roman's hands touched her—a warm reassurance on her hips—and she held her breath deep in her chest as she moved. The discomfort sharpened but soon dulled, blooming into something luminous as they fully came together, tangled in the sheets. As they found a rhythm between them, one that only they could know. She felt safe with him, skin to skin. She felt full and complete; she felt the wholeness in the dark, this weaving together of vows and body and choice.

"*Iris,*" he whispered when she had nearly reached the end of herself.

It was agony; it was bliss.

She could hardly breathe as she gave herself up to them both.

I am his, she thought as he suddenly sat forward to hold her close, their hearts aligned. She felt how he trembled in her arms.

"Roman." She spoke his name like a promise, her fingers lost in his hair.

A sound broke from him. It could have been a sob or a gasp. She wanted to see his face, but there was no light between them save for the fire hiding in their skin.

"*Roman,*" she said again.

He kissed her, and she tasted salt on his lips. The wave began to ebb; the pleasure turned leaden, making their limbs heavy.

She held him as the warmth faded. Her thoughts were bright, illuminating the dark.

And he is mine.

They lay entwined for a long while afterward, his fingers tracing the wild waves of her hair. Iris had never loved a silence more. Her ear was pressed to his chest; she listened to the steady beat of his heart. An endless, faithful song.

His fingers eventually drifted down her arm to find her hand, leaving a trail of goose bumps in their wake.

"Tomorrow," Roman said, lacing his fingers with hers, "I want your hand to be in mine, no matter what comes. Just like this. We have to stay together, Iris."

"Don't worry," she said. Little did he know she had already planned this. To stay close to him. To be ready to support his weight all the way to the lorry if he needed her. To keep him alive.

She opened her eyes to the night and drolly said, "It'll be quite hard to get rid of me now, Kitt."

His laughter was beautiful in the dark.

40

To Wake in Another World

Iris woke to the faint wash of dawn, her cheek pressed to Roman's chest. His arm was wrapped around her and his breaths rose and fell slowly in sleep. After she got over her shock at how good his body felt against hers, she realized her face and hands were like ice, even though the blankets were draped over them and Roman was hot as a furnace.

It was far too cold for late spring, Iris thought, carefully rising.

She walked to Roman's window, moving the curtain to peer beyond the glass panes. She couldn't see any of the soldiers who were supposed to be guarding this side of town. The world looked gray and withered and empty, as if a frost had fallen.

"Kitt?" Iris said, urgent. "Kitt, get up."

He groaned, but she heard him sit forward. "Iris?"

"Something's not right." No sooner had the words left her mouth than she heard distant shouting outside. She couldn't see what was inspiring the commotion from this vantage point and she turned to face him. "We need to get dressed and go downstairs. See if Marisol knows anything. Did you hear me, Kitt?"

Roman was staring at her as if he were in a daze. She stood naked before him, wearing nothing but morning light on her skin.

"We need to get dressed!" she repeated, rushing to gather their garments, which were strewn all over the room.

He continued to sit in their bed, watching her every move. He seemed frozen, as if she had cast a spell on him, and Iris brought his belt and jumpsuit to him. She drew him up to his feet, the blankets falling away from his waist.

He was perfect, she thought with a sharp inhale. Roman watched her study his body, his cheeks flushed. And when her gaze finally returned to his, he whispered, "Do we have time?"

"I don't know, Kitt."

He nodded his disappointment, reaching for his jumpsuit. She helped him step into it, her fingers swiftly buttoning up the front, cinching the belt. She wished they had more time. She wished they could have woken up slowly, and her hands shook as she struggled to hook her bra. Roman stepped forward to help her, his fingers warm against her back. He was fastening the buttons of her jumpsuit when a knock sounded on the door.

"Iris? Roman?" Attie called. "Marisol is asking us to come down to the kitchen. Don't touch any of the curtains. Eithrals have been spotted, heading to town."

"Yes, we'll be right down," Iris said, her blood going cold.

There had been no siren. And then she remembered that Clover Hill was gone. A shudder passed through her as Roman finished buttoning her clothes and buckling her belt. They quickly laced their boots.

"Let's go," he said, and he sounded so calm that it eased Iris's fears.

He wove his fingers with hers and led her down the stairs. She could tell his leg was still bothering him, even as he tried to hide it. There was a slight limp in his gait as they walked into the kitchen. Iris was beginning to wonder if he'd be able to run through the streets and climb over the barricades, but she chased those thoughts away as they joined Attie by the table.

"Good morning," she said, Lilac purring in her arms. "I hope the two of you lovebirds had a good night's rest."

Iris nodded. She was about to thank Attie for all her help yesterday when the house suddenly rocked on its foundation. A splitting boom shook the walls and the ground, and Iris fell to her knees, hands clapped over her ears. She didn't even remember ripping her fingers from Roman's. Not until he knelt behind her on the kitchen floor and drew her into his arms, holding her back against his chest.

He was saying something to her. His voice was low but soothing in her ear. "We'll get through this. Breathe, Iris. I'm here and we'll get through this. *Breathe.*"

She tried to calm her breaths, but her lungs felt locked in an iron cage. Her hands and feet were tingling; her heart was pounding so hard she thought it would split her open. But she slowly became aware of Roman. She could feel his chest against hers—deep, calm draws of air. Slowly, she mimicked his pattern, until the stars that danced at the edges of her vision began to fade.

Attie. Marisol. Their names shot through Iris's mind like sparks, and she lifted her chin, searching the kitchen.

Attie was on her knees directly across from them, her mouth pressed into a tight line as Lilac screeched in fear. Everything was trembling. Paintings fell off the walls. The pot rack shook. Herbs began to rain down. Teacups shattered on the floor.

"Marisol," Iris panted, reaching for Attie's hand. "Where is Mari—"

Another bomb fell. A loud peal of thunder not that far away, because the house shook even harder, down to its roots. The timber beams overhead groaned. Plaster from the ceiling began to fall in chunks around them.

The B and B was going to collapse. They were going to be buried alive.

The fear burned thorough Iris like a coal. She was trembling, but she breathed when Roman breathed, and she held fiercely to Attie's hand. She closed her eyes, envisioning the night before. A wedding in the garden. Flowers in her hair. A dinner of candlelight and laughter and nourishing food. That warm feeling, like she had finally found her family. A place where she belonged. A home that was about to crumble.

Iris opened her eyes.

Marisol was standing a few paces away. Her revolver was holstered at her side, the dash-packs in her hand. Her dress was red, a striking contrast to her long black hair. She was like a statue, staring into the distance as the house rocked for the third time.

Dust streamed down. The windows cracked. The tables and chairs inched along the floor as if a giant was pounding the earth.

But Marisol didn't move.

She must have felt Iris's gaze. Through the chaos and devastation, their eyes met. Marisol slowly knelt beside Roman and Attie, their bodies creating a triangle on the kitchen floor.

"Have faith," she said, touching Iris's face. "This house will not fall. Not while I'm within it."

Another bomb exploded. But it was as Marisol swore: the B and B shuddered, but it didn't crumble.

Iris closed her eyes again. Her jaw was clenched, but she envisioned the garden, the life that grew within it. Small and seemingly fragile, yet it flourished more and more with each passing day. She envisioned this house with its many rooms and the endless people who had come and found solace here. The love that this ground had been claimed by. The green castle door that had seen sieges of an older era. The way the stars shined from the rooftop.

The world was becoming silent again.

A heavy, dust-laden silence that made Iris realize the air was warmer. The light shone brighter through the seams in the walls.

She opened her eyes. Marisol stood amid the debris, glancing at her wristwatch. Time felt distorted, the seconds spilling through fingers like sand.

"Stay here," Marisol said after what could have been two minutes or a full hour. She glanced at the three of them, a dark fire shining in her eyes. "I'll return soon."

Iris was too shocked to say anything. Attie and Roman must have been the same, because they were quiet as Marisol departed.

"Iris," Attie said a few moments later, her voice strained, "Iris, we can't . . . we have to . . ."

They couldn't let Marisol out of their sight. They were supposed to protect her, ensure she was taken to safety in the lorry. They had made a binding vow.

"We should go after her," Iris said. Now that she had a task, a mission to focus on, she could take control of her thoughts. She pushed herself up, letting Roman help her when she stumbled. Her knees felt watery, and she took a few deep breaths. "Where do you think we should look first?"

Attie stood, petting a disgruntled Lilac. "Keegan was stationed on the hill, wasn't she?"

"Right."

"The let's start there. But let me put Lilac somewhere safe."

Iris and Roman waited in the foyer while Attie closed the cat in one of the downstairs rooms. A beam of light snuck through a crack in the mortar, cutting across Iris's chest. The front door sat crooked on its hinges; it creaked open beneath Roman's hand.

Iris wasn't sure what she would find beyond the threshold. But she stepped into a sunlit, steaming world. Most of the buildings on High Street were unscathed save for shattered windows. But as Iris and Roman and Attie walked deeper into town, they began to see the radius of the bombs' destruction. Houses were leveled, lying in piles of stone and brick and glittering glass. A few had caught on fire, the flames licking the wood and thatch.

It didn't feel real. It felt like the wavering colors of a dream.

Iris walked around the barricades, around soldiers who were either holding fast at their posts or rushing to put out the flames. She watched through billows of smoke, her heart numb until Roman brought her to the foot of the bluff. Their summit.

She felt his hand tighten on hers, and she looked up to what remained.

The hill had been bombed.

There was a crater in the street. The buildings were heaps of rubble. Smoke rose in steady streams, smudging the clouds and turning the sunlight into a dirty haze.

From the bluff looking down on Avalon, there seemed to be a pattern to the destruction, as if Dacre had cast a web of ruin. Although the longer Iris stared at the bisecting lines of unscathed homes and the corresponding pockets of debris, the stranger the sight seemed to be. She struggled to make sense of how one home was standing while its next-door neighbor was demolished. But when she squinted, she could almost see pathways. Routes that were protected from the bombs. Marisol's B and B was on one of them.

Iris had to turn away from the uncanny observation. She released Roman's hand to help the wounded.

There were more than she could count, lying on the cobblestones. Broken and moaning in pain. Her gorge was rising; she had a moment of panic. But then she saw Keegan farther up the road. Moving and bleeding from a wound on her face but wondrously alive. Iris felt her resolve trickle back through her. She knelt beside the nearest soldier, pressing her fingertips to his neck. His eyes were open, fixed on the sky. Blood had poured from a wound in his chest, staining the street.

He was dead, and Iris swallowed, moving over loose cobblestones to reach the next soldier.

She was alive but one of her legs was splintered below the knee. She was struggling to rise, as if she didn't feel the pain.

"Just lie back for a moment," Iris said, taking her hand.

The soldier released a shaky gasp. "My legs. I can't feel them."

"You've been wounded, but help is coming." Iris glanced up again, watching as Keegan helped a few nurses lift a wounded soldier onto a stretcher. And then she caught a glimpse of Marisol's red dress as she assisted a doctor in a white coat with another wounded soldier. There was Attie, racing up the hill to give aid to a nurse who was shouting for it, and Roman, a few paces away, tenderly wiping the grime and blood from a soldier's face.

She hadn't been expecting this.

Iris had expected a siege or an assault. She had expected gunfire in the streets and the flash of grenades. She hadn't believed that Dacre would send his eithrals and his bombs.

A war with the gods is not what you expect it to be.

"My legs," the soldier rasped.

Iris tightened her grip on the girl's hand. "The doctors and nurses are coming. Hold on, just a moment longer. They're almost here to us." But a barricade and countless bodies lay between them and the medical help, who were methodically making their way down the street.

"She's losing too much blood," Roman whispered in her ear.

Iris turned to find him kneeling next to her, his gaze on the girl's mangled leg. Roman eased closer to the soldier, removing his belt to cinch it tightly on her left thigh.

A chill raced up Iris's spine. Her hands and feet suddenly felt cold again. She worried she was descending into shock.

"I'm going to see if I can get a stretcher for her," Iris said, rising. "Will you stay beside her, Kitt?"

Roman's lips parted, as if he wanted to argue. She knew his thoughts, the reason why he was frowning. He didn't want any sort of distance to come between them. But the soldier groaned and began to thrash, and he quickly gave her his attention, talking to her in a soothing tone. Reaching for her hand to help her through the waves of pain.

Iris turned and stumbled up the hill. She needed a stretcher. A plank of wood would even work. Anything that she and Roman could use to carry the soldier to the infirmary.

Should she search the rubble for something? Should she pull a board free from the barricade? She paused before it, rife with uncertainty even as her thoughts roared at her to *hurry*.

At the corner of her eye, a wounded soldier was bowed over, weeping for his mother. His agony pierced Iris, and she decided she would take a board of wood from the barricade. There was no time for her to chase down the nurses or the doctors, who were already overwhelmed. There was no time to find a stretcher. She began to claw at the structure, determined to work a plank free.

She didn't feel the shadows or the cold that rippled through the smoke. She was so intent on liberating this piece of wood that she failed to realize that the wind had ceased and frost had spangled the cobblestones at her feet.

"Down, down, *down!*"

The command cut through the mire and the chaos like a blade.

Iris froze, lifting her eyes to the churning sky. At first she thought the clouds were moving. A thunderstorm was building. But then she saw the wings, long and pronged, transparent in the fading light. She saw the monstrous white bodies emerge as they flew closer, nearly upon the town.

She had never seen an eithral before. She had never been this close to one. Even as she had once lain sprawled in the field with Roman, she had never been so close as to taste the rot and death in their pinions. To feel the beat of their wings.

"*Down and steady!*" The command came again. It was Keegan's voice, hoarse and frayed and yet powerful enough to knock everyone's sense back into place.

Iris turned, frantically searching for Roman.

She found him five paces away, standing frozen, but it was evident he had been coming to her. Wounded soldiers and rubble lay between them. There was no clear path, and his eyes were wide, his face pale. He had never appeared so afraid, and Iris had to resist the temptation to run to him.

Don't move, Iris, he mouthed to her.

She drew a deep breath. Her hands twitched at her sides as the creatures flew closer. Any minute now. Any minute, and they would be overhead.

"Mum," the soldier beside her moaned, rocking on his heels. "*Mum!*"

Iris glanced at him with alarm. So did Roman, a vein pulsing at his temple.

"You must be quiet," she said to the soldier. "You must stop moving."

"I need to find my mum," the boy wept, beginning to crawl over the ruin. "I need to go home."

"Stay down!" Iris cried, but he wasn't listening. She could see her breath; she could feel her heart pounding in her ears. "Please stop moving!"

A shadow of wings spilled over her. The stench of decay stole through the chilled air.

This is the end, Iris thought. She looked at Roman, five paces away.

He was so close, and yet too far to reach.

She imagined their future. All the things she wanted to do with him. Experience with him. All the things she would never taste now.

"Kitt," she whispered. And she didn't think he could hear her, but she hoped he could feel the force of such a whisper in his chest. How deep her love was for him.

Something small and shiny was falling from the clouds. But Iris didn't let its descent draw her eyes from Roman.

She held his steady gaze, waiting for the bomb to hit the ground between them.

41

Your Hand in Mine

She saw her nan. It was Iris's birthday—the hottest day of summer. The windows were thrown open, the ice cream had left a sticky spot on the kitchen floor, and her grandmother was smiling as she brought her typewriter to Iris.

"Is this really for *me?*" Iris cried, bouncing on the balls of her feet. She was so excited it felt like her heart might burst.

"It is," Nan said in her raspy voice, dropping a kiss in her hair. "Write me a story, Iris."

She saw her brother. Forest was with her at the riverbank, cupping something small in his hands. This was one of their favorite places in Oath; it almost felt as if they were no longer in the city, but deep into the countryside. The rush of the currents masked the clamor of the busy streets.

"Close your eyes and hold out your hands, Little Flower," he said.

"Why?" Iris asked, but it was no surprise. She always asked *why*. And she knew she asked too many questions, but she was often filled with doubt.

Forest, knowing her well, smiled. "Trust me."

She did trust him. He was like a god to her, and she closed her eyes and held out her hands, dirty from exploring the moss and the river rocks. He set something cool and slimy on her palm.

"All right, take a look," he said.

She opened her eyes to see a snail. She laughed, delighted, and Forest tapped her on the nose.

"What will you name it, Little Flower?"

"How about Morgie?"

She saw her mother. Sometimes Aster worked late at the Revel Diner, and Forest would walk Iris there after school, taking her for dinner.

She sat at the bar, watching her mother deliver plates and drinks to customers. Iris had her notebook open before her, desperate to write a story. For some reason, the words were like ice.

"Working on a new assignment, Iris?" her mother asked, setting down a glass of lemonade before her.

"No, I have all of my schoolwork complete for the day," Iris said with a sigh. "I'm trying to write a story for Nan, but I don't know what it should be about."

Aster leaned on the counter, quirking her lips and gazing down at the blank page in Iris's notebook. "Well, you're in the perfect place, then."

"The perfect place? How so?"

"Look around you. There are quite a few people here that you could write a story about."

Iris's eyes flickered around the diner, taking in the details she had never noticed before. When her mother strode away to take an order, she took up her pencil and began to write.

She saw Roman. They were alone in the garden again, but it wasn't in Avalon Bluff. It was a place Iris had never seen before, and she was on her hands and knees, weeding. Roman was supposed to be helping her, but he was only a distraction.

He tossed a clump of dirt at her.

"How dare you!" she said, glaring up at him. He was smiling, and she felt her skin flush. She could never stay angry at him for long. "I just washed this dress!"

"I know you did. It looks better off you anyways."

"Kitt!"

He tossed another dirt clump at her. And another, until she had no choice but to abandon her task to tackle him.

"You're impossible," she said, straddling him. "And I win this round."

Roman only grinned, his hands tracing up her legs. "I surrender. How shall I pay my penance this time?"

She waited for the bomb to fall. She waited for the end, and her mind flashed with memories, dragging her through the past with lightning speed. People she loved. Moments that had shaped her. She saw a glimpse of something to come, and that was where her thoughts stayed. On Roman and the garden they had planted together and how he was now standing five paces away from her, watching her as if he saw the same future.

At last, the bomb hit the ground.

There was a clatter as it rolled on the cobbles, eventually coming to rest in the crook of a soldier's body.

Iris glanced at it, disbelieving. She studied the way it caught the light. A metal canister.

Her thoughts were slow and thick, still hung upon the *what could have been,* but the present returned to her like a slap to her face, waking her up.

This was not a bomb.

This was—she didn't know what it was. And that frightened her even more.

The eithrals swarmed overhead. Their wings beat cold, rotten air and their talons dropped canister after canister, up and down the street. Panicked voices began to rise. The nurses, doctors, and soldiers who had been holding still broke into frantic motion.

"*Iris!*" Roman shouted, tripping over the rubble to close the gap between them. "Iris, take my hand!"

She was reaching for Roman when the gas hissed, spilling out of the canister in a green-hued cloud. It hit her like a fist, and she coughed, scrambling away from it. Her nose was burning, her eyes were burning. She couldn't see and the ground felt like it was lurching beneath her.

"Kitt! *Kitt!*" she screamed, but her voice stung her throat.

She just needed some clean air. She needed to get away from the cloud, and she frantically moved forward, eyes clenched shut and hands outstretched, uncertain which direction she was heading.

Tears spilled down her face. Her nose was running. Iris coughed and tasted blood in her mouth.

She fell to her knees. She pulled the collar of her jumpsuit up to cover her nose and crawled over twisted pieces of metal and shards of glass and the remnants of destroyed homes, over soldiers who had died. She had to keep moving; she had to stay low.

"Kitt!" She tried to call to him again, knowing he had to be nearby. But her voice was shredded. She could scarcely draw half a breath, let alone shout.

Get to clean air. Then you can find him and Attie and Marisol.

She continued to crawl, blood and drool dripping from her lips as she panted. The temperature was getting warmer. Through her eyelids, she could see the light strengthening, and she pushed toward it.

She tested the air, drawing a deeper breath. Her lungs blazed as she coughed, but she knew she had escaped the gas.

Iris stopped, daring to open her eyes. Her vision was watery, but she blinked and let the tears slip down her cheeks. She coughed again and spit blood onto the ground, sitting back on her heels.

She had crawled to a side street.

She glanced behind to see the cloud of gas and the people crawling out of it, just as she had.

I should be helping them, she thought.

As soon as she made to rise, the world spun. Her stomach rolled and she heaved onto the cobblestones. There wasn't much in her, and she had no choice but to sit back down, leaning against a pile of stone rubble.

"Keep moving," a soldier croaked to her as he crawled by.

She didn't think she could. Her limbs were tingling, and a strange taste was haunting her mouth. But then the wind began to blow. She watched in horror as the breeze carried the gas toward her, down the winding side street.

Iris staggered to her feet and ran. She made it a few strides before her knees gave out, and she crawled until she felt like she could stand again. She followed a string of soldiers downhill. She thought she would be safe in the lower side of town, but more gas was rising on High Street, and she ended up turning around and racing toward the market, where the air looked clean.

"Iris!"

She heard someone calling her name. She spun and searched the crowd that had gathered around her, frantically looking for Roman, for Attie, for Marisol, for Keegan. It was time for them to flee. She felt it in her gut, and she remembered what Attie had told her the day before.

I'll grab Marisol. You grab Roman. We'll meet at the lorry.

"Kitt!" she shouted.

She was standing in a sea of olive uniforms, a sea of splattered blood and coughs and boots squeaking on the stones. A few of the soldiers now wore gas masks, their entire faces concealed as they rushed back toward the deadly streets. She had a moment of icy fear that she would be trampled if she was misfortunate enough to fall.

There was a flicker of red at the corner of her eye.

Iris turned toward it just in time to see Marisol and Attie weaving through the crowd. They hadn't seen her; they were moving away from her position toward the east side of town, and she knew they were heading to the lorry.

The relief softened her, to know they were all right. But then her dread returned, sharp enough to slice her lungs. She had to find Roman. She couldn't leave without him, and she began to push her way through the throng, shouting his name until her voice was hoarse.

She needed to stand on one of the barricades. He would never see her like this, adrift in the crowd.

Iris began to work her way to one of the structures, shuddering when she finally broke away from the chaos. She took a moment to lean on her knees, to take deep breaths.

A firm hand grasped her arm, so hard that she knew she would be bruised by tomorrow.

She yelped and turned, frightened when she saw it was a masked individual. Their face was entirely concealed by a gas mask made of fabric, two round amber lenses, and a cylindrical gear for breathing clean air. She couldn't see their face, but she could hear them inhaling, exhaling. They also wore a helmet, which hid their hair, and her eyes traveled down, taking in the jumpsuit they wore.

"Kitt! Oh my gods, *Kitt*!" Iris fiercely embraced him.

His hold on her arm loosened, but only for a moment. He stiffly created some space between them, and she frowned, confused, until he said, "Put this on."

His voice was distorted from the mask, and it made her flinch. He sounded robotic, as if he were made of metal pieces and winding gears. But she saw that he had found a mask for her and she slid its leather thongs over her head.

It was like being in a bubble. The mask affected her every sense, and the world turned to shades of amber, slightly blurred. At first it was beautiful, but then Iris felt her panic rising. She felt like she was about to suffocate.

She clawed at the edges of the mask. Roman reached for her, turning the cylinder that rested near her chin. Cool air began to flow.

"Take a deep breath," he said.

She nodded, sweat trickling down her back. She breathed and calmed the tide of her panic. She could keep it at bay, because she had him now. They would be safe.

"Kitt," she said, wondering how her voice sounded to him. If it sounded like she was composed of sharp edges and cold steel. "Kitt, we——"

He took her hand. His grip was tight again, almost punishingly so, as his fingers wove with hers. *I want your hand to be in mine, no matter what comes.*

"We need to go," he said, but she had the sense that he wasn't looking at her but at something beyond her. Perhaps he saw Keegan, giving them the sign to flee. As Iris began to turn to see for herself, Roman tugged on her arm. "Come with me. We'll be faster if you don't look behind."

He dragged her around the barricade, into the shadows of a quiet side street. She felt dizzy, but she focused on her breathing and followed him.

Her hearing was not as keen in the mask, but she could hear her boots pounding on the street and a distant shout.

Roman paused at the intersection. She thought he was catching his breath until he glanced behind again and hurried to pull her onward, into a street that was swarming with gas. Iris winced as she followed him into the cloud, waiting to feel its sting in her lungs and her eyes. But the mask shielded her, filtering the air, and they emerged on the other side of High Street.

Roman hesitated again, as if he were lost.

Iris finally gained her bearings. They were far from the lorry, and she felt a cold prickling at the nape of her neck. Something didn't feel quite right.

"Kitt? We need to go east. Attie and Marisol are waiting for us. Here, this way."

She began to guide him in the correct direction, but he jerked her back to his side. "I'll lead us, Iris. This way is faster."

He hauled her onward before she could protest. She tripped over her boots, trying to keep pace with him. He must be scared, but it still struck her as odd. He wasn't acting normal. She tried to study him as they ran, but the mask softened everything, and it hurt her eyes to strain them.

"Where did you get the masks?" she asked. "Shouldn't we be using them to help those trapped in the gas?"

He didn't answer. He only progressed to a faster run.

She finally realized it when they reached the edge of town. Her mind sharpened as they ran into the golden field. Roman was no longer limping. He was running as he had before his injuries.

She couldn't catch her breath as she watched him sprint, cutting through the sweep of the grass. Powerful and strong, dragging her in his wake. The wind began to blow at their backs, as if pushing them onward.

"Kitt . . . Kitt, *wait*. I need to stop." She pulled on his hand, which continued to hold hers like a vise.

"It's not safe yet, Iris. We have to keep moving," he insisted, but he eased to a jog.

They were almost to the place where they had once collided. Where Iris had covered his body with hers, desperate to keep him alive.

She would no longer be dragged by him like this. Something wasn't right.

She sank to a walk, which forced him to also slow down. He glanced at her, and she wished she could see his face. She wished that she could see where his gaze was resting, because his hand tightened on hers.

"We need to hurry, Iris. It's not safe."

Why did he continue to say those words?

She had the overwhelming urge to look behind her. And she gave into it, angling her body so she could glance over her shoulder. The mask made it awkward, but she saw something in the field. A moving shadow, as if someone was chasing them.

He yanked on her arm. "Don't look behind you."

"Wait." She dug her heels into the soil and fully faced the town. Her eyes focused on that strange shadow, which she realized was a man. A tall man with dark hair, running after her in a stilted gait.

She ripped her gas mask away, desperate to see without the distortion of the amber lens. The world flooded around her, bright and sharp. Yellow and green and gray. Her hair tangled across her face.

She saw her pursuer with shocking detail, even as twenty meters of golden grass stretched between them.

It was Roman.

"Iris!" he screamed.

Her heart stalled. Her blood turned to ice as she watched him run, his face anguished. Blood stained the front of his jumpsuit. He stumbled as if his leg was ailing him, but he regained his balance, pushing himself to keep running. To close the distance between them.

But if that was Roman, then *who was she with*? Who was holding her hand, dragging her across this field to the distant woods?

Iris looked at the masked stranger, wide eyed with fear. His chest was heaving, and he was speaking in that distorted tone.

"Iris? Stay with me. I'm trying to help you. *Iris!*"

She ripped her hand from his and spun, dashing toward Roman.

She took three strides before the stranger's arms came around her, hauling her backward. Her anger burned like wildfire, and she fought him. She kicked and swung her elbows and dashed the back of her head against his mask, provoking grunts and curses from him.

"What do you want with me? Let me go! *Let me go!*" She dug her nails into his hands, drawing blood. She raged, keeping her gaze on Roman as he collapsed in the grass.

He was only fifteen meters away.

The wind gusted, blowing the gas in their direction. She froze when she could no longer see Avalon Bluff but only a wall of green, steadily making its way to them.

Roman needed to get up. *Get up, get up!* Her heart screamed, and she watched as he rose again, limping to her.

"Run, Kitt!" she shouted. Her voice was hoarse, frayed by terror.

The man holding her turned her around and gave her shoulders a good shake. Her neck snapped, her thoughts rolling through her like marbles.

"Stop fighting me!" he demanded. But he must have seen the fear that was shining within her, because his voice gentled. "Stop fighting me, Little Flower."

Her world cracked in two.

And yet . . . hadn't she hoped for this?

She found his name, hidden deep in her heart. A name that burned her throat. "Forest?"

"*Yes,*" he said. "Yes, it's me. And I'm here to keep you safe. So stop fighting me and come on." His hand found hers again, lacing their fingers. He tugged, expecting her to willingly follow him now.

She stiffened, pulling back. "We have to get Kitt."

"There's no time for him. Come on, we need to run——"

"What do you mean there's no time for him!" she cried. "He's right there!" She turned, desperate to see him again. But there was only the dance of the grass, bending to the wind, and the swirl of gas, creeping closer.

He must have fallen. He must be on his knees.

I can't leave him like this.

Iris raged again, desperate to break away from Forest's hold.

"Enough of this!" her brother growled. "It's too late for him, Iris."

"I can't leave him," she panted. "He's my *husband*! I can't leave him. Forest, let me go. *Let me go!*"

He wasn't listening. He refused to release her. It felt like her fingers were about to fracture, but she fought him. She yanked and pulled and she didn't care if it broke every bone in her hand. She finally slipped away from him.

She was free. The gas blew closer; she lurched toward it, defiant.

"KITT!" she screamed as she ran, her eyes searching the grass.

Where are you?

She thought she saw a shadow moving in the stalks just a few paces away. Hope sang through her until Forest's hand found her neck, drawing her back to him. His thumb and fingers pressed down hard on her throat. Stars began to flare in her vision.

"Forest," she wheezed, clawing at his ruthless grip. "Forest, *please*."

A cold pang of terror shot through her. It was a fear she had never felt before, and her hands and feet began to go numb.

My brother is about to kill me.

The words reverberated through her. Echoed down her arms and legs as she flailed against him.

The light dimmed. The colors were melting. But she saw Roman rise from the grass. He was only five meters away. He could no longer run; he could hardly walk. Her heart broke when she realized he had *crawled* through the gold to reach her.

Blood dripped from his chin.

The wind swept the dark hair from his brow.

His eyes smoldered, burning a path to her. She had never seen such a fire within him, and it called to her, stirring her blood.

"Iris," he said, his hand outstretched.

Four meters. He was almost to her, and she scrounged up the last of her strength.

Her hand was trembling, bruised and numb. But she reached for him, the silver ring on her finger catching the light. The ring that bound her to him. And she thought, *I'm so close. Just a little farther* . . .

She was suddenly hauled backward. Forest swore as the wind blew harder against them. The air began to sting her eyes, her lungs. The distance between her and Roman swelled again.

She tried to call his name, but her voice was gone.

She was fading.

The last thing she remembered seeing was the green cloud spin over the field, swallowing Roman Kitt whole.

42

All the Things I Never Said

Iris woke with a splitting headache.

Her eyes cracked open; late afternoon light played over her face. Branches swayed in the breeze above her. She watched them for a moment before realizing she was surrounded by trees and the air smelled like evergreen and moss and damp earth.

She had no idea where she was, and her hands reached out, passing over pine needles and leaves. The stained linen of her jumpsuit.

"Kitt?" she rasped. It hurt to speak, and she tried to swallow the splinter in her throat. "Attie?"

She heard someone shifting nearby. They came into her field of vision, hovering over her.

She blinked, recognizing the wavy chestnut brown hair, the wide-set hazel eyes, the dusting of freckles. They were so much like her own features. They could have been twins.

"Forest," she whispered, and he reached for her hand, gently helping her sit forward. "Where are we?"

Her brother was silent, as if he didn't know what to say. But then he brought a canteen to her mouth. "Drink, Iris."

She took a few sips. As the water washed through her, she began to remember. She remembered mistaking her brother for Roman and how he had been determined to drag her away from town.

"Kitt," she said, pushing the canteen aside. She was worried, hungry for answers. "Where is he? Where's my husband?"

Forest glanced away. "I don't know, Iris."

It took everything within her to *stay calm, stay calm* as she stated through her teeth, "You saw him in the market. He was shouting for me then, wasn't he?"

"Yes." Forest's tone was unapologetic. He held her eyes, his face emotionless.

"Why didn't you tell me who you were, Forest? Why didn't you let Kitt join us?"

"It was too much of a liability, Iris. My only plan was to get you out of there safely."

She began to rise. Her legs were shaky.

"Sit down, Little Flower. You need to rest."

"Don't call me that!" she snarled, reaching out to balance herself on the nearest pine. She blinked and studied her surroundings. The woods stretched on and on, and the light looked older, richer. It must be late afternoon. She took a step toward the west.

"And where do you think you're going?" Forest asked, standing.

"I'm going back to the field to find Kitt."

"No you're not. Iris, stop this!" He reached out to grasp her arm and Iris jerked away.

"Don't touch me." She leveled him with a glare.

Forest let his hand drop. "You can't go back there, sister."

"And I can't abandon him. He could still be in the field."

"Chances are, he's not. Listen to me, Iris. Dacre will have stormed into Avalon Bluff by now. If he catches sight of us, he'll take us as prisoners. Are you listening to me?"

She was walking toward the west. Her heart was pounding, aching with possibilities, when she tripped over something soft. She paused, glancing down at it. Two dash-packs. The two that Marisol had been missing.

So it had been him. Her brother had tromped through the garden and trespassed into the B and B, stealing two of the bags and Roman's jumpsuit.

She felt betrayed. She felt so angry she wanted to strike her fists against him. She wanted to scream at him.

He appeared before her, holding his hands up in surrender.

"All right, I'll make a deal with you," he began. "I'll take you back to the field to look for Kitt. But we can't go beyond it; we can't stray into the town. It's too dangerous. And after we search the field, you will agree to let me take you somewhere safe. You'll follow me home."

Iris was silent, but her mind was reeling.

"Do you agree to my terms, Iris?" Forest prompted.

She nodded. She had every faith Roman was still in the field, waiting for her to come to him. "Yes. Take me there. Now."

They reached the field by evening. Forest had been right; Dacre's forces now ruled Avalon Bluff. Iris crouched in the grass, staring at the town. Fires were lit and music was pouring like a stream. Smoke still rose from the ashes, but Dacre was celebrating. His white flag with the red eithral eye was raised, flapping in the wind.

The gas was long gone by now. As if it had never been.

"We'll have to crawl through the grass," Forest said, his words clipped with tension. "It looks like Dacre isn't expecting any retaliation from Enva's forces. I don't see any sentries, but that doesn't mean they aren't stationed as snipers. So move very slowly, and stay down. Do you hear me?"

She nodded. She didn't spare her brother a glance. She was too focused on the sway of the grass as the wind raked over it. On the place she believed Roman to be.

She and Forest crawled side by side through the field. She moved gentle but swift, as he instructed. She didn't wince when the stalks cut her hands, and it felt like a year passed before she reached the place where she had fought her brother, hours ago. She recognized it easily. The grass was broken here, trampled by their boots.

She swallowed the temptation to call for Roman. She remained low, crawling on her belly. The stars were beginning to wink overhead. The music from Avalon Bluff continued to echo, a fierce beating of drums.

The light was almost gone. Iris strained her eyes, looking for him amongst the flax.

Roman!

Her breaths were shallow and painful. Perspiration dripped from her brow, even as the temperature dropped. She searched for him, knowing this had been the spot. She searched, but there was no trace of him. Only his blood, staining the grass.

"We need to go, Iris," Forest whispered.

"Wait," she pleaded. "I know he has to be here."

"He's not. Look."

Her brother pointed at something. She frowned, studying it. There was a ring drawn in the dirt. It encircled them both as they paused, still lying low.

"What is this, Forest?" she asked, finding more of Roman's blood on the ground. It looked like spilled ink in the dusky light.

"We need to go. *Now,*" he hissed, grabbing her wrist.

She didn't want him touching her, and she lurched away. Her hand still ached, as did her neck. All due to him.

"Just a minute longer, Forest," she begged. "Please."

"He's not here, Iris. You have to trust me. I know more than you."

"What do you mean?" But she had a terrible inkling. Her heart was beating, hummingbird swift in her throat. "Do you think he's in Avalon Bluff?"

Guns fired in the distance. Iris startled, pressing deeper into the earth. Another round of shots, and then came peals of laughter.

"No, he's not there," Forest said, his eyes sweeping their surroundings. "I promise. But it's time for us to go, as you agreed, sister."

She glanced around the grass one last time. The moon hung above, watching as she sagged, as she crawled back to the woods with her brother.

The stars continued to burn as the last of her hope waned into despair.

He chose a place deep in the woods to make camp, where the mist curled around the trees. It gave Iris the chills, and she remained close to the small fire he built.

They had put several kilometers between them and Avalon Bluff, but Forest was still on edge, as if he expected Dacre's forces to emerge from the shadows at any moment.

Iris had endless questions for him, but the air between them was tense. She held her tongue and accepted the food he handed her—food from Marisol's kitchen—and she ate it, even though there was a lump in her throat.

"Where is Kitt?" she asked. "You said you know more than me. Where can I find him?"

"It's not safe to talk about it here," Forest said tersely. "You should eat and go to bed. We have a long walk ahead of us tomorrow."

Iris was quiet, but then murmured, "You should have let him come with us."

"This is *war*, Iris!" Forest cried. "This isn't a game. This isn't a novel with a happy ending. I saved *you*, because you are all I care about and you were all I could manage. Do you understand me?"

His words pierced her. She wanted to remain frozen and guarded, but she felt incredibly fragile in that moment. She kept seeing Roman rise from the grass. The way he had looked at her.

A sob hitched her breath. She drew her knees to her chest and began to weep, covering her face with her dirty hands. She tried to suck everything back in, to press it down to her marrow where she could handle it in private. But it was like something had broken in her, and things were spilling out.

Forest sat across from her, deathly quiet. He didn't offer her any comfort; he didn't embrace her. He didn't speak kind words to her. The things he would have done in the past. But he remained near her, and he bore witness to her grief.

And all she could think through her tears was *He feels like a stranger to me now.*

He was paranoid about something. He had Iris up and walking early the next day, and by the slant of the sun, she judged they were traveling east.

"We could go to the road," she suggested. "We could catch a ride with one of the lorries." She wanted, more than anything, to find Attie and Marisol. To continue her search for Roman.

"No." Forest's reply was curt. He quickened his pace, glancing behind to make sure Iris was still following him. Twigs cracked beneath his boots. Iris thought the jumpsuit fit him poorly, and she wondered how she hadn't seen it before.

"So we're going to walk all the way to Oath?" she asked, a bit snidely.

"Yes. Until it's safe to board a train."

They traversed the next few hours in silence, until her brother was ready to make camp.

Perhaps Forest would finally explain himself here.

She waited for it, but her brother remained quiet, sitting on the other side of the fire from her. She watched the shadows dance over his lean, freckled face.

Eventually she could bear it no longer.

"Where's your company, Forest? Your platoon? A lieutenant wrote to me, explaining that you joined another auxiliary force."

Forest stared at the flames, as if he hadn't heard her.

Where is your uniform? she inwardly added, wondering why he had gone to such lengths to steal one of Roman's jumpsuits. Although it was becoming more evident that her brother was a deserter.

"They're gone," he replied suddenly. "Every last one of them." He threw another branch on the fire before lying down on his side. "You can take the first watch."

She sat quietly, her mind racing. She wondered if he was speaking about his Fifth Landover Company. The one that had been slaughtered at Lucia River.

She didn't feel it was right to press him for clarity, and so she thought of other things.

Attie and Marisol most likely got away in the lorry. They would be driving east. Iris knew she could eventually find them at River Down, with Marisol's sister.

But she wasn't sure about Keegan's fate.

She wasn't sure about Roman's.

Her stomach ached. Everything within her ached.

The fire was beginning to burn low.

Iris stood and brushed pine needles from her backside, looking for a new stick to add to the flames. She found one on the edges of the darkness, a shudder racking her spine as she returned to the camp, feeding the fire.

Forest was awake, staring at her over the sparks.

His gaze startled her at first, until she lowered herself back down to the ground. Her brother shut his eyes again.

She realized he thought she was attempting to run.

Dear Kitt,

I returned to the field to find you. I crawled through the gold, felt the grass cut my hands to ribbons. I strained my eyes for a glimpse of you, and only found traces of your blood and a circle in the dirt that I can't explain.

Are you safe? Are you well?

I don't know what happened after my brother took me away from Avalon Bluff. I don't know if you survived the gas, and while it seems impossible, I feel like you did. I feel like you are sitting somewhere safe, wrapped in a blanket and sipping a bowl of soup, and your hair is even more tangled than before, bordering on rogue at the moment. But you are breathing beneath the same moon, the same stars, the same sun as me, even as the kilometers are growing between us.

In spite of all of that hope, my fear is sharper. It's a knife in my lungs, cutting me a little more, a little deeper with each breath I take. I fear I will never see you again. I fear that I won't get the chance to say all the things I never said to you.

I don't have my typewriter. I don't even have pen and paper. But I have my thoughts, my words. They once connected me to you, and I pray that they'll reach you now. Somehow, someway. An old trace of magic in the wind.

I'll find you whenever I can.

Yours,

Iris

On the fourth day of traveling with Forest, the road came into view. Iris tried to tamp down her excitement, but it must have been evident when she suggested they walk along it.

"It'll be faster, Forest," she said.

He only shook his head, as if he was loath to be seen by anyone but her.

He made sure to pull them deeper into the woods. And while they could hear the lorries rumbling by, Iris couldn't see them.

Attie and Marisol.

Their names rolled through her like a promise. She hoped Attie hadn't waited too long for her. That Attie had sensed the awful truth—that she and Roman weren't coming—when the minutes had continued to pass without them appearing. Or perhaps Attie had found Roman, and he was currently with them.

I will find you at River Down, Iris thought, watching the wind whisper through the trees. *Keep going, Attie. Don't slow down for me. Don't worry about me.*

That night, Forest moved slowly when he built the fire. He moved like he was wounded, and when patches of blood began to seep through the chest of his jumpsuit, Iris jumped to her feet.

"Forest . . . you're bleeding."

He glanced down at the bright red spots. He winced but waved her away. "It's nothing, Iris. Eat your dinner."

She stepped closer to him, dismay eclipsing her thoughts. "Let me help you."

"No, it's fine, Iris."

"It doesn't look *fine.*"

"It'll stop in a moment."

She bit her tongue, watching him touch the blood. "I didn't know you were wounded. You should have told me."

Forest grimaced. "They're old wounds. Nothing to worry about." But his voice was ragged, and she was sorely worried about him.

"Sit down," she said. "I'll fix your dinner."

To her relief, Forest heeded her. He settled close to the fire, his shoulders hunched as if he was holding the pain close.

Iris opened a tin of beans and found a wedge of cheese in the dash-pack. She thought of Marisol, and her eyes stung as she brought the food to her brother.

"Here. Eat this, Forest."

He accepted her offering. His movements were choppy, as if the pain in his chest was overwhelming. Her eyes drifted to the chords of his throat, to the open collar of his jumpsuit. She could see a flash of gold around his neck.

Iris paused. Her eyes narrowed, watching the necklace gleam in the firelight.

It was her mother's locket. The one Iris had worn ever since her death.

"Forest," she breathed. "Where did you find it?" She reached out to touch the taunting gold, but Forest leaned back, his face pallid.

He said nothing as he stared at Iris.

She had lost it in the trenches. When the grenade's blast had pushed her to the ground.

She had lost it in the trenches, which meant Forest had been there. He had found it after she had retreated, and the truth unfolded with a brutal, cold scrape to her ribs.

Iris met her brother's bloodshot gaze.

At last, she understood his hesitance to be seen by Enva's army, his constant worry. Why he stole Roman's jumpsuit. Why he was running. Why he had never written to her.

He had been fighting for Dacre.

"Forest," Iris whispered. "*Why?* Why Dacre?"

He pushed upward to his feet, trembling. She remained on her knees, gazing up at him, incredulous.

"You don't understand, Iris," he said.

"Then help me!" she cried, throwing her arms wide. "Help me understand, Forest!"

He walked away without another word.

Iris watched as he melted into the night. Her breaths turned ragged as she slid to lie facedown on the ground.

He walked away, but he soon returned to her.

She was lying next to the fire when he came back to the camp. Her eyes were closed, but she listened as he settled on the other side of the flames.

He sighed.

And Iris wondered what her brother had lived through. She wondered what other wounds he was hiding.

Dear Kitt,

I should have known my brother wasn't you. I should have known the moment he took hold of my arm. His touch was too hard, too firm. As if he was terrified I would slip through his fingers. I shouldn't have taken the mask. I should have insisted we give them to the soldiers who actually needed them, using them to draw survivors from the gas. I should have insisted that my brother stop his frantic running. I should have looked behind me.

I am broken, full of contradictions.

I wish I were brave, but I am so afraid, Kitt.

They boarded a train, but not before Forest took a day to wash his jumpsuit in a river.

Iris caught a glimpse of his bare chest as he scrubbed the blood from the linen. She saw the scars on his skin. They didn't look like recent wounds, and yet they had bled the other night. She counted three of them, and she could only imagine what it must have felt like to have those bullets pierce his skin.

Once the jumpsuit was clean and dry, they walked into a town on the other side of the woods. To any observer, they were two war correspondents heading back to Oath. Forest held her hand, his palm clammy. Iris had a creeping feeling that he was worried she would make a run for it.

She didn't.

She had given him her word, and he owed her more answers.

She sat across from him in the train compartment. And while she kept her gaze on the window, watching the land pass by in a blur . . . she thought about Forest's scars. One just below his heart. One where his liver rested. One even lower, striking his intestines.

They had been fatal wounds.

He should be dead.

He shouldn't be here with her, breathing the same air.

She didn't know how he had survived them.

Dear Kitt,

 I never told you how relieved I was to discover you were Carver.

 I never told you how much I loved those morning runs with you.

 I never told you how much I loved to hear you say my name.

 I never told you how often I reread your letters, and how I now feel agonized, to know they are lost to me, scattered somewhere in Marisol's B and B.

 I never told you that I think the world of you, that I want to read more of your words, that I think you should write a book and publish it.

 I never thanked you for going to the front lines with me. For coming between me and the grenade.

 I never told you that I love you. And I regret that, most of all.

Oath was exactly as she had left it.

The streets were crowded, the pavement gleaming from a recent rain. The trams ran their courses, bells ringing. The buildings were tall and the shadows were cold. The air smelled like a rubbish bin and sugared bread.

The war felt distant, no more than a dream.

Iris followed her brother to their flat.

She was exhausted. They had been traveling in near silence for days now, and it had worn her down. She hadn't told him yet about their mother. The words suddenly beat in her chest, frantic to find their way out.

"Forest." She took hold of his sleeve, stopping him on the pavement before their building. "I need to tell you something."

He waited, his eyes on her face.

It began to rain softly. Mist beaded in their hair, gathered on their shoulders. It was eventide, and the lamps began to flicker to life.

"Mum's not here," Iris said.

"Where is she?"

"She passed away, weeks ago. It's why I left Oath. It's why I became a correspondent. There was nothing left for me here."

Forest was silent. Iris dared to glance at his face. She was terrified she would find blame in his eyes, but her brother only sighed and pulled her close. She was stiff until his arms wrapped around her, enveloping her in a warm embrace. His chin rested on her head and they stood entwined as the last of the light dwindled.

"Come on," he said, relinquishing her when he felt her shiver. "Let's go home."

Iris found the spare key, hidden behind a loose stone in the lintel. She was reluctant to step into the flat's empty darkness first. She gave that honor to Forest, who instantly reached for the light switch.

"The electricity's off," he mumbled.

"There are a few candles on the sideboard. To your left," Iris said, closing the door behind them.

Her brother fumbled in the dark, finding the matches from one of the dash-packs. He struck a flame and lit a host of candles. The light was weak, but it was enough.

Iris glanced around the room.

The flat was just as she remembered, only dustier. More cobwebs hung in the corners, and it smelled musty and sad, like spoiled paper and drenched wool and decaying memories.

The box with her mother's belongings still sat on the tea table. Forest noticed, but he didn't touch it and he said nothing as he collapsed on the sofa with a groan.

Iris remained standing, feeling strangely out of place.

"Do you want to sit down?" Forest asked.

She took that as an invitation to finally talk, and she gingerly crossed the room, sitting beside him.

The silence was awkward. Iris cracked her knuckles, wondering what she should say. Her hands were still covered in small lacerations, from when she had crawled through the rubble of Avalon Bluff, the grass of the field.

She stared at the silver ring on her finger. In some terrible way, it felt as if Roman was nothing more than a feverish dream. This ring was the only proof she had, the one tangible thing to whisper to her, *Yes, it happened, and he loved you.*

Forest thankfully broke the quiet.

"I found the locket in the trenches," he began. "I was with Dacre's forces. We were driving forward, and I nearly passed over it. The gleam of gold caught my eye at the last minute, and I stopped, to see what it was." He paused, pulling a loose thread from his sleeve. "As soon as I recognized it, I knew you had been wearing it, Iris. It devastated me in a way I can't describe. And I was determined that I would find you and we would both escape the war. I was . . . I was *so* tired and exhausted. It took everything within me to break away from Dacre's command. If not for the locket, I don't think I could have done it."

Iris was quiet. She watched her brother closely in the candlelight. The emotion he had been burying for days was stirring. She could hear it in his voice, see it in the deep lines of his brow.

"I made it my mission to find you," Forest continued in a hushed tone. "It was surprisingly easy. After I deserted, I fled to Avalon Bluff. I caught wind that correspondents resided there and that's when it hit me. You weren't fighting as a soldier, but as a reporter. But I couldn't simply walk up to you and announce myself. I knew I would have to wait and bide my time. That I would most likely have to wait until things got bad, when Dacre tried to take the town. And so that's what I did. I lived on the outskirts, but I kept watch over you. I saw you that afternoon, in the garden with Kitt."

Iris flushed. Her brother had seen her on Roman's lap, kissing him. She had no idea what she thought about it.

"I know he means a great deal to you, Iris," Forest whispered. "And I'm sorry, Little Flower. I'm sorry I couldn't save him as I saved you. But I need you to understand that it took *every* fiber within me to desert, to defy Dacre's command. It took everything within me to run to safety with you."

He met her gaze. Iris glanced away, unable to withstand the pain in his eyes.

"It wasn't your choice to fight for Dacre?" she asked.

"No."

"I . . . I still don't understand, Forest. I received news that you had been wounded, but evacuated in time. That you were fighting with another company of Enva's."

"Part of that is true," Forest replied. "I was wounded at Lucia River, so badly that I was supposed to die in the Meriah infirmary. I held on for days, but was too weak to be evacuated, and when Dacre came to take Meriah . . . he healed me before I died. He held me by the debt of my life, and I had no choice but to fight for him."

The words chilled her. They suddenly spun strange thoughts in her mind. Images of Roman, wounded. Struggling to breathe in the cloud of gas that had swarmed him in the field. Would she rather him dead or taken by the enemy?

"I've done things, Iris," Forest continued, bringing her back to the present. "I've done things that I can barely live with. And I know you may want to leave me. I can see it in your eyes; you want to find Kitt and your other friends. But I need you. I'm asking you to stay here with me, where it's safe."

She nodded, even though her heart was sinking. "I won't leave you, Forest."

He closed his eyes, relieved.

He looked like he had aged an entire decade. She caught a fleeting glimpse of him as an old man, worn and weathered and somber.

"Get some sleep, brother," she said. "We can talk more tomorrow."

She rose and left Forest on the sofa. The very place he had once slept before the war, when he was a horologist's apprentice with bright eyes and a quick laugh and bear hugs that always made Iris feel better after a hard day.

She took a candle and retreated to her bedroom, leaning against the door for a moment. She had to drop these fears about Roman, captured. Roman, dead. Roman, suffering. She had to have faith, and she needed to sleep. She needed her mind sharp and her body rested so she could forge a new plan to find her way to him.

She soaked in the forlorn truth that she was back where she started. She was "home," and yet she felt like a stranger here. She felt like an entirely different person. Iris shut her eyes, listening to the rain tap on the window.

Slowly, she took in her old room.

The blankets on her bed were wrinkled. Books were strewn over her desk, which was draped with gossamer. Her wardrobe door was open, revealing a glimpse of the clothes she had left behind.

And there, on the floor, was a piece of paper.

Iris froze, staring at it.

She had left it there, untouched. She had chosen not to read it months ago, fearing Carver would alter the course she was determined to take.

She walked to the folded paper. She bent down and picked it up from the floor, carrying it to her bed. She set the candle aside, the light flickering around her.

Iris stared at the paper, nearly holding it over the flame to burn. She didn't know if she was strong enough to open it. She worried it would break the last of her, to read his words now.

In the end, she couldn't resist.

The paper unfolded like wings in her hands.

His words met her like a blade. She bowed over them.

Iris! Iris, it's me, Kitt.

Epilogue

DACRE

D acre waited for his eithrals to retreat for the second time before he began his approach to Avalon Bluff. His pets returned to their resting place underground, and he walked across the lush valley, full of hope.

The gas rose, limning the town in green. Green like the mountains, like the emeralds he wore on his fingers. Green like Enva's eyes, which he still saw some nights when he slept below.

The mortals had done a fine task of creating this weapon for him. And he decided he wouldn't burn this town, because he had other plans in mind.

With a graceful flick of his fingers, his motioned for his soldiers to rush ahead to scavenge. Sometimes they were good at picking the right ones. But other times, they chose poorly, and he was left with scraps of a being.

The secret was this: the will had to still be present in the spirit. It usually shined brightest right before death. Mortals ran either cold or hot, their souls like ice or fire. He had discovered long ago that ice served him best, but every now and then, fire would surprise him.

Dacre chose to take a long walk around the town. The wind was beginning to blow the gas to the wayside, and he followed its path to a golden
field. He felt the staggering, gasping soul before he saw it. This one was
made of ice—a cold, deep spirit like the northern sea.

It drew him closer. His feet made no sound, left no impression as they
walked over the earth, seeking this dying mortal.

At last, Dacre found it.

A young man with raven dark hair was crawling through the grass. Dacre
stood over him, measuring what remained. The mortal had a minute and
thirteen seconds left before his lungs filled with blood and he expired. There
were also wounds on his right leg.

Dacre was in a good mood that day. Or else he might have let the ice in
this one melt away.

"My lord?"

Dacre turned to see Val, the strongest of his servants, standing in his
shadow.

"My lord, we have almost secured the town. But a few of the lorries have
escaped."

The news should have angered Dacre, and Val was prepared for it, cring-
ing when the god stared at him.

"So be it," Dacre said, glancing back at the gasping mortal on the ground.
Blood was dripping from his chin as he raised his head, eyes closed. He
sensed Dacre's presence. "This one."

"Yes, what of this one, my lord?"

Dacre was quiet, watching the man crawl. What was he seeking? Why
didn't he just lie down and die? His soul was so anguished, nearly rent in
half. It made Dacre wince.

But he could heal those wounds. He was a merciful god, after all. The
god of healing. This mortal, once mended, would do very well in his army.
Because Dacre suddenly realized with delight . . . this was no soldier, but a
correspondent. And Dacre had never had one of those before.

"Take him below."

Val bowed before he drew a ring in the ground, encircling the mortal. A quick way to open a portal, to pass below.

Satisfied, Dacre set his eyes eastward, on the path that would lead him to Enva.

Acknowledgments

"A girl who writes letters to her missing brother, and the boy who reads them." I wrote that line down in my brainstorming journal on November 20, 2020, uncertain of where it would lead me. Of whether this enticing story morsel had enough magic to grow wings and become a novel. And yet here we are, Iris and Roman. I've always believed the right books find you at *just* the right moments, both as a reader and as an author, and I will never get over this wonder.

What a journey this novel has been, from its origins as a stray thought in my journal to a finished product that you're now holding in your hands or listening to or reading on a screen. There are countless people who have invested their time, love, and expertise into this story and into me as an author, and I want to illuminate them here on these pages.

First, to Ben, my better half. You were with me every step of the way with this novel, and I would be remiss if I didn't acknowledge here that you wrote soul-stirring love letters to me when we were dating. When I was in the mountains of Colorado and you were in the golden fields of Georgia. We didn't have enchanted typewriters, but we had paper and pens and stamps, and it was all the magic I ever needed. And even now, years later, you continue to leave me notes here and there to find around the house. I love you.

To Sierra, for being the best watchdog and making sure I leave my desk to go for walks. Also, for cuddling next to me on the couch while I was revising this book.

To my Heavenly Father, who continues to take these small dreams of mine and multiplies them beyond anything I could ever imagine. Who loves me just as I am, and always has. You remain the strength and the portion of my heart.

To Isabel Ibañez, my soul sister and critique partner. You read this book while I was drafting it, and your insights and notes transformed the story from a messy draft into something I am incredibly proud of today. Thank you for all the hours you've poured into my stories, and for giving me a second home in Asheville. You truly are the best.

To my agent, Suzie Townsend. Words could never describe how thankful I am for you and all you do in making my dreams a reality. For being my champion and my rock in the ocean that is publishing. To the amazing Sophia Ramos and Kendra Coet—thank you for reading my drafts and providing notes and encouragement, as well as keeping me organized. A heartfelt thank-you to Joanna Volpe and Dani Segelbaum, who were there to guide me when this book went on submission. To Veronica Grijalva and Victoria Hendersen, my subrights team, who have helped my books find the perfect homes overseas. To Kate Sullivan, who read this book in preparation for submission, and who always has the best notes. To the amazing team at New Leaf—I'm so honored to be one of your authors.

To Eileen Rothschild, my inimitable editor. I'm beyond excited to be working with you on this series and am so thankful for how much you love Roman and Iris's story. Thank you for helping me make this story the best it could be. To the incredible team at Wednesday Books who have been an absolute delight to work with on this duology: Lisa Bonvissuto, Alexis Neuville, Brant Janeway, Meghan Harrington, Melanie Sanders, Lena Shekhter, Michelle McMillian, Kerri Resnick. My eternal gratitude to Olga Grlic for designing the beautiful cover for this story. A huge thank-you to Angus Johnston for copy editing.

To Natasha Bardon and Vicky Leech—I'm so honored this story has found a home at Magpie Books in the UK. Working with y'all and your team is such a dream come true.

To Leo Teti, who has championed my books in the Spanish market. Thank you for helping my stories find their readers overseas, and for inviting me to take part in so many amazing trips.

To Adalyn Grace, Isabel Ibañez, Shelby Mahurin, Rachel Griffin, Ayana Gray, and Valia Lind, for taking the time out of your busy schedules to read an early copy and provide amazing blurbs. To Adrienne Young and Kristin Dwyer, for encouraging me countless times and for cheering me on when I first told you about this book.

To my local independent bookstores that have been and continue to be integral to the success of my books: Avid Bookshop in Athens, Little Shop of Stories in Decatur, The Story Shop in Monroe, and The Inside Story in Hoschton. Thank you for being light and magic in our communities.

Two books were incredibly helpful when it came to my research for trench warfare: *Warrior* by R. G. Grant and *World War I* by H. P. Willmott. I also want to acknowledge two films that I found deeply moving, heartbreaking, and atmospheric: *1917* and *Testament of Youth*.

To my family: Mom and Dad and all my siblings. To my grandparents, who continue to inspire me daily, and to the Ross, Wilson, and Deaton clans. All of you hold me together and make me stronger.

And to my readers, for all the love and support you have given to me and my books. I'm so honored that my stories have found a home with you. Thank you for going on this journey with me.